PENGUI...

Membe...

Leonie Fox is a former magazine journalist. She lives in Kent.

Members Only

LEONIE FOX

PENGUIN BOOKS

PENGUIN BOOKS

Published by the Penguin Group
Penguin Books Ltd, 80 Strand, London WC2R ORL, England
Penguin Group (USA), Inc., 375 Hudson Street, New York, New York 10014, USA
Penguin Group (Canada), 90 Eglinton Avenue East, Suite 700, Toronto, Ontario, Canada M4P 2Y3
(a division of Pearson Penguin Canada Inc.)
Penguin Ireland, 25 St Stephen's Green, Dublin 2, Ireland (a division of Penguin Books Ltd)
Penguin Group (Australia), 250 Camberwell Road, Camberwell, Victoria 3124, Australia
(a division of Pearson Australia Group Pty Ltd)
Penguin Books India Pvt Ltd, 11 Community Centre, Panchsheel Park, New Delhi – 110 017, India
Penguin Group (NZ), 67 Apollo Drive, Rosedale, North Shore 0632, New Zealand
(a division of Pearson New Zealand Ltd)
Penguin Books (South Africa) (Pty) Ltd, 24 Sturdee Avenue,
Rosebank, Johannesburg 2196, South Africa

Penguin Books Ltd, Registered Offices: 80 Strand, London WC2R ORL, England

www.penguin.com

First published 2009
2

Set in Monotype Garamond
Typeset by Rowland Phototypesetting Ltd, Bury St Edmunds, Suffolk
Printed in England by Clays Ltd, St Ives plc

ISBN: 978-0-141-02808-8

www.greenpenguin.co.uk

Acknowledgements

My thanks to all at Penguin, especially Mari Evans, Natalie Higgins, Nikki Dupin and last – but certainly not least – Naomi Fidler, Ana Maria Rivera and their excellent sales team.

One

Amber Solomon settled into the soft leather armchair and set her Balenciaga handbag on the floor. Her expression as she surveyed her cosmetic surgeon was inscrutable (not that Amber's face had much choice in the matter these days).

Dr Peter Lawrence, perching on a corner of his desk, as was his habit during consultations, smiled pleasantly. 'So, what brings you here today, Mrs Solomon? I do hope there aren't any problems with the chin implant.' He dipped his head, inspecting his recent handiwork. 'It's certainly healing well. The scar's practically invisible already.'

Amber raised a languid hand and stroked her new chin with her fingertips. 'It's perfect,' she said. 'Just how I imagined it.'

'Excellent,' said Dr Lawrence, beaming delightedly.

'It's my nose that's the problem.'

'Oh?' The surgeon's intelligent grey eyes clouded over.

'I think I'd like it to be smaller still, and just a touch more retroussé.'

Dr Lawrence folded his arms across his chest and studied the forty-eight-year-old former actress dispassionately. Amber had been an attractive woman when she'd first walked into his surgery, fifteen months earlier. Her forehead had been a little lined and her eyelids a little saggy, but that was only to be expected in a woman of her age. Now, however, eleven surgical procedures later, the face that looked back at him seemed barely human. A series of facelifts had left her skin so taut she could barely crack a smile, while silicon injections and lipo-suction had bestowed her with obscenely swollen lips and cheekbones sharp as steak knives. Most dramatic of all were the slanted, cat-like eyes, which gave her a perpetually haunted look, like an animal caught in a trap.

'Mrs Solomon,' he began in a gentle tone, 'we've already performed two previous rhinoplasties. Your nose is perfectly delightful as it is; a further reduction would make your face look quite –' The word on the tip of Dr Lawrence's tongue was 'freakish', but he managed to check himself just in time – '*unbalanced,* in my professional opinion.'

Amber sighed in annoyance. 'Let's remind ourselves what we're working towards, shall we?' She reached into her handbag and removed a manila envelope. 'Here,' she said, handing it to Dr Lawrence. 'As I told you when we started out on this journey together, I won't be happy until I look like that.'

The surgeon opened the envelope and withdrew a laminated clipping from *National Geographic.* It bore a large colour photograph of one of the most recognizable sculptures in the world: the bust of Queen Nefertiti, discovered in 1912 and now housed in Berlin's famous Egyptian museum. Although he was already familiar with the face in the picture, Dr Lawrence studied it again for politeness' sake, taking in the perfect nose, full lips and wide-set, feline eyes. He could understand Amber wanting to recapture her youth, but not why she insisted on making herself a grotesque parody of an ancient queen. 'Are you sure this is what you want?' he asked her.

Amber rolled her eyes impatiently. 'Quite sure. And if *you* won't help me, I shall have to find a surgeon who will.'

At this, Dr Lawrence – who was forking out a hefty four-figure sum in alimony every month and paying to put three children through private school – leapt from the desk and placed a hand on Amber's shoulder. 'That won't be necessary, Mrs Solomon,' he said smoothly. 'Why don't we book you in at the end of the month?'

Outside Dr Lawrence's city-centre clinic, a sleek black Mercedes waited on double yellow lines. The minute Amber appeared on the surgery doorstep, its uniformed driver sprang into action.

'Where to now, Mrs Solomon?' the driver asked as he opened the door for his employer. 'Harvey Nichols?'

Amber smiled weakly. 'No, Stephen, I've changed my mind about that shopping trip. I can feel one of my head-aches coming on; I'd like to go straight home, please.'

The driver gave a deferential nod. 'Right you are, Mrs Solomon.'

Half an hour later, the Mercedes was driving through the picturesque village of Kirkhulme, which boasted more millionaires per square mile than anywhere else in the country. As soon as Amber caught her first glimpse of the Old Manor through a gap in the trees, the corners of her mouth curled upwards. Even now, eighteen years after she'd first stepped over the threshold as a new bride, the house still had the power to take her breath away. Nestling in a tranquil woodland setting, the sprawling mansion was built of rich, plum-coloured Cheshire brick, and came complete with tennis court, swimming pool, extensive garaging and assorted outbuildings. The four-acre plot occupied a prime position next to St Benedict's Country Club & Spa, and a private gate in the secluded gardens offered direct access to the club's famous golf course. No wonder the Old Manor was widely regarded as one of the most desirable pieces of real estate in Kirkhulme. But when the Solomons took it on it was a wreck.

Built by a wealthy clothing merchant in 1582, the house stayed in private ownership for centuries until it was bought by a conglomerate in the late fifties and converted into a boys' boarding school. Much patronized by families in the Armed Forces, the school was eventually forced to close after a series of unsavoury incidents involving the matron and a number of sixth-form boys. Afterwards, it languished on the open market for the best part of two years before the Solomons snapped it up at a knockdown price. They didn't see what other prospective buyers had seen: a shabby white elephant, ravaged by three decades of rough treatment at the hands of a horde of unruly army brats. What *they* saw was a beautiful and important piece of history, desperately in need of a loving touch – and, back then, the Solomons had love in spades. For the next three years, the couple dedicated themselves to bringing the Old Manor back to its former glory and once the restoration was complete both agreed they could never imagine leaving it.

Amber thanked Stephen as he dropped her off at the front door. 'I won't be going out again today,' she told him. 'So you can put the car in the garage.'

'And *Mr* Solomon?' the driver enquired.

'He's at the office all day. He said he was going to get a taxi home. Oh, and, Stephen . . .'

'Yes, Mrs Solomon?'

'The cushions in the back seat need plumping.'

The driver smiled. 'I'll see to it right away.'

Unusually, there was no one to greet Amber when she pushed open the Old Manor's studded oak door. It was the housekeeper's day off and Calum, Amber's teenage son, was at college, studying for the A levels he seemed certain to fail. She stepped into the imposing entrance hall and slung her handbag on a Louis XV chair, where it would remain until the housekeeper came to tidy it away. Behind her, the front door slammed shut with a dull thud. Shuddering, Amber massaged her temples. The two aspirin she'd taken in the car didn't seem to be having much effect. In a minute, she would go upstairs for a lie down, but first there was someone she must see. She went to the drawing room, which gave out on to a spectacular orangery, modelled on the one at Kensington Palace. Kept at a constant temperature all year round and filled with an abundance of exotic palms and cacti, it was home to the third dearest creature in Amber's life, after her husband and her hairdresser.

'Couscous,' she said in a sing-song voice as she made her way towards a large metal cage in the corner of the room. 'Mummy's home.' At the sound of her voice, a high-pitched chattering struck up. Amber smiled as she flipped the bolt and opened the door. Immediately, the cage's inhabitant flew from the branch of a leafy fig and landed on her shoulder.

'Hello, little man,' Amber cooed as she nuzzled her face against his soft fur. 'Has Mummy been gone a long time? Have you missed her terribly?'

Couscous was an eight-year-old capuchin, more commonly known as an organ-grinder monkey. Bred in captivity, he'd been a gift from Amber's husband Daniel on their tenth wedding anniversary. The pair had been inseparable ever since. To Amber's mind, Couscous made the perfect companion. He was loving, fiercely loyal and, most importantly, never answered back.

'Let's go upstairs for a lie down,' she told the monkey as they made their way back into the drawing room. 'Mummy's head's *throbbing*.'

Suddenly, Couscous spotted a tempting dish of jellied fruits lying on an occasional table. Leaping from Amber's shoulder, he bounded over to the dish and snatched up one of the crystalline candies.

'Bad Couscous!' said Amber, wagging her finger. 'You know you're not supposed to eat sugar.' She bent down and held out her palm. 'Give it to Mummy.' The capuchin looked at her quizzically for a moment before stuffing the jellied fruit into his cheek for safekeeping and scampering towards the door.

Amber shook her head, more in amusement than anger, and followed Couscous into the entrance hall, just in time to see his long tail disappearing down the winding corridor that led to Daniel's study.

'Don't you dare,' Amber threatened. There was a stern

note in her voice now. Daniel wouldn't be at all pleased if he discovered that the pampered pet had violated his inner sanctum. Amber hurried down the corridor, tutting as she saw Couscous spring into the air and grab the study's door handle with his prehensile fingers, using his weight to draw it down, then bracing his feet on the door frame to give him the leverage he needed to push it open. Knowing that her husband's office contained a number of valuable artefacts, Amber broke into a jog.

Daniel Solomon had been fascinated by ancient Egypt ever since a boyhood trip to the British Museum. An art enthusiast and avid collector, he now owned one of the largest private collections of Egyptian antiquities in the north-west of England. Most of the items – all of which were carefully catalogued and generously insured – were kept in secure storage under strict conditions of temperature and humidity. But some of his favourite pieces were on permanent display at the Old Manor, housed in custom-made glass exhibit cases and mounted on the walls of his study.

When Amber entered the room, she found Couscous squatting on one of the cases that was home to a twenty-fourth dynasty lapis lazuli scarab. The monkey had the jellied fruit between his paws and was gnawing on it with gusto.

Smiling indulgently, Amber scooped him up and set him on her hip. 'Mummy will be very cross if you won't eat your dinner later,' she told him, planting a kiss on top of his tiny head. She glanced at Daniel's desk to check that nothing had been disturbed. Her husband was anal about his office and would notice if anything was a millimetre out of place. His Lalique crystal paperweight sat in its usual place beside the Rolodex and the crocodile leather blotter was lined up precisely with the desk's tulipwood inlay. Next to it, a finger's width away, lay a limited edition Mont Blanc. Satisfied that everything was in order, Amber began walking towards the door with Couscous. Then suddenly she stopped, turned round and walked slowly to another one of the dozen or so exhibit cases, this one mounted on the opposite wall to the scarab. Bending her knees slightly, she surveyed the limestone funerary sculpture inside. The face that stared back at her was cool and aloof, its expression as impenetrable as the Mona Lisa's. On Amber's hip, Couscous squeaked impatiently. Having devoured his sugary prize, he was now growing bored.

'Shhh, baby,' Amber murmured. Leaning forward, she studied the sculpture even more intently, remembering how thrilled Daniel had been when he had secured the fifteen-inch likeness of Queen Nefertiti at auction. Unpainted and not as finely worked as the famous Berlin tribute, it was an arresting piece all the same.

To say that Daniel held the legendary royal consort in high regard was an understatement. He was, to put it bluntly, obsessed with her. 'Nefertiti is the ultimate vision of female beauty,' he told the friends who came to admire his artefacts. 'And she wasn't just a pretty face ... all the evidence suggests Nefertiti had almost as much influence as her husband, the heretic king Akhenaten, and even served for a short time as ruler after his death,' at which point, most people tended to glaze over.

Amber had always been happy to indulge her husband's unusual hobby. After all, it wasn't *she* who had to polish the exhibit cases on a daily basis with a mixture of one part vinegar and two parts water. That tedious duty, like so many others at the Old Manor, fell to the housekeeper. Over the past year or so, however, Daniel had become increasingly distant, and Amber had begun to resent anything that took his attention away from her. His business interests meant he was often away for days at a time, and when he *was* at home he spent hours holed up in his office, purportedly scouring websites and auction catalogues in search of obscure Egyptian treasures.

In an attempt to regain her husband's interest, Amber splashed out on a pair of handcuffs and a thousand pounds worth of designer lingerie – but to her horror Daniel fell asleep before she could seduce him, having explained that he was too old and too tired for such antics. And so, in desperation, she turned for help – not to her friends, who were few and far between and who, in any case, would take great delight in broadcasting her marital difficulties to anyone who cared to listen, but rather to a long-dead member of Egyptian royalty.

And so, supervised by one of the most eminent cosmetic surgeons in the county, Amber set about metamorphosing into her husband's ideal woman. It was, she reasoned with her peculiar twisted logic, the only way to ensure the survival of their marriage. Amber was no stranger to surgery – there had been liposuction in her early forties, followed by a discreet breast augmentation a few years later – but she'd never attempted anything on this scale. At first, she didn't reveal her long-term plan to Daniel; she wanted to surprise him. And when she returned home after her second eye lift, surprise him she did. 'You look scary,' he'd said, as he gazed in horror at her curiously elongated eyes.

If Amber could have cried, she would have, but unfortunately her tear ducts still weren't working properly after the operation. 'I did it for you,' she said. 'I did it so I'd look like Nefertiti. What was it you called her – "the ultimate vision of female beauty"?'

At this, Daniel had held up his hands, palms turned towards her defensively. 'Whoa there,' he said. 'If you want to mess with what God's given you, fine – but don't drag me into it.'

Following that unpleasant little scene, Daniel seemed uninterested in his wife's quest for physical perfection and, after her subsequent surgical procedures, he made no comment beyond the occasional 'very nice, dear' platitude. For Amber, it was a crushing disappointment and now, as she caught sight of her reflection in the glass of the exhibit case, she found herself wondering if all the pain and money had been worth it. Feeling the invisible band round her head tighten, she winced.

'Come on then,' she said to Couscous. 'Let's go upstairs.'

Together, they ascended the cherrywood staircase, which was one of the Old Manor's splendid late-Georgian additions. When they reached the first-floor landing, Amber pushed open the door to the master-bedroom suite. As she released her grip on Couscous, he jumped out of her arms and on to the balustrade, dancing along it like a tightrope walker. When he reached the end, he stared hard at the upper staircase, which led to the second-floor guest bedrooms, head cocked inquisitively. Amber held out her arms. 'Mummy's not in the mood to play, darling. Come back here, please.'

Couscous flashed his mistress a mischievous look and darted up the staircase. With a weary sigh, Amber followed him. She found him sitting on the carpet at the top of the stairs waiting patiently for her, but the minute she reached out her arms he set off again, scampering to the end of the hall, where the largest of the half a dozen guest bedrooms was located. The monkey waited until his mistress was an arm's length away, then he jumped on to the door handle and braced his feet against the frame. A second later the door swung open to reveal the magnificent Jacobean-style mahogany half-tester bed, handmade by a local craftsman at vast expense. The silk eiderdown had been tossed carelessly on the floor and on top of the linen sheets, a pair of hairy buttocks, covered in a light sheen of sweat, could be seen pumping up and down furiously. Mesmerized, Amber took a step closer. Now she noticed a set of spread legs, their sturdy shins stippled with dark stubble. As she watched in stunned silence, two hands appeared and gripped the buttocks forcefully, kneading them like mounds of dough. Both participants seemed completely unaware of her presence. Suddenly, the woman let out a long, low moan. At this, Couscous, who had been watching proceedings from the top of the door, leapt soundlessly from his perch, ran over to the bed and began tugging at the sheets as if it were all part of some elaborate game.

Daniel Solomon stopped, mid-thrust, and turned his

head forty-five degrees to see Couscous performing a series of excited backflips. 'You little shit,' he said crossly. 'Who let you out?'

'I did.' Amber's tone would've frozen hot water.

At the sound of his wife's voice, Daniel's entire body seemed to go into spasm, and he rolled off his partner with such force that he ended up on the floor amid a tangle of damp sheets. While her husband wrestled to free himself, Amber marched up to the bed. Lying on the pillows, her mottled face frozen in embarrassment, was a woman Amber trusted, a woman she saw almost every day, a woman who knew her most intimate habits. Finding her in bed with Daniel was shocking enough, but what disturbed Amber even more was the fact that her rival wasn't even attractive. Although she was roughly the same age as her employer, she had pendulous breasts and a crooked nose. *And* her roots were showing through a do-it-yourself blonde rinse.

'Nancy,' said Amber coolly. 'I thought it was your day off.'

The housekeeper grabbed a pillow and clasped it over her chest. 'It was – I mean, it *is*,' she stammered.

By this juncture, Daniel had staggered to his feet. Noting the condom drooping ridiculously from the end of his flaccid penis, Amber raised a disdainful eyebrow. 'I see you used protection,' she snapped. 'I suppose I should be grateful for small mercies.' Then, without another word, she turned round and walked out of the room.

Two

The shop at St Benedict's Country Club & Spa was unusually quiet for a Friday lunchtime. Outside, it was raining cats and dogs, and the club's famous golf course – which had played host to two Ryder Cups and ten British Opens in its illustrious 111-year history – was deserted. Ace Cox, who had been promoted to shop manager eight months earlier, stood patiently beside a changing cubicle while inside, one of his regular customers wrestled with the zip on a too-small tennis skirt.

'How are you doing in there, Mrs M?' Ace called out after a decent interval.

There was a loud tut. 'The damn zip's stuck. I'm doing my best to free it, but I don't want to tear the fabric.' Then a well-timed pause. 'Perhaps you could lend some assistance.'

Ace rolled his eyes. This turn of events wasn't entirely unexpected. 'Of course, Mrs M,' he said cheerily. 'Here I come.'

He pushed aside the curtain and stepped into the cubicle. Forty-five-year-old divorce lawyer Fiona Mortimer was wearing nothing but the tennis skirt and a sheer black bra that left little to the imagination.

'I knew I should've got the size sixteen,' she said with a coy smile. 'Only I've lost a bit of weight recently and I thought I might just be able to squeeze into the fourteen.'

She glanced down. 'I do hope I haven't broken that zip.'

Ace waved a hand. 'Don't worry about it. Let's just concentrate on getting you out of there.' The young manager dropped to his knees so he was eye level with the roll of fat that bulged unappetizingly over the skirt's waistband. Holding the fabric around the zip taut, he gave it a few sharp tugs, but it refused to budge. He leaned forward for a closer inspection. Above him, Fiona's bosoms loomed like two enormous boulders. 'Ah, I see what's happened,' he said. 'The zip's got caught in your underwear.' He looked up. 'Do you think you could breathe in for me?'

Fiona nodded, eager to please. She took a deep breath and the roll of fat receded, allowing Ace to slip two fingers of his right hand inside the waistband.

'Ooh, your hands are lovely and warm,' Fiona chuckled.

Ace smiled lazily. 'We aim to please.' He gripped the zip with his left hand and worked it up and down, while simultaneously easing out the silky stuff of Fiona's under-wear with his left. A few moments later, the zip came unstuck. 'There we go; job done,' said Ace, rising to his feet.

'My, aren't you a clever boy?' Fiona took hold of the zip and pulled it up and down a few times. 'Yes, that's working fine now, isn't it?' Suddenly, she pulled the zip down as far as it would go and gave a little shimmy. The pleated tennis skirt went parachuting to her ankles, revealing a pair of black lace-trimmed cami-knickers. 'Oops, naughty me!' she exclaimed. Without looking down, she stepped out of the skirt. 'There, that's better.'

She stared at Ace provocatively, her thickly glossed lips slightly parted.

Ace rubbed his jaw. 'I guess I'll leave you to get dressed now, Mrs M.'

As he turned to go, Fiona stepped in front of the curtain, effectively blocking his escape route. Placing her hand in the centre of his muscular chest, she pushed him against the cubicle's flimsy rear wall. 'You know I find you very attractive, don't you?' she said breathily.

'Yeah, I kinda gathered that,' the manager admitted.

The lawyer pressed her semi-naked body against him. As she turned her face upwards, Ace caught a garlicky whiff – the remnant no doubt of a thrusting power lunch. He knew it would be an easy matter to escape Fiona's clutches but he hesitated, wanting her to enjoy the feel of the rock-hard pectorals beneath his polo shirt. The way Ace saw it, it was all part of the shop's unique service.

'I realize I'm quite a bit older than you, but I am at my sexual peak, you know,' Fiona said, pushing her breasts against his chest so that they spilled over the top of her bra.

'I don't doubt it, Mrs M,' said Ace, whose jaw ached with the effort of trying to keep a straight face.

Fiona batted her eyelashes at him. 'I bet I could show you a thing or two,' she murmured. Her hand moved to his crotch.

'I really am very flattered,' Ace lied, as he took Fiona by the shoulders and gently pushed her away from him. 'But, as you know, I already have a girlfriend.'

Fiona arched a disbelieving brow. 'You're still with the masseuse?'

'Yep, it's our year anniversary in a couple of weeks' time.'

'That shouldn't be a problem,' Fiona said, tracing the line of Ace's cheek with her index finger. 'I've no doubt that a fit young man like you would have no trouble keeping two women satisfied.'

'Sorry, Mrs M, no can do. I love Astrid; I wouldn't dream of cheating on her.'

Fiona sighed. 'How incredibly unimaginative.'

Ace decided to throw the old girl a bone. 'Of course, if I was single, things might be very different. You're a good-looking woman, Mrs M – and obviously very intelligent too. I hear you string ex-husbands up by the balls in that law firm of yours.'

Fiona – who had already seen off three husbands and was, according to rumour, on the lookout for a fourth – smiled. 'Well, I do pride myself on negotiating a healthy settlement for my clients.' Having accepted defeat, she pulled a purple track top from a hook on the wall. 'Can you wrap this for me while I get dressed?'

'Good choice,' said Ace, nodding appreciatively as he took the top. 'That's a great colour for you. It'll go really well with that gorgeous Titian hair of yours.'

Fiona patted her dyed auburn pageboy. 'Yes, I thought the same thing.'

Ace bent down to retrieve the tennis skirt. 'Do you want to try this in a sixteen?'

'No thanks, I'd better get back to the office.'

'Right you are, Mrs M. I'll have that track top waiting for you at the till.' The manager turned to go.

'Oh, and, Ace?'

'Yes, Mrs M.'

'Can I get a little something for the weekend? I'm hosting a dinner party and I want to serve something special with the digestifs.'

Ace rubbed his hands together. 'Of course. How much? Five grams?'

'Better say ten. You know what healthy appetites we lawyers have.'

Ace was smiling as he made his way to the till. He played out the same charade with Fiona Mortimer every time she came into the shop. She'd lure him into the changing cubicle on some flimsy pretext and then proceed to give him the come-on. Quite frankly, he'd sooner shag his own grandmother, but the lawyer was a good customer so he had to indulge her a little.

Behind the counter, sales assistant Harry Hunter was polishing a new consignment of silver-plated golf-ball keyrings.

'Hey, Harry,' Ace said in a low voice. 'Ten grams of coke for Mrs Mortimer, please.'

His colleague tossed down his jeweller's cloth. 'Sure thing, boss.'

'Oh, and tell Dylan to get a move on with those Ralph Lauren sweaters. He's been in the stockroom for ages.'

'I think he's having a sly kip. He was out last night with Sorrel. You know ... that ashtanga yoga teacher he met on the staff away-day.'

'Showing him her legs akimbo pose, was she?'

Harry grinned. 'Something like that.' He walked to the

rear of the shop and pushed open a door marked STAFF ONLY.

As he passed the stockroom, he stuck his head round the door. His fellow assistant Dylan was lying on the floor, his head resting on a makeshift pillow of bubble-wrap.

'Oi, Dylan, wakey wakey,' said Harry, banging the wall with his fist.

Dylan woke with a start. 'Fuck,' he said, rubbing his eyes. 'You frightened the crap out of me. Where's the fire?'

'Come on, mate, look lively. The boss wants those Ralph Lauren sweaters out front, pronto.'

Dylan struggled to his feet. 'Okay, okay.'

'Good night last night, was it?'

'Bloody amazing; Sorrel's into that tantric sex malarky.' He grinned lazily. 'And she's very flexible. Have you ever seen a naked woman with both legs behind her ears?'

'Er no, mate. Can't say I've ever had the pleasure,' said Harry. 'You can tell me all the gory details later. I've got to get some coke for a customer.' He raised a hand in farewell and continued down the corridor to the office. This small, windowless box was where all the shop's admin was done. It also served as a handy storeroom for a second, more lucrative merchandising business.

Harry made straight for the safe and punched in the combination, which was known to only two other people beside himself: Ace and Dylan. Reaching inside, he removed a pre-weighed package of high-grade cocaine. It wasn't the only drug on the menu: cannabis, ecstasy, LSD, ketamine, Viagra ... the boys in the shop could lay their hands on just about anything – and club members were prepared to pay top dollar for a discreet, reliable service.

A former private investigator, Harry had been hired the previous summer by St Benedict's general manager, Anthony Lanchester. Masquerading as Lanchester's god-son, Harry worked undercover in the shop for three months, charged with the task of collecting evidence to support his employer's suspicion that the shop was a front for drug dealing. He quickly discovered two things: one, that his colleagues were indeed up to no good; and two, that he was a natural-born salesman. Before long, he felt completely at home in the shop's louche atmosphere and quickly formed a close bond with Ace and Dylan. Unwilling to grass up his new-found friends, Harry – who'd never been cut out to be a private investigator – had brokered a deal with Lanchester. He agreed to forgo his fee, but only if the general manager allowed him to carry on working in the shop as a regular employee. What's more, he persuaded Lanchester that it was in the club's interests to allow the drug-dealing to continue unchecked. It was an arrangement that suited everybody.

A month or so later, as he shared an after-work beer with Ace and Dylan in the village pub, Harry finally plucked up the courage to come clean about his past as a PI. They'd been pissed off at first, which was under-standable – but once they realized that his intervention had effectively protected their livelihood, they accepted him as one of their own. Soon afterwards, Ace offered to cut him in on the drugs deal. They were, after all, one man short after the shop's previous manager had been sacked in the wake of a messy sex scandal. Harry hesitated – but not for very long. The financial rewards were considerable and, besides, he fancied living dangerously for a change.

By the time Harry returned with the ten grams, a fully dressed Fiona Mortimer was at the till with Ace, paying for her purchases. 'There you go, Mrs M,' Harry said, thrusting his balled-up fist into the burgundy-and-gold carrier bag lying on the counter. 'Any complaints, don't hesitate to return the goods for a full refund.'

Fiona smiled. 'I'm sure that won't be necessary.' She took the carrier bag from Harry's outstretched hand. 'Thanks, boys, it's been a pleasure, as always. Oh, and one more thing.' She took a business card out of her purse and slid it across the counter towards Ace. 'Just in case you change your mind.'

Ace picked up the card. 'Okey-doke, Mrs M,' he said with a wink. 'Enjoy your dinner party now.'

The minute the door had closed behind her, Harry leaned across the counter. 'What the fuck were you two *doing* in that cubicle?' he asked Ace. 'You were in there ages. Copping a feel, was she?

Ace smiled. 'Something like that.'

'Aren't you even tempted? I've heard Fiona Mortimer's loaded.'

Ace looked at him aghast. 'Why would I make do with scrag end of mutton when I've got fillet steak at home?'

Harry frowned. 'Sorry, mate, you've lost me.'

Ace jerked his thumb towards the window. On the shop's front steps, an Amazonian blonde was shaking the rain from her umbrella. 'Is that the best-looking woman you've ever seen, or what?'

Harry nodded. 'Ah . . . now I get you.'

Ace scooted round the counter and opened the door for the blonde. 'Astrid baby, this is a nice surprise,' he said as he kissed her on the lips.

'I'm on my break,' Astrid replied, tossing her umbrella in the brass stand by the door. 'I just thought I'd come and say hi.'

Ace glanced around the shop and, seeing that his sole customer was engrossed in a display of golf bags, gave his girlfriend's arse cheek a surreptitious squeeze. 'What time shall I pick you up tonight?'

'Seven?' Astrid lowered her voice. 'I said we'd meet the other couple in the pub – and then if we like the look of them we can take them back to ours.'

'Perfect.'

'Hey, Astrid,' Harry called out from behind the counter. 'How's it going?'

'Good thanks.' Astrid smiled, displaying a row of perfect white teeth. 'Ace tells me you've got a new girlfriend.'

'I'm seeing someone, yeah.'

Astrid smiled. 'Nice, is she?'

'Yeah, she is pretty hot, as a matter of fact. Spanish.' He outlined a female form in the air. 'Curves in all the right places. Bright too.'

'Oh, Harry, that's great. I'm so pleased for you.'

The man looking at the golf bags raised an arm in the air. 'Any chance of some assistance over here?' he called out.

'Of course, sir,' said Harry, walking over to him.

21

Astrid turned back to Ace. 'Listen, sweetheart, I'd better get back to the spa.' She lowered her voice. 'I've got one of my special clients in half an hour and I have a little treat for him. It's going to require a detour to the compost heap behind the greenhouse.'

Ace wrinkled his nose. 'Blimey, what on earth are you planning to do to the poor guy?'

'He'll get exactly what he's paid for, nothing more and nothing less.'

'Is it anyone I know?'

Astrid gave her boyfriend a wry look. 'You know better than to ask.'

'Oh yeah, client confidentiality and all that.' Ace snaked an arm round his girlfriend's waist. 'Just don't be too hard on him, okay? You need to save your energy for tonight.'

Harry called out, 'Ace, there's a scuff mark on this Titleist bag. Can we offer this gentleman a discount?'

'I'm sure we can. I'll be with you in a minute,' Ace replied. He smiled at Astrid. 'See you at seven then.' He gave her a wink. 'I think it's going to be fun.'

The rain was easing as Astrid began making her way across the sweeping lawn towards St Benedict's vast greenhouse. Because of the weather, a significant number of grounds staff had been deployed to the 17,000-square-foot building, which provided the 180,000 flowers planted at the club every year. As she approached, Astrid could see them working, hunched over seedling trays and sacks of fertilizer. She used her umbrella to shield her face as she walked past the windows. Not that any of the greenhouse's inhabitants would have cared less if they'd known what she was up to. All kinds of strange and unusual things went on at St Benedict's and the staff – much like the management – were well practised in the art of turning a blind eye. No wonder the club's invitation-only memberships were as highly prized as bottles of 1961 Chateau Latour.

Behind the greenhouse lay a large compost heap, which kept the club's 200 acres of gardens and undulating parkland exceptionally well nourished. Astrid's interest lay not in the compost heap itself, but in the small patch of uncultivated land just beyond it, which was home to a dense patch of *Urtica dioica*, otherwise known as the common-or-garden stinging nettle. But before she could claim her prize, there were certain precautions to be taken. After folding her umbrella and tossing it on the ground, Astrid reached into the small canvas bag she wore slung across her chest and removed a length of kitchen towel, a pair of latex gloves and some scissors. She slipped on the gloves, squatted down and cut half a dozen nettle stems. These she wrapped in the kitchen towel, taking great care not to crush the soft green leaves, mindful that such an action would disable the tiny hollow stinging hairs. It was these hairs that contained the trio of chemicals – histamine, acetylcholine and serotonin – which were capable of triggering a temporary and painful skin rash. Her mission complete, Astrid hurried back to St Benedict's luxurious spa complex.

Although she was one of the club's top-earning practitioners of Swedish massage, Astrid's talents extended far beyond effleurage and petrissage. Before, after – and even, on occasion, *during* – her regular shifts, she administered her own, unique brand of treatment to a select group of private clients. A monthly backhander to the spa's senior receptionist was all it took to ensure this *tukta* therapy (*tukta* being the Swedish word for discipline) remained a secret from the management. In the early stages of their romance, Astrid had also kept Ace in the dark about her little sideline, fearful of scaring him off. But then, as their relationship grew increasingly serious, she knew she had to come clean. She'd fallen in love with him and she didn't want there to be any secrets between them. At first, Ace had been shocked by her confession. And then turned on.

Back at the spa, Astrid went directly to the staff comfort suite, where she took a quick shower and changed into a fresh uniform and a pair of white leather regulation clogs. Afterwards, she spent some time in front of the mirror, scraping her hair back into a severe ponytail and applying black eyeliner, mascara and a slick of ruby lipstick. Satisfied with her appearance, she went to her locker and removed a small polycarbonate suitcase. She wheeled it back to her treatment room, which was situated at the end of a long corridor and separated from the other therapists' rooms by a heavy glass fire door, making it virtually soundproof. Once inside, she opened the suitcase and started to unpack. Her client had highly unusual requirements, but Astrid was nothing if not broad-minded. First came a yoga mat, filched from the club's fitness studio, which she placed on the floor beside her treatment couch. Then she produced a five-foot-square piece of sturdy plastic sheeting, of the sort used by painters and decorators, and positioned it close to the mat. Next came several lengths of braided nylon cord, a bowl of assorted fruits, a squeezy tube of caramel dessert sauce, some black silk hold-ups and a pair of red patent leather court shoes with diamante ankle straps and four-and-a-half-inch heels. She placed the items on a stainless steel trolley, which had been emptied of its usual cargo of massage oils. These were joined by a single latex glove and the stinging nettles, arranged artistically on a glass dish (presentation was very important to Astrid). Now she was ready to receive her client.

William Farquharson was the manager of Clayborne & Co, one of Cheshire's leading private banks. A tall man with a lugubrious manner, he was well known in Kirkhulme, where he lived with his wife and their three children. As chairman of the Rotary Club and a leading light in the village history society, he was widely regarded as a pillar of the local community and a man whose morals were beyond reproach. But Astrid – or Mistress Valkyrie as she was also known – knew better than anyone that appearances could be deceptive.

After greeting her client in reception, Astrid led him to the treatment room, taking care to lock the door behind them. When she turned round, she saw William looking at her expectantly, his hands stuffed in the pockets of his impeccably cut suit trousers. All at once, Astrid's beautiful face twisted into a mask of disgust.

'You insolent worm,' she snarled. 'Take your hands out of your pockets this instant.'

William did as he was told and clasped the offending appendages together penitently in front of his crotch. 'I'm sorry, Mistress,' he said in a low voice that was far removed from the booming tone he used to address his minions at the bank.

'Take care that it doesn't happen again, or the consequences will be very serious,' Astrid hissed. She directed her client to a hospital screen in the corner of the room. 'Strip down to your underpants – and be quick about it. Mistress Valkyrie does not like to be kept waiting.'

William walked briskly to the screen, eager for the session to begin.

As she waited for him to undress, Astrid made some preparations of her own, kicking off her clogs and lowering the treatment couch so that she when she sat on it, her bare feet rested on the tiled floor.

After a few moments, the bank manager emerged from behind the screen. He was wearing a pair of black Calvin Klein boxers that made his milky skin look even paler.

Astrid pointed to the yoga mat. 'Lay on the floor,' she commanded.

When William was prostrated, Astrid performed a slow circuit of the mat, eyes fixed on her client's narrow ribcage. 'What a pitiful specimen of manhood you are,' she said witheringly.

'Yes, Mistress.'

'I think you need to be taught a lesson.' She stopped pacing and sat down on the edge of the treatment couch. Extending a long leg, she began stroking William's impressive mat of chest hair with the tips of her French-manicured toes. A small moan of pleasure escaped from the bank manager's lips. The masseuse flashed a superior smile – then, quite without warning, she caught a curl of hair between her toes and tweaked it as hard as she could.

William's body jerked as if an electric current had passed through it. 'Oh, Mistress,' he murmured. 'You're most cruel.'

'Silence!' Astrid cried. 'You must speak only when spoken to.' Seizing another curl, she tweaked again. This time, William accepted his punishment without complaint. Astrid's foot moved northwards with practised ease and commenced roughly kneading the bank manager's bony shoulder. A minute or so later, she turned her attention to his face, smacking his cheek with the sole of her foot – lightly at first and then more roughly. Unable to stop himself, William reached out a hand to caress the instrument of torture.

'Bad boy!' Astrid cried as she jerked her foot away. 'No touching – not until Mistress Valkyrie says so.' She thrust her chin out haughtily. 'I think you should be punished for that transgression.' She stood up and went to the trolley. Picking up the bottle of dessert sauce, she carried it over to the plastic sheeting and proceeded to empty half the contents over the toes of her right foot. She glanced at William. A line of drool was leaking from the corner of his mouth. Tossing the bottle aside, Astrid stuck out her foot and began moving it in a circular motion above William's head. 'You're going to lick this clean. Do you understand?'

'Yes, Mistress.'

Astrid brought her foot to William's mouth. Without hesitation, he began licking it enthusiastically, pushing his tongue in the crevices between her toes like a chameleon foraging for locusts. The masseuse observed his activities approvingly. Sexually speaking, the act of foot worship did nothing for her, but that wasn't to say she didn't enjoy it. 'You may touch me if you wish,' she said archly.

Cupping the sticky foot tenderly in his hands, William took Astrid's big toe in his mouth and began sucking it rhythmically. He repeated the same process for each toe until the foot was clean. Then he kissed Astrid's instep and placed her foot carefully on the floor as if it were a priceless piece of Fabergé.

'Excellent,' said Astrid, turning the foot from left to right as she inspected her client's handiwork. 'You are a most diligent Footboy.'

William's caramel-covered mouth broke into a grateful smile. 'Thank you, Mistress; it's a privilege to serve you.'

'And now,' said Astrid as she returned to the trolley. 'I have a special treat for you.' She picked up the latex glove, stretching it between her two hands before releasing it with a menacing snap. She pulled the glove on to her right hand and picked up a sprig of stinging nettles, before returning to William's prone form. 'See what a thoughtful mistress I am?' she said, presenting the sprig as if it were a wedding bouquet.

'Oh yes,' the bank manager whimpered.

Reaching down, Astrid brushed the nettles back and forth against her client's left nipple. William cringed as the leaves delivered their stinging payload. 'How does that feel?' said Astrid, as she stroked the nettles around the other nipple.

'Delicious,' the bank manager whispered as a livid rash began to spread across his chest.

Astrid returned the nettles to the glass dish, peeled off the glove and reached for one of the black silk hold-ups.

She pulled it over her toes then, resting her foot on the bottom tier of the trolley, she began to slowly roll the stocking upwards. William had lifted his head from the mat for a better view and his eyes followed her movements hungrily. The masseuse reached for the second hold-up and slipped her foot inside. 'This silk feels *soooo* soft against my skin,' she gasped as she drew it towards her thigh.

William stretched out an arm. 'May I stroke it, Mistress?'

Astrid smiled benevolently. 'In a moment.' She pointed to the patent leather stilettos. 'But first I think a little trampling's in order, don't you?'

Her client nodded his head vigorously. 'Yes, Mistress.'

'Excellent,' said Astrid with a glacial smile. 'Then roll on to your stomach, you vile creature.'

Fifteen minutes later, William's entire back, from the base of his spine to the tip of his shoulders, was studded with indentations and red marks, some of which were already darkening into bruises. They were wounds that would sting gratifyingly for several days to come – and Astrid hadn't finished with him yet.

'I have a special treat for you today,' she said, using the pointed toe of her stiletto to flip him over on to his back.

William winced as his sore back smacked against the yoga mat. 'Oh, Mistress, you *are* spoiling me,' he cooed in delight.

'Get your scrawny arse on here,' Astrid said, patting the treatment couch.

The bank manager rose to his feet and mounted the couch in one swift movement.

Astrid snapped her fingers impatiently. 'On to your stomach ... come on, come on – I haven't got all day.'

'What are you going to do to me, Mistress?'

'Wait and see, you impertinent wretch,' Astrid barked.

Once the bank manager was in position, the masseuse went to her trolley and selected several lengths of nylon cord. She held one up in front of William's face, tugging on the ends as if she were wielding a garrotte.

'Cross your ankles,' she ordered.

William did as he was told, whereupon Astrid wrapped the cord round his ankles several times and tied it securely.

'Now put your hands behind your back.'

With a second length of rope Astrid tied his hands, deliberately scraping her long nails against the tender undersides of his wrists as she did so.

'And now for the fun part,' she said, taking a third length of rope and using it to link the ties on his ankles and wrists together. She tied a loose slipknot then pulled the cord tight. William let out a cry as the manoeuvre caused his body to arch backwards.

Astrid looked at him enquiringly. 'Is that too tight?'

'If it's not too much trouble, Mistress, may I have it a little tighter?' the bank manager gasped.

Astrid obliged. Then she stepped back to admire her willing prisoner, who was now trussed up like a hog, ready for the spit. 'You look wonderful,' she told the bank manager. 'But there's something not quite right.' She held a finger in the air. 'I know.' Returning to the trolley, she took a Cox's orange pippin from the fruit bowl. 'Now, which orifice shall I stuff this in?' she said, tossing the apple into the air and catching it in one hand.

'Any orifice you like, Mistress,' the bank manager replied without hesitation.

Astrid smiled as she eased the apple into his open mouth. 'Why thank you, William. You really are a good and faithful servant.'

The bank manager fluttered his eyelashes. Given his current indisposition, it was the only way he could show his appreciation.

Three

Laura Bentley collapsed on to the kitchen table and buried her head in her arms. Upstairs in the jungle-themed nursery, her infant son Tiger Somerset Bentley was bawling his lungs out. All babies cried; Laura, who'd given birth to three children, was well aware of the fact. But this was no colicky wail, no wah-wah of boredom, no desperate appeal for feeding or nappy changing or blanket removal. Instead, Tiger wielded his voice like an instrument of torture, his howls slicing through the calm like a machete through a melon. Sighing, Laura snatched up a pair of striped oven mitts and pressed one to each ear. 'Please shut up,' she whispered. Ignoring his mother's plea, Tiger continued to scream. A few moments later, Laura hurled the mitts across the room. 'Shut the fuck up, you little shit,' she cried shrilly, 'or so help me, God, I won't be responsible for my actions.'

To say that Laura was struggling to cope was something of an understatement. In the six weeks since giving birth, she'd turned from a relaxed, easy-going earth mother into an exhausted, irritable grouch who seemed to be permanently on the edge of tears. With her daughters, Carnoustie (named for the legendary Scottish golf course) and Birdie (a hole played one stroke under par), it had been love at first sight. The minute the midwife had deposited each damp and bloody creature on her breast,

Laura had been choked with emotion – rendered speechless by a wonderment that couldn't be articulated. But with Tiger it was very different. The pregnancy was unplanned, for one thing. Still, Laura was happy enough to learn she was expecting again and she'd been looking forward to welcoming her first son into the world. But when he was born she'd felt nothing for him; nothing, that is, except a curious detachment – a sense that, while he might have emerged from the ragged wound between her legs (a wound that required stitches and a course of stinging salt baths) he belonged to somebody else entirely.

She thought the situation would improve once she got her son home, that somehow the sight of him in his new nursery, with its hand-painted *Jungle Book* mural and menagerie of stuffed animals, would kick-start her maternal instincts. The opposite was true, for instead of simple indifference, Laura found herself actively resenting him. Try as she might, she couldn't help viewing the new arrival as an intruder, a cuckoo in the nest who was hell-bent on destroying the harmony of the Bentley household. She did her best to hide her feelings, putting on an enthusiastic falsetto as she waggled a teddy over his cot, and forcing herself to smile when he latched on to her breast, even though the sight and sensation of him sucking on her sore nipples made her lip curl in disgust. But the harder she tried the more she felt like a fraud.

By contrast, Laura's husband, Sam, seemed to have no trouble bonding with his newborn son, strapping on the Bill Amberg baby sling at every opportunity and generally behaving as if he'd sired the heir to the throne. But then, Laura told herself, Sam – a professional golfer, who spent at least eighty per cent of his waking life on the golf course – generally saw Tiger when he was at his best: drowsy and docile first thing in the morning, or sweet-smelling and freshly talcumed after his evening bath. Once or twice, Laura had tried to broach her concerns with Sam. 'He cries a lot more than the other two ever did,' she'd remarked the other day over dinner as upstairs, Junior's caterwauling threatened to break the nursery windows.

'Do you think so?' Sam had said as he got up from the table to turn down the volume on the baby monitor. 'I can't really remember what the other two were like when they were tiny.'

'Oh, Carnie was a very easy baby – you must remember that,' Laura said, smiling at the memory. 'And as for Birdie ... she's always been such a sunny-natured little thing.' She twisted a mound of spaghetti Bolognese absent-mindedly round her fork. 'I must say, I'm finding motherhood much more difficult this time round. It's almost as if –' she hesitated – 'he isn't my child.'

Sam stared at her in shock. 'What are you saying, Laura? That you don't love your own son?'

'Gosh no, of course not. I love Tiger to bits.' Laura stared at her plate, unable to look her husband in the eye as she uttered the deliberate untruth. 'It's just ...'

'Go on.'

'Bringing up three children under five ... it's tough, even with Marta helping out.'

'But you've always wanted a big family; you know you have.'

Laura rolled her eyes. 'Seriously, Sam, we're not having any more after this.'

'Chance would be a fine thing.' Sam pointed to his crotch. 'It's been nearly two months now, Laura, and my balls are just about ready to explode.'

Laura sighed. 'To be honest, sex has been the last thing on my mind; I just feel so tired all the time.'

'Maybe you should start going to the gym again. They do say exercise is a great aphrodisiac.' Sam's eyes flitted to Laura's slack stomach, which was still encased in a pair of the comfy drawstring trousers she'd worn throughout her pregnancy. 'And of course it'll help you get the old bod back in shape.'

And maybe you should think about spending less time on the sodding golf course and more time with your family, Laura thought to herself. 'I'm going to the club on Friday to meet the girls for lunch. Perhaps I'll speak to someone about renewing my membership.' She set down her fork. All of a sudden, her appetite had disappeared.

It was a full twenty minutes since Laura had been sitting in the kitchen, listening to Tiger's frantic sobs, and she knew from past experience that he had at least another twenty minutes left in him. Sighing, she pushed her chair away from the table, causing its feet to scrape unpleasantly across the limestone flags. As she headed out into the hall, she was aware of a familiar knot tightening in her stomach: a kind of nameless dread, tinged with nausea. 'Relax, Laura,' she said as she climbed the stairs with leaden feet. 'He's only a baby.' The words sounded hollow and strangely meaningless.

In the nursery, Tiger lay in his shabby chic cot, his face red with exertion as he forced out each ear-splitting yelp.

Laura leaned over the bars and stared at her offspring, hoping for a rush of maternal affection. None was forthcoming. 'What is it this time?' she said through gritted teeth. At the sound of her voice, Tiger's crying eased a little. He opened his tear-filled blue eyes and regarded his mother accusingly. 'Don't look at me like that,' Laura snapped. At this, the baby screwed up his eyes again and began howling at full throttle. Sighing, Laura scooped him up from the cot. He looked tiny and helpless in her arms. She jiggled him up and down half-heartedly a few times. 'You can't possibly be hungry,' she told him. 'I only fed you an hour ago.' Tiger, unfortunately, was giving nothing away.

Laura carried him over to the changing table and lay him on his back. As she started to undo the fasteners on his Peter Rabbit sleepsuit, he squirmed on the plastic mat, flailing his fists as if beating an invisible drum. 'Stay still, can't you?' Laura said irritably, popping his feet out of the sleepsuit. When she pulled back the tapes on his nappy, she saw it was bone dry. Frowning, she picked up Tiger's ankles and lifted them in the air, intending to check his bottom for redness. As she did so, a fountain of urine shot vertically upwards and splashed across her chin. With a shriek, Laura stepped back from the table. 'You little horror,' she said, reaching for a wet wipe. 'You did that on purpose, didn't you?' She watched in distaste as Tiger proceeded to shower the changing table and the cream Axminster carpet with piss.

'Great,' Laura said, when he'd finally finished peeing. '*More* work for Mummy. Thanks a lot.' She pulled Tiger's soiled sleepsuit off and tossed it in the laundry basket.

'As if I haven't got enough to do already.' She yanked another wet wipe out of the dispenser and began cleaning Tiger up. As she did so, his sobs turned to whimpers. 'Hallelujah!' Laura cried. Afterwards, she fastened him into a fresh Pampers and carried him over to his cot. The instant she lay him down on the mattress, he started crying afresh, indignant squawks that made the hairs on the back of Laura's neck stand on end.

'You're not very creative, are you?' she said, walking back over to the changing table to swab the pools of urine with a fistful of wipes. 'Can't you do anything else?' Her voice was cold and scornful. 'Gurgle perhaps. Or even, God forbid, crack a smile every once in a while.' She hunkered down on the floor and began scrubbing at a wet patch on the carpet. 'It's a battle of bloody wills, that's what it is. But I'm not going to let you get the better of me.'

For a few minutes, Laura cleaned in silence, her jaw tightening as Tiger's cries grew in pitch and intensity. At last she rose to her feet. 'Right then, what shall we do now?' She turned towards the cot. 'How about a nice game? Let's see if we can give you something else to think about besides making Mummy's ears bleed.' She went to the cot. Tiger's cries didn't let up. All Laura's instincts were telling her to run away, but she ignored them, gripping the bars of the cot so hard her knuckles turned white.

'What shall we play?' she said with the ersatz enthusiasm of a children's TV presenter. 'I've got a good idea!' She reached down and cupped Tiger's left foot in her hand. Instead of pausing to marvel at the miniature toes

37

and perfect creamy skin, as she would have done with her daughters when they were babies, she cleared her throat in a business-like fashion. 'This little piggy went to market,' she half-spoke, half-sang, taking his big toe between her forefinger and thumb. 'This little piggy stayed at home.' Tiger's cries juddered to a halt. Laura breathed a sigh of relief. 'This little piggy had roast beef.' Suddenly, Tiger grabbed one of Laura's dark corkscrew curls and yanked it hard. 'Ouch!' she cried as she disengaged the tiny fist. 'That hurt.' She narrowed her eyes. 'Why do you always have to spoil things? You hate your mummy, don't you? You want to make her life a misery.' Tiger opened his mouth and let out a yowl. 'Go on, you little cry baby. Do your worst. See if I care.' Laura squatted down beside the cot so that her face was level with the baby's. 'You've got your daddy wrapped round your little finger, haven't you? But he doesn't know what you're really like. He's not the one who's stuck at home with you day after day, feeding you and wiping your shitty arse – *is* he? No, my precious little bundle of joy, that wonderful honour falls to Mummy.'

All at once Laura heard the sound of the front door opening, signalling that Marta, the au pair, was back from taking four-year-old Carnie to nursery. She jumped to her feet. 'Come on, whingebag,' she said, scooping Tiger out of the cot and wrapping a blanket around him. 'The cavalry's arrived.'

Downstairs, in the hall, Marta was lifting Birdie out of her pushchair. Laura's face lit up at the sight of her eighteen-month-old daughter. 'Hi, darling,' she called out from the top of the stairs. 'Have you had a nice walk with Marta?'

'Yeth,' Birdie lisped. 'We thaw the duckths in the park.'

'Did you now?' said Laura as she walked down the stairs. 'Did you give them some bread?'

Birdie nodded solemnly before tottering down the hall towards a toy bus that was parked under one of the radiator covers.

'We took the long way home,' said Marta in her husky, heavily accented English. 'I thought I'd give you two a bit of peace and quiet.'

'Peace and quiet? You're joking, aren't you?' Laura nodded at Tiger, who was still grizzling in her arms. 'This one hasn't stopped crying since you left.'

'What's wrong with him?'

Laura shrugged. 'Christ knows.' She held out her arms. 'Do you mind taking him for a while? He's doing my head in.'

'Sure.' Marta took the infant and settled him into the crook of her arm. Instantly, he fell silent.

Laura gave an exasperated sigh. 'Look at that … bloody typical.'

'Are you okay, Laura?' Marta asked, her pretty face creasing with concern. 'Only you seem a little tense.'

'Tense? Of course I'm tense. This little fucker's ruining my life.'

The Spanish girl looked shocked.

'Only joking!' Laura chirruped. 'I'm just tired, that's all. Tiger had me up five times last night. I just couldn't work out what was wrong with him. He was fed, winded, changed . . . I checked he wasn't running a fever.'

'Sometimes babies cry when all they want is a cuddle,' said Marta.

Laura felt a rush of guilt. The truth was she didn't enjoy physical contact with Tiger. She found it boring and uncomfortable. 'I realize that,' she said, rather more sharply than she intended. 'I have got two other children, in case you hadn't noticed.'

Marta looked at the floor. 'I wasn't criticizing, Laura. I was just trying to help.'

'Yes, I know you were,' Laura said in a softer voice. 'Sorry, Marta, I didn't mean to bite your head off. I don't know what's wrong with me; I've been really short-tempered lately. I think I need to get out more.' She broke into a smile. 'Speaking of which, I've got a hair appointment this afternoon. I'm ridiculously excited about it . . . It's going to be nice to have someone pamper *me* for a change. I might even push the boat out and have a facial while I'm in town.' Laura paused. She noticed that Marta was looking distinctly uncomfortable. 'Is that okay? You'll be able to manage on your own with the kids, won't you? I'll be back in time to pick Carnie up from nursery.'

Marta grimaced. 'Sorry, Laura, I can't. Don't you remember, I'm finishing at lunchtime today?'

Laura's face fell. 'Damn, I forgot.'

'I'd offer to have tomorrow afternoon off instead, but I'm meeting Harry. He's taking me for a picnic.'

'Don't be silly, I wouldn't dream of asking you to change your plans.' Laura put her arm round Marta's shoulders. It wouldn't do to alienate the one person who

40

made the job of being Tiger's mother just about bearable. 'How's it going anyway? This'll be your what … *third* date?'

'Fourth,' said Marta, smiling shyly. 'I really like him, Laura. I know we've only just met, but I have a good feeling. I think he could be, how do you say it in English … The One.'

At this, Laura felt a wave of panic rising up inside her. The notion that Marta might fall in love and abandon the Bentleys to start a family of her own was too awful to contemplate. 'Yes, but you don't want to jump in with both feet,' she said hastily. 'I know you Spaniards are a passionate race, but it doesn't hurt to be a little aloof. English men like that sort of thing.'

Marta frowned. 'Do they?'

'Absolutely. In any case, it won't hurt to keep your options open. I'm sure Harry's a nice enough lad, but he is only a shop assistant after all. I'm sure you can do a lot better.'

'Harry's very smart. I don't think he will be a shop assistant forever.'

Laura looked doubtful. 'Maybe.' She looked down at her infant son, lying in Marta's arms. He was fast sleep. She shook her head disbelievingly. 'Well, would you look at that?'

On the other side of Kirkhulme, in the pretty Victorian church of All Hallows, Marianne Kennedy was arranging a display of mixed summer blooms. She worked quickly and carelessly, cramming the flowers into the glass vase with no thought for symmetry or colour coordination.

Her friends would doubtless have been shocked to see her there, standing at the foot of the pulpit, modestly dressed in an Alberta Ferretti taupe linen dress and flat pumps. A handsome woman in her early fifties, Marianne had not hitherto exhibited the vaguest spiritual tendency. Generally speaking, her interests were of an altogether more carnal nature.

'Bugger,' she said out loud, as she snapped the neck of a gerbera.

Daphne Hammond, who was on her knees beside the altar, putting the finishing touches to an ambitious display of calla lilies, glared at her fellow volunteer. 'Marianne, language! Please try to remember that we're in the Lord's house.'

'Sorry, Daphne, I wasn't thinking.' Marianne plucked the drooping gerbera from the vase and offered it up for inspection. 'I seem to have been a little heavy-handed.'

Daphne, who had been doing the flowers at All Hallows for the best part of two decades, gave Marianne's vase a pitying look. 'Hmm. I don't think you're really cut out for floristry, are you, dear? Perhaps you should think about offering your services elsewhere. I hear they're looking for people to help clear the bindweed from the graveyard.'

Marianne shuddered. 'And ruin a perfectly good manicure? I don't think so.' She picked up a sunflower and forced it into the already overcrowded vase. 'This is only my second week on the job. I just need a bit more practice, that's all.'

As the two women worked, Daphne flung sly sideways glances at her companion, taking in the sleek platinum chignon and expensive jewellery. Marianne wasn't the usual type they got helping out at All Hallows. To the best of Daphne's knowledge, she didn't even attend Sunday service. Still, the church's Volunteer Coordinator never turned down any offer of help.

Marianne stepped back to admire her handiwork. 'Where's the Rev this morning?' she enquired casually.

Daphne frowned at the casual form of address. 'I expect *Reverend Proctor* is in the vestry, enjoying a few moments of quiet contemplation ahead of Morning Prayer,' she said. 'Perhaps you'd like to join us for the service.'

'No thanks, praying's not really my thing. When I finish up here, I'm heading into town for a spot of retail therapy. I'm looking for some shoes to go with my new Miu Miu shirt dress.'

Daphne, who detested avarice in all forms, gave a disparaging sniff. 'I'm afraid I've never been able to get very excited about fashion.'

Marianne stared at the other woman's baby-poo-coloured cords and shapeless turtleneck. 'Really, Daph? I'd never have guessed.'

Suddenly, the door to the vestry swung open. The Reverend Simon Proctor appeared on the threshold, dressed in cassock and surplice. As he made his way towards the women, the shafts of sunlight shining through the stained-glass windows caught the blond high-lights in his thick, tawny hair, giving him a celestial glow. Marianne smiled when she saw him approach, pleased that her – frankly boring – floral endeavours hadn't been for nothing.

To say that Marianne had a voracious sexual appetite was something of an understatement. Since the death of her husband, four years earlier, she'd had dozens of lovers. She picked men up wherever she could – at the club, in the off-licence, waiting in line at the butcher's. She seduced the postman, the pool boy, the man who delivered her groceries. In Marianne's book, anyone with a pair of testicles and a firm set of abs was fair game. There had been only one serious affair, the summer before, with a young golf pro at St Benedict's. It was good while it lasted, but after six months Marianne had grown bored of getting into bed with the same man, night after night. The truth was, she functioned perfectly well on her own. She didn't want or need a relationship. All she wanted was high-quality, uncomplicated, fast and furious, down and dirty sex. And her next lover was going to be the Reverend Proctor. She'd stake her blue crocodile Fendi Spy bag on it.

Simon Proctor had arrived in Kirkhulme a month earlier. Marianne had first spotted him when she attended the funeral of an acquaintance – Bunty Cowper, a champion Crown Green bowler, who'd choked to death on a bottle cap while celebrating her win at the Cheshire Ladies' Open. As Marianne peered through the black spotted lace of her veil – which was attached to a darling Dior pillbox she'd found in a vintage clothes store – she had been transfixed by the vicar's bottomless brown eyes and warm manner, as he recited a moving tribute to a woman he'd never met. After carrying out some discreet enquiries, Marianne discovered that Simon was forty-two, unmarried and had been transferred from his old parish in Oxford, where he'd served for ten years and had been exceedingly well liked. One week and a generous cash donation later, and Marianne had inveigled a place on All Hallows' coveted flower-arranging roster. After that, she told herself, it was only a matter of time before she inveigled herself into the Reverend Proctor's affections.

'Good morning, ladies,' the vicar said as he drew level with the women. His voice was fruity and well modulated and bore a faint country burr. 'You're doing a terrific job with those flowers.' He inhaled deeply. 'And they smell wonderful.'

Daphne beamed with pride. 'That'll be my lilies, Father.'

The reverend looked at the flowers admiringly. 'Oh, Mrs Hammond, what a wonderful display. You really do have quite a talent.' He nodded towards Marianne. 'And I see you have a new assistant today.'

'That's right Father. This is Mari–'

Quick as a flash, Marianne stepped in front of Daphne and held out a tanned arm. 'Hello, Father. Marianne Kennedy, novice florist at your service.' She nodded towards her own amateurish arrangement, which sat on a folding table at the foot of the pulpit. 'Although, as you can see, I've still got a lot to learn.'

The Reverend Proctor took her hand in a firm grip. He smiled, causing the skin around his eyes to crinkle attractively. 'I don't know,' he said. 'I think your display is rather arresting. I love all the different colours.'

'Ahhh,' Marianne breathed. 'That's very kind of you to say so.' As their hands fell apart, she allowed her middle finger to graze the centre of his palm. She just had time to catch his slightly startled expression, before casting her eyes demurely to the floor.

There was a brief silence before the reverend spoke. 'Will you both be joining us for Morning Prayer?'

'*I* will, Father,' Daphne piped up, 'but Marianne is planning a shopping trip.'

'I have to buy a christening gift for my godson-to-be,' said Marianne.

Daphne frowned. 'But I thought you said –'

Marianne cut across her. 'I take my duties as a god-mother very seriously, Reverend.'

'I'm pleased to hear it. When's the christening?'

'Next month. As a matter of fact, you're going to be doing the honours.'

'Wonderful!' said the vicar, clasping his hands together beatifically. Who's the little chap?'

'Tiger Bentley . . . Sam and Laura Bentley's little boy.'

'Ah yes, that's right. A photographer from the *Kirkhulme Gazette*'s already been in touch to ask if he can take some pictures outside the church. I believe Mr Bentley's quite the celebrity in these parts.'

Daphne made a harrumphing noise. 'It certainly won't be the first time he's made the headlines . . . although he does tend to attract the sort of publicity the village could well do without.'

Marianne's jaw tightened. 'I assume you're referring to the deaths of Abi and Xavier Gainsbourg.'

Daphne wrung her hands. 'It was a terrible business, Father, absolutely terrible. I daresay you've heard all about it.'

The vicar cleared his throat. 'Yes, my predecessor, Father John, did make reference to it. It sounds like a tragic waste of two young lives.'

'Of course, Sam Bentley wasn't responsible for their deaths,' Marianne said quickly. She didn't want the reverend thinking she socialized with murderers.

'Not directly, no,' agreed Daphne. 'But, let's face it, if he hadn't been having an affair with Abi, they'd both still be alive.' She sighed and shook her head. 'Then there was that ... ooh, I don't know if I can bring myself to say it in the Lord's house.' She gave a little shudder and mouthed the word *dogging.*

The Reverend Proctor looked confused. 'I'm sorry, I'm not sure I'm familiar with the term.'

Daphne chuckled. 'You don't want to be, Reverend. Suffice to say, it's a thoroughly unnatural practice that no decent Christian soul would ever think about engaging in.'

Marianne gave her a withering look. 'I bet you enjoyed reading about it in the *Sunday Herald*, though, didn't you, Daphne?'

At this, Daphne's cheeks turned pink. 'Well, I may have glanced at an old copy in the surgery waiting room. Anyway,' she said, clearly keen to change the subject, 'how are you settling in at the vicarage, Reverend?'

'Very well, thank you. It's a beautiful old house and I think I shall be very comfortable there.' He made a face. 'Mind you, my washing machine gave up the ghost at the weekend and I've a pile of dirty cassocks in the vestry, so I think a trip to the village launderette will be in order this afternoon.' He smiled. 'It was wonderful to talk to you ladies, but I wonder if I might excuse myself. I need to run through this morning's hymns with Jenny.'

'Of course, Father,' said Marianne, laying a hand on the reverend's arm. 'Don't let us keep you.' She ran the tip of her tongue around her top lip. 'It was wonderful to meet you.'

The vicar patted her hand. 'Likewise, Mrs Kennedy.' Then he gave a small bow and set off in the direction of the winding oak staircase at the far end of the nave.

'Who's Jenny?' Marianne asked, as soon as he was out of earshot.

'Our organist,' Daphne replied. 'She's been helping out at All Hallows longer than I have, which is saying something.'

Right on cue, the air was filled with the opening bars of 'Abide With Me'. Daphne stopped speaking and closed her eyes. 'She plays beautifully, don't you think?'

Marianne shrugged. 'I suppose it's okay . . . if you like that sort of thing.'

Suddenly, Daphne's eyes snapped open. 'I'm not usually one to gossip,' she said in a low voice, 'but a little bird told me that the reverend and Jenny have become very close.'

Marianne looked at her, aghast. 'What?'

'Jenny deserves a bit of happiness,' Daphne continued, seemingly unaware of Marianne's disquiet. 'She's been very low since her divorce last year. Mind you, if you ask me, she's better off without that husband of hers. A drinker he was. And he had an eye for the ladies. I don't know why she stuck it out as long as she did.'

Marianne waved her hand impatiently. 'Never mind

48

him. What about the vicar? Is he having it off with Jenny or not?'

Daphne's hand flew to her mouth. 'Ooh, Marianne, you are awful,' she exclaimed.

Marianne sighed impatiently. 'Oh, come on, Daffers. You're practically part of the furniture at All Hallows. I bet you know everything that goes on.'

Daphne pinched her lips together sanctimoniously. 'Not at all, I respect other people's privacy.' She folded her arms across her shelf-like bosom. 'All I know is Jenny's cooked dinner for Simon a couple of times.'

Marianne's nostrils flared as she stared up at the organ loft. 'Has she indeed?'

'Right then,' Daphne said, as she bent down to pick up a stray sprig of gypsophila. 'You can get off into town if you like. I'll finish this last bit of clearing up.'

'Okay. Same time next week?'

Daphne's eyes flitted to Marianne's display, which was already beginning to wilt. 'Super,' she said, without conviction.

Marianne nodded and set off down the aisle towards the main door, her ballet flats barely making a sound on the tiled floor. She'd only taken a few steps when she stopped and turned to look over her shoulder. Daphne was bending over, dustpan in hand, broad arse straining the seams of her sensible slacks. Quickly, Marianne slipped between two rows of pews and crept along the side wall of the church towards the vestry. The door was shut. She waited until the organist was in full flow before turning the handle and pushing open the door. The room was modest and bare, save for a sink, a writing desk and a large wardrobe. She crossed the room to the wardrobe. A variety of ceremonial vestments in various colours were hanging up, some plain, others richly embroidered. On the floor of the wardrobe was a wicker linen basket. When Marianne flipped the lid, she saw that it contained half a dozen black cotton cassocks. With a satisfied smile, she bundled up the garments and tucked them under her arm. Less than two minutes later, she was walking briskly through the graveyard.

Four

Fiona Mortimer gazed out of the window of her office, which occupied a prime corner position on the fifteenth floor of Delchester's most prestigious high-rise. On a fine day like today, the view was spectacular. There was the cenotaph, standing proudly in Town Hall Square, and beyond it the medieval cathedral with its pointed spires and spectacular rose window. In the distance, she could just make out the docks, whose Victorian warehouses were now home to thrusting financiers and where the lawyer herself owned two profitable buy-to-lets, purchased with the proceeds of her first high-profile court victory – a £7 million settlement for the wife of a philandering footballer.

Deep in thought, Fiona wandered back across the room and sank into her Mies van der Rohe cantilever chair. 'So,' she said, uncapping her fountain pen, 'in the absence of any pre-nuptial agreement, what are you prepared to settle for?'

Amber Solomon cleared her throat. 'Having given the matter considerable thought, I've drawn up a list of my demands.' She flipped a page in the pale blue pigskin notebook resting on her lap. 'I'd like a sizeable cash settlement – let's say fifteen million for the sake of argument – plus five thousand a month living expenses, full medical benefits and an annual allowance of ten thousand pounds for personal upkeep.'

Fiona raised an eyebrow. 'Personal upkeep? Would you mind elaborating?'

'Manicures, dermatology consultations, bikini waxing . . . that sort of thing.'

Fiona stared at her client, taking in the puffy lips and obscenely elongated eyes, and tried to understand what would motivate a perfectly attractive woman to mutilate herself in such a fashion. 'And would you include cosmetic surgery in that category?'

Amber thrust out her new chin implant imperiously. 'It's a distinct possibility.' She turned back to the notebook. 'I want to keep all my jewellery, including the pieces given to me by Daniel's mother, and the Mercedes, of course; I wouldn't be able to function without that. Oh, and a basic staff: housekeeper, cook, driver, gardener.' She fastened her cat-like eyes on the lawyer. 'I don't think I'm being unreasonable, do you?'

Fiona smiled benignly. 'Not in the least. After all, you did devote eighteen years of your life to this man.'

'You're damn right I did,' Amber hissed. 'I raised his son, I organized his social life, I hosted dinner parties for his bloody business associates. Hell, I even gave up my career for him.' She leaned forward. 'Did you know I used to be a household name?'

'Of course,' said Fiona. Like millions of others, she'd once been a big fan of *Highfield Hill*. Set in a close-knit farming community, the primetime soap had run for nearly two decades, until budget cuts and a series of increasingly implausible plotlines forced the network to pull the plug. For nearly three years during the show's late-1980s heyday, Amber had played Clemency Curtis, an upwardly mobile former prostitute who'd bagged a millionaire landowner and was hellbent on sending him to an early grave.

'So that's why you left the show,' Fiona said. 'Because of Daniel?'

Amber nodded. 'I was at the height of my fame when I first laid eyes on Daniel at a mutual friend's Christmas party. We spent the entire evening together, talking and dancing – and then he took me back to his hotel room.' She gave a sad sigh. 'After that, we were virtually inseparable, and six months later he asked me to marry him. He said he wanted us to have a quiet life and that me being in the public eye made that impossible. So I told the producers I was quitting and decided to channel my energies into being the best wife and mother I could.'

'That was some sacrifice.'

'You're telling me.'

Fiona regarded her client thoughtfully. 'And you haven't appeared on television since?'

Amber shook her head.

'Are you still in touch with your old agent?'

'We send each other Christmas cards, nothing more.'

'Perhaps you should think about paying him a visit.'

'Whatever for?'

'To let him know that you might be available for work – if the price was right.'

Amber gripped the edge of the black lacquer desk. 'Have you gone mad? I haven't worked in eighteen years.'

'Yes, and hopefully you won't have to start now.

Believe me, I'm going to work very hard to get you the most generous settlement I can,' said Fiona in a reassuring tone. 'However, it doesn't hurt to have a back-up plan.'

'I love acting,' said Amber. 'I always have and I always will. But it would be like starting from scratch again. I'd be a nobody ... a tiny minnow in a vast ocean, and I don't think I could bear that.'

'Actually, I wasn't thinking about acting.'

Amber frowned. 'No? Then what *were* you thinking about?'

'Reality shows. As a former soap star with a very, er, distinctive look ... you'd be perfect for them. And, best of all, you could earn tens of thousands for only a couple of weeks' work.'

Amber recoiled in horror. 'You want me to shit in a jungle, or kowtow to some ghastly bullyboy chef on national television? You have *got* to be kidding. I trained at RADA, you know. I'm an actress, not a performing seal.'

'Okay, okay ... it was only an idea. Let's put it on the back burner for the time being.' Fiona tapped her pen on her jaw. 'Tell me something, Amber – was Daniel already a successful entrepreneur when you two got together?'

Amber shrugged. 'You *could* say that. He owned a chain of budget hotels. You know, those dreadful places at the side of the motorway with polycotton sheets and complimentary custard creams.' She gave a derisory sniff. 'They made good money, but they were hardly aspirational. I was the one who suggested he go down the boutique hotel route. He took a fair bit of persuading, but in the end I convinced him that people would pay over the odds for Frette bed linen and gourmet food. And I was right. Within five years, his turnover had quadrupled.

Fiona scribbled something on her legal pad. 'Excellent. Since you significantly contributed to your husband's success, we'll be able to argue that you're entitled to not only a portion of your joint capital assets, but also a stake in Daniel's future earnings.' She glanced down at her notes. 'You've made no mention of the family home. Does that mean you're happy for Daniel to retain it?'

Amber shrieked in horror. 'Don't be ridiculous! Of course I want the Old Manor; that goes without saying. Where there are children are involved, the woman always gets to keep the house . . . *doesn't she?*'

'Not necessarily. After all, it's Daniel's home too.'

Amber's hand flew to her throat. 'But I can't leave the Old Manor. I put so much of myself into that place. I chose every light fitting, every metre of carpet, every piece of porcelain. It's my sanctuary, my shangri-la, the only place I feel truly secure. Besides which, the house is all I have to show for the past eighteen years.'

'*And* your son of course.'

Amber rolled her eyes. 'Yes, there is Calum. Not that he's been much comfort to me. He's refusing to take sides, even though I've been at great pains to explain exactly what a lying, cheating scumbag his father is.'

'Just remind me how old Calum is.'

'Seventeen.'

'So he's still technically a minor. Will you be seeking sole custody?'

'God, no – joint custody. I can't cope with that boy's raging hormones twenty-four/seven.'

Fiona made a corresponding note in her pad. 'So at the moment, all three of you are residing at the Old Manor?'

'That's right, though Daniel and I are barely on speaking terms.'

'Have you asked your husband to leave?'

'Yes, but it seems his lawyer has advised him not to.'

'That must be awkward.'

'It's a nightmare. Daniel's being incredibly childish; he's even barred me from certain areas of the house.'

Fiona frowned. '*Barred* you?'

'I know, it's perfectly ridiculous when I've as much right to be there as him.' Amber drew her pashmina more tightly about her shoulders. 'Daniel's taken over the entire second floor. He's threatened me with a restraining order if I so much as set one toe on the staircase.' She pursed her lips, causing the skin around her surgically enhanced jaw line to tighten uncomfortably. 'I really am under a great deal of strain. I used to be such a happy-go-lucky person, but now I'm a bundle of nerves.' She held out her hand. 'See . . . I'm shaking.'

The lawyer nodded sympathetically as she scrawled the words *emotional wreck* on her pad.

'Daniel's also forbidden the staff from serving me. He threatened to sack them if they even make eye contact with me.'

'So you're having to take care of yourself now – cook, clean, drive and so on?'

'Yes, and it's so humiliating; it's been years since I so much as picked up a kettle.' She leaned forward. 'But do you know what the most humiliating thing of all is?'

'No,' said Fiona. 'Why don't you tell me?'

'He's shagging Nancy under my roof.'

'Ah, his mistress.'

'Well, that's one word for her.' Amber's eyes narrowed. 'Scheming little whore is a more accurate description. I can hear them banging away when I'm lying in bed at night. How inconsiderate is that?'

'Extremely inconsiderate,' Fiona agreed. 'Is your husband serious about her?'

'The stupid fool says he's in *love* with her.' Amber gulped. She could feel hot tears pricking the back of her eyelids. It was two weeks since she'd discovered her husband *in flagrante* and she was still having trouble accepting the fact her husband had been unfaithful. And not with a high-breasted, velvet-skinned, thirty-something fox, which would have been easier to stomach – but homely Nancy, with her weightlifter's thighs and hairy top lip. At first, Amber had assumed Nancy was simply a fleeting aberration; that her husband would soon be begging for forgiveness and trying to make it up to her with a string of expensive gifts. So she had been stunned when Daniel had explained, in an exceedingly cold and unapologetic fashion, that he wanted a divorce. And when tears, tantrums and bitter recriminations failed to move him, Amber immediately set about hiring the best divorce lawyer her husband's hard-earned money could buy.

Seeing her client's distress, Fiona reached into her desk drawer and removed a box of Kleenex. 'Help yourself,' she said, pushing the box across the table.

'Thank you,' said Amber, reaching for a tissue.

'So you really don't think there's any chance of a reconciliation.'

Amber shook her head. 'Not unless hell freezes over.'

'And you're adamant that you want the house?'

'I'd sooner die than let him get his filthy hands on it.'

'What if Daniel offered you half the value of the Old Manor?'

Amber's nostrils flared. 'Absolutely not. I don't want half the value; I want the Old Manor, every last brick and slate of it. Daniel cheated on me; he made me a laughing stock.' She wiped her tears away angrily. 'After all the pain and suffering he's put me through, I've bloody well *earned* that house – and I'm quite sure any judge in their right mind would share my opinion.'

Fiona smiled. She liked fighting talk. The way things were shaping up, Solomon vs Solomon could well turn out to be her biggest payday yet.

Cindy McAllister looked at the platinum watch encircling her slender wrist and sighed in irritation. She'd arranged to meet her friends for lunch in the opulent surrounds of St Benedict's Ladies' Lounge – but, as always, the others were late. As a highly sought-after interior designer, Cindy's time was very precious and in less than two hours she had a meeting with a mobile-phone mogul who had commissioned her to make over his guest annexe. Unless her friends arrived soon, she'd barely have time to wolf down a goat's cheese and quail egg salad before making her excuses.

When she glanced up, a handsome olive-skinned waiter in a Nehru jacket was standing by her side. 'Can

I get you a drink while you're waiting, madam?' he said, bowing obsequiously. 'A glass of champagne perhaps?'

Cindy smiled. 'Just some sparkling water, thanks.' She would need to keep a clear head if she were going to convince the mobile-phone mogul that the remote-controlled toilets he'd set his heart on would be horribly *de trop*.

'Very good, madam,' the waiter said, before he turned and glided away across the polished walnut floor.

As she waited, Cindy surveyed her fellow diners with interest. A native Californian, she had moved to Kirk-hulme the previous summer with her pro-golfer husband Kieran. Ever since her arrival, she'd been fascinated by the not-so-subtle divisions in the English class system – and nowhere were these more apparent than in the lunchtime hubbub of the Ladies' Lounge. Two tables away sat a clutch of twenty-something aristo-brats, braying loudly over sashimi and dressed in an expensive uniform of designer jeans and Barbour gilets. Cindy had learned to identify this breed as 'old money'. Next to them, a group of horribly tanned identikit blondes with acrylic nails and credit card cleavages were attacking a bottle of Cristal with gluttonous abandon, each one flashily dressed in this season's Versace or Roberto Cavalli. These were the North Cheshire *nouveau riche*. Both groups were equally wealthy, equally fashion conscious and equally vacuous – and yet, for reasons Cindy was still struggling to grasp, they'd sooner stick Asprey & Garrard brooch pins in their eyes than socialize with one another.

All at once, Cindy caught a familiar whiff of Gucci

Envy. Looking over her shoulder, she saw Marianne walking towards her, a row of crisp, rope-handled carrier bags ranged up her arm to the elbow.

'Darling, I'm so sorry to keep you waiting,' Marianne said as the pair exchanged air kisses. 'Keeley and I have been shopping in town and our cab got stuck in traffic. Kee won't be a moment, she's just powdering her nose.' Realizing that Cindy was alone, Marianne's Botoxed forehead attempted a frown. 'Isn't Laura here yet?'

Cindy shook her head. 'She texted me ten minutes ago to say Tiger threw up all over her just as she was about to leave.'

Dropping her shopping bags on the floor, Marianne sank on to the velvet banquette. 'The poor love has really got her hands full with those three children; we've hardly seen hide nor hair of her since Tiger was born. Personally, I think she made a big mistake getting pregnant so soon after she and Sam decided to make a go of things. In fact . . .' She pursed her lips. 'I think she made a big mistake deciding to make a go of things with Sam, full stop. But that's strictly between you and me.'

Cindy nodded. 'I feel the same way, honey. But, given the alternative, I guess Laura was just trying to do the best thing for the kids, and nobody can blame her for . . .' Cindy's voice tailed off as a volley of expletives rang out. Turning towards its source, she caught sight of her friend, Keeley Finnegan, standing beneath the room's elegant arched entrance. At her feet, a pile of shopping bags lay in a tangled heap as if she'd just thrown them up in the air. Beside her was one of the shiny-haired aristo-brats Cindy had spotted earlier. Judging by their angry expressions and hands-on-hips stances, the two women were engaged in some sort of face-off.

'I'll say this for Keeley,' Marianne remarked. 'She knows how to make an entrance.'

Cindy craned her neck to get a better view. 'What do you reckon they're arguing about?'

'God only knows. You know how sensitive Keeley can be.'

'Sensitive?' Cindy made a face. 'Belligerent, more like.' No sooner had she finished speaking than Keeley shoved her adversary into a dining chair, prompting its occupant to choke on a forkful of potato rösti.

Cindy, who hated 'scenes' of any sort, stood up. 'Perhaps we should go and rescue her, before she does something *really* stupid.'

Marianne grabbed Cindy's arm and drew her back down. 'Absolutely not, darling; Keeley would never forgive us.' She nodded towards their fellow diners, most of whom were watching the proceedings with interest. 'Besides, look at how much pleasure she's providing. Even the waiting staff don't want to break it up.'

Cindy followed Marianne's pointing finger and saw that two waiters – including the one who was supposed to be bringing her sparkling water – had abandoned their duties and were watching the catfight with obvious relish. 'Sick sonsofbitches,' she muttered. 'I expect they're finding this a real turn-on. They're probably hoping those girls are about to start grappling on the floor.'

Marianne gave a little snort. 'The way things are going, I'd say it's only a matter of time.'

She wasn't wrong: seconds later the aristo-brat flew at

Keeley, grabbing her hair with both hands and yanking it hard.

'You fucking slag!' Keeley shrieked as her elaborate up-do exploded in a shower of hairpins. Without a moment's hesitation, she swung her arm back and brought the palm of her hand down hard on the girl's cheek.

Cindy covered her eyes with her hand. 'This is horrible; I don't think I can bear to watch any more.'

'Hmm ... it looks as if you've got your wish,' said Marianne. 'Look who's come to spoil the party – just as things were getting interesting.'

Cindy peeked through her fingers. Jeremy, St Benedict's veteran maître d', had just come storming through the swing doors that led to the kitchen. 'Ladies, please!' he bellowed as he strode towards the entrance arch. 'I must ask you to desist.'

Keeley thrust out her lower lip sulkily. '*She* started it,' she said. 'She came flying round the corner at a hundred miles an hour and ran straight into me. She didn't even have the decency to help me pick up my bags.'

The aristo-brat jabbed a finger in Keeley's face. 'If you hadn't been too busy gabbing on your mobile, you would've seen me coming,' she said in a cut-glass tone.

Keeley pushed a skein of blonde hair out of her eyes. 'Stuck-up cow,' she muttered.

'Common little slapper,' came the retort.

Jeremy placed a hand on each girl's shoulder. 'You're disturbing our other diners. If you don't say sorry and shake hands nicely, I'm afraid I'm going to have to ask you both to leave.'

Keeley folded her arms across her chest and looked away.

The aristo-brat's nostrils flared. 'Apologize to *her*? You must be joking. Anyway, I was just leaving.' With that, she gave Keeley one last lingering look of disgust and flounced off.

The crisis averted, a relieved Jeremy clapped his hands at the waiters. 'Look lively,' he snapped. 'You're not paid to stand around gawping.'

When she arrived at her friends' table, Keeley wore a thoroughly unrepentant air. 'God, those bloody toffs get on my tits,' she cried as she flung her shopping bags down beside Marianne's and began combing her fingers through her dishevelled hair. 'Just because I haven't got a trust fund and a flaming Range Rover doesn't mean she can look down her nose at me.'

'Of course not, darling,' said Marianne. 'And I think you made that point quite beautifully.'

Cindy, who refused to condone violence of any sort, studiously avoided commenting. 'I know Laura isn't here yet, but is it okay if we go ahead and order?' she said, picking up a menu. 'Only I'm meeting a client at three.'

'Good idea – I'm starving,' said Keeley. 'Spending money always gives me an appetite.' She grinned impishly. 'Especially when I'm spending somebody else's.' A former model, Keeley now earned a modest living, buying and selling designer clothes and accessories on eBay. However, her predilection for rich boyfriends meant she was able to live well above her means – and for the past nine months she'd been going out with Delchester United goalkeeper Ryan Stoker.

Cindy waved at a passing waiter, indicating that they were ready to order. 'Oh, the joys of dating a Premiership footballer,' she said sarcastically. 'What's the occasion this time?'

'It's one of the other players' thirtieth birthday party next weekend. Ryan bunged me a few thou to buy myself something nice, so I can give those other WAGs a run for their money.'

'Oh?' said Cindy, arching a well-shaped eyebrow. 'You make it sound like some sort of competition.'

'That's precisely what it is,' Keeley deadpanned. She clasped her hands together. 'I've bought *the* most gorgeous Alaia cocktail dress. It fits me so well it could be a couture piece; all the other WAGs are going to be green with envy. Then, of course, I had to splash out on matching Louboutin shoes. And a Bottega Veneta clutchbag. Not to mention an adorable charm bracelet from Bulgari.'

Cindy, who privately thought Keeley's predilection for sticking together a load of designer labels in a cacophonous mix was more than a little trashy, smiled insincerely. 'Well, in that case, I daresay you're going to be the belle of the ball.'

The women had just started their main course when Laura finally arrived, full of apologies. She seemed harassed. A pink spot of colour adorned each cheek and the buttons of her cardigan were done up the wrong way. 'I'm so sorry, girls,' she said as she took a seat at the table. 'It's Tiger's fault. There I was, bag in hand, ready to go, when the little shit went and projectile vomited his breakfast all over my brand-new blouse.' She reached for the ice bucket where a bottle of rosé was chilling. 'He did it on purpose, I swear.'

Keeley giggled. 'That's what six-week-old babies do, isn't it – eat, sleep, shit and puke?'

Laura filled her glass almost to the brim and returned the bottle to the ice bucket. 'Yes, I suppose so, but ...' She leaned forward, as if worried she might be overheard. 'Tiger isn't like other babies. He's very – how can I put this diplomatically? – *challenging*.'

'Oh?' said Cindy, her face filled with concern.

Laura took a gulp of wine. 'He never stops crying, for one thing. I've had the doctor out more than once, but there's absolutely nothing wrong with him.' She chewed the inside of her cheek. 'At least not *physically*.'

Marianne's forkful of radicchio stopped halfway to her mouth. 'What, you mean you think Tiger might be mentally subnormal?'

Laura shook her head. 'No, it's not that; it's just that there's a sort of slyness about him. Whenever he's with me, he's always grizzly and awkward, but the minute Sam or Marta pick him up, he stops crying and turns into the proverbial ray of sunshine. It's almost as if he's trying to punish me.'

'Why would he want to do that?' asked Keeley.

'Because he's got the devil in him.'

Keeley began humming the theme tune from *The Omen*.

'It's no laughing matter,' Laura said. '*You* try being stuck at home with three kids under the age of five.'

Keeley gave a stagy shudder. 'Ugh, perish the thought.'

'I mean, I'm trying my hardest with him, I really am, but we're just not bonding,' Laura said disconsolately. 'The truth is, I don't think Tiger likes me very much.' She sighed. 'And I have to say, the feeling's mutual.'

Marianne put down her fork. 'Nonsense, darling. Plenty of women don't bond with their babies instantly; you just need to give it time.' She pushed a menu across the table. 'Here, why don't you order some food? You'll feel better once you've had something to eat.'

Laura took a slug of wine. 'No thanks, I'm not really hungry.'

'I don't think it's a good idea to skip meals,' Cindy admonished her. 'You need to keep your strength up.'

Laura grabbed her spare tyre and wobbled it up and down. 'Just look at this; I hardly think I'm in danger of starving to death – as my dear husband is fond of reminding me.'

Marianne gave her a sharp look. 'That man should take a lesson in tact. You've just given birth for heaven's sake.'

'Oh, *you* know Sam,' said Laura. 'He's a perfectionist and he expects everyone around him to be the same. Of course, if he spent more time looking after the kids and less time on the golf course, I'd have more opportunity to get my fat arse down the gym.'

'Sam's never been what you might call a hands-on dad, has he?' said Marianne witheringly. 'I rather thought he might have bucked up his ideas after what happened last year.'

There was a brief silence as the four friends contemplated the tragic events Marianne was referring to. The previous summer, Sam and Laura had both embarked on torrid affairs, as a consequence of which, two people – Sam's young mistress Abi Gainsbourg and her husband Xavier – had lost their lives. A third – Laura's lover, ex-Formula One star Jackson West – had wound up paraplegic. In the grim aftermath, Sam and Laura had decided to try and make a go of their marriage, and Laura had fallen pregnant almost immediately.

Cindy was the first to speak. 'Do you ever think about Jackson?' she enquired gently.

'Sometimes, but I don't regret my decision to stick with Sam. For all his faults, he's a good provider and he loves the kids to bits. To be honest, I was glad when Jackson decided to leave Kirkhulme and go back to France. It would've been tough seeing him in that wheelchair.' Laura took a piece of ciabatta from the bread basket and began loading it with butter. 'I wish Sam and I could move house. Our place is gorgeous, but it's just not big enough for the five of us.'

'Then why *don't* you, darling?' said Marianne. 'I was looking in the window of Woodward & Stockley the other day and I noticed that lovely old coach house down by the river is up for sale. It's got six bedrooms – four en suite – two receptions, a billiard room, wine cellar and a very spacious conservatory. That would suit you down to the ground, wouldn't it?'

'Too right,' said Laura. 'But thanks to that conniving slut, we just can't afford to move right now.'

Marianne rolled her eyes. 'Ah yes, Elissa Jones. I was forgetting about that grubby business.'

An erstwhile waitress at St Benedict's, Elissa Jones had

allegedly been impregnated by Sam after a three-minute, cocaine-fuelled, stag-night encounter in the club's video-conferencing suite. Initially, Elissa was threatening to keep the baby and demanding a hefty monthly maintenance. But, after lengthy negotiations by Sam's lawyer, she had finally accepted a six-figure pay-off in exchange for a termination – even though there was no proof the baby she was carrying was indeed Sam's.

Cindy pushed her salad bowl to one side. 'C'mon, guys, we're supposed to be having fun here. Can't we talk about something more upbeat? I know . . .' She clapped her hands together. 'The christening!'

'Ooh yes,' said Keeley. 'That was so sweet of you to ask all three of us to be Tiger's godmothers, Laura; I know exactly what I'm going to wear.'

'Well, I hope it's not one of your fancy designer numbers,' said Laura dryly. 'Because it's probably going to end up covered in baby sick.'

'Now, now,' said Marianne. 'I'm sure it's going to be a fabulous occasion. For all sorts of reasons.' Her eyes misted over. 'For those of you who haven't met him, the vicar of All Hallows is practically edible.'

'Marianne!' Cindy exclaimed. 'You cannot be serious.'

'I'm perfectly serious,' the older woman replied tartly. 'Despite his innocent exterior, I reckon the Reverend Simon Proctor's a bit of a beast on the sly. What's more, I intend to find out.'

'Well, good luck to you,' Laura said. 'He's a good-looking bloke. If I wasn't feeling so fat and frumpy, I might even be tempted to have a go myself.'

Cindy sighed. Sometimes it felt as if she were the

only happily married woman in Kirkhulme. The thought reminded her of something. 'Hey, you'll never guess who called me yesterday.' She paused for dramatic effect. 'Amber Solomon.'

'What, Catwoman? No way!' Keeley squealed.

'It's true,' said Cindy, smiling smugly. 'She's planning some cosmetic alterations at the Old Manor and she's booked a consultation with me.'

'What's she got in mind?' asked Laura. 'The poor woman's in the middle of a divorce; I would've thought a redesign would be the last thing on her mind.'

Cindy shrugged. 'I'm not sure; she was pretty cagey on the phone.'

'*Poor woman*, my arse,' said Keeley. 'I, for one, don't blame Daniel Solomon for shagging the hired help – not when his wife looks like the bastard child of Aslan and CoCo the Clown. I saw Amber in the village the other day . . . I swear to God, small children were running away from her screaming.'

'Hear, hear,' said Marianne. She drew the back of her hand across her jaw. 'I know *I've* had a few nips and tucks in the past, but at least my face hasn't changed beyond all recognition.'

'There's absolutely no comparison,' Cindy told her friend. 'You look fantastic.'

'For your age,' Keeley added, rather cruelly. 'How old are you now, Marianne? Fifty-six?'

'Fifty-*two*,' Marianne snapped.

'I've heard the Solomons' divorce is turning really ugly,' said Laura. 'Apparently, they're both refusing to move out of the house. It's their poor son I feel sorry for.' She drained the contents of her wineglass. 'It's always the kids who suffer in the end.'

Cindy sighed in exasperation. 'Look ... we're doing it again.'

'What?' said Laura.

'Being negative.' She smiled. 'I know what'll cheer us up.' She waved their waiter over. 'Could we see the dessert menu, please?'

Five

It was a warm Saturday in early June and the golf course at St Benedict's was teaming with players. Beneath the cloudless sky, the tenth green stretched like a green velvet carpet, its lush appearance maintained by daily mowing and a state-of-the-art, computer-controlled irrigation system. Squinting against the morning sun, Sam Bentley gripped the tempered steel shaft of his custom-made putter and tried to focus. The hole was less than twelve feet away. A golfer of his calibre, playing on home turf, should be able to take the shot with his eyes closed. Rocking from his heels to the balls of his feet, Sam moved the putter in a pendulum motion and struck the ball with a well-timed flick, then watched in disgust as it trickled straight past the pin.

'Bad luck,' an American-accented voice called out.

Sam frowned. He hated it when other players commented on his game, even if they were only commiserating; it upset his concentration. He glanced over his shoulder, ready to fire an icy glare in the culprit's direction. There were several players within hailing range and at first he wasn't sure which one had spoken. Then he looked towards the row of mature beech trees that guarded the green's southern boundary and saw a familiar five-foot-ten-inch brunette, dressed in a cute ensemble of pink polo shirt, teeny white skirt, white knee-high socks and pink golf shoes. Instantly his expression softened.

The girl nodded towards the ball. 'I think you had a bit of cross-wind to contend with.'

Sam knew she was being kind. The winds were light, and in any case the green was sheltered from the elements by a series of grassy hummocks. 'Or maybe I'm just not on form today,' he said with a rueful grin. He walked over to the girl and stood in front of her, legs spread wide to emphasize his masculinity. 'Hi, Taylor, I heard you were training at St Benedict's. I was hoping our paths would cross.'

The American looked him up and down. Sam enjoyed the feel of her eyes exploring his body. He knew he cut an impressive figure with his muscular forearms, dazzling blue eyes, and the five o'clock shadow spreading across his jaw like a bruise. 'I'm sorry, I don't believe I know you,' Taylor said at last.

'Sam Bentley,' he replied, swapping his putter to his left hand and extending his right towards her. 'I'm the European number forty-five,' he added, keen to identify himself as a fellow pro and not one of the power-mad, distance-obsessed golf punks who flocked to St Benedict's at the weekend and insisted on playing well above their handicap.

Taylor eased off her pink golf glove and took Sam's hand, gripping it with surprising force. 'Oh yeah, I know you by reputation. Didn't you win the Scottish Stroke Play Championship a couple of years back?'

Sam nodded. 'Yep, I carded a three-under-par sixty-nine for a one-over total of two eighty-nine.'

'*Verrry* impressive,' said Taylor flirtatiously. 'I bet you could teach me a thing or two.'

Sam laughed. 'Somehow, I doubt it.'

At nineteen years old, Taylor Spurr was one of the most precocious talents on the American golf circuit. Having turned professional two years earlier, she was currently sitting at number twenty-nine in the women's world rankings. But it wasn't just her explosive swing that had tournament photographers rushing after her in droves, so much as her megawatt smile, voluptuous figure and eye-catching outfits, which always included a splash of her favourite pink. Normally based in her hometown of Dallas, Taylor was spending the summer at St Benedict's, training with Stanley Rose, a British golfing legend and one of the world's top coaches.

'How are you finding life in the Cheshire countryside?' Sam asked, flipping his golf club over his shoulder in a casual display of athleticism.

Taylor reached for the glossy ponytail that snaked through the back of her pink baseball cap and pulled it over her shoulder, twirling the tip round her index finger. It was a coy, girlish gesture that Sam found curiously arousing. 'I've only been here a couple of weeks, so I'm still finding my feet,' she said. 'It sure is different to Dallas though.'

'Are you staying in the village?'

Taylor nodded. 'Uh-huh. I'm renting a cottage overlooking the river; it's real pretty.'

'Oh yes, there are some wonderful properties in Kirk-hulme,' said Sam. 'It's a great place to live, very peaceful and quiet.'

Taylor wrinkled her freckled nose. 'If you ask me, it's a little *too* quiet. What do folks do for fun around here?'

It was the opening Sam had been waiting for. 'Oh, there's tons going on. You just have to know where to look.' He paused for a beat. 'I'd be happy to show you around, if you like.'

Before Taylor could answer, a husky voice called out across the green. 'Hey, Taylor! Get your ass over here.'

Scanning the landscape for the source of the interruption, Sam saw a powerfully built woman in a pair of purple twill plus-fours striding towards them. As she drew nearer, he saw that she was hauling a professional golfbag, emblazoned with the name of Taylor's sponsor.

Taylor's face fell. 'I wish that woman would leave me alone for one minute,' she said through gritted teeth. She cupped her hands round her mouth. 'Can't you see I'm having a conversation?' she called back.

'You're supposed to be practising,' came the terse reply.

Sam looked aghast. 'Jesus, how can you let your caddie speak to you like that?'

Taylor made a face. 'Because my caddie also happens to be my mom. And she still treats me like I'm ten years old.'

'Surely she can't object to you talking to a fellow pro.'

'If he's a guy and he's as good looking as you are, she can. Mom's a total slave driver; she disapproves of anything that takes my mind away from golf.'

Sam smiled, basking in the compliment. 'Oh well, she's only looking after your best interests.'

'Trying to stop me enjoying myself, more like,' said

Taylor, glowering. Her mother was now less than twenty feet away. 'Why does she always have to spoil *everything*?'

'Don't worry,' said Sam soothingly. 'I'll take care of her.' He held out his putter. 'Hold this for a minute, will you? Oh, and what's your mother's name?'

'Kristina,' said Taylor as she took the club. 'But her friends call her Kris.'

Sam turned and began walking towards Taylor's mother. 'Kris, how lovely to meet you,' he said as he drew level with her. 'Here, let me take that.' Before she could object, he'd wrested the handle of the pink golf bag from her grasp. 'I was just warning your charming daughter about the perils of the tenth,' he said, hauling the bag back towards Taylor. 'There's a stretch of dead ground just in front of the green that makes the hole play longer than it appears.'

Kris eyed him warily. 'And who are you?'

'Sam Bentley, at your service, ma'am.' The golfer ran a hand through his thick dark hair and treated her to one of the killer smiles he usually reserved for members of the press and adoring fans. Despite her naturally suspicious nature, Kris couldn't help smiling back.

'He's one of the UK's top players, Mom,' said Taylor.

'And I know the course at St Benedict's better than anyone,' Sam added. He gave Kris a lingering look. She was a striking woman – tall and muscular, if a little weather-beaten. He estimated her age at forty-eight, which would make her eleven years older than him. 'I can't believe you two are mother and daughter,' he said. 'If I didn't know any better, I'd swear you were sisters.'

Kris sucked her cheeks in. She knew it was a line, but

she couldn't help feeling flattered. It was coming up to the tenth anniversary of her divorce and during that time she'd been so busy looking after Taylor's career she'd barely had time to think about finding a new love interest. Her eyes flitted discreetly to Sam's left hand. She saw that he wasn't wearing a wedding ring. 'I've heard about you English guys,' she said.

'Oh yes?' said Sam. 'What have you heard? Nothing bad I hope.'

'That you're a bunch of smooth-talkin' bastards.'

'Mom!' Beneath her deep Texas tan, Taylor blushed a fetching shade of crimson.

Sam laughed. 'She's a smart woman, your mother.' Reaching out he took his putter back from Taylor. 'It was great meeting you girls, but I guess I'd better let you get back to your practice round.'

Kristina silently cursed herself for the putdown. She'd meant to be playful but now it seemed she'd driven the handsome Englishman away. 'I expect we'll run into you again some time,' she said.

'I expect you will. I'm on the course most days.' Sam raised his hand in farewell and began walking away towards the eleventh green. Mother and daughter stared after him. If Sam had bothered to look over his shoulder, he would have seen that both women's eyes were filled with longing.

Less than half a mile away, Marianne was parking her Audi in a leafy lane, just off Kirkhulme's bustling high street. Normally groomed to within an inch of her life, she'd opted for a more natural look, with loose hair and subtle make-up, even foregoing her usual designer frock in favour of a pair of skinny cargo pants and a cotton camisole. On this particular occasion, she told herself, less was definitely more. Before pulling the keys out of the ignition, she applied a fresh slick of nude lipgloss and pushed her hair back behind her ears. Satisfied with her appearance, she got out of the car and went round to the boot to retrieve a pile of clothes that she'd just collected from the dry cleaner's. Draping the plastic garment bags over her arm, she slammed the boot shut and activated the Audi's alarm. Even in Kirkhulme, where crime figures were low, one couldn't be too careful. As she made her way towards a large double-fronted property set well back from the road, she felt a twinge of excitement. For a woman like Marianne, the thrill of the chase was almost as enjoyable as the act of devouring the spoils. When she pushed open the garden gate and began walking up the crazy-paved pathway, she saw that an upstairs window was open, indicating that the occupant was at home. She smiled to herself, pleased that she hadn't had a wasted journey.

Although Marianne had driven past the house countless times, she'd never seen it at such close quarters. It was an imposing – if austere – piece of Victorian architecture with a wealth of original features, including, above the front door, a stucco plaque bearing the words *The Vicarage* in Gothic script. Marianne took a deep breath and pushed the doorbell. A few moments later, she found herself face to face with the Reverend Simon Proctor. It was several days since the pair's last meeting and the vicar looked even more handsome than Marianne remembered. He was wearing a dark suit, complete with dog collar, and his cheeks were flushed, as if he'd just stepped out of a warm bath.

'Mrs Kennedy,' he said with a bewildered smile. 'This is an unexpected pleasure.'

'Good morning, Reverend, and what a glorious morning on God's earth it is too.' Without waiting for an invitation, Marianne stepped over the threshold. The hallway was narrow and she was close enough to see that the vicar's deep brown eyes were tinged with flecks of green. 'I hope you don't mind me dropping by like this,' she continued. 'I just wanted to return something of yours.'

The vicar frowned. 'You did?' He closed the front door behind Marianne. When he turned back to her, she was already halfway down the hall. 'The living room's just off to the right,' he called out. 'It's rather untidy, I'm afraid. I wasn't expecting company.'

'Oh, don't you worry about that,' said Marianne as she pushed open the stripped pine door. 'A little bit of mess never hurt anyone.'

The room was cool and spartan. A faint smell of disinfectant hung in the air. The Reverend Proctor didn't care for comfort. He felt easier in his soul when he was hungry, or tired, or when his lower back ached. Marianne, who had a keen sense of aesthetics, tried to mask her dismay as she took in the mismatching furniture and the pile of newspapers heaped messily on the coffee table. Still, she noted, the room was well proportioned and contained some fine original features, including a cast-iron fireplace and an ornate ceiling rose.

'This is the first time I've seen inside the vicarage,' she remarked, mentally working out how much the house would be worth in the unlikely event it ever came on to the open market. 'It's much grander than I imagined.'

'It's beautiful, isn't it?' Simon replied. 'I'm afraid my furnishings don't do it justice. A priest's life must, by necessity, be a simple one.'

'Oh, I don't know,' said Marianne, eyeing the lumpy settee. 'I think it has a nice homely feel.'

'Thank you, Mrs Kennedy; that's kind of you to say so.'

'Please, Reverend, call me Marianne.'

'The vicar smiled. 'Very well – and you must call me Simon.'

'Well, *Simon*,' Marianne said. 'I trust I haven't called at an inconvenient time.'

'No, no, I was just doing some paperwork upstairs in my office.'

'I won't stay long, I promise. I just wanted to return these.' Marianne walked over to a saggy, rust-coloured armchair and draped the dry cleaning bags over its tall back. The vicar looked at her quizzically. 'Your cassocks,' she said. 'I've had them dry-cleaned.'

Simon looked at her in surprise. 'So it was you who took them from the vestry,' he exclaimed.

Marianne nodded. 'I know how busy you are, tending to your flock, so I thought I'd save you a trip to the launderette.' She smiled, waiting for Simon to praise her thoughtfulness. But, instead, his face took on a serious cast.

'The vestry is off limits to the general public,' he said firmly. 'It houses the sacred vessels.'

'Really? I had no idea.' Marianne bowed her head contritely and murmured: 'Forgive me, Father, for I have sinned.'

The vicar seemed embarrassed by her declaration. 'Please, there's no need for that. You made a mistake, that's all.'

Marianne looked up at him, her eyes wide and innocent. 'I'm so sorry, Simon; I thought I was doing my Christian duty.'

Simon patted the top of her arm. 'Let's forget about it, shall we? My cassocks have been returned and that's the main thing.' He smiled. 'And just to show there are no hard feelings, why don't we have a nice drink?'

Marianne was thrilled. She'd been in the vicar's house for less than five minutes and already he was asking her out on a date. 'I'd like that very much,' she said.

'Good. I'll go and put the kettle on then. Tea or coffee?'

Marianne's face fell. She appeared to have jumped the gun. 'Tea, please. Lapsang souchong, if you have it.'

'Oh. I'm afraid I don't. Is PG Tips okay?'

'Fine. I take mine black – with a slice of lemon.'

Simon grimaced.

'No lemon? Not to worry.'

The vicar gestured to the settee. 'Make yourself comfortable. I'll be back in a jiffy.'

While her host was absent, Marianne took the opportunity to nose around. In her experience, a bit of background information was never a bad thing. She went to the deeply unfashionable sideboard and opened the top drawer. It contained a set of tarnished cutlery and a well-thumbed hymnal. The second drawer was filled with prayer cards, packed in plastic boxes. Disappointed, she wandered over to the bay window and stared out across the garden. It was a generous size, with some pretty planting, but the scrubby lawn needed mowing and the door to the shed was hanging off its hinges. Marianne sighed. The vicarage could clearly do with some TLC – and so, she suspected, could the vicar.

By the time Simon returned with two steaming mugs of tea, Marianne had taken up position on the settee. 'How are you settling in to the parish?' she asked as she accepted one of the mugs. 'I trust you've been made to feel welcome.'

'Oh yes, you're a friendly bunch all right.' The vicar sat down beside his guest and proffered a half-empty packet of Bourbons, sending a shower of crumbs between the gap in the cushions as he did so. 'Biscuit?'

'No thanks, I've got to watch my figure.' Marianne's figure was spectacular for a woman of her age – indeed, for a woman of any age – thanks to a strict regime of yoga, swimming and gym workouts. She was hoping the remark would elicit a compliment, as it usually did, but Simon, who was singularly ill versed in the art of flattery, failed to take the bait.

Marianne sipped her tea tentatively. It was slightly stewed and hot enough to take the roof off her mouth. 'I gather you've hit it off with one female parishioner in particular,' she said lightly.

Simon bit down on a Bourbon. 'And which lady might that be?'

'Come, come, there's no need to be coy,' said

Marianne. 'I'm sure you know perfectly well who I'm talking about . . . Jenny, the church organist.'

Simon cleared his throat. 'Ah yes, Mrs Branscombe. A very talented lady.'

'And does she cook as well as she plays the organ?' Marianne cocked her head to one side. 'A little bird told me you've been sharing intimate dinners *à deux*.'

'Jenny's been good enough to cook a meal for me on one or two occasions, that's all,' said Simon.

Marianne fixed the vicar with a penetrating stare. 'So you two aren't an item?'

The vicar began scraping at an imaginary stain on the arm of the settee. 'You know, Marianne, discussing my private life makes me feel dreadfully uncomfortable. I'm not sure that I –' Out in the hall, the telephone began to ring. Simon made a wry face. 'Saved by the bell, eh?' He stood up. 'Will you excuse me for a moment?'

Marianne was annoyed by the interruption. What's more, she was beginning to think that her visit was a waste of time. The Reverend Proctor wasn't giving much away. In fact, he seemed rather uptight – in which case, they weren't going to be sexually compatible. His voice began to drift through the open door of the living room. 'The church charges a basic fee of five hundred pounds, payable in advance,' he was saying. 'That covers the marriage licence, floral decorations, organist and car park attendant, but *not* the choir and bell ringers.'

'Fools,' Marianne muttered. *She'd* been married once – for twenty-two long years, and the experience had left her determined never to be beholden to another man so long as she lived. The way she saw it, the male of the species was good for one thing and one thing only.

The vicar was now embarking on a precis of All Hallows' five-week marriage preparation course. Sighing, Marianne set her mug down on the coffee table. It was time to cut her losses. She must have been mad, thinking that a man of the cloth would ever be able to match her sexual appetite. No, she comforted herself, Simon Proctor was probably better off with the likes of mousey Jenny Branscombe, who probably wore a pie-crust collar nightie to bed and would only do it in the missionary position with the lights out. She picked up her car keys and went out into the hall. When Simon saw her, he covered the mouthpiece of the phone with his hand.

'I'll leave you to it,' she whispered. 'Is it okay if I use your loo before I go?' The vicar nodded and pointed above his head before resuming his conversation with the bride-to-be.

The upper part of the vicarage was just as uninviting as the downstairs. The gloomy landing with its badly worn carpet seemed to stretch endlessly ahead and offered no clue to the bathroom's location. The first door Marianne tried turned out to be a bedroom. It was bare, save for an old oak wardrobe and a single bed, covered in mustard-coloured candlewick. Above the bed was a plain wooden cross, the sort of thing you'd expect to find in a Benedictine monk's cell. Shuddering in distaste, Marianne closed the door and tried another. This time, she found herself in an office. There was a filing cabinet in the corner and, opposite it, a tall bookcase that leaned perilously to one side. In between the two was a desk and on it a surprisingly modern PC. The vicar's face stared out from the flatscreen. Intrigued, Marianne went over to the computer for a closer look. The screen saver showed Simon standing on a windswept beach, his arm curled round the shoulders of a middle-aged man. The pair shared the same Roman nose and strong, almost simian, brow. As she leaned on the desk, Marianne inadvertently nudged the mouse. Instantly, the photograph disappeared. To her surprise Marianne found herself staring at an enormous pair of naked breasts. Their owner was sprawled across an unmade bed, gazing up at the camera, wet-look lips slightly parted. A caption beneath the bosom screamed: *See live cam cuties ready to bare all and take direction!* Marianne tutted. 'Doing paperwork', indeed. No wonder Simon's cheeks had been flushed when he came to the door. 'Oh, Reverend,' she said, shaking her head. 'You wicked, wicked man.'

By the time Marianne reappeared at the top of the stairs, the vicar was bidding the caller goodbye. Marianne waited until she heard the click of the receiver being replaced and then began her descent. At the sound of her footsteps, the vicar came to greet her. 'Sorry about that,' he said, his eyes fixed on the scrap of paper in his hand on which he'd scrawled the woman's details. 'It was an out-of-towner wanting to know if she could book All Hallows for her wedding.' When Marianne failed to reply, Simon glanced up. 'Saints preserve us!' he cried, staggering backwards and gripping the balustrade for support.

In all his forty-two years, the Reverend Simon Proctor had never seen a vision quite so lovely as the one in front of him. He swallowed hard, drinking in the sight of

Marianne floating down the staircase in nothing but a white broderie anglaise basque and matching knickers, somehow managing to look wanton and virginal all at the same time. 'Where are your clothes?' he stammered.

'On the floor of your office,' she replied matter-of-factly. 'I was looking for the bathroom, but instead I found myself staring at a naked lady on your computer screen.' She widened her eyes. 'That's an interesting hobby you have there, Reverend.'

The vicar let out a loud groan.

'There's no need to be embarrassed,' said Marianne as she descended the final few steps. 'I'm very broad-minded. As you're about to find out.' Reaching up, she gently drew Simon's hand away from his face and placed it on her breast. He stared at her in mute disbelief, but didn't try to move his hand away. Marianne leaned towards him and brushed her lips against his. The vicar hesitated for a fraction of a second, then pushed his tongue into the soft, moist cavern of her mouth and began kissing her more passionately than he'd kissed any woman before.

Six

Cindy felt a delicious sense of anticipation as she stood on the well-worn front step of the Old Manor. She'd been thrilled when she received the phone call inviting her to the house – and not from some secretary or flunky, but from Amber Solomon herself. After all, what designer wouldn't give her eye teeth to work on such a fine historic building? Cindy's interest in the Solomons was more than just professional, however. Whether or not she cared to admit it, a significant proportion of her excitement stemmed from the prospect of rubbing shoulders with one of Kirkhulme's most illustrious families. Daniel Solomon was a local legend, thanks to his chain of award-winning hotels, not to mention his fleet of supercars, which at last count included a Maserati GranSport, a Lamborghini Miura and a Jaguar XKSS. His wife, Amber, meanwhile, had gained a notoriety all of her own, courtesy of her erstwhile showbiz career, startling facial features and the lavish parties she was fond of throwing. Not that there had been much partying of late – for, as Cindy and everyone else in the village knew, the Solomons were in the midst of a bitter divorce.

News of the couple's split had sent the village gossip-mongers into a veritable frenzy. One reliable source claimed Amber had been stripped of her couture wardrobe and banished to the basement, a virtual prisoner in her own home. Others theorized that Daniel's new love, Nancy, was a white witch who had slipped a home-brewed love potion into her employer's morning cappuccino – for how else, they reasoned, could a woman with wiry hair and thick ankles have bagged such a prize? With such extravagant rumours doing the rounds, Cindy had no idea what to expect as she grasped the heavy brass knocker and let it fall against the Old Manor's ancient front door.

It was Amber who came to greet her, wearing dainty embroidered slippers and a full-length summer gown, fashioned from some diaphanous material. Even though Cindy had seen several pictures of her prospective client in 'Jemima's Diary', the *Kirkhulme Gazette*'s twee weekly gossip column, nothing could have prepared her for her first face-to-face encounter with the infamous Cat-woman. Everything about Amber's face was odd, but it was her eyes Cindy noticed first. It wasn't so much their alien-esque shape, as their deeply pained look, which suggested their owner were nursing some sort of injury – a broken toe perhaps, or, at the very least, a nasty corn. Beneath the eyes was the smallest nose Cindy had ever seen, its tip dangerously tilted upwards like the end of a ski jump. It contrasted frighteningly with the grotesquely swollen lips, which put her in mind of a pair of sausages, fit to burst as they cooked on a barbecue. And then, all once, the lips began to move.

'Hello there, you must be Cindy.' Despite the friendly tone in her voice, Amber's features remained curiously static.

'And you must be Amber,' Cindy replied with a wide

Californian smile. 'It's great to meet you in the flesh. I've heard so much about you.'

Amber's pencilled-on eyebrows moved a fraction of a millimetre. 'So my reputation precedes me.'

Cindy's smile faltered as she struggled to remember some piece of information that portrayed Amber in a flattering manner. 'I hear you're a leading light in the Kirkhulme Ladies' Guild,' she said after a slight pause. 'I'm a big fan of their bake sales.'

Amber sighed languidly. 'As a matter of fact, I've just given up my seat on the board.'

'Really?' said Cindy. 'Oh well, I expect you have a lot of demands on your time.'

Amber sighed again. 'It's not that; it's just that I haven't felt very sociable of late.' She stepped back from the door. 'Please, won't you come in?'

The entrance hall was even more spectacular than Cindy had imagined and resembled a medieval banqueting chamber, with its polished sandstone floor and a magnificent staircase leading to a lofty minstrel's gallery. 'You have a beautiful home,' Cindy said, as she stared up at the beamed ceiling with its roughly worked wattle and daub reveal. 'Have you lived here long?'

'Eighteen years. The house was in a very shabby state when we bought it. My husband and I spent a great deal of time and money bringing it back to life.' Amber rubbed her arms through the thin fabric of her dress, as if she'd suddenly felt a chill. 'It would break my heart to leave it now.'

'I'm sure it would.' Cindy's gaze was drawn to a feature wall, which was covered above the wainscoting with some unusual embossed wallpaper. She brushed her fingertips against it. It felt soft and leathery. 'This is an interesting wall covering. What's it made from?'

'Hand-gilded kidskin,' Amber replied. 'I found it in a little shop in Paris.'

Cindy was seriously impressed. It was becoming clear that Amber was a woman of exceedingly good taste. 'I've never seen anything quite like it,' she said, letting her hand fall away. 'It's utterly gorge—'

Suddenly, Cindy froze in horror. A ball of fur was bounding across the floor towards her, its nails beating out a sinister tattoo on the stone floor. Cindy let out a shriek as the creature launched itself at her shoulder bag, grabbing the strap with its bony fingers and swinging beneath it like a tiny trapeze artist.

'It's okay — he won't hurt you,' Amber said as she extended her arms towards the capuchin. 'Come on, Couscous, come to Mummy.' The ball of fur obligingly let go of Cindy's bag and leapt into his mistress's arms.

Cindy held her hand over her pounding heart. 'You have a pet *monkey*?' she said, trying to mask her horror.

'Yes, I've had him since he was a baby,' said Amber, nuzzling her chin against the primate's soft head. 'I'm afraid he can be a little mischievous at times.'

'So I see,' said Cindy, surreptitiously checking her shoulder bag for damage. 'Is he house-trained?'

'Of course he is,' Amber replied indignantly. She planted a kiss on the monkey's head. 'Couscous is a wonderful companion. I don't know what I'd do if anything happened to him.'

'Well, he's absolutely adorable,' said Cindy – who, truth be told, had never been a great animal lover.

With Couscous's arms clasped round her neck, Amber led the way to the drawing room. 'Make yourself comfortable,' she said. 'I'd better put this little attention-seeker back in his cage, otherwise he'll just make a nuisance of himself.'

Cindy watched as Amber disappeared through a set of double doors that gave on to a grand conservatory. In the far corner, she could see a large metal cage, filled with tropical foliage. It didn't seem right to her that a wild animal – even one bred in captivity – should be kept as a pet. Cindy knew on which side her bread was buttered, however, and she wasn't about to jeopardize a possible commission by articulating her views. As she made her way towards a wing chair, she noticed a cluster of photographs in silver frames, ranged on top of a decorative radiator cover. A wedding picture caught her eye and, with Amber busy in the conservatory, she couldn't resist taking a closer look.

Despite his youth, the groom was easily recognizable as Daniel Solomon. Cindy had seen him around the village once or twice, most recently in the Fox & Hounds when, celebrating a prestigious hotel industry award, he'd generously stood a round for the entire pub. Beside him was his pretty – but not beautiful – bride in a beaded, empire-line gown, her dark hair piled into an elaborate up-do and studded with tiny white rosebuds. Cindy squinted at the woman's face. It must surely be Amber, and yet she looked completely different. Her face was a delicate oval, the eyes alert and wide-spaced, the cheeks softly curving above an elfin chin. Although the woman's nose was broad and rather prominent, it gave her a look of fierce intelligence that might otherwise be lacking.

'I remember it as if it were yesterday; it truly was the happiest day of my life.' The voice made Cindy start. She looked up. Amber was watching her from the doorway. 'And now,' her hostess continued. 'My marriage lies in tatters.' She walked over to join Cindy. 'I daresay you know all about it.'

Cindy chewed her lip. 'I did hear you were going through a divorce.'

'And did you also hear that my louse of a husband is refusing to move out of the Old Manor until the case is settled?'

'Er, yes, I believe I did.'

Amber sighed. 'Is the entire village talking about me?'

'*Noooo*,' Cindy gushed. 'Of course not.'

Amber's lips tightened. 'I appreciate your diplomacy, but if we're going to work together I shall require complete honesty from you.'

Cindy took a deep breath. She'd already made up her mind that she'd do anything – short of sacrificing a limb – to win this commission, even though Amber had yet to reveal its precise nature. 'Okay then, I'll give it to you straight,' she said decisively. 'The village is agog. Barely a day goes by without me hearing some outrageous new piece of gossip about your marital difficulties.'

'I see,' said Amber. 'And what's the *most* outrageous thing you've heard?'

Cindy thought for a moment. 'That when you found

out about your husband's affair, you hired a muck spreader and sprayed the exterior of his business premises with half a ton of well-rotted horse shit.'

Amber clapped her hands together. 'What a fabulous idea! I only wish I had the imagination to dream up something like that.' Her cat-like eyes glinted. 'Still, there's always time.'

Cindy nodded her approval. 'You go, girl. In my book, a cheating husband deserves everything he gets.'

'You know what,' Amber said. 'I think you and I are going to get along famously.'

Delighted by the compliment, Cindy decided to drive her advantage home. 'Of course, if you did decide to commission me, you could rely on my utmost discretion,' she said. 'And I'd be more than happy to sign a confidentiality agreement, if it made you feel more comfortable.' She held out the leather-bound book she was carrying under her arm. 'Here, why don't you take a look at some of my work?'

Amber took the portfolio and sank on to a nearby chaise, her dress settling about her ankles in gauzy drifts. 'I must say, I've heard some good things about you. My friend Pamela was very pleased with the transformation you wrought on her dining room.'

Cindy beamed. 'Yes, that was a very challenging project,' she said, remembering the job she'd had trying to convince Pamela to install a canopy of twinkling diodes in the ceiling to simulate the night sky. 'Mrs Lamont initially had a fairly conservative scheme in mind, but I managed to persuade her to be a little more adventurous.'

Amber opened the portfolio and began flipping its

thick pages, pausing every now and then to study a particular photograph more closely. 'Your style's very eclectic,' she said as she examined a clipping from *Cheshire Life*, which detailed Cindy's makeover of a theatre impresario's boudoir, in which she had daringly combined ethnic and modernist influences.

'It's my trademark,' said Cindy. 'I'm afraid I've never been much of a traditionalist, at least not where design's concerned.'

'Me neither,' said Amber. 'My husband, on the other hand, is terribly unimaginative. If he had his way, the house would be done out from top to bottom in Laura Ashley. As it was, I've been forced to compromise on an awful lot of things, decor wise.' She patted the chaise's damask covering. 'This reproduction furniture, for example. Awfully chi-chi, don't you think?'

Cindy pursed her lips. 'It is a little fussy.'

'Still, now that Daniel's my soon-to-be *ex*-husband, I no longer have to pander to his vile tastes, do I?' Although she spoke the words confidently, Amber's voice was tinged with sadness.

'I guess not.' Cindy ran a hand over her poker-straight hair. 'It must be very difficult for you guys . . . living in the same house, I mean.'

'It's perfectly hellish,' Amber admitted. 'Especially since we're barely on speaking terms. We communicate mainly through our teenage son.'

'Gee, it must difficult for him, being caught in the middle like that.'

'I suppose so,' said Amber. 'Although it's difficult to tell with Calum; he's very self-contained. I've tried talking to him about the divorce, but he just gets embarrassed – you know what teenagers are like.' She snapped the portfolio shut and rose to her feet. 'Anyway, I won't bore you with the details. Let's go the library and I'll tell you all about my little design project.'

A few moments later, Cindy found herself standing outside what those in her trade called a 'feature door'. Short and squat, it was wrapped in brown leather and secured with brass rivets, like an antique trunk.

Amber reached for the sturdy doorknob. 'This is Daniel's favourite room in the entire house,' she said, flinging the door open. 'After you.'

Cindy stepped across the threshold. For a moment she stared about her in wonder, breathing in the distinctive smell of old paper. The room must have contained close to five thousand books, all neatly ranged in alphabetical order on sturdy beechwood shelves, which extended from floor to ceiling. 'What a stunning room,' she said, letting her hand brush against a row of exposed spines.

'My husband loves books,' said Amber as she joined Cindy in the centre of the room. 'A lot of these are first editions. I daresay they'd fetch a tidy sum at auction.' She gave a derisory sniff. 'Anyway, it's not going to be a library for much longer.'

'It's not?'

'I plan to turn it into a music room.'

'I see.' Cindy couldn't help frowning. It seemed a shame to destroy something so beautiful.

'As a child, I played the viola and now I plan to start taking lessons again,' Amber continued. 'God knows, I need something to take my mind off this dreadful

94

divorce.' She put her hands on her hips. 'So, what do you think?'

Cindy forced a smile. If she were going to win this commission, she would have to tell Amber precisely what she wanted to hear. 'I think that would work really well,' she said brightly. She gestured towards the large leaded-light windows, which had views across the sweeping front lawn. 'This room has a beautiful outlook. I'm sure that any musician would find it very inspirational.' Cupping her chin in her hand, she tried to imagine the room without the shelves. 'I can see utilitarian furniture working really well in this space.' she said. 'Biedermeier or something similar – and perhaps some surrealist artwork to encourage your creativity.'

Amber nodded her head. 'Yes, I like the sound of that.'

'Those are just my initial thoughts. I need to think about it some more . . . take some pictures . . . draw some sketches.'

'Of course,' said Amber. 'I want this room to be utterly unique, so feel free to let your imagination run wild.'

'Great,' said Cindy. This was just the sort of commission she liked. 'Can you give me some idea of budget?'

'Oh, I don't know . . . fifteen thousand?' Amber shook her head. 'No, let's make it twenty. It is Daniel's money I'm spending, after all.'

Cindy began wandering around the room, absorbing its atmosphere, and taking note of key features and proportions. 'What's your husband going to do with all these books?' she asked, as she snapped away with her Polaroid camera.

Amber waved a dismissive hand, as if the whole lot

could go up in flames for all she cared. 'I haven't got a clue,' she said. 'Put them into storage, I expect. I'm very keen to get this project underway as soon as possible. When would you be able to start?'

'I'm quite busy at the moment; in fact, I'm already taking commissions for six months from now.'

Amber touched Cindy's forearm lightly. 'Oh, but surely you can squeeze me in sooner than that,' she said in a wheedling tone. 'I really am very keen to use you, and I'd be sure to recommend you to all my friends.'

'Well ...' said Cindy, breaking into a smile. 'I may be able to move one or two things around. Let me see what I can do.'

'Excellent,' said Amber, beaming delightedly. 'I think that calls for a celebration. If you've finished your recce, why don't we go to the kitchen for a nice glass of wine? It *is* nearly lunchtime after all.'

It was obvious to Cindy that the Old Manor's kitchen, with its ruby quartz work surfaces and top-of-the-range Aga was just as expensive as the rest of the house. She watched as Amber produced two wine glasses the size of soup bowls and then went to a wooden trapdoor in the floor. 'This is Daniel's other pride and joy,' she said, hauling open the door to reveal a circular aperture, cut into the limestone tiles. 'His wine cellar.'

Intrigued, Cindy walked to the edge of the aperture. She found herself staring into a two-metre-deep cavern. At its centre was a spiral staircase surrounded by a honeycomb of shelves. 'What an ingenious design,' she said. 'There must be hundreds of bottles in there.'

Amber began to descend into the cavern. 'Five hundred and sixty-two at the last count.' She scanned the shelves and made her selection. 'Better make that five hundred and sixty-one.'

Back in the kitchen, Amber put the wine on the counter while she fetched a corkscrew. Cindy glanced at the label on the bottle and saw that it was a 1981 Chateau Margaux. 'Gee, Amber, are you sure you want to be quite so generous?' she said. 'I'd be fine with a glass of Merlot.'

'Don't be silly,' said Amber as she removed the cork. 'Daniel's being so bloody-minded about this whole divorce business, I don't see why we girls shouldn't treat ourselves at his expense.' She poured generous measures into their wine glasses. 'It's just a pity I don't have Aldo any more. He could have made us a nice lunch.'

'Aldo?'

'Our chef. He's from Puglia; his homemade pasta is to die for.'

'What happened? Did he quit?'

Amber shook her head. 'No, he still works here, but my husband's banned him from cooking for me. It's the same with all the staff – from now on, they only take orders from Daniel. In fact, he's threatened to fire them if they so much as exchange pleasantries with me.'

Cindy looked at her in disbelief. 'Can he *do* that?'

'He can do what he likes. After all, he's the one who pays their wages.'

'But that's so petty.'

'Tell me about it. He even threatened to sack Stephen, my driver, until *my* lawyer reminded *his* lawyer that I lost the peripheral vision in my left eye after my last cheek implant. Driving in my condition would be downright dangerous.'

'How awful for you.' Cindy picked up her wine glass and took a sip. The Chateau Margaux tasted every bit as good as its £200 price tag suggested.

'I know, it's an absolute outrage. Daniel's determined to make me suffer; he knows I can hardly boil an egg. I've been living off Marks & Spencer ready meals for the past month.'

'No,' said Cindy. 'I wasn't talking about Aldo. I meant how awful that you lost your peripheral vision.'

Amber shrugged. 'You get used to it.'

Suddenly a teenage boy appeared at the kitchen door. He was wearing low-slung jeans and a baggy T-shirt and his lank hair fell forward, obscuring most of his face. He raised a hand in greeting when he saw the two women, but didn't say anything. As he drew nearer, Cindy caught a distinct whiff of cannabis.

Amber smiled. 'Calum, darling, I'd like you to meet Cindy.'

Ignoring her, the boy went to the fridge and removed a block of cheese wrapped in clingfilm.

'Calum!' Amber repeated in a much louder voice.

The teenager turned round and plucked a pair of earphones from his ears. 'What?' he said moodily.

'I'd like you to meet Cindy; she's an interior designer.'

With a show of reluctance, Calum shuffled over. 'All right?' he said, tossing his hair back to reveal a surprisingly handsome face, framed by fashionably long sideburns and a goatee beard.

'Hi,' Cindy replied. She nodded towards the earphones,

which were now dangling round his neck. 'What are you listening to?'

Calum stared at Cindy's hourglass figure, which was encased in a black silk shirtdress. 'The Chili Peppers,' he mumbled.

'Cool,' she said. 'They're one of my favourite bands too.'

Smiling shyly, Calum reached into the steel breadbox and removed a sliced wholemeal loaf. Then he noticed the bottle of wine. 'Can I have some of that?'

'No, you can't,' Amber said. 'Anyway, aren't you supposed to be at college?'

'Double free period,' Calum said as he began cutting thick slices of Cheddar straight on to the worktop.

'Calum's studying music and art at A level,' Amber explained. She sucked in some air. 'He's not terribly academic, are you, darling?'

Calum made no reply, but Cindy could see he was annoyed by the set of his jaw.

'He's in a band and he's labouring under the illusion that he's going to be able make a living from it,' Amber continued, seemingly oblivious to her son's discomfiture.

Calum stabbed the knife into what was left of the cheese and picked up his sandwich.

'Do get a plate, Calum. I don't want you dropping crumbs all over the house.'

The boy glared at his mother and walked over to the hand-painted Smallbone dresser, where a rack of colourful plates was displayed. Cindy felt a twinge of sympathy for him.

'Where's your father?' Amber asked.

'Dunno.'

'Well, when you see him, tell him the catch on the airing cupboard door needs fixing. It won't close properly and you know how noisy that water tank is. It kept me awake half the night.'

'Can't you tell him yourself?'

'No, I cannot!' Amber said shrilly. 'What's wrong with you, Calum? You know I'm going through a very traumatic time. Can't you just do one small thing for me?'

Calum sighed. 'This whole situation is totally ridiculous. Why can't you two act like grown-ups for a change?'

Amber turned to Cindy. 'See what I have to put up with?' she asked. 'Honestly, he's as bad as his father.'

Feeling awkward, Cindy stared into her wine glass.

'You can slag me off as much as you like, but I'm still not doing it,' said Calum, stuffing his earphones back into position. He picked up his sandwich and walked out of the kitchen.

Cindy glanced at Amber, who seemed to be on the verge of tears. 'Well, I suppose I'd better get going,' she said, setting her glass down on the counter. 'I'll get some sketches to you by the middle of next week, but bear in mind that it's just a starting point. If there's anything you're not happy with, anything at all, we can work on it.'

'I'm sure I'm going to love your ideas.' Amber gave a loud sniff. 'I can tell already that you and I have a lot in common.'

Cindy smiled uncertainly, not sure whether to be flattered or repulsed by the suggestion.

'Well, it was good to meet you. Don't worry about showing me to the door; I know the way.'

'Are you sure?'

'Yeah, you stay here and finish your wine.'

As Cindy made her way along the corridor she heard the sound of the front door slamming. She continued walking, her heels making no sound on the Old Manor's plush burgundy carpet. As she emerged into the entrance hall, she saw a man and a woman standing beside the antique coat stand in the far corner of the entrance hall. The man was holding the woman's face in his hands and kissing her passionately. Cindy cleared her throat to give them some warning of her approach. Instantly the woman's head snapped round.

Cindy smiled at the couple. 'Hi,' she said. 'I'm Cindy McAllister. I've been visiting with Amber.'

The man released his lover and turned towards her. 'Hello there,' he replied pleasantly. 'I'm Amber's husband, Daniel.'

'Yes, I know,' said Cindy, and then thought immediately how silly she sounded.

'You wouldn't by any chance be related to Kieran McAllister, would you?'

Cindy nodded. 'Why yes, as a matter of fact I'm married to him.'

Daniel's face lit up. 'Well, in that case, I must shake your hand.' He strode across the room and took Cindy's dainty hand in his two large ones. 'I'm a huge admirer of Kieran's. I often see him up at St Benedict's. He's competing in the Scottish Open next month, isn't he?'

'He sure is, and I'll be going with him. I'm very excited; it'll be my first trip to Scotland.'

'Oh, you'll have a wonderful time; Loch Lomond is beautiful at this time of year.' It was Daniel's companion who had spoken. She stepped forward and Cindy got her first good look at the woman who was threatening to usurp Amber's position as lady of the manor. She'd heard that the housekeeper was no looker – and, while Cindy tried never to judge by appearances, she had to admit that Nancy was striking for all the wrong reasons. For starters, she was tall. Very tall ... around six feet by Cindy's estimation. She was also blessed with a lantern jaw, overgrown eyebrows and a cloud of frizzy brown hair, threaded with silver strands. But, despite her obvious lack of grooming, she was expensively dressed in a caramel-coloured crêpe de Chine dress and dainty pearl-drop earrings. But it was what was in Nancy's hand that made Cindy's heart beat just a little bit faster. Unless she was very much mistaken, the humble housekeeper was the proud owner of an exceptionally rare and highly collectible crocodile-skin Hermès Kelly bag.

As if aware that Cindy was coveting her designer accessory, Nancy pushed the bag up her arm.

'I'm Nancy,' she said. She ran her tongue round her chapped lips and added, rather unnecessarily it seemed, 'Daniel's girlfriend.'

'Pleased to meet you,' said Cindy.

Nancy cocked her head to one side. 'I didn't know you and Amber were friends.'

'We're not. I'm here in a professional capacity.'

Nancy's bushy brows shot up. 'Oh? And what *is* your profession, if you don't mind me asking?'

Cindy thought about saying something vague to protect Amber's interests, but then thought better of it. 'An interior designer.'

Daniel's craggy forehead crumpled into a frown. 'Is my wife planning some work on the house?'

'I think it's probably best if you ask *her*,' said Cindy neutrally.

There was a brief, awkward silence and then a shrill voice came echoing down the corridor. 'Cindy, are you all right? Who are you talking to?' A few moments later, Amber appeared. Her slanted eyes flickered in a cobra-like fashion from Cindy to Daniel to Nancy and back to Cindy again. 'I thought I heard voices,' she said in a sharp voice. 'I do hope these people aren't bothering you, Cindy dear.'

'We were just getting acquainted,' said Nancy with a superior smile. 'Cindy's presence rather suggests you're planning a little redesign. Presumably you were planning to tell Daniel about your plans at some point. After all, as co-owner he's a right to know about any changes that might affect the value of the Old Manor.' She sidled up to Daniel and looped her arm round his possessively.

'What the hell's it got to do with you?' Amber said, placing her hands on her hips aggressively.

Daniel took a step forward. 'Please don't speak to Nancy like that,' he said tightly.

'She's in *my* house, which gives me the right to speak to her any way I like,' Amber snarled. 'Of course, if you had any sort of decency, you wouldn't bring that trollop back here at all.'

'And if *you* had any sort of decency, you wouldn't be trying to turn my own son against me by making me out to be some sort of sex maniac.'

'I haven't got the faintest idea what you're talking about.'

Nancy snorted. 'Don't play the innocent. Calum's told us what you've been saying about Daniel.'

Amber held up a palm. 'Talk to the hand, bitch.'

'Apparently, I'm operating some sort of harem,' Daniel said.

'That isn't what I said at all,' Amber snapped. 'I simply speculated aloud that, if you were enough of a sleazeball to shag the housekeeper behind my back, then you probably had a whole string of women on the go.'

'Amber, you know that's ridiculous,' Daniel said wearily. 'Why do you always try and twist things?'

Amber took a step towards her husband. 'Do you know what I'd really like to twist right now?'

Daniel sighed. 'No. But I expect you're about to tell me.'

Amber pointed to her husband's crotch. 'I'd like to put your genitals in a Black & Decker vice and twist it tighter and tighter until your cheating dick turns blue and drops off.' Amber folded her arms across her chest, waiting for Daniel's reaction. But before it could come Amber spotted something that made her erupt in fury. 'You thieving cow!' she cried. 'That's *my* Hermès bag.'

Nancy's reactions were lightning quick and, as Amber lunged for the bag, she twisted the strap round her wrist. For ten seconds or so, the pair wrestled like children in the playground for ownership of the item. 'Let go!' Amber was shouting. 'You'll break the strap.' But Nancy hung on for grim death and eventually, realizing she was no match for Nancy's muscular forearms, Amber let go.

'Tell her, Daniel, tell her to give it back to me,' she whined. 'That bag was in my dressing room; she must've gone in there and stolen it; there's no other explanation.'

'No, she didn't,' Daniel said calmly. 'I gave the handbag to Nancy.'

Amber shot him a look of pure hatred. 'But it belongs to me.'

'Actually, it belonged to my late mother.'

'Yes, and she left it to me in her will.'

'No, Amber, Mother left all her personal effects to *me*. I simply allowed you to borrow that handbag. And now I've given it to Nancy. As a gift.'

'You removed it from my dressing room without so much as a word to me?'

'Yes, that's precisely what I did.'

Amber's face turned an alarming shade of puce. 'Why don't you tear the clothes off my back and be done with it?' she shrieked, clutching her breast dramatically.

'Now, now, there's no need for histrionics.'

'You think you can steal my dignity, my chef, even my handbags,' Amber sobbed. 'But you know what, Daniel, you'll never take the Old Manor away from me. Never!'

Daniel's nostrils flared. 'We'll let the courts decide that, shall we?'

Throughout this entire exchange, Cindy had been rooted to the spot in horrified silence. Now, she decided, it was high time to make a getaway. While the feuding pair continued to hurl brickbats, she slipped through the front door unnoticed. As she hurried to her car, she thanked her lucky stars that *her* marriage was a peaceful and happy one.

Upstairs, Calum followed Cindy's progress from his

bedroom window, mesmerized by the sway of her hips and the way the silky stuff of her dress strained against her rounded bottom. She really was quite the loveliest creature he had ever seen and, as he mentally undressed her, he found himself nursing an erection. He leaned forward so that his groin pressed against the edge of the window sill. One day, he told himself, one day he'd get his hands on a woman like that.

Seven

The house was huge – a proper country pile – and much grander than either of them had imagined. As Ace slid his Mini Cooper in between a top-of-the-range Lexus and a BMW convertible, he half expected to see a uniformed valet appear. He turned to Astrid, who was peering into her compact as she made subtle adjustments to her make-up. 'Are you sure this is the right place, babe?'

The masseuse grimaced, checking her teeth for lipstick marks. 'Quite sure; we followed Damian's directions to the letter, didn't we?'

Ace stared out across the expansive grounds, which were ringed by towering leylandii, presumably to protect the mansion from prying eyes. In the last rays of the setting sun, he could just make out a summer house with a wide verandah and flowing voiles at the windows. 'I didn't think it would be this fancy, that's for sure.' He chewed his lip for a few seconds, lost in thought. 'Do you think we're going to fit in with these people?'

'Of course,' said Astrid. 'Let's face it, we're all here for the same reason, so we know we're going to have at least one thing in common.' Sensing her boyfriend's nervousness, she leaned over and kissed him gently on the mouth. 'We don't have to go to this party, you know. We can turn round right now and go home, if that's what you want.'

Ace smiled. 'Don't be silly. I've been looking forward to this for ages.'

'Me too.' Astrid snapped the compact shut and began raking her fingers through her long blonde hair. 'Do I look okay?'

Ace's eyes roamed her body, his gaze finally settling on the V of her crisp white blouse, which was buttoned low, so the black lace of her bra could be clearly seen. 'Fan-bloody-tastic. Trust me, every guy in that house is going to be drooling over you.'

Astrid gave him a wry half-smile. 'Well, that is the object of the exercise.'

Moments later they were standing on the doorstep, overnight bags at their feet.

A tall, sandy-haired man in his mid-forties, casually dressed in linen trousers and an open-necked shirt came to greet them. 'Hello there,' he said pleasantly. 'I'm Damian. Welcome to Tall Trees.'

Astrid handed him the bottle of wine she was carrying. 'Thank you so much for inviting us. I'm Astrid and this is Ace.'

The man smiled. 'Yes, I recognize you from your photos.'

A petite woman in a strapless summer dress appeared over his shoulder. 'Hi,' she said. 'I'm Nikki; we spoke on the phone.' She took Astrid's hand and began leading her down the hallway. 'Damian, sweetie, will you take their bags upstairs while I give them the guided tour?'

'Yes, dear.' Damian took the bags from Ace and patted him on the shoulder. 'Don't look so scared, old man. You're in good hands.'

Nikki led the couple to a comfortable lounge, dominated by a huge corner sofa. At one end of the room, various drinks and professional-looking canapés were laid out on a farmhouse table. 'What can I offer you to drink,' said Nikki. 'Champagne, wine, beer?'

'A glass of champagne would be lovely,' said Astrid. 'Ace?'

'I think I'll stick to sparkling water, thanks.'

'Good idea. It's nice to have a couple of drinks to relax, but we don't encourage our guests to get too tiddly.' Nikki giggled. 'We don't want any *flagging* spirits, if you know what I mean.'

'How long have you and Damian been hosting these parties?' Astrid asked.

'Gosh, now there's a question. Absolute yonks – ten or eleven years, I should think. We're quite picky about who comes – that's why I subjected you to a bit of a grilling on the phone. And now that I've met you in the flesh, I have no doubt you're both going to be very popular indeed.' She reached out and stroked the back of Astrid's head in a tender, almost maternal, way. 'You have beautiful hair. Is that your natural colour?'

Astrid nodded. 'I'm Swedish. All my family are blonde.'

'Lucky you,' Nikki murmured. Her hand fell away. 'There's a nice mix of people here tonight – mainly couples, although we do have one or two singles. Would you like to meet some of them?'

Ace nodded. 'Great,' he said, sounding rather more confident than he felt. 'Lead the way.'

Nikki took them through to a second, smaller reception

room, where a dozen or so people of varying ages were mingling. The lighting was low and Diana Krall was playing softly in the background. Nikki was silent for a few moments as she scanned the room. 'Ah yes, I know. Let me introduce you to Hugh and Caroline,' she said. 'They're a lovely couple, very intelligent. He's a university lecturer and she's an artist.' She led them towards an attractive couple in their thirties, who were standing slightly apart from the others. 'Darlings, I'd like you to meet Ace and Astrid. It's their first time, so we need to be gentle with them.'

Hugh's face lit up. 'Newbies, how exciting!' He took Ace's hand and pumped it vigorously. 'What do you do for a living?'

'I'm the manager of a golf shop.'

'Oh yes? Jolly good . . . I like a game of golf myself.'

Hugh turned to Astrid. He took her hand and raised it unselfconsciously to his lips. '*Enchanté.*'

'Astrid's a massage therapist,' said Nikki.

'A massage therapist!' Hugh repeated lubriciously, as if there were something inherently risqué about such an occupation. 'Now there's a skill worth having.'

Somewhere in the distance, a telephone began to ring. Nikki made a face. 'I'd better get that. I daresay one of our guests has got lost; somebody usually does.' She squeezed Astrid's upper arm. 'I'll catch up with you later, but for now I'll leave you in Hugh and Caroline's capable hands.' As she drew away, her hand grazed Astrid's breast – whether by accident or design, it was impossible to say.

For several minutes, the two couples made stilted small talk and then Caroline, sensing a way to break the ice, pointed to the French windows. 'There's a fabulous hot tub out here,' she said. 'Shall we take a look?'

She led the way out on to a decked area, decorated with pots of fragrant jasmine and nemesia. Dusk was falling and the garden was illuminated by a series of low-voltage spots, cleverly concealed in fibreglass rocks. In the centre of the deck, the cedar hot tub had pride of place.

'Damn, I didn't bring my swimming trunks,' Ace remarked.

Astrid smiled. 'Somehow, I don't think that's going to matter.'

'Have you two been together long?' Caroline enquired casually.

'Just over a year,' Astrid replied. 'We work at the same country club. Ace chatted me up in the staff canteen.'

'And whose idea was it to come tonight?'

'Astrid's,' said Ace. 'She's pretty adventurous, aren't you, babe?' As he spoke, he saw Astrid and Hugh exchange a look. He felt a prickle of jealousy and tried to swallow it down.

'What about you, Ace?' Caroline said, twisting one of her dark curls coyly. 'Are *you* the adventurous type?'

Ace grinned. 'Oh yeah, I'm up for most things. How about you guys; how long have you been an item?'

'We've been together for four years and married for two. We actually met at one of these parties.'

'Wow, really?'

Caroline nodded. 'We'd both gone as singles and we just hit it off.'

'And you've been partying ever since?'

'That's right,' said Hugh. 'But we don't go too mad. Once every two or three months is about average for us.'

'And it hasn't done your relationship any harm?'

'Not at all; in fact, I'd say it's brought us closer together, eh, Caro?'

His wife stared up at him adoringly. 'Absolutely.'

Astrid ran her tongue around her pink-painted lips. 'I don't know about anyone else, but I'm starting to find that hot tub irresistible,' she said. Without waiting for a response, she began unfastening the buttons of her shirt. Hugh stared at her as she shrugged the shirt off and tossed it over the back of a teak recliner.

'If you don't mind me saying so, you have the most magnificent breasts, Astrid,' Hugh said, ogling her ample bosom, encased in Rigby & Peller lace.

'Of course I don't mind; I enjoy receiving compliments.' Astrid glanced at Ace. He rubbed the side of his nose. It was a pre-arranged signal they'd devised in the car on the way to the house. 'Why don't you and Caroline get some more drinks, sweetie? I think Hugh and I are going to take a little dip.'

'Good idea,' said Caroline as she linked her arm through Ace's. 'Have fun you two. I know we will.' And with that the two began walking back towards the house. Neither of them looked back.

While Hugh and Astrid were getting acquainted in the hot tub, back at St Benedict's Sam Bentley was hoping to indulge in a little foreplay of his own. It was more than a week since he'd met Taylor on the golf course and he'd been keeping a close eye out for her ever since. Earlier that day, his patience had been rewarded when he'd spotted her on the driving range, looking good enough to eat in a pair of pink hotpants. He'd waited until she was replenishing her stock of golf balls before strolling over. 'Hey, Taylor, how's it going?' he said, ultra-casual.

She seemed pleased to see him. 'Sam, what a nice surprise.'

He made a pretence of looking around, though his covert observations had already revealed that Taylor was unaccompanied. 'Isn't your mum with you today?'

'No, thank God. She's back at the cottage, updating my website.'

Sam smiled. 'She takes good care of you, doesn't she?'

'Oh yeah, Mom's a regular whirlwind.' Taylor's tone was deeply sarcastic. 'She likes to get involved in every aspect of my career. I swear, she'd sack my damn agent and do the job herself, given half the chance.'

'You two must be very close.'

Taylor nodded. 'We're more like sisters really. She drives me mad sometimes, but I know she only has my best interests at heart.'

'What about your dad? Is he staying in Kirkhulme too?'

'My parents got divorced ten years ago. My dad's a surgeon; he ran off with his scrub nurse. Mom's only just gotten over it.'

'It's taken her *ten* years to recover?'

'The scrub nurse was a man.'

Sam suppressed a smirk. 'Ah, right. I expect that would take some getting over.'

At this point, Taylor gave him a coy little smile.

'Speaking of *marriages*,' she said with an exaggerated emphasis on the final word, 'how's your wife – Laura, isn't it?'

Sam felt a mixture of emotions – pleasure that Taylor had obviously been making enquiries about him; irritation that she'd found out he was married. He didn't wear a wedding ring; it interfered with his grip – or that's what he told Laura – and he'd been hoping to keep his wife a secret from Taylor, at least until he'd had a chance to work his legendary charm on the young golfer.

'She's fine . . . I think.'

'You *think*?'

Sam lowered his voice. 'I feel a bit awkward saying this but, to be perfectly honest, my wife and I pretty much lead separate lives these days.'

Taylor seemed amused by his admission. 'Is that a fact?'

'Yeah, I mean we're good friends and everything, but the spark went out of our marriage a long time ago.'

'Really?' The golfer folded her arms across her chest. 'It's just I heard that your wife had had a baby recently.'

Sam rubbed his chin. Taylor was sharp as a tack; he liked that in a woman. 'That's right,' he said. 'Tiger's nearly two months old now. He's a great kid.' He covered his eyes with his hand, as if recalling some embarrassing faux pas. 'Laura and I had had a few too many glasses of wine the night he was conceived . . . you know how it is.'

Taylor made a face. '*Ewww!* Thanks for over-sharing.'

Now Sam's embarrassment was genuine. Deftly, he switched the conversation to safer ground: golf. For a few minutes they chatted about Taylor's training programme and her chances of winning a place on the Curtis Cup team. Then, when she picked up her bucket of golf balls and announced she'd better get back to her swing practice, Sam decided to make his interest clear.

'So listen, Taylor, if you're not doing anything this evening, how do you fancy meeting me for a drink? I could give you the lowdown on village life, recommend some good pubs and places to eat and tell you which places to avoid like the plague.'

She didn't answer him straight away. Instead, she grabbed her ponytail, twisting the end round her forefinger . . . making him wait. At last she spoke. 'Sure.' And then, almost as an afterthought, 'I thought you'd never ask.'

Now it was evening and Sam was occupying a corner booth in St Benedict's wood-panelled Chukka Bar, eagerly awaiting Taylor's arrival. He'd just texted Laura to tell her he was having a drink with some golfing buddies and wouldn't be home for dinner. As he switched off his phone to prevent any unwanted interruptions he didn't feel the slightest bit of remorse. Make no mistake about it, Sam loved his wife, but the life of a professional sportsman was a stressful one and he needed some way of releasing the tension – this was how he managed to justify his numerous affairs in his own mind. He usually went for much younger women, who tended to be more impressionable and were easily dazzled by his good looks and celebrity status – though none, admittedly, had been quite so young as Taylor. Still, he told himself, there was a first time for everything.

Sam glanced at his watch. Taylor was already fifteen minutes late. He drained his vodka martini and was thinking about ordering another when he saw Kristina Spurr walk into the bar. She was wearing gabardine trousers and a cropped jacket that made her sturdy frame look unappealingly mannish. Sam's jaw tensed. He scanned the room, looking for Taylor. He was sure he hadn't misread the signals, but the presence of Kristina seemed to suggest one of two things: that Taylor was nervous about being alone with an attractive older man, or that she simply wasn't interested in him sexually.

Kristina caught his eye and waved. A few seconds later, she was at his table.

'Kris,' Sam said, forcing a smile. 'This is an unexpected pleasure. What can I get you to drink?'

She nodded at his glass. 'I'll have whatever you're havin'.' Her Texan accent was much stronger than Taylor's, and soft as molasses.

'Vodka martini, cool.' He looked around. 'Where's Taylor – powdering her nose?'

Kris pulled out a chair and sat down opposite him. 'My silly daughter forgot that she'd arranged to have dinner at her coach's house tonight. She had no way of gettin' in touch with you, so I offered to come to the club and pass on her apologies.' She looked at him from under her eyelashes. 'I hope you're not too disappointed.'

Sam smiled, trying not to let his displeasure show. He wondered if Taylor had got cold feet and the dinner was just an excuse. 'Oh well, another time perhaps.' He got up from the table. 'Anyway, thanks for coming all the way down here to let me know she wasn't coming. I appreciate it.'

Kris reached across the table and laid her hand on top of his. 'Ain't you gonna buy me that martini?'

Sam hesitated. If he were going to win Taylor over, he needed to keep Kris onside. 'Of course – that's the least I can do.'

When he came back with their drinks, Kris had taken off her jacket to reveal a low-cut silk blouse. She'd obviously made an effort with her appearance, and it suddenly dawned on Sam that Kris had taken a bit of a shine to him herself. Oh well, he told himself, she was only human. Unfortunately, however, she wasn't his type – not by a long shot. She was too old, too butch and, judging by the way she was batting her over-made-up eyes at him, too desperate.

'Bottoms up,' he said.

Kris clinked her glass against his. 'Cheers.'

'So, are you enjoying your stay in our humble village?'

'I sure am. I'll be real sorry when the summer's over and me and Taylor are headin' home.'

Sam raised an eyebrow. 'Does that mean you've revised your opinion of British men since the last time we met?'

Kris shook her head. 'Nope.'

'Well, we'll have to see what we can do about that, won't we?' Despite himself, Sam was slipping into flirt mode. He couldn't help it.

His companion responded by leaning across the table, exposing a vast Grand Canyon of a cleavage as she did so. 'I'd like to see you try.'

Sam beamed. 'How about Taylor? I bet she's got British blokes falling at her feet,' Sam said, keen to get some idea of the competition.

'Oh, you know how it is – guys try to hit on her all the time, but Taylor's got no time to be thinkin' 'bout boys; she's gotta keep her mind on her game.' She flashed Sam a grateful smile. 'I wanna thank you for taking her under your wing, Sam. She hasn't had a father figure in her life for a very long time.'

At this, Sam, who had just taken a sip of his drink, exploded in a coughing fit.

Kris reached across the table and administered a series of short, sharp slaps to his upper back. 'Are you okay, darlin'?'

He looked at her through watery eyes. 'Fine, thanks. I think my martini went down the wrong way.' For Sam, *father figure* was nothing short of an insult. Still, he comforted himself, if Kris knew what his real motives were, she'd probably take out a restraining order on him.

With the subject of Taylor clearly off limits, the conversation drifted to golf. Kris had plenty of amusing anecdotes about life on the PGA tour and, as the evening wore on, Sam found himself warming to the outspoken American. When he noticed that her glass was empty, he ordered two more martinis from a passing waiter.

'Are you tryin' to get me drunk?' Kris said playfully.

'Of course not,' he said with mock indignation. 'The rest of Britain's male population may be complete cads but I, my dear, am a gentleman.'

Kris giggled. 'Too bad.'

The next hour or so passed perfectly pleasantly and then Sam decided it was time to make his excuses. 'I think it's time I was heading home,' he said. 'I'll go to reception and get them to order a couple of cabs, shall I?'

Kris looked him right in the eye. 'Or we could just get a room?' She ran her tongue round her lips. 'They do have rooms here, don't they?'

Sam smiled. Despite Kris's flirtatious behaviour throughout the evening, he hadn't expected her to be quite so forward. 'Are you trying to seduce me, Mrs Spurr?'

Kris laughed. 'Well, it sure would be a fine end to a fine evenin'.'

'Listen, Kris, I can't pretend I'm not flattered, but I'm a happily married man.'

She seemed taken aback. 'You're married? But you don't wear a weddin' ring.'

''Fraid so,' said Sam, grimacing apologetically. 'And a dad of three to boot.'

'Oh okay, I'm sorry, I just thought ...' Kris's voice tailed off. 'Never mind, just forget I asked, okay?'

'It's forgotten already.' Sam patted her on the shoulder. 'I'll go and order those cabs, shall I?'

Eight

The ballroom at St Benedict's was almost unrecognizable. An avalanche of polystyrene boulders littered the parquet floor and the magnificent hand-painted wall murals were disguised with animal skins and fur rugs. Beside the elegant arched entrance doors was a life-size woolly mammoth, while overhead several pterodactyls swooped, suspended on invisible wire. In the centre of the room, on a raised dais, was a cave and a small fire with silk flames fluttering beneath a crudely fashioned cooking pot. Standing in front of this prehistoric backdrop and posing for all she was worth was a petite brunette in a suede bikini and fur bootees. Her hair had been backcombed into a sexy bouffant and the necklace of plastic bones that hung round her neck contrasted sharply with her chicken tikka tan.

'Doesn't it make you sick?' Keeley muttered as the girl thrust out her chest provocatively for the half dozen or so photographers who stood at the foot of the dais, worshipping her with their cameras. 'This time last year Joely Archer was a nobody, and now look at her.'

'Mmmm,' Marianne agreed as she looked down at the hardback book in her hands. The cover showed a grinning Joely. She was wearing the same skimpy outfit and her right foot was balanced, somewhat incongruously, on top of a football. Marianne traced the embossed title with a well-manicured finger. '*Cavegirl Cuisine: How A WAG Beat The Flab.*' She shuddered. 'Isn't it amazing how one can be famous for doing so very little these days?'

'Tell me about it,' said Keeley. 'It's not even as if she's lost that much weight. She went from a twelve to an eight. Big fucking deal. And what does this paleolithic diet consist of anyway?' She took the book from Marianne's hands and scanned the back cover. 'Wholegrain bread, brown rice, seeds, fish and root vegetables,' she read aloud. 'Puh! Hardly rocket science, is it?'

'I thought you and Joely were friends.'

'I wouldn't go that far. Our boyfriends play for the same football team, that's all.'

'Where *is* Ryan anyway?' said Marianne, looking around the room.

Keeley shoved Joely's book in between two boulders. 'Fuck knows; he should've arrived an hour ago and he hasn't even had the courtesy to text me to say he's running late.'

'Oh well, I expect he'll be here soon.'

A waiter bearing a silver tray of canapés appeared beside the women. 'Can I tempt you?' the waiter said, lowering his tray with a flourish.

Marianne looked him up and down. He was young – mid-twenties at most – with broad shoulders and smooth skin. She ran her tongue slowly and deliberately across her front teeth. 'That rather depends on what you're offering.'

The waiter blushed. 'Er ... we have a fantastic selection of paleolithic delicacies,' he said, as if reading from an invisible autocue. 'Wholegrain blini with sunflower seed paté, sea kelp koftas, and carrot and rutabaga skewers with acacia honey dipping sauce.'

Keeley opened her mouth and made a jabbing motion towards the back of her throat with two fingers.

'I think that's a no,' said Marianne.

The waiter gave an understanding smile and turned to go.

'Hang on a second,' Marianne said. She reached into her handbag and pulled out a pad of Post-It notes and a pen. After scribbling down her mobile number, she peeled off the Post-It and stuffed it into the waiter's trouser pocket. As she withdrew her hand, she brushed it fleetingly across his crotch, almost causing him to drop the tray of canapés. 'Call me if you fancy some fun, darling,' she said. 'No strings attached.'

The startled waiter nodded mutely before scurrying back to the kitchen to compose himself.

'Marianne!' Keeley squealed. 'That bloke's young enough to be your son. In any case, I thought you only had eyes for the vicar these days.'

The older woman fluttered her eyelashes. 'What can I say? I've got a very high sex drive; I need constant stimulation.' Running a hand absent-mindedly across her creamy décolletage, she glanced towards the vast crystal chandelier in the centre of the room. Beneath it, the Reverend Simon Proctor was deep in conversation with St Benedict's general manager, Anthony Lanchester. 'In fact, I can feel my sap starting to rise already. I may have to take Simon somewhere quiet later. We'll need to be discreet, though; Simon's awfully keen that we keep our relationship under wraps.'

'Things are still going well then?'

'Couldn't be better, darling. The sex is simply divine, if you'll pardon the pun. Simon has introduced me to practices I didn't even knew existed.'

'Oh?' said Keeley, her interest piqued. 'Would you care to elaborate?'

Marianne gave a little smirk. 'Come over here.' She took Keeley's arm and led her to a quiet spot behind an MDF megalith. 'Look at this,' she said, extending her left leg and raising her Anna Sui skirt by a few inches. Halfway up her bare thigh was a highly unusual garter. It was made of animal skin and tightly secured with a leather cord.

Keeley wrinkled her nose. 'What's that?'

'A goat-hair cilice, made in Italy by Carmelite nuns. Simon gave it to me. Cute, isn't it?'

'What's a cilice when it's at home?'

'It's a religious thing ... an object that induces discomfort. Simon says it teaches humility.'

Keeley frowned. 'When you say "discomfort" ...'

'Here, I'll show you.' Marianne loosened the leather tie and pushed the cilice down to reveal a two-inch band of flesh that had been rubbed red raw.

'Ugh,' said Keeley. 'That's gross; how can you do it to yourself?'

'Don't knock it till you've tried it,' said Marianne, as she pushed the cilice back into position, wincing as the rough material cut into her inflamed flesh. 'Believe it or not, it's actually quite a turn on. It's really no different to those *tukta* sessions you have with Astrid.'

'I suppose so,' Keeley replied, remembering how good

it felt to hear the satisfying thwack of a birch paddle against her buttocks. Suddenly, she spotted a familiar figure entering the throng. 'Oh my God,' she said, clutching Marianne's arm. 'Look who's just walked in.'

Following her friend's gaze, Marianne saw Amber standing beside the woolly mammoth, her almond eyes flickering as she scanned the room. Compared to the other guests, she seemed overdressed for the occasion in skin-tight satin trousers, strappy sandals and a silky, off-the-shoulder top, across which a jewel-encrusted panther reared menacingly.

'Talk about mutton dressed as lamb,' Marianne remarked, as Amber – her movements somewhat restricted by the satin trousers – began walking across the room with the stiff-legged gait of an SS commandant. 'Though I must say, it's awfully brave of her to show her face at all. She must be feeling wretched about the divorce. If I were in her shoes, I'd want to keep a low profile.'

The women watched as Amber accepted a Bellini from a passing waiter before positioning herself beside a large Perspex bookstand. Although the Catwoman was drawing plenty of interested glances, nobody approached her and after a little while, clearly self-conscious, she picked up a copy of *Cavegirl Cuisine* and began flicking through its pages.

'Do you think we should go over and introduce ourselves?' asked Keeley. 'I've always wanted to see what she looks like close up.'

'Why not?' said Marianne. She turned towards the ballroom's grand French windows. Beyond them, on the terrace, Daniel Solomon was chatting to an attractive older man in a well-tailored suit. 'I wonder if Amber knows *he*'s here.'

'I doubt it; according to Cindy, they can't stand being in the same room together.' Keeley looked Daniel's companion up and down. 'Who's that guy in the suit?'

'Alistair Gluck. He owns Gluck's ... you know the luxury hotel guide. He's notoriously selective – only one or two new places a year make it into the guide. I suspect Daniel's on a serious schmoozing offensive tonight.'

'Hmm ... in that case he's not going to be happy when he sees Amber.' Keeley glanced back towards the hotelier's wife and saw, to her annoyance, that she was now chatting to a statuesque blonde carrying a Marni patent-leather clutch under one arm and a tiny rat-like dog under the other. Amber appeared visibly relieved to have some company and had suddenly become very animated, waving her arms around and laughing rather too loudly as if it were quite the best party she'd ever been to, which seemed unlikely.

'Oh,' said Marianne. 'It looks as if we've been beaten to it.'

Keeley scowled. 'Vienna Beauchamp ... trust her to muscle in. That stuck-up society cow always has to be the centre of attention.'

'And why does she have to take that disgusting animal everywhere she goes?' said Marianne. 'I'm quite certain members aren't supposed to bring dogs on to the premises.'

'Because when you're born with a silver spoon in your mouth, you grow up thinking it's perfectly acceptable to piss all over other people's rules.'

Marianne looked thoughtful. 'I wonder what those two are talking about.' She linked her arm through Keeley's. 'Come on, let's move a little closer.'

With exaggerated nonchalance, the pair walked across the room and took up a prime eavesdropping position behind the bookstand.

'I was dreadfully sorry to hear about your divorce,' Vienna was saying. 'It must be awful being single at your age. You must feel as if your life is so, like, totally over.'

'Ah well, you know what they say about every cloud having a silver lining,' Amber replied. 'Now that I don't have a husband to look after, I'm thinking about relaunching my acting career.'

Vienna sniggered. 'Oh, Amber, do you really think that's a good idea?'

'Yes, as a matter of fact I do.'

'A lot's changed since you were last on TV,' said Vienna. 'And let's face it, you certainly look a whole lot different.'

'I've aged a little, of course I have,' said Amber. 'But there are still plenty of roles out there for good, middle-aged character actresses.'

'Er, I was referring to your surgery,' said Vienna tactlessly. 'I shouldn't think there's much demand for actresses with your unusual look.' She paused cruelly before delivering her punchline. 'Not unless the BBC are planning a new adaptation of *Bride of Frankenstein* and they want to save on special effects.'

The two eavesdroppers winced simultaneously. 'With friends like those, eh?' Marianne muttered.

'Anyway, I mustn't monopolize you,' Vienna continued. 'I'm sure you've got tons of people to catch up with. *Ciao*.'

Marianne and Keeley watched as the heiress strutted away.

'Come on,' said Keeley, beckoning to Marianne. 'Now's our chance to nab Amber.' But by the time the two women had emerged from behind the bookstand, Amber was nowhere to be seen.

Marianne sighed. 'Where'd she go?'

Keeley pointed towards the French windows. Daniel and his companion were now stepping back inside the ballroom and their entrance hadn't gone unnoticed.

'Daniel!' Amber cried with artificial enthusiasm as she goose-stepped towards them.

The hotelier stiffened. 'Hello, dear. I didn't know you'd been invited tonight.'

'I wasn't.'

'So what are you doing here?'

'Pamela gave me her invitation. She was supposed to be coming with me, but she's laid up in bed with the flu.'

Daniel looked surprised. 'You've come alone?'

'Yes, and why shouldn't I?' Amber thrust her miniscule nose in the air. 'After all, *I've* got nothing to be ashamed of. *You're* the one who should be crawling under the nearest rock.'

Daniel ground his teeth together as he struggled to keep his cool. 'I need to chair a meeting in twenty minutes, so we'd better make a move. Enjoy the rest of your evening.' He touched his companion's elbow and began guiding him away. 'We've just got time for a quick drink in the Chukka Bar, before your cab arrives.'

In one swift movement, Amber had stepped in front of them, effectively blocking their escape route. 'Not so fast,' she said – and then, in a syrupy tone – 'Not until I've had a chance to renew my acquaintance with the lovely Alistair.'

Daniel's companion looked confused. 'I'm sorry, have we met before?'

'Why yes, you came to the Old Manor for dinner last summer. You brought me *the* most delicious box of hand-made chocolates.' Amber pouted outrageously. 'Surely you haven't forgotten already.'

Alistair's mouth dropped open as he stared at the grotesque face of the woman in front of him. 'My God, Amber ... is that really you? You look so ... so ... *different*.' To mask his shock, he leaned forward and kissed her on both cheeks.

'I've had a little bit of work done, just to keep me looking my youthful best,' Amber simpered.

'Well, it's lovely to see you again, it really is,' said Alistair. 'In fact, seeing as your friend has deserted you, why don't you join us for a drink?'

'Why thank you, Alistair. I'd love to.'

At this, Daniel launched into a coughing fit. 'I, er, don't think that would be a very good idea,' he said when he'd recovered his composure.

Alistair looked from one to the other. 'Oh? Why not?'

'We're going to be talking shop,' Daniel said quickly. 'My wife will be bored rigid.'

Amber shot her husband an Arctic look, then turned

back to Alistair. 'He's lying,' she said. 'The real reason he doesn't want me to join you is because he finds me repulsive.'

Alistair gave a nervous laugh.

'I'm serious,' Amber continued. 'Otherwise why would he have dumped me for the housekeeper?'

Alistair's eyebrows shot up. 'You two have split up?'

'Oh yes, didn't Daniel tell you?'

Alistair shook his head. 'No . . . he didn't.'

'I expect he didn't want to ruin his image as a nice, respectable family man – isn't that right, dear?'

Daniel's Adam's apple bobbed up and down furiously. 'I simply didn't feel it appropriate to divulge that information to a business contact,' he said stiffly.

'Ah, but you *did* feel it was appropriate to give the housekeeper a good seeing to right under my nose,' Amber snapped. 'And then make my life an absolute misery by refusing to let me have the house so I can raise our son with a bit of dignity.' She wiped her eyes, though they were quite dry. 'Honestly, Alistair, I'm in pieces; Daniel's being an absolute pig about the divorce. All I want is what's rightfully mine, but he seems determined to make things as difficult for me as possible . . . as if I haven't suffered enough already.'

Alistair removed the crisp purple handkerchief from his breast pocket and handed it to Amber. 'There, there; don't get upset.'

'Once an actress, always an actress,' Daniel said witheringly. 'Don't pay any attention to her, Alistair. It's all a pantomime; she's only trying to make you feel sorry for her.'

'And don't you think I deserve a bit of sympathy, after everything I've been through!' Amber shrieked.

Daniel looked around anxiously. Their little trio was starting to attract attention and several clusters of guests had moved closer, not wanting to miss out on any drama. 'Why don't we discuss this later, Amber?' he said briskly. 'In private.'

'I'm not interested in discussing anything with you. From now on, anything you want to say to me you can say through my lawyer.'

'Fine,' said Daniel. 'If that's the way you want to play it.'

As she looked at Daniel's cold, calm expression, something inside Amber flipped. Spotting an abandoned glass of red wine on a nearby table, she picked it up and hurled it in her husband's face.

The move took Daniel by surprise and, temporarily blinded, he stumbled backwards into a boulder, scraping his Achilles heel painfully. 'You fucking bitch,' he spat as he wiped his face with his sleeve. 'What did you do that for?'

'Because you deserve it,' said Amber, who was now crying for real. 'And if I was the owner of Gluck's, I wouldn't touch any of your bloody hotels with a bargepole.'

'Well then, it's damn lucky you're not, isn't it?' said Daniel. He looked around and realized that Alistair had left his side and was heading towards the door. 'Hey, Alistair, wait a second. I'll be right with you,' he called out.

Alistair turned over his shoulder. 'Sorry, Daniel, I think we'd better call it a night.'

'But I haven't told you about the new hotel I'm building on the south coast. It's going to have a heli-pad and a saltwater infinity pool.'

'Don't listen to him, Alistair,' Amber cried. 'He doesn't deserve to be in your guide. He doesn't even like you very much. He thinks you're a boring old fart — he's told me so on several occasions.'

Alistair's face grew dark as thunder. 'I see,' he said. 'In that case, this boring old fart is going to have to think long and hard about including any of your hotels in Gluck's in the future. Good evening to you.'

'Alistair, please ...' Daniel begged. But it was too late: Gluck was gone. Daniel glared at Amber, who was dabbing her heavily mascaraed eyes with Alistair's hand-kerchief. 'Bravo, Amber,' he said, as he began a slow handclap. 'Brav-fucking-o.'

Marianne and Keeley had been agog throughout the emotional vignette, but now that it was over they melted discreetly away. As they headed to the ladies' to powder their noses, Keeley spotted Ryan walking towards them, talking into his mobile phone. He waved when he saw her but seemed in no hurry to end his call.

'About bloody time,' Keeley said crossly, looking at her watch.

Marianne touched her friend on the shoulder. 'I expect you two would like some time alone. I think I'll go and see what Simon's up to.'

'Okay,' said Keeley, 'I'll catch up with you in a little while.' She went over to meet Ryan and stood beside him, hands on hips, as she waited for him to finish his call.

'Who was that?' she said when he finally took the phone away from his ear.

'A friend,' he replied.

'What friend?'

Ryan scowled. 'Why do you always have to know *everything*?'

'I'm just curious, that's all.'

'If you must know, it was my sister.'

Keeley gave a disparaging snort. 'Then why didn't you just say that in the first place?'

'To make a point.'

'Sometimes, Ryan Stoker, I really don't understand you,' Keeley said. 'Why are you so late anyway? Marianne and I have been here for ages.'

'What is this – the Spanish Inquisition? I got held up in traffic, okay?'

'For an hour and a half?' Keeley said in a disbelieving tone.

The footballer raked his fingers through his hair. He was fond of Keeley. At one point he even thought he might be falling in love with her. But their relationship, which had been fun and easy-going at the start, was now getting too heavy for his liking. When he wasn't with her, Keeley always wanted to know what he was doing and who he was doing it with, and if there were other females involved she was prone to sulks and standoffishness. Even more worryingly, a couple of weeks earlier he'd been at her flat watching TV while she showered, when he'd spotted a copy of *Cosmo Bride* in the magazine rack. He'd pulled it out for a closer look and was horrified to find that a handful of pages had been deliberately dog-eared. The thought that she might be planning a wedding – *their* wedding – had totally freaked him out. He was only twenty-six, and in his book that was far too young to be settling down.

The footballer gave his girlfriend a stern look, determined to stamp his authority. 'Are you going to carry on like this all night?' he said. 'Because, if you are, I'm off.'

Instantly, Keeley crumpled. 'Oh, babe, I'm sorry,' she said as she flung her arms round his neck. 'I was just worried about you, that's all. I thought you might have had an accident.'

'Yeah, well as you can see, I'm fine.' Ryan unwrapped her arms. 'Come on, let's go in; I'm gasping for a drink.'

Meanwhile, not so very far away, Marianne was seeking her own entertainment. Unable to suppress her womanly urges a moment longer, she'd gone in search of Reverend Proctor. She found him chatting to a well-known TV presenter – a skinny streak of dandy with thrombosis-inducing jeans and bird's-nest hair, who had exchanged bodily fluids with at least half of Kirkhulme's twenty-something female population.

The Reverend smiled when he saw his lover, but was careful to keep his tone cool and light as if they were nothing more than casual acquaintances. 'Ah, Mrs Kennedy, how lovely to see you. Have you met Ross Butler?'

'No, I do believe I'm one of the few women in the village who hasn't,' said Marianne mischievously. Personally, she couldn't see what the appeal was. To her eye, Ross Butler looked as if he could do with a square meal and a good wash. Her opinion didn't improve when she accepted the presenter's outstretched hand. His grip was soft and limp – the handshake of someone who didn't care whether or not you liked the impression he was making.

'Mr Butler and I have been having an interesting discussion about the vow of chastity,' said Simon.

Marianne gave the vicar a sharp look. 'Why, are you thinking of taking one?'

'No,' said Ross. 'I am.'

Marianne exhaled in relief. 'That's very brave of you. But how on earth are you going to fill all those long, lonely nights?'

Ross grinned, revealing a row of tombstone teeth. 'Blimey, is my reputation really that bad?'

''Fraid so,' said Marianne. 'But it's nothing to be ashamed of, darling. By all accounts, you've made a lot of women very happy.' She smiled back at him. 'Would you mind if I steal the reverend away for a few minutes? There's a spiritual matter I need to discuss with him rather urgently.'

Without waiting for a response, she swiped the glass of champagne from Simon's hand and set it on top of the nearest window sill. 'Let's go somewhere more private, shall we?'

A minute later, they were walking out of the ballroom. 'Where are we going?' Simon asked as they set off down a long corridor.

Marianne licked her lips in anticipation. 'Somewhere I can take advantage of you.' They rounded another corner. 'We're here,' she said, gesturing to the smooth, mahogany-lined wall.

Simon looked around. 'You're not seriously suggesting we do it in the corridor.'

'No, silly ... watch this.'

Marianne reached out a hand and pushed a seemingly random section of wood panelling at about chest height. At her touch, it sprang open smoothly to reveal a concealed cupboard, which was lined with shelves laden with cleaning materials. 'After you.'

The vicar was suitably impressed. 'Hey, this is clever,' he said as he stepped into the cupboard. 'You wouldn't know it was here from the outside.'

'It's great, isn't it? Keeley discovered it last year.'

Marianne shut the door behind them and flicked a light switch. 'That light's awfully bright, isn't it?' she said, wincing at the naked bulb suspended a few inches above their heads. She undid her chiffon blouse and draped it over the bulb, filling the small space with a peachy glow. 'There, that's better. Now we can get down to business.'

Without further ado, she unzipped her skirt and let it flutter to the scuffed linoleum. At the sight of Marianne's goatskin garter, the vicar's lips began to quiver. Falling to his knees, he began to gently unlace the cilice, gasping in delight when he saw the wound that lay beneath. 'Oh my love,' he murmured as he began to shower her reddened skin with tiny kisses. 'It's such a wonderful sacrifice you're making, my love.'

Marianne smiled. 'Actually, I'm really rather enjoying it,' she said. 'Every time I feel it chafing, I think of you.'

The vicar flung the cilice to the ground. 'You really are the most terrible distraction,' he said, stroking his hand across his lover's flimsy lace briefs. The Bishop would be horrified if he knew my mind was filled with such impure thoughts.'

'Perhaps we should ask him if he'd like to watch,' said Marianne, as she guided Simon's hand between her legs.

The reverend laughed softly. 'You wicked, wicked woman.' Suddenly, his hand froze.

'Don't stop,' Marianne said in a breathy voice.

'I thought I heard a noise outside.'

'Ignore it,' said Marianne, grabbing his hand and moving it up and down.

The vicar cocked his head. 'Listen, there it is again.'

This time, Marianne heard it too: a squeaking sound, like rubber on wood, with an accompaniment of tuneless whistling.

Simon rose to his feet, pulling Marianne's skirt up with him. 'Here, put this on,' he said as he yanked her blouse from the lightbulb.

'Oh, Simon, there's no need to be so jumpy. No one's going to disturb us; the cleaners went home hours ago.'

'Please, my love; do it for me.'

Sighing, Marianne pushed her arms into the sleeves of her blouse. She barely had time to fasten the top button before the cupboard door was flung open. There on the threshold stood Alf Joiner, St Benedict's veteran head caretaker. In his hand was a mop stuffed into a metal bucket on wheels. He jumped back when he saw the vicar. 'Reverend Proctor!' he exclaimed. 'You nearly gave me a heart attack. Whatever are you doing in *there*?'

Simon's mouth gaped as he tried to come up with a plausible excuse. 'I was just, erm . . .'

'He was just hearing my confession.' Marianne stepped

out from behind the vicar and flashed an apologetic smile at Alf.

The caretaker scratched his head. 'Confession? In *my* broom cupboard?'

'Yes,' said Marianne, crossing her arm across her body to disguise her unbuttoned blouse. 'I was attending a function in the ballroom when I spotted Reverend Proctor across the room and realized there was something I simply had to get off my chest.' She paused. 'Immediately.'

Alf looked from one to the other, not sure whether or not he believed them. 'I see.'

'Anyway, we mustn't keep you from your work,' said Marianne, taking a step towards the door. 'Come on, Reverend, we'd better get back to our friends in the ballroom.'

The caretaker shook his head as he watched them walk down the corridor together. He'd seen some strange sights during his thirty-one-year tenure at St Benedict's, but this was one of the strangest. Still tutting, he wheeled his mop and bucket into the cupboard. As he rested the mop handle against a shelf, he spotted a scrap of fabric lying on the floor. He bent down to pick it up, frowning as he turned it over in his hands. It was a piece of animal skin by the looks of it, with something like a leather bootlace threaded through it.

'Heavens to Betsy,' Alf said out loud. 'What in God's name is this?'

Sighing, he stuffed the cilice in the pocket of his overalls and exited the cupboard. His next port of call was one of the private rooms further along the corridor where a strange and unusual secret society was holding its regular monthly meeting – a meeting that had only just started when, according to Alf's ancient Timex, it should have broken up half an hour ago.

Alf's boss, Anthony Lanchester, general manager of St Benedict's, was always urging him to be more flexible in his dealings with members, but the caretaker was already annoyed about the use of his cleaning cupboard for unauthorized purposes and he was buggered if he was going to be taken advantage of twice in one evening.

As Alf approached the room in question, the exotic sound of chanting reached his ears. The society, which was made up entirely of men, had been meeting at St Benedict's every month for years, but Alf still didn't have the faintest idea what they were about – or even what they were called. What he did know was that they left the room smelling of incense and candlewax, and once, after they'd gone, he'd found a thick paper scroll, marked with obscure hieroglyphs, lying under the table.

After a quick glance around to check that he was unobserved, Alf pressed his ear to the door. What he heard seemed to make no sense at all:

'Oh, Nefertiti, Daughter of the Gods, Nubian Queen, Lady of Beauty and Grace,' a lone voice intoned.

'Awake in peace!' chorused the others.

'Your belly that contains the perfect womb.'

'Awake in peace!'

'Your breasts of abundant milk.'

'Awake in peace!'

'Your arms that give life to the faithful.'

'Awake in peace!'

'The regent in the west and in the east.'

'Awake in peace!'

Alf had heard quite enough. Raising his fist, he rapped sharply on the door. Instantly, the chanting stopped. Without waiting for an invitation, the caretaker entered the room. A very peculiar sight met his eyes: twelve middle-aged men were seated at the conference table, all wearing long white shifts tied with red sashes. Their eyes were rimmed with dark kohl and they wore poker-straight black wigs that were cut just above the shoulder. The overhead lights had been turned off and the room was lit by dozens of votive candles.

At the head of the table sat a man Alf recognized – despite the wig – as Daniel Solomon. Beside him, on an ornate pedestal, stood a large and ancient-looking plaster bust of a beautiful woman wearing a tall, blue headdress. The millionaire hotelier was clearly annoyed at the interruption – and also a little embarrassed, judging by the red streaks above his cheekbones.

'Mr Joiner, how dare you barge in here like this,' he said, snatching off his wig and throwing it on the table. 'This is a private meeting.'

'That's as may be, but your meeting's running well over,' Alf said gruffly. 'This room should've been vacated half an hour ago.'

Daniel glanced at his watch. 'Oh gosh, there must be some mistake with the booking. I was under the impression we had the room for another hour.' He forced a smile. 'I'm sorry if we've inconvenienced you, Mr Joiner – but is there any chance you could let us stay for a bit longer? We've only just started our incantation, you see.'

Alf held up a hand. 'I don't want to know what you were doing, Mr Solomon. Just make sure you're out of here in the next twenty minutes. I've got to polish this floor before I clock off.'

'Yes, of course,' Daniel replied. 'Thank you very much – and I'll make sure I double check the booking next time.'

As Alf turned to go, he noticed a small ornament sitting in the middle of the conference table. Made of a dull greenish stone, it depicted a seated male figure. An enormous phallus projected from between his legs and on top of the member, a small jar was balanced.

'It's beautiful, isn't it?' said Daniel, noting Alf's interest. 'An exceedingly rare example of ancient Egyptian erotica.' He gestured to the man sitting on his left. 'One of my brothers here purchased it at auction last week and kindly brought it in to show us.'

Alf averted his eyes from the object. 'It's bloody disgusting, if you ask me.'

Daniel's smile disappeared. 'Ah well, not everyone appreciates fine art.'

As Alf made his way back to the cleaning cupboard, he mulled over what he had just seen and heard. 'Men in make-up and dresses,' he muttered as he pushed his floor polisher back along the corridor. 'Flaming perverts, the lot of them.'

Nine

Marta woke with a start. The sun was streaming in through the thin cotton blind, filling the room with shimmering dust motes. Beside her, Harry, her boyfriend of four weeks, lay fast asleep, one arm flung above his head like a child. Recalling the energetic sex they'd had the night before, Marta smiled and rolled over, so her breasts pressed against her lover's torso. At the same time, she caught sight of the alarm clock's digital display. '*¡Mierda!*' she cried, flinging back the duvet.

Harry stirred. 'What's up?' he said, his voice thick with sleep.

'I should've been at work half an hour ago,' Marta said as she rolled out of bed and began gathering up the clothes that were scattered across Harry's floor.

'Why don't you phone in sick?'

'I can't. Laura's taking Tiger to a baby yoga class this morning. She needs me to look after the girls.'

Harry hauled himself on to one elbow and regarded his naked girlfriend. 'What about her husband? Can't he keep an eye on them?'

Marta made a huffing noise as she stepped into her knickers. 'You don't know Sam. Anyway, even if he did agree to stay home, he wouldn't be able to cope. The last time Laura left him on his own with the girls, he managed to lose Birdie.'

'*Lose* her?'

'Yes. She crawled under the dining-room table and fell asleep. The tablecloth was so long, Sam couldn't find her for two hours. Laura was furious that he'd let her out of his sight. She's only tiny; anything could have happened to her.'

Harry smiled sleepily, watching as Marta struggled with her bra. 'Here, you look as if you could use some help with that.'

The au pair went over to him and sat on the edge of the bed with her back to him. 'There you go,' Harry said as he fastened the hooks with surprising deftness. 'Not quite as much fun as taking it off, admittedly.'

'Thank you.' Marta turned round and brought her lips down on the end of her boyfriend's nose. 'When will I see you again?' she murmured.

'How about tomorrow night?' He ran his hand over the soft curve of her hip. 'Do you have to go right this second? If you're going to be late, you may as well be *really* late.'

Marta looked at the alarm clock again. 'Laura's going to kill me.'

'You'd better think up a good excuse then,' said Harry, as he began unfastening her bra.

By the time Marta finally arrived at the Bentley's elegant Georgian home, it was gone ten. The minute she heard the au pair's ancient 2CV chugging up the driveway, Laura came rushing out to meet her. 'Thank God you're here!' she cried as Marta emerged from the car. 'I was starting to think you'd had an accident.'

'Sorry, Laura, I had a flat tyre,' Marta lied. 'Harry had to help me change it.'

'You might have called me. I was worried about you.'

Marta looked sheepish. 'Yeah, you're right; it was thoughtless of me.'

'So you stayed the night at Harry's again, did you?' Laura said as they went into the house.

'He made me dinner for the first time. I couldn't believe how much trouble he'd gone to. There were candles and flowers on the table, and white linen napkins; it was *sooo* romantic.' Marta sighed. 'Honestly, Laura, he's my dream man. I'd see him every night if I could.'

Laura felt a tightening in her chest. Marta's relationship was moving far too quickly for her liking. At this rate, she'd be getting engaged and handing in her notice by the end of the summer. 'I'm very pleased for you,' she said, trying to sound sincere. 'But you don't want Harry thinking he's got you at his beck and call. Remember what I said ... play a little bit hard to get. It'll make him twice as keen.'

'You're probably right, but I don't think I've got the willpower. We can hardly keep our hands off each oth–' She paused and looked at the ceiling. Upstairs, Tiger had begun one of his high-decibel workouts. 'Should I go up?'

'Ignore him; he's just doing it to annoy me,' Laura said petulantly. 'He's had me up and down those stairs all morning and there's absolutely nothing wrong with him. He's been fed, winded, changed ... the works.'

'Maybe I should check on him anyway.'

Laura shrugged. 'If you like. While you're up there,

would you mind getting him dressed? We're going to have to leave for yoga in half an hour. I've laid out the Baby Dior dungarees on the changing table.'

'Denim – is that going to be appropriate for baby yoga?'

Laura frowned. 'What do you suggest?'

'Something lightweight and tight-fitting, like a baby-gro.'

'Okay. Stick him in the Ralph Lauren romper suit – you know, the blue and white striped one with the Peter Pan collar.' Suddenly, Laura clutched her hair. 'Shit, he puked on it last week; it's still in the laundry hamper.'

'Don't worry, Laura, I'll find something.'

'Yes, but do make sure it's designer. You know how competitive the Kirkhulme mums are; I don't want them looking down their noses at us.' As Tiger's cries reached fever pitch, Laura put her hand to her forehead. 'I really hope this yoga class works; I'm running out of ideas.'

Marta stroked Laura's upper arm soothingly. 'I'm sure they'll help Tiger feel more relaxed, but don't expect miracles after just one session. It's going to take time.'

'I haven't got time,' Laura said shrilly. 'I just want my life back. That's not too much to ask, is it?'

Just then a sing-song voice called out from the kitchen. '*Mumm-eee*. Birdie's spilled her drink.'

'Okay, sweetheart; I'm coming.' Laura gave Marta a thin smile. 'I'll go and see to the girls.' She pointed to the ceiling. 'Sing the little sod a nursery rhyme or something, will you? Anything to shut him up.'

'I'll do my best.' As Marta watched Laura disappear

down the hallway, a wave of sadness washed over her. In her native Spain, children – whatever their appearance or disposition – were cherished and doted upon. It was becoming increasingly obvious that Laura didn't love her baby. In fact, the way she was acting, Marta was beginning to suspect she didn't even *like* him.

The yoga class was being held a short drive away in Kirkhulme's village hall. Having been calmed by Marta, Tiger remained mercifully quiet throughout the journey. Laura thought he must have fallen asleep, but when she glanced at the car seat he was staring at her, wide-eyed and solemn. As she turned her gaze back to the road, she found herself wishing – and not for the first time – that her offspring was more attractive; perhaps then she'd feel more kindly disposed towards him. Tiger wasn't cute like other babies, with fat pink cheeks and long eye-lashes. Instead, he had the wispy hair and wrinkled skin of a little old man – and Marta hadn't helped matters by dressing him in a lemon DKNY sleepsuit that made his complexion look even more sallow than usual.

When they reached their destination, Laura switched off the engine and turned to her son. 'You're doing very well,' she said in a jolly tone. 'If you can keep your gob shut for the next hour, you're going to make your mother an exceedingly happy woman.'

Tiger jerked his head upwards, as if to say, '*You'll* be lucky.'

Inside the village hall, eight women on yoga mats were ranged in a circle. Some were chatting; others were play-ing with their babies, who lay in the centre of the circle on a patchwork of ethnic rugs. All the women were slim, well coiffed and fashionably dressed, with immaculate French manicures and expensive earrings. Laura felt frowsy by comparison in her two-seasons-old Paul Smith palazzo pants and an oversized T-shirt that, despite several washes in biological detergent, still bore a faint stain of baby sick.

At the head of the group, a middle-aged woman with long wavy hair and a rainbow-coloured tunic sat in the lotus position. 'Welcome!' she exclaimed as Laura approached with Tiger in her arms. She gestured to the circle. 'Please, make yourself comfortable on the floor with baby. We'll be starting soon; we're just waiting for one or two more people.'

Laura settled on one of the spare yoga mats and lay Tiger down on the nearest rug. He hadn't made a sound since emerging from the car: so far, so good. She looked furtively at the other babies who were all gurgling contentedly; there wasn't a grizzler among them.

'Hi, I'm Alex,' said the woman on Laura's right. Her skin was the colour of honey and she wore a figure-hugging black leotard and matching leggings.

Smiling, Laura introduced herself and her son.

'Tiger ... that's a cute name.' Alex reached out and stroked his cheek. 'Hello, little wildcat.'

To Laura's amazement, Tiger's lips formed a gummy smile. 'He never does that for me,' she remarked.

'Never does what?'

'Smiles. He's nearly two months old and he's never once smiled at me.'

'Really? I wonder why that is.'

Feeling she ought to reciprocate Alex's interest in Tiger, Laura leaned towards the other woman's baby. 'And who do we have here?'

'This is Maddy. She'll be six months old tomorrow.'

Laura stared at the infant jealously, taking in her blonde curls and pink-checked Burberry dress. 'She looks just like you.'

'Everyone says that.' Alex adjusted the red bow in her daughter's hair. 'I haven't seen you at baby yoga before. Is this your first time?'

Laura nodded. 'Tiger's quite a difficult baby. He's always crying and he never sleeps for more than a couple of hours at a stretch. I'm hoping the yoga will help us both relax.'

'Oh, it will; you'll notice the difference right away,' Alex gushed. 'We've been coming to baby yoga since Maddy was ten weeks. After every class, without fail, she falls into a deep sleep, which means I can go home and get loads of stuff done.'

Laura's eyes widened. 'Gosh, how wonderful; I just hope it has the same effect on Tiger.'

While they'd been talking, two more women had joined the group and now every yoga mat was taken. The teacher stood up and began fiddling with a CD player. A moment later, some new-agey music, complete with wind chimes and weird dolphin noises, struck up.

'Okay, ladies,' the teacher said, resuming her position on the floor. 'I'd like you all to sit cross-legged, pick up your baby and hold him close to your chest.'

All the mothers did as they were told. The teacher smiled. 'Good. Now circle gently on your hips, just like

I'm doing, first right and then left. Excellent ... keep that rhythm going.'

Laura's movements were tentative at first. Tiger usually objected when she held him close, squirming in her arms as if he were desperate to escape. But just for once his limbs were still; it seemed that he, like Laura, found the warm-up exercise soothing. After a few minutes of hip circling, the teacher ordered them to stop. 'Let's pause now and close our eyes for a silent moment of gratitude, to give thanks to the universe for bringing our babies into our lives.'

Laura wanted to think positive thoughts, but when she shut her eyes she found herself cursing the two consecutive days she'd forgotten to take her contraceptive pill – an oversight that had resulted in Tiger's conception. She pushed the thought to the back of her mind and tried to imagine a great tidal wave of love rising up from her heart and washing over Tiger. Instead, she felt vaguely seasick.

'And open!' The teacher picked up the large fabric doll that was lying beside her yoga mat. 'We're going to start off with the locust pose. For those of you who haven't been to baby yoga before, this posture encourages movement in the organ- and gland-packed upper belly and will help your baby develop a sense of his or her own power and will.'

Laura smirked. It seemed to her that Tiger didn't need much help in that department.

'Watch me do it first.' The instructor positioned the doll on its back in front of her. 'Lay your baby on their back and slip your hands under their knees, like so.

Then, in one smooth motion, slide your hands towards their feet, lengthening the legs and lifting them about one inch off the floor. Next, we gently lower the legs. Remember, never force baby's limbs; gently coax them into position. And that's all there is to it.' She smiled at her pupils. 'Okay, time for you to try.' She watched carefully as her pupils performed the exercise. 'Good work, ladies. Okay, we're going to repeat that five times, nice and slowly.'

Unfortunately for Laura, Tiger wasn't very receptive to the idea of having his limbs manipulated. On the second repetition, his face began to crumple. On the third, he opened his mouth wide.

'Please, Tiger, no,' Laura whispered, but it was too late. A loud wail sliced through the air. Laura sighed. It never ceased to amaze her how such a tiny pair of lungs could produce such an almighty racket. She looked around the group and grimaced apologetically.

'It's all right, keep going,' the teacher urged. 'He's just feeling a little insecure.'

Obediently, Laura continued raising and lowering Tiger's legs. His crying continued, and soon his sobs were so loud, they all but drowned out the music. Laura could feel a hot flush creeping up her neck and radiating across her face. Whatever had she been thinking, bringing Tiger here? She should've known he would make a show of her.

'Why don't you pick baby up?' the teacher suggested. 'Give him a nice cuddle.'

Laura didn't need to be asked twice, knowing she could muffle Tiger's cries against her shoulder. She scooped him up, but in her haste she forgot to support his head and it lolled backwards.

There was a sharp intake of breath from Alex. 'Watch his head!'

'He's fine,' Laura said stiffly as she pressed Tiger to her breast.

Alex turned back to Maddy, who had begun a kittenish whimpering.

'Let's try the boat pose,' said the teacher, now shouting to be heard above the sound of Tiger's squalling. 'This chest expansion exercise will open the heart centre and keep your baby's energy flowing.'

As she began demonstrating the manoeuvre with her doll, Maddy started crying. Alex looked horrified. 'Oh, darling,' she cried. 'Whatever's the matter?'

Next to her, Laura was rocking Tiger frantically from side to side. Her underarms were damp and she could feel her heartbeat racing. She'd always been such a laid-back, capable mother, but somehow Tiger had the ability to make her feel totally inadequate. And then a third infant started crying.

'Goodness,' the teacher declared. 'This is a first. Our babies are usually so well behaved.' Her eyes alighted on Tiger. From her strained expression, Laura knew what she was thinking: *disruptive influence.* The class limped on for another two minutes, but when a fourth infant joined the cacophony, the teacher stood up. 'I'm sorry, ladies, I think we're going to have to take a break.'

A couple of the women groaned in disappointment, while another glared at Laura accusingly. It was too much. Blushing furiously, Laura scrambled to her feet and began walking towards the door with Tiger. The teacher made no attempt to stop her.

When she got back to the car, Laura erupted in a fit of anger. 'You little wretch,' she snarled, depositing Tiger in his car seat. 'You do realize I'll never be able to show my face in that class again, don't you?' The baby flailed his tiny arms, his face bright red with the effort of crying. Laura regarded him dispassionately. 'You can complain all you like, but I'm not taking you home. I've been stuck in that house all week; we're going for a walk, whether you like it or not.'

Leaving the car door open, she stomped round to the boot where Tiger's pram was stored. Even though the girls' old pram was perfectly serviceable, Sam had insisted on spending a small fortune on a new one. A ludicrously sophisticated affair with the torque and suspension of a Ferrari, it took Laura several minutes – and half a dozen choice swear words – to erect. Once Tiger was on board, a fleece blanket tucked tightly round him, she set off down the high street at a brisk pace. Lulled by the smooth motion of the pram's chunky all-terrain tyres, it wasn't long before Tiger's cries slowed to a hiccup. A very relieved Laura offered up a silent prayer of thanks.

Kirkhulme's shopping thoroughfare was small, but well suited to the needs of the local community. There was an organic butcher, two hairdressers, three designer boutiques, a patisserie-cum-deli, an off-licence (which did a brisk trade in Cristal rosé at £300 a pop) and a charity shop, which, at first glance, looked like any other but step inside and you could have been in New Bond Street, with its minimalist decor and rails of Armani, Versace and Miu

Miu. Despite the numerous temptations, Laura didn't break stride until she reached the plush offices of Woodward & Stockley. A couple of days earlier, one of the estate agent's FOR SALE boards had appeared outside a house at the end of Laura's street, and she was keen to find out what it was on for. Property prices in the village never ceased to amaze her and, at £1.5 million, her neighbour's house turned out to be one of the cheapest on offer in Woodward & Stockley's window. When she moved closer to inspect the recently remodelled kitchen-breakfast room, Tiger started fretting. Without taking her eyes off the property details, Laura began pushing the pram back and forth. But it was too late: a minute later, Tiger's mewls had escalated into a full-blown aria. 'I knew it was too good to be true,' Laura said through gritted teeth. She peered into the pram. 'I must've done something very bad in a previous life to wind up with a brat like you.'

A few feet away, a middle-aged lady who had been inspecting a barn conversion – a snip at two million – turned to her with a disapproving frown. 'You really shouldn't speak to him like that, dear.'

Laura glared at her. '*You* try living with a crying child twenty-four/seven.' She pushed the pram towards the woman. 'In fact, why don't you take him, if think you can do better?'

The lady looked at her as if she were some sort of lunatic. 'You shouldn't joke about things like that.'

'But I'm not joking; I want you to have him. Honestly, you'd be doing me a favour.'

'Well, really!' the woman exclaimed. With a supercilious toss of her head, she turned on her heel and walked away.

Laura turned back to Tiger. 'Oh well, it was worth a try, eh, kiddo?' She pulled a tissue from her pocket and wiped a drizzle of snot from his nose. 'Come on then, Grumpy. Let's get moving.'

They continued walking for half a mile or so until the village gave way to open countryside. On a whim, Laura turned off the main road on to a footpath, which led to a local beauty spot – a dramatic sandstone escarpment known as Devil's Ridge. It was an uphill climb, but Laura welcomed the opportunity to burn off some of the pounds she'd struggled to shed since giving birth. Tiger quickly nodded off and, with the sun rising ever higher in the sky, Laura raised the pram's hood to protect him from the sun. As she walked, she tried to analyse her antipathy towards her newborn son. It wasn't that she hated him exactly – just that she wished he'd never been born. She didn't know why she felt this way; it seemed to her to be nothing more sinister than a simple clash of personalities. It *had* crossed Laura's mind that she might be suffering from post-natal depression, but she didn't feel depressed, just irritable and full of resentment. She'd meant what she'd said to the interfering busybody outside the estate agent's. She would gladly put Tiger up for adoption but, knowing such an act would be wholly socially unacceptable, there seemed to be only one option open to her. 'Boarding school,' she said to her son's sleeping form. 'That's where you're headed the minute you're old enough.'

Eventually, the footpath opened out into a plateau,

which offered magnificent views across the valley below. Breathing heavily from her exertions, Laura activated the brake on the pram and went to the edge of the escarpment. Beneath it, the ground fell sharply away and the undulating landscape was littered with sharp-edged boulders, the legacy of ancient quarry workings. She stood there for several minutes, enjoying the scenery and breathing in deep lungfuls of gorse-scented air. It was such a peaceful spot and, apart from a couple of dog-walkers she'd passed on the way up, there was no one else in sight. For one blissful moment, standing there on Devil's Ridge with the wind whipping her dark curls across her face, Laura felt utterly free. In the distance she could see a vast shimmering lake, surrounded by sturdy Scots pines. She and Sam had taken the girls for a picnic there on a blazing hot bank holiday, just a week before Tiger was born. How happy and carefree she'd been that day, oblivious to the black cloud that was about to descend. Suddenly, an idea flashed into Laura's mind; perhaps there was another option after all. She mulled it over for several minutes, working out the consequences. It was a risky move, no doubt about it. The question was, was it a risk worth taking?

Laura looked around. There was no one in sight; even the dog-walkers had vanished from view. Quickly, she walked over to the pram. Tiger was still fast asleep, his breathing deep and even. One sturdy push was all that stood between her and freedom. She raised her foot, intending to deactivate the brake, when suddenly she heard a voice.

'Hello.'

Laura's foot froze in mid-air. She looked over her shoulder. A boy of six or seven stood on the other side of the plateau. He had an ice lolly in his hand and his mouth was ringed with a blackcurranty stain.

Laura held up a warning hand. 'Don't come too close to the edge; it's dangerous.'

The little boy stared at the pram. 'What are you doing?'

'None of your business.'

The boy frowned, as if he were thinking. 'Are you going to push it over the edge? Can I watch?'

'Goodness, no,' said Laura, moistening her dry lips with the edge of her tongue. 'What a ridiculous suggestion.'

'So what's your pram doing there then?'

Laura glared at him. 'You ask too many questions. Where's your mother anyway?'

He pointed towards the footpath. 'Down there with Megan.'

Laura crossed to the other side of the plateau where she had a better view of the footpath. Some distance away, she could see a blonde-haired woman holding the hand of a small girl.

'Hey, there's a baby in here.' Laura turned to look back. The boy was now standing next to the pram.

'Get away from there,' Laura shrieked. 'I told you – it's dangerous.'

The boy started backing away from the pram. '*Ummm* . . . I'm telling on you,' he said in a smug voice.

Laura sighed, thoroughly exasperated. 'What's to tell?' she said as she grabbed the pram handle and pulled it further back from the edge of the escarpment.

Ten

The saleroom was packed. Lazenby's was hosting one of its twice-yearly antiquities sales, and hopeful bidders had descended on the Delchester auction house from far and wide. With the temperature in the nineties, the portable air-conditioning units were struggling to cope. Sweat-soaked buyers fanned themselves with their auction catalogues as they waited for the sale to begin, but none was willing to risk their seat by stepping outside where it was cooler. Three rows from the front, Amber Solomon sat quietly. A wide-brimmed straw hat was pulled low over her forehead and her distinctive eyes were hidden behind enormous sunglasses. Usually, she liked being the centre of attention, but today, just for once, she was going incognito. Until that morning, Amber had been in two minds about whether or not to attend the auction. But, after being forced to listen to Daniel and Nancy's lovemaking for the second night on the trot – a lovemaking so violent it had caused the crystal teardrops on the rococo chandelier above her bed to tremble – Amber's mind had been made up.

Suddenly, an audible ripple of excitement radiated through the room. Amber turned her head just in time to see her husband enter the room. Daniel Solomon was a well-known figure on the antiquities scene and his presence at auction always added an extra frisson to proceedings. With him was his accountant, Kelvin, a grey, humourless man whom Amber had never liked. Daniel, however, trusted Kelvin implicitly and rarely made a financial decision without first seeking his approval. Amber watched as her husband slid into a reserved seat a dozen or so rows back where several of his cronies were already sitting – men she recognized as members of an informal Nefertiti tribute society Daniel had set up years earlier. They all shook hands with each other and one of them gave the hotelier a hearty pat on the back, as if to say, *You go, big boy!* Daniel gave him a wide, relaxed smile in response. *He reckons it's in the bag,* Amber thought to herself. *Poor, deluded fool.*

At 11 a.m. precisely, the auctioneer, immaculate in a Savile Row suit and silk tie, stepped up to the rostrum. Amber waited patiently, her numbered paddle resting on her lap, as lot after lot went under the hammer. Bidding was brisk and by eleven thirty, the auction house had already netted more than £100,000 in commission alone. Finally, it was time for lot number nineteen. The auction-eer cleared his throat discreetly. He, like Amber, knew that this was the big one.

'And now we come to one of our most eagerly antici-pated lots.' On the big screen, a close-up of a chunky gold ring appeared. 'A large and exceedingly rare Egyptian gold stirrup ring, dating from the reign of Akhenaten. The bezel bears the face of the pharoah's legendary wife, Queen Nefertiti, together with a hieroglyphic inscription.' The auctioneer glanced at his paperwork. 'I already have interest on the book ... I'm starting the bidding at fifteen thousand pounds. Fifteen thousand with me ... who'll give me twenty?'

There was a moment's silence and then the auctioneer pointed towards the back of the room. 'Thank you, sir.' Amber looked over her shoulder. Just as she had predicted when she'd browsed through the Lazenby's catalogue that had been carelessly left lying on the hall console table, Daniel's paddle was in the air. She smiled tightly and turned her attention back to the auctioneer.

'Twenty-five thousand anywhere?' The auctioneer pointed to the row of porters in the gallery, each of whom had a phone clamped to their ear. 'I have twenty-five thousand on the telephone. I need thirty thousand to advance.'

A woman in the front row with mousey hair piled into a towering bun raised her paddle. 'Thank you, madam. I have thirty thousand in the room. Do I have thirty-five? Thank you. Thirty-five in a new place. Yes, the gentleman at the back ... forty thousand pounds, thank you, sir. Do I have forty-five?'

With a pounding heart, Amber watched as the bidding rose steadily in £5,000 increments until finally only two bidders were left: Daniel and the woman with the bun.

'I have sixty thousand against you, madam. Do I have sixty-five thousand? No? Sixty-three thousand, if you like.'

The woman with the bun shook her head.

'Sixty-one thousand?'

Another shake of the head.

'All done at sixty?' The auctioneer looked out hopefully at the sea of faces before him. 'I will sell then at sixty thousand pounds to the gentleman at the back.'

Amber sneaked another glance at Daniel. He was smiling, certain that the ring was his. Her fingers closed round her paddle. 'Going once, going twice ... last call.' At the precise moment the auctioneer raised his gavel, Amber's hand shot in the air.

A collective gasp went up from the room. Even the auctioneer, who was used to such last-minute dramas, looked surprised. 'Sixty-one thousand from a new place ... just in time.' He looked to Daniel. 'Do I have sixty-two? Thank you, sir. It's sixty-two thousand with you. Madam? Sixty-three thousand, thank you. Sixty-four ... sixty-five ... do I have sixty-six, sir?'

Daniel felt Kelvin's arm on the sleeve of his Armani suit. He brushed it away impatiently.

'Sixty-six thousand. Thank you, sir. Sixty-seven ... it's with you, madam. Sixty-eight?'

Daniel looked at his accountant, his eyes large and pleading. Kelvin made a cutting motion under his neck. Daniel chewed his lip. Then he slowly shook his head.

'No?' said the auctioneer.

Amber kept her eyes fixed firmly to the front and held her breath.

'Sixty-seven thousand then, with the lady. All done at sixty-seven thousand? Going once, twice, three times.' The auctioneer brought his gavel down with a flourish. 'Sold to paddle number one-three-three.'

Amber exhaled noisily. Victory was hers. True, it had come at a hefty price, but she'd checked their joint account that morning and it contained more than enough funds to cover the purchase.

By the time Amber's driver returned her to the Old Manor, Daniel was already home. What's more, he was in a foul mood – Amber could tell by the skid marks in the gravel and the careless way his Bentley Continental was parked at an angle with its rear wheels in a flowerbed. She smiled as she let herself into the house, knowing Daniel was going to be even more pissed off when he discovered *she* was the one who'd swiped the Nefertiti bauble from under his nose.

In the hall, Amber removed her disguise. As she set her hat and sunglasses down on the console table, she caught sight of her reflection in the ormolu mirror that hung above it. Despite the thrill of the auction, she looked drained and there were dark shadows under her eyes. She would have to speak to Dr Lawrence about another round of dermabrasion, and quite possibly a third eye lift too. With a long sigh, she opened her Zac Posen handbag, which she now kept under lock and key in her dressing room, together with anything else she thought Nancy might take a fancy to. Removing a small, suede-covered box, she slipped it into the breast pocket of her linen shirt and went to the drawing room. Hearing her approach, Couscous began chattering in an excited falsetto.

'Hello, my precious,' Amber cooed as she slid back the bolt on his cage. 'Sorry Mummy's been so long; she had some very important business to attend to.' She patted her shoulder and Couscous leapt obligingly on to it, flinging his arms round the top of her head. 'I expect you're hungry, aren't you?' she said, stroking his soft back. 'Mummy's got some delicious wasp larvae for your lunch, but first there's something she must do.' The monkey let out an indignant squeal. 'Yes, all right then, Couscous can come too.'

Together, they made their way to the study. Amber knew her husband would be there – it was his sanctuary, the place he always went to lick his wounds. Knowing it would annoy him, she didn't bother knocking before she entered. He was sitting at his desk, head in his hands.

'Just barge in, why don't you?' Daniel said irritably. He glowered at Couscous. 'You'd better keep a tight hold of that monkey. If he damages any of my treasures, I'll wring his verminous neck.'

'Don't worry, he won't go anywhere near your wretched artefacts.' As Amber spoke, she glanced at the nearest exhibit case and saw that the top was covered with a thin film of dust. 'Goodness, standards *are* slipping,' she said, running a forefinger along the top of the glass. She held it up for inspection. 'Don't tell me Nancy's so busy servicing you she hasn't got time to lift a duster.'

Daniel gritted his teeth. 'Was there something you wanted in particular?'

'I was just wondering how the auction went, that's all,' Amber said, batting her eyelids innocently.

Daniel gave her a hard look. 'How do you know about that?'

'You left the catalogue lying around, and when I flicked

through it I couldn't help noticing that you'd circled lot number nineteen. What was it now? Ah yes, that's right, a fourteenth-century Egyptian gold stirrup ring, bearing the likeness of your favourite lady – your favourite lady after that little scrubber Nancy, that is.'

'Don't speak about Nancy like that,' Daniel said wearily. 'You don't know the first thing about her.'

'What a ridiculous thing to say,' Amber snapped. 'Of course I know her. She cleaned my toilet bowls for the best part of three years.'

'But you didn't make much of an effort to find out about her as a person, did you?'

Amber snorted. 'What, like *you* did you mean?'

Daniel chewed the inside of his lip, trying not to rise to the bait. 'I'm really not feeling at my best, Amber, and the last thing I want is an argument. So, if there's nothing else, kindly remove yourself and that repulsive primate from my study.'

'Aw, poor bunnykins,' Amber taunted him. 'What's the matter? Didn't Danny-wanny get the pretty ring he'd set his heart on?'

'No, Amber, if you must know, I didn't get it. I was outbid. Are you happy now?'

'Oh yes, I'm very happy; never felt better as a matter of fact.' Amber reached into her pocket and removed the box. 'You see, my darling, I've just become the proud owner of a very beautiful, very old and very rare piece of jewellery.'

She opened the box and removed the ancient ring from its velvet mount. Then she slipped it on to her middle digit and held out her hand, waggling her fingers like a bride-to-be showing off her engagement ring. 'It suits me rather well, don't you think?'

Daniel was wearing a peculiar strangulated expression, as if an invisible elastic band were tightening round his windpipe. 'Let me see that!' He made a sudden lunge for the ring, causing Couscous to clutch his head in alarm.

'Ah-ah, not so fast, mister,' said Amber, whisking her hand behind her back. 'This is *my* ring; I won it fair and square. You should know that; after all, you watched me do it.'

Daniel stared at her in disbelief. 'That was you in the auction room, sitting at the front in the straw hat?'

Amber nodded. 'I think I did rather well for a novice.'

'But, but ... I don't understand,' Daniel stammered. 'You haven't even the vaguest interest in Ancient Egypt. Why on earth would you pull a stunt like that?'

Amber looked at him, her eyes glittering like diamonds. 'Because you've degraded and humiliated me, and because you continue to rub my nose in your grubby little affair, even though my lawyer has asked you on more than one occasion not to bring Nancy to the house.' She rolled her eyes. 'Honestly, I thought you two were going to bring the ceiling down last night.'

'You're saying you bought the ring just to spite me?' Daniel said incredulously.

'Got it in one.'

'You conniving bitch.' Daniel slowly flexed his fists, furious that his wife had not only outbid him, but out-witted him too. 'Have you any idea how valuable that ring is?'

Amber pursed her giant lips. 'I'd hazard a guess at sixty-seven thousand pounds, or thereabouts.'

'I wasn't referring to its monetary value; I was talking about its historical significance. That ring is one of the most important Ancient Egyptian artefacts to have come on to the open market for twenty years. It's said to have belonged to one of Akhenaten's most powerful generals.'

'You don't say?' Amber replied in a bored tone.

'That ring is more precious than you can possibly imagine; it's vitally important that it's looked after properly.' There was a catch in Daniel's voice; he seemed close to tears.

For one fleeting moment Amber almost felt sorry for him. Then she remembered how, earlier in the week when she'd lain in bed all day with a migraine, he'd spitefully allowed her daily goat's milk delivery to languish on the doorstep, so it curdled in the heat.

'Oh well, look on the bright side. It's one less thing for you to worry about.'

A blue vein began jumping at Daniel's temple. 'So what do you intend to do with the ring?'

Amber shrugged. 'I hadn't thought about it.'

'If you decide to sell it, will you give me first refusal?'

'Hah!' said Amber. 'I'd give it away to some old dosser in a street doorway before I'd let you get your philandering hands on it.'

Daniel slumped back in his executive chair and ran a manicured hand through his hair. 'What exactly is it you want from me?'

'It's perfectly simple. I want the house and everything

in it.' Amber waved a hand at the exhibit cases. 'Apart from those manky old relics; you can keep those.'

'I am *not* moving out,' said Daniel, banging his fist on the desk for emphasis. 'I love this place every bit as much as you do.'

'But you're the one who was unfaithful,' said Amber, jabbing an accusing finger. 'I've never been anything other than a dutiful and loving wife. Remember all those gourmet dinner parties I hosted for your boring business associates? Remember how I attended every single one of our son's parents' evenings alone because you were too busy working? Remember the time I drove you to the hospital in the middle of the night when you thought you had appendicitis and it turned out to be trapped wind?'

'Thanks for reminding me,' said Daniel, wincing at the memory.

'And what about the hotels?' Amber continued, her voice growing angrier. 'Are you forgetting that it was me who persuaded you to get rid of those miserable motels and go into the luxury end of the market? Who chose the bed linen, interviewed the staff, helped design the brochures?' She drew herself up to her full height. 'Surely I deserve some sort of recompense for all those years of dedicated service.'

'Yes, yes, there's no need to get hysterical. It's not as if I'm refusing to pay you any alimony at all; I fully intend to make sure that you and Calum are well provided for. But I'm not giving the house to you on a plate. If you want it, you're going to have to fight me for it.'

'Then fight you I will,' Amber screeched. On her

shoulder, Couscous started whimpering. 'It's all right, Couscous; just ignore the nasty man.'

'Your relationship with that creature is nauseating,' Daniel spat. 'He's an animal, for Christ's sake. Why do you persist in treating him like a child?'

Amber threw up her hands. 'Surely you don't begrudge me a bit of companionship. Honestly, I hardly recognize you any more, Daniel. You used to be such a kind, thoughtful man, but ever since Nancy got her claws into you, you've turned into a monster. One day, you're going to come to your senses and realize she's nothing but a common little tart and then you're going to come crawling back to me with your tail between your legs.'

Daniel gave a bitter laugh. 'I don't think so. Meeting Nancy certainly hastened the demise of our relationship, but even if she and I hadn't got together we'd have ended up in the divorce courts eventually.'

Amber looked at him aghast. 'What are you talking about?'

'Oh, come on, you know as well as I do that our marriage had been falling apart for years.'

Amber frowned. 'I don't know any such thing. I thought we were perfectly happy together.'

'Happy? How could I be happy with a woman like you?'

'And what sort of woman is that, pray tell?'

'Take a long, hard look at yourself, Amber. You're a freak, a laughing stock. They call you Catwoman in the village – did you know that?'

Amber bit her bottom lip to stop it from trembling.

'No, I didn't think so. All those whippet-thin airheads

who pretend to be your friends . . . they're laughing at you behind your back.'

'Stop it, stop it!' Amber cried shrilly.

'No, I won't stop. You not only look inhuman, Amber – you *are* inhuman, and that Oscar-winning performance at the auction shows just how evil you truly are.'

Amber took a step closer to her husband and leaned over him, gripping the arms of his chair, while Couscous clung on to her neck for dear life. 'Oh, my love, that was nothing,' she hissed. 'Believe me, this is just the beginning.'

'I'm not scared of you,' Daniel said. 'I'm going to fight you every step of the fucking way and I don't intend to lose. From now on this is war – and you'd better not forget it.'

Eleven

A smug smile played about Keeley's lips as she stepped across the threshold of the church. She knew without looking that her fellow guests were staring – not just because she looked stunning in a Chloé mini-dress and Fendi peep-toe stilettos, but also because she had a Premiership footballer on her arm. As she proceeded towards the altar – slowly, so that everyone could get a good look at her – Keeley found herself hoping it wouldn't be too long before she was walking up the aisle at All Hallows again. For perhaps the first time in her twenty-eight years, she was *genuinely* in love. Even more thrilling, the object of her affection, Delchester United goalkeeper Ryan Stoker, was *genuinely* loaded. They'd been seeing each other for less than a year, but Keeley felt sure it was only a matter of time before Ryan popped the question. Today, however, the village church was playing host not to a wedding, but to Tiger Bentley's christening, and for the past fifteen minutes his squawks had been ricocheting unpleasantly around the vaulted nave.

In the front pew, Laura was fast reaching the end of her tether. She'd had a terrible night's sleep – not because of Tiger who, for the first time in his short life, had unselfishly slept right through till morning. Rather, she'd been fretting about the christening, wondering how on earth she was going to maintain a facade of maternal devotion in front of all her friends and family. To make her task even more difficult, Tiger had started snivelling as she forced his stiff limbs into the antique christening gown and matching lace-trimmed bonnet that had been handed down through three generations of Bentleys. He fell asleep in the car, but the minute they took their places in the church, he started up again, crying and dripping snot over Laura's freshly dry-cleaned trouser suit. She'd rocked him, rubbed his back, whispered soothing lullabies in his ear, but nothing would shut him up. She wished she could offload him on to Marta, who was sitting at the far end of the pew, but the au pair already had her hands full looking after Carnie and Birdie, both of whom were nursing summer colds. Finally, in desperation, Laura thrust Tiger into Sam's arms.

'Take him for a wander around the graveyard, will you?' she whispered. 'See if you can get him off to sleep.'

Sam scowled. 'Can't you take him?'

'I've had him all bloody morning; it's your turn.'

Sighing, Sam pulled a muslin square from the changing bag and draped it over his shoulder to protect his suit jacket. 'Come on then, Tiger,' he said, hoisting his son on to his chest. 'Let's go and look at the dead bodies.' He set off down the aisle, smiling at Keeley and Ryan as he passed them. 'Morning guys, I'm just taking this noisy fella for a breath of fresh air,' he told them. 'See you in a bit.'

Behind Sam's back, Ryan pulled a face. 'Rather him than me,' he muttered.

'I don't know, I think you'd be a brilliant dad,' said Keeley, staring up at him adoringly.

The footballer shrugged. 'Maybe, but that's a long, *long* way off.' He couldn't help noticing the look of disappointment that flitted across Keeley's pretty face. It made him feel panicky and slightly sick. First weddings, now babies . . . was there no end to his girlfriend's ambitions?

As soon as she spotted the final member of her triumvirate of godmothers, Laura jumped to her feet. 'You look gorgeous,' she said, kissing her friend on the cheek.

'So do you,' Keeley replied – though, truth be told, she didn't mean it, for Laura's taste in fashion fell far short of her own exacting standards. 'I've really been looking forward to today. Nobody's asked me to be a godmother before; it's such an honour.'

Laura sighed. 'Believe me, you wouldn't be quite so enthusiastic if you'd ever spent an evening in Tiger's company.'

'Don't be silly. Ryan and I are happy to babysit any time, aren't we, babe?'

The footballer tugged at his shirt collar. 'Mmmm.'

'Thanks, the next time I'm tearing my hair out, I might just take you up on that offer.' Laura pointed to the pew behind. 'Do you want to join Cindy and Kieran over there? Marianne's here too . . . somewhere.'

Keeley took a seat beside her fellow godmother. 'Hey, Cindy, how are you?'

'Good thanks.' The Californian nodded towards the lush arrangements of white roses that decorated the altar and font. 'Doesn't the church look pretty? Marianne and the other volunteers have done a fabulous job with the flowers.'

Keeley raised an eyebrow. 'Didn't you hear? Marianne's do-gooding days are over.'

'Oh? Why's that?'

'Well, let's face it, her sudden interest in floristry was only ever a way of getting into the vicar's knickers. She made that perfectly plain from the outset.'

Cindy blanched. She didn't like vulgar talk, especially in a place of worship. 'I thought she was joking.'

'Marianne never jokes about sex; you should know that by now.' Looking over her shoulder, Keeley scanned the pews of guests. 'Where is the old dear anyway?'

'She said she needed to use the bathroom, but that was ages ago. I can't think where she's gotten to.' Cindy frowned anxiously. 'Maybe I should go and look for her; the service will be starting soon.'

Keeley laid a hand on her friend's arm. 'I shouldn't bother. I've got a fair idea what she's doing.' She gave Cindy a wink. 'Put it this way, the service won't be starting until she's completely satisfied.'

In the vestry, the Reverend Simon Proctor was prostrated on the floor. 'This is so wrong,' he groaned as he thrashed his head from side to side.

'Then why does it feel so right?'

Simon stared up at the vision of loveliness that was straddling his torso, her pencil skirt bunched round her hips and her cream blouse unbuttoned to the navel. He had to admit she had a point. Gasping with pleasure, he gripped his lover's buttocks as she rode him like the accomplished horsewoman she was.

The vicar's affair with Marianne was less than a week

old, but already they'd had sex in every room of the vicarage, not to mention up against the rear wall of the church, while inside the weekly choir practice took place. Put simply, Simon couldn't get enough of the comely – and exceedingly uninhibited – widow, but even *he'd* been startled when she'd slipped into the vestry ten minutes earlier. Mindful that his congregation was sitting mere feet away, he tried to send her away. But Marianne was very persuasive, and in the end he'd been powerless to resist her many and varied charms.

Sensing that the vicar was close to climax, Marianne reached behind her to gently massage his balls. As her hand closed round his pendulous sac, there came a knock at the door.

'Reverend?'

Recognizing the voice of Paul, the head altar server, the vicar's eyes widened in alarm. Marianne, by contrast, barely broke rhythm.

The door handle began to turn. Thankfully, Marianne had taken the precaution of locking it. 'Reverend Proctor?' the voice came again. 'Are you in there?'

Simon put his hands on Marianne's hips, slowing her pace.

'Yes, Paul, I'm here.' The vicar was aware that he sounded breathless, but it couldn't be helped. 'Can you give me five minutes? I'm just rehearsing my sermon.'

'All right, Reverend. I'll go and light the candles, shall I?'

'Good idea, thank you, Paul.'

Simon waited until he could hear the teenager's footsteps receding on the flagstone floor before closing his eyes and surrendering to Marianne as she urged him towards the finishing post. And he wasn't the only one with carnal matters uppermost in his mind. Out in the graveyard, Sam's thoughts had turned to sex as he paced up and down between the well-maintained graves. He and Laura had not made love since before Tiger's birth and he was growing increasingly frustrated. There were plenty of golf groupies at St Benedict's – bunker babes, as they were known – who would happily spread their legs for a good-looking high-profile player like Sam. But that would be too easy. Sam liked women who were slightly out of his league, because of their age or their looks or because they were married. And in his opinion no one on his current radar presented more of a challenge than Taylor Spurr. After she'd sent her mother to meet him in the Chukka Bar, Sam had come to the conclusion that Taylor wasn't interested in him sexually – perhaps, even, that she was trying to throw him and Kristina together. But the previous day, one of the receptionists at the club had pushed an envelope across the desk as he signed in. 'For you, Mr Bentley,' she'd said, eyes lowered discreetly. 'One of our other members asked me to pass it along.' Inside the envelope was a note from Taylor. *Sorry about the other night*, she'd written in a neat cursive. *Can you meet me at the eighteenth hole on Monday at nine a.m.? I'll explain everything then.* She'd signed her name, and next to it there was a kiss. It seemed the hot Texan filly hadn't given up on him after all.

Back in the vestry, Simon and Marianne lay in a tangled heap, both panting heavily. 'Saints preserve us,' the vicar muttered as Marianne rolled off him. 'My legs have turned to jelly. How am I to conduct a christening ceremony after that?'

'I'm sure you'll manage, darling.' Marianne stood up and began adjusting her clothes, pulling her skirt down so it covered her knees, which bore the criss-cross marks of the vestry's herringbone floor. 'Are you going to come to the Bentleys' garden party afterwards?'

'I'm afraid not. I shall be taking communion to some housebound parishioners this afternoon.'

'That's a shame. I was rather hoping we could squeeze in a repeat performance.' She smiled saucily. 'Laura's got plenty of spare bedrooms.'

Simon reached for his cassock. 'We mustn't be too flagrant, Marianne. Goodness knows what the Bishop would say if he found out about us.'

'Why would he care? We're both free agents.'

'Yes, but sex outside marriage … it's not appropriate for a man of the cloth.'

Marianne arched an eyebrow. 'You're not complaining, are you?'

'Of course not; we just need to be careful, that's all.' Simon kissed the tip of Marianne's nose. 'And now, my sweet, you need to make yourself scarce.' He went to the door and unlocked it. 'I'll chcck to see if the coast's clear.' He stuck his head out and looked from left to right. 'Okay, off you go.'

Marianne slipped through the narrow aperture. 'I'll see you soon, darling.' She smiled. 'And don't forget to wash that lipstick off your face, or the Bishop will probably have you excommunicated.'

*

The christening ceremony went smoothly enough. Much to Laura's relief, Tiger was quiet for most of the service, erupting into anguished howls only when the vicar sprinkled cold water over his head. For one fleeting moment as she stood at the font, surrounded by her family and friends, Laura could almost have imagined she were a normal mother. But when the Reverend Proctor asked her if she repented of her sins and renounced evil, she felt a hot flush of embarrassment. Whatever would the vicar think if he knew how she'd stood on the edge of a cliff, cold-bloodedly contemplating the delicious prospect of a life *sans* Tiger?

Afterwards, the christening party descended on the Bentleys' elegant Georgian home, where a team of party planners had transformed the garden into a Moroccan hideaway, complete with olive trees, leather ottomans, gushing mosaic fountains and even a Berber tent, decorated with brass hookahs and sheepskin rugs. While waiting staff dressed as bedouins moved among the guests with trays of canapés and Pimms served in painted tea glasses, Laura did the rounds with Tiger. As her eager guests queued for cuddles and photographs with the tiny guest of honour, Laura wore her brightest smile and responded enthusiastically when asked about his bowel frequency and sleeping habits. But she was relieved when the meet and greet was over and she could foist Tiger on to Marta, with strict instructions to banish him to the nursery the instant his good mood evaporated.

As she helped herself to a well-earned glass of wine from a passing waiter, Laura felt a light touch on her arm. She turned to see Marianne.

'Lovely party, darling,' the older woman said.

Laura beamed. 'Thanks. Oh, and thank you for the christening gift too. A whole case of port ... that's very generous. It'll be aged to perfection by the time Tiger hits eighteen.' As she spoke the words, her smile faded. Eighteen years. It was a very long time. The thought was enough to make her shiver.

Marianne gave her a sharp look. 'What is it, Laura? You look as if somebody's just walked over your grave.'

'Nothing; I'm just a bit chilly.'

Marianne had known Laura long enough to know when she was lying. 'But, darling, it's eighty degrees in the shade.' She gave her friend a probing look. 'Are you still finding motherhood tough going?'

'It's not motherhood, *per se*,' Laura said wistfully. She gazed across the lawn to where Carnie and Birdie were galloping around with butterfly nets. 'Whenever I look at the girls, I experience this flood of emotion that's almost overwhelming. And if anyone ever harmed them, I'd be perfectly capable of murder; I know I would. But with Tiger ... well, it's just not the same.' She met her friend's gaze. 'I may as well be honest, Marianne; I know I can trust you to keep it to yourself. The truth is, I don't feel *anything* for him; not a single scrap of affection. I've been tying myself up in knots over it, but I can't go through my entire life feeling guilty. After all, there's no law saying that a mother *has* to love her child, is there?'

'No, you're absolutely right,' Marianne said carefully. 'But it *is* the normal course of events.'

Laura looked affronted. 'I'm not mad, if that's what you're saying.'

'Darling, of course you're not. But, all the same, it might be worth sharing your anxieties with someone.'

Laura sighed. 'I've tried talking to Sam, but he doesn't understand; he dotes on Tiger.'

'I meant a professional.'

'A psychiatrist?'

'I'd start off with your GP. He'll be able to refer you to someone else if needs be.'

Laura looked doubtful. 'I'll think about it,' she said. Keen to change the subject, she nodded at Marianne's empty tea glass. 'Let's get you another drink, shall we?'

Inside the house, Keeley had just finished freshening her make-up in one of the Bentleys' en suites. As she made her way back down the stairs, she noticed Harry Hunter emerging from the kitchen. The pair were friends, after a fashion, and the previous summer they'd had a brief sexual relationship. Harry had always hoped it would develop into something more and he was gutted when Keeley hooked up with Ryan and put an end to their weekly arrangement.

Seeing his former lover on the staircase, Harry stopped and smiled. 'So,' he said, resting an elbow on the banister. 'How does it feel to be a godmother?'

'Kinda cool, actually.' Keeley eyed the front of Harry's blue chambray shirt, which was soaking wet. 'Had a little accident, have we?'

'Yeah, I tripped over a tent peg and managed to pour a whole glass of Pimms over myself.'

'That'll teach you to look where you're going.'

Harry grinned sheepishly. 'Too right it will.' He looked

at Keeley and felt the same twinge of desire he always felt whenever he set eyes on her. 'I haven't seen you in the shop for a while.'

'No, I'm not going to the club as often as I used to. I spend most of my spare time at Ryan's.'

'I saw you two together in the church. That was a nice suit he was wearing.'

'It's Prada; I helped him choose it.'

Harry raised an eyebrow. 'It sounds as if it's going well with you two.'

'Couldn't be better; I reckon I've hit paydirt this time.' Keeley paused, suddenly aware that her comment could be misconstrued, especially given her previous form. 'Not that I'm with Ryan just because of his money.'

'Perish the thought,' said Harry in a teasing tone. He plucked at his wet shirt. 'I put some water on this, but I've only succeeded in making it worse.'

'I think I saw a hairdryer upstairs. You could use it to dry your shirt.'

'Hey, that's a good idea. Are you sure Laura won't mind?'

'Don't be silly.' Keeley grabbed Harry's hand. 'Come on, I'll show you.'

A few minutes later, Harry was standing topless in one of the guest bedrooms. 'I was surprised to see you in the church,' Keeley remarked as she spread his shirt on the bed and began blasting it with hot air from the hairdryer. 'I didn't think you knew Sam that well.'

'I don't,' Harry replied. 'I've come with my girlfriend.'

Keeley looked up. 'Girlfriend? I didn't know you had one.'

'Yeah, I'm seeing the Bentleys' au pair.'

'Marta? Well, well, well.'

'She's a nice girl.'

'I'm sure she is. I know Laura thinks very highly of her.' Keeley turned her attention back to the shirt. 'Look, this is nearly dry already.'

Harry smiled. 'Thanks for doing this for me, Keeley.'

'No problem.'

Keeley turned off the hairdryer and picked up the shirt. 'Here you are. There's only a faint stain; I shouldn't think anyone will notice.'

As she handed the shirt to Harry, she couldn't help noticing his toned physique. She'd always found Harry attractive, and he was certainly much better looking than Ryan. But, unlike Ryan, Harry was only a lowly shop assistant and therefore well below Keeley's minimum requirement. 'Have you been working out?' she said in a faintly amused tone.

Harry tightened his pectoral muscles. 'Yeah, one of the personal trainers in the club gym is a mate of mine. He's been giving me some free sessions.'

Keeley reached out and stroked her fingertips down Harry's sternum towards his impressive six-pack. 'Hmm ... well it's certainly paying off.'

Harry caught her hand. 'Don't be a tease.'

'I wasn't teasing.' Keeley pouted.

'Oh no?'

Through a crack in the door, Marta observed the couple's flirtatious exchange. She'd just settled her young charge down for his afternoon nap when she'd heard voices further down the landing. Thinking it was Laura, she'd gone to tell her that Tiger was sleeping soundly. She'd been surprised to see Keeley and Harry together. She didn't know they were friends – certainly Harry had never mentioned knowing Keeley – but, judging by what she'd just witnessed, the pair were intimately acquainted. As she shifted her weight, one of the floorboards beneath her foot emitted a loud creak. Keeley turned towards the door. 'Laura, is that you?'

'No.' Marta stepped into the room. 'It's me. I'm not disturbing anything, am I?'

'Don't be silly,' Harry said as he pushed his arms into the sleeves of the shirt. 'I spilled a drink over myself. Keeley was just helping me dry off.'

'I see.' Marta leaned against the door jamb and folded her arms across her chest. She looked at Keeley who, she had to admit, looked absolutely stunning in the sort of designer dress her au pair's wages would never stretch to. Although the former model was one of Laura's best friends, Marta had never warmed to her. She found Keeley vacuous and rather hard-faced. 'I didn't realize you two were so close,' she said pointedly.

Harry began buttoning up his shirt. 'We're not.'

'We're friends, that's all,' Keeley said as she unplugged the hairdryer and replaced it on the walnut dressing table. 'Nothing for you to worry about, Marta. I've got a boyfriend of my own, remember.'

Patronizing bitch, the Spanish girl thought to herself as she forced a smile.

As day turned to night, the Bentleys' guests drifted away one by one. By ten o'clock there were only a dozen or so people left and all of them, including Sam and Laura, were pretty drunk. The children were in bed, the waiting staff had been sent home and now the garden was illuminated by dozens of twinkling candles, housed in hanging lanterns. Ace and Astrid were among the stragglers. The shop manager was good friends with Sam and he kept the golfer well supplied with cocaine and the occasional tab of recreational Viagra. True to form, he hadn't come empty-handed, and when he judged that the mood was right he held up a clear plastic bag filled with grassy material. 'I'm going to the tent for a smoke,' he said casually. 'Would anyone care to join me?'

Astrid, who was sitting on one of the hand-woven kelims dotted about the lawn, raised a languid arm. 'I will,' she said. As she unfolded her long legs, Sam, who was sitting directly opposite her on a wrought-iron chair, realized she wasn't wearing any underwear. Immediately, he felt a stirring in his groin. He'd gone without sex for so long his cock was liable to respond to the slightest provocation. Astrid caught his eye and smiled. Sam smiled back. He wondered what Laura would think if she knew he occasionally took advantage of the masseuse's unique *tukta* therapy. Thankfully, he didn't have to worry about such an eventuality, for Astrid's discretion was beyond question.

Sam leaned forward in his chair, his gaze lingering on the stunning Swedish girl. 'I think I could be tempted.'

Laura, sitting opposite him, cleared her throat. Sam knew what that meant. His wife didn't approve of drug taking. She knew he sometimes indulged, but she would have been horrified to discover quite how often. 'On second thoughts, I think I'll give it a miss,' he said quickly.

On another kelim, Ryan sat with his arms wrapped round Keeley. 'Fancy it?' he murmured into her hair.

She nodded. 'Yeah, go on then.'

With no other takers, the foursome began making their way towards the Berber tent, which was pitched at the end of the garden and afforded a good degree of privacy. As soon as she stepped inside, Astrid kicked off her shoes and collapsed on to a leather ottoman. 'Isn't this gorgeous?' she said, reaching out to stroke one of the swathes of jewel-coloured fabric that lined the walls. 'The Bentleys must've spent a fortune on this party.'

'They're pretty flush at the moment,' Keeley said, sinking on to a sheepskin rug next to Astrid's ottoman. 'Sam's just signed a six-figure sponsorship deal with one of the big sportswear companies.'

Ace went to a mosaic table and immediately set about rolling a fat joint. 'It's all right for some, eh?'

'I'm sure you're not doing too badly yourself, mate,' said Ryan who, in common with a good proportion of the members of St Benedict's, made regular sorties to the club shop for drugs and knew that Ace must be raking it in.

Ace smiled. 'Yeah, business is pretty good. What about you? I heard on the radio that your agent's in talks with Delchester about a new two-year contract.'

'That's right,' said Ryan, taking a seat at the table next to Ace. 'Nothing's been signed yet. In fact, we've reached a bit of a stalemate; the money isn't right.'

'But you performed brilliantly last season. Surely it's just a matter of naming your price.'

'You would've thought so, but the new chairman's a tight bastard.'

At the mention of money, Keeley was suddenly alert. 'You didn't tell me you were renegotiating your contract,' she said lightly.

Ryan shrugged. 'That's because you think football's boring.'

'True,' Keeley conceded. 'But this is a really big deal, isn't it? You're happy at Delchester; you wouldn't want to leave, would you?'

'Mmmm ...' Ryan shifted in his seat, suddenly feeling uncomfortable. He was glad when Ace finished rolling the joint and held it up for inspection. Everyone eyed it hungrily, the subject of Ryan's new contract instantly forgotten.

As they passed the joint round, they talked of random things, as drunk and stoned people often do. After a little while, Astrid began giving Keeley a head massage. 'You have such beautiful hair,' she said, her fingertips gently kneading the other woman's scalp. 'It's so soft and silky.'

Keeley smiled and let her head loll back against the ottoman. 'Ahh ...' she sighed. 'That's lovely. It's making me feel all sleepy.'

Ace drew a mouthful of smoke deep into his lungs. 'Astrid's got the magic touch.'

'She certainly has,' Keeley agreed, closing her eyes. 'Astrid's massages are legendary.'

'It must be strange ... touching naked bodies all day long,' said Ryan, taking the joint from Ace.

Astrid's hands moved to Keeley's temples, where she began moving the pads of her fingers in a circular motion. 'It's quite fascinating, actually. There's such incredible variety in the human form.'

Ryan looked at Ace through heavy eyelids. 'Do you ever get jealous at the thought of Astrid running her hands over another bloke's glutes?'

'I used to, but not any more. It's just a job at the end of the day.'

Ryan passed the joint to Astrid. 'But you must be ... you know ... physically attracted to some of your clients. There are some very fit blokes at St Benedict's.'

'Of course,' Astrid replied. 'I'm only human.' She licked the Cupid's bow of her lips with the end of her tongue. 'There are some very fit women too. Keeley, for example, has a fantastic body.'

Keeley frowned. 'Oh, come on, mine's nothing special.'

'Oh, but it is,' Astrid murmured. She leaned down to Keeley on the floor and held the joint to the other girl's lips. It was an intimate and entirely unnecessary gesture that both men found curiously arousing.

Keeley inhaled deeply and tilted her head back so she was looking directly into Astrid's eyes. 'My body's not a patch on yours, though,' she said, holding the smoke in her lungs. 'Your legs are so long, and as for those boobs ...' She turned her head and exhaled. 'They're enough to make a girl turn lesbo.'

Astrid gave a throaty laugh. 'I can't think of a nicer compliment.' She moved her hand so it was resting on Keeley's collarbone. 'You know, smoking this stuff always makes me feel horny.'

Keeley giggled as she stubbed the joint out in an empty tea glass. 'Me too.'

'Well, don't let us stop you two ladies getting it on,' said Ace, throwing a sly sideways look at Ryan.

It was meant as a joke, but Astrid didn't need a second invitation. The next minute, she was beside Keeley on the sheepskin rug, squatting on her haunches like a cat about to pounce on a bird. For a brief moment, they stared into each other's eyes and then their lips locked together. Ryan and Ace watched in amazement as the two girls shared a lingering, open-mouthed kiss.

'Mmmm ... that was nice,' said Keeley when they finally drew apart. She looked across at the men, smiling when she saw their slack-jawed expressions. 'It certainly looks as if you two enjoyed it.'

'Yep,' said Ace, nodding towards the tent in his trousers. 'Any time you want to give us a repeat performance, feel free.'

Astrid flipped her long, blonde hair over her shoulders. 'You know, we should all go out as a foursome one evening.'

'I'd be up for that,' said Ryan, who knew nothing of Keeley's bisexual tendencies and still couldn't quite believe what he'd just witnessed. 'I can get us into the VIP room of pretty much any nightclub in Delchester.'

'Sounds great,' said Astrid. She frowned, as if she were thinking. 'Actually, Ace and I have been invited to a party on Friday. It's going to be lots of fun. Why don't you join us?'

Ace looked at his girlfriend in surprise. 'Er, I'm not sure it's going to be their cup of tea, babe.'

'Nonsense,' said Astrid. 'Keeley's very broad-minded and I have a feeling Ryan is too.'

'Where is this party?' Keeley asked.

'In the village; do you know that fabulous art deco place backing on to the park?'

Keeley gasped. 'I love that house; I've always wanted to see inside.'

'So you'll come then?'

Keeley looked at Ryan. 'We're not doing anything on Friday night, are we?'

'No, I don't think –'

'Hang on a minute,' said Ace, cutting across the footballer. He gave Astrid a loaded look. 'Don't you think we should tell them what *sort* of party it is? After all, it's only fair they know what they're letting themselves in for.'

Astrid sighed, as if Ace were over-reacting. 'Trust me, guys – you'll have a brilliant time.'

Keeley looked from one to the other, confused. 'Does one of you want to tell me what's going on?'

There was a long silence, and then Ace spoke. 'It's a swinging party.'

Ryan coughed. 'A what?'

'A swinging party,' Astrid repeated.

Keeley looked shocked. 'I didn't know you two were into all that stuff.'

'We're novices really,' said Ace quickly. 'We've only done it a couple of times.'

'But we really enjoyed ourselves, didn't we?'

Ace nodded. 'Yeah, it was a laugh.'

'You wouldn't believe how many people around here do it,' Astrid went on. 'Some of Kirkhulme's biggest movers and shakers are involved in the scene. And it's not at all seedy; we're talking million-pound-plus houses, champagne and canapés, attractive and articulate people. It's just like a regular party, except —'

'You all shag each other,' said Ryan, smirking like a schoolboy.

Astrid smiled patiently. 'Not quite. It's completely up to the individual what he or she does, and with whom. Forget all this throwing your car keys into a fruit bowl malarkey. Swinging's evolved; it's all about freedom of choice now.'

'Hmmm . . .' said Keeley, not convinced.

'Look, guys, if you don't want to come, it's no problem,' said Ace, who had begun rolling another joint.

'I think it sounds great,' said Ryan.

Keeley glared at him. 'But what if someone recognizes you and goes to the papers?'

'Believe me, that wouldn't happen,' Astrid interjected. 'There's a strict code of conduct. These parties are full of rich and influential people — headmasters, barristers, civil servants. No one's going to blab. They've all got too much to lose themselves. And it's not as if people can come in off the street; it's strictly invitation-only.' She looked at her friends hopefully. 'So, are you up for it?'

'I'm really not sure,' Keeley began.

'Oh, go on,' said Ryan. 'Let's live dangerously. We've got nothing to lose — and if we get there and decide we don't fancy it, we can always make our excuses and leave, right, Astrid?'

'Right,' Astrid said firmly.

Keeley looked at Ryan. He was smiling at her, willing her to agree. She didn't know why she felt so reluctant; she'd always regarded herself as quite adventurous, sexually speaking. But she wasn't sure she wanted to share Ryan with anyone else. 'Okay,' she said. 'I'll give it a go.'

'Brilliant,' Astrid said. She placed a hand on Keeley's knee. 'And don't worry, Kee, Ace and I will take good care of you.'

Suddenly, there was a rattling noise as a hand swept aside the beaded curtain that hung at the entrance to the tent. It was Sam. He caught a heady whiff of marijuana and smiled.

'What's been going on in here then?' he demanded. 'Have I missed out on all the fun?'

Ace stared at him, glassy-eyed. 'No, mate, you've arrived just in time.' He held up the joint he'd just rolled. 'Why don't you make yourself comfy?'

Sam turned to stare back out into the garden. Laura had gone into the house to check on the kids. He let the beaded curtain fall behind him. 'Don't mind if I do ... while the cat's away, eh?'

Twelve

A shrill ringing exploded in Calum's head. Badly hung-
over after a heavy session with his bandmates the night
before, it took him a few seconds to realize what the
sound was. Groaning loudly, he reached out an arm and
groped on the bedside table until his fingers made contact
with the alarm clock. It was seven forty-five and, to
Calum's mind, unfeasibly early to be awake. Usually, he
didn't emerge from his bedroom until at least noon on a
weekend – but today was different; today, he had plans.
Shucking back the duvet, he hauled his leaden limbs out
of bed, gripping the back of a chair for support as the
room swam in front of his eyes. He staggered to the en
suite and opened the bathroom cabinet, hunting for
painkillers. Locating a half-empty blister pack, he popped
a couple of tablets into his mouth, washing them down
with a handful of water from the tap. If he were going to
fully enjoy the treat that lay in store, he would need a clear
head. He'd laid the groundwork the day before, filching an
electric drill from his father's toolkit and sneaking out into
the garden unobserved. Most of what Calum did these
days was unobserved. His parents were far too busy with
their own complicated lives to pay much attention to him.
Sometimes – quite often, in fact – he used this state of
affairs to his advantage, but that wasn't to say he didn't
feel horribly neglected. After blasting a jet of deodorant

into each armpit, he went back into his bedroom and pulled on last night's beer-stained jeans and a hoodie, then picked up his trainers and made his way downstairs.

Outside, the sun was shining weakly through the clouds. Calum shaded his eyes with a hand as he squinted up at his father's bedroom window on the second floor. Noting that the curtains were still drawn, he shoved his hands deep into his pockets and set off across the manicured lawn.

At the bottom of the garden, partially concealed behind a screen of copper beeches, lay the swimming pool. Housed in a converted hay barn, it had been installed twelve years earlier, using money Calum's father had inherited from a distant cousin. Daniel Solomon was a man with high-end tastes, and no expense had been spared in the pool's construction. Forty feet long, it boasted underwater halogen lighting, a surround of Bavarian fossil stone – and, on the bottom, a mosaic design that incorporated Daniel and Amber's intertwined initials. Beside the barn was a rustic, red cedar cabana with luxurious his-and-hers changing facilities, designed and accessorized by Amber herself. A keen swimmer, she normally used the pool every day during the summer, but recently her activities had been curtailed. Following his wife's unexpected appearance at the auction, Daniel had changed the lock on the barn door, arguing that, since the pool had been bought with his inheritance, he had every right to decide who could – and, more importantly, who *couldn't* – enjoy it.

Amber had gone ballistic when she'd discovered what he'd done. Calum had watched from the kitchen window

as she ran around the garden in her Chanel bikini, screaming like a banshee, until Daniel – rather insensitively, in
his son's opinion – threatened to have her sectioned. So
now, much to Amber's chagrin, Nancy had exclusive
rights over the swimming pool. Although she owned an
ex-council flat in a nearby village, the former housekeeper
stayed over at the Old Manor a couple of nights a week –
and, as Calum's discreet surveillance had revealed, there
was nothing she liked better than an early morning dip.

When he reached the row of copper beeches, Calum
made straight for the cabana, which was set directly behind the pool house. He walked round to the rear of the
single-storey structure where, the previous day, he had
drilled three small holes in the soft wood at approximately
chest height. After removing the cork plugs he'd
fashioned to fill the holes, he retraced his steps across the
lawn, stopping when he reached an ancient willow, in the
leafy canopy of which was a tree house. A gift for his tenth
birthday, the elaborate hideaway, fashioned to look like a
pirate ship, had provided endless hours of enjoyment for
Calum and his friends. He still went there occasionally
when he wanted to be alone, away from his bickering
parents and the increasingly tense atmosphere in the Old
Manor.

After climbing the wooden ladder, Calum took up
position in the tree house's highest point – the crow's
nest – which offered sweeping views across the entire
garden. Kneeling down on a beanbag, he trained his gaze
on the house, waiting for his prey to break cover. He
didn't have long to wait. Just after eight thirty, he spotted
Nancy walking across the lawn in a pair of flip-flops and a

tight purple tracksuit that showed off every bulge of her ample figure. Hanging from one shoulder was a small rucksack, which doubtless contained her swimming costume and goggles. She was whistling while she walked, as she often did around the house. That was one of the things Calum liked about Nancy. She was always in a good mood, unlike Amber, who seemed genetically predisposed to irritability. Of course, his mother would've said that Nancy's high spirits resulted from the fact she'd bagged a multi-millionaire, but Calum preferred to give her the benefit of the doubt. The funny thing was he'd never really noticed Nancy when she worked as their housekeeper. For almost three years, she had moved silently around the house in her blue-and-white checked overall, keeping the Old Manor spick and span with the minimum of fuss. That was the way his mother liked her staff to be: seen and not heard.

Calum had been shocked when he'd discovered that his father was sleeping with Nancy – but, when he thought about it, it made perfect sense. It had been obvious to him for ages that his parents had grown apart. They were always sniping at one another, and more than once he'd caught his father rolling his eyes behind his mother's back. Daniel's working life was very stressful and, in Calum's opinion, Nancy was exactly the sort of easy-going, low-maintenance woman he should have married in the first place. Instead of hating his father for breaking up the family, he was glad that at least one of his parents had found happiness. If only his mother would too, and then all this stupid warring over the house could come to an end. Calum didn't see what all the fuss was about. The

Old Manor was, after all, only a pile of bricks and wattle-and-daub. If his parents agreed to sell it and split the proceeds, they could both make a fresh start. Surely that would be the best thing for all concerned.

With a growing sense of excitement, Calum watched as Nancy strode athletically towards the cabana and pulled open the door. The minute she was safely inside, he leapt from the tree house and crept across the grass, crouching down low, so Nancy wouldn't spot him through the small front windows. His heart was racing as he put his eye to one of the newly drilled holes. Through it, he had a clear view of the two shower cubicles and a shelf piled high with fluffy white towels. There was no sign of Nancy, but he could hear her moving about. He went to the second hole, and instantly his pulse rate quickened. His mother's nemesis was standing beside the steel changing bench with her back to him. She'd already removed her tracksuit top and now she was reaching behind to unclip the sturdy white bra that, by some miraculous feat of engineering, supported her giant bosom.

Calum watched in awe as the bra fell away to reveal one of Nancy's low-slung breasts in profile. On her back, he could see the red marks left by her bra straps and a large raised mole, from which a single dark hair sprouted. He licked his dry lips, willing her to turn round. Ignoring his silent plea, Nancy kicked off her flip-flops and hooked her thumbs round her elasticated waistband. A moment later, the tracksuit bottoms were off, and she was naked except for a pair of knickers. They were large and cottony, the sort of thing a middle-aged woman *should* wear – quite unlike the impractical scraps of gauze Calum had seen in his mother's underwear drawer. After another surprisingly elegant shimmy, the pants were off and Calum found himself ogling a generous pair of arse cheeks, richly dimpled with cellulite.

As Nancy bent down to rummage in her rucksack, he caught sight of the silken cleft between her legs. It was, in all his seventeen years, quite the most thrilling sight he'd ever seen. Calum, who was still a virgin (though not for want of trying), had never seen a woman stark naked, except in the pages of the magazines his father kept in the bottom drawer of his desk. He hadn't found his father's taste in pornography especially arousing. The girls in the pictures were too perfect, with their fake tits and shiny hair. Calum much preferred Nancy's Rubenesque figure with its fleshy hips and well-developed thigh muscles. She was a *real* woman, the sort who could keep a man in check.

All too quickly, Nancy was stepping into the leg holes of her swimming costume – a jolly, jungle-print affair – hauling it up over her slack stomach and using her hands to shoehorn her breasts into the reinforced cups. Once dressed, she pulled her goggles over her head, pushed her feet into her flip-flops and moved out of sight. A moment later, Calum heard the cabana door creak open. Sweating like a fugitive, he flattened himself against the rear of the building, not that there was any real danger of him being seen. He waited a few minutes, then tentatively stuck his head round the corner of the cabana. The pool house lights were on, indicating that Nancy was safely inside. With a satisfied smile, Calum scuttled back to the tree house, where he intended to sit out the next half hour or so, until Nancy came back to take a shower. Flushed with success, he strutted around his eyrie, his head filled with lustful thoughts. From the rear verandah, he could see over the garden wall and out across the stunningly well-maintained golf course at St Benedict's. If he'd looked carefully enough, he would have been able to make out Sam Bentley, striding impatiently up and down the eighteenth green.

Taylor was ten minutes late and Sam had all but convinced himself she wasn't going to show. Realizing he was starting to draw attention to himself with his incessant pacing, he pulled a mallet-shaped putter out of his carry bag and pretended to be practising. He'd just holed an easy five-foot shot and was bending down to retrieve his ball when he spotted Taylor emerging from the clubhouse. Grinning, he rested his hands on his putter as he tracked her bouncy progress across the green. She looked stunning as usual in baby-pink capri pants and a tight white singlet, her eyes shaded by huge, white-framed sunglasses. He noticed that she wasn't carrying any clubs, which suggested she'd come on the course simply to see him. For an unashamed egotist like Sam, it was a deeply pleasing thought.

'Hey,' said Taylor when she arrived at the hole. 'I'm glad you're here. I wasn't sure whether or not you'd gotten my message.'

'It's nice to see you too,' Sam replied. 'I thought for one horrible moment you were going to stand me up again.'

Taylor removed her sunglasses and pushed them up

into her hair. 'I didn't stand you up last time,' she said. 'My mom locked me in my bedroom.'

Sam frowned. 'She did *what*?'

'You heard,' said Taylor with a wry half-smile.

Sam glanced around. He and Taylor were well-known figures at St Benedict's and several of their fellow golfers were already casting interested looks in their direction. 'Let's go somewhere more private, shall we?' he said. Picking up his carry bag, he took Taylor's elbow and led her to the dense row of conifers that guarded the entrance to the green. Satisfied that no one could see them, he rested his carry bag against a tree. 'Okay, now tell me exactly what happened.'

Taylor cleared her throat prettily. 'I was really looking forward to seeing you. There I was, in my room, putting on my make-up, when my mom came in and asked me where I was going. I told her the truth – that I was meeting you for a drink – but if I'd known how she was going to react, I'd have kept my mouth shut.'

'She wasn't happy about it then?'

Taylor sighed. 'She went apeshit. She said you were a distraction I couldn't afford, that I'd come to England to improve my game, not hook up with the local Romeos.'

Sam curled his lip. 'She said that?'

'Yep.' Taylor dropped her chin and regarded him from under her eyelashes coquettishly. 'She also said you were too old for me.'

'Did she now?' said Sam, remembering that night in the Chukka Bar. So he was too old for Taylor – but not, apparently, too *young* for Kris.

'*I* don't think you're too old,' Taylor said, pushing out her small breasts provocatively. 'I like older guys. They have more *experience*.' She placed extra emphasis on the final word, leaving Sam in no doubt as to the kind of experience she was referring to. 'Anyhow, when she told me I couldn't go out with you, I laughed, thinking it was a joke, and carried on fixing my make-up. That was when she walked out of the room, slammed the door and turned the key in the lock.' Taylor scowled. 'Up until that point, I hadn't even noticed the dumb door *had* a lock.'

'I'm shocked,' said Sam, shaking his head disbelievingly. 'Kristina doesn't seem the type.'

'You don't know my mom. Trust me, she can be a real bitch when she puts her mind to it.'

'So what happened then?'

'I was pretty mad, as you can imagine, so I started kicking the door and screaming at her to unlock the door, but she wouldn't listen. All I could do was sit tight until she came to let me out – three hours later.'

'You *do* know she came to the club in your place, don't you?' Sam said.

'Uh-huh. She told me she'd head down there and tell you I wasn't coming.' Taylor cut her eyes to the side. 'Which I thought was real big of her. *Not*.'

'She said you were having dinner at your coach's house.'

'That was *her* idea. I wanted her to tell you the truth, but I guess she didn't want to make herself look like a total control freak.'

Sam frowned. 'Why do you let her treat you that way?'

he said. 'You seem like the sort of girl who can stand up for herself.'

'I can with most people. But my mom and I . . .' Taylor shrugged. 'We have a weird relationship. It's what you might call love-hate.'

'But locking you in your room . . . that's pretty heavy. You're a grown woman; surely you have the right to pick and choose who you want to see.'

Taylor scuffed her foot in the loose earth. 'It's awkward, what with her being my caddie an' all. She's good at her job; she's kinda like my lucky charm out there on the golf course. I don't want her to quit, which is why every so often I have to let her get her own way, just to fool her into thinking she's the boss. That's why I promised her I wouldn't see you again.'

Sam's face fell. 'Is that why you've come here today – to tell me you can't see me?'

'Jeez no,' said Taylor breaking, into a creamy smile. 'All Mom's succeeded in doing is making me even more determined to get my own way. We'll just have to be careful, that's all.' She began strumming her collarbone with her fingertips. 'Do you know how long it is since I got laid?'

Sam shook his head, pleased at the direction this conversation was taking.

'Two whole months.' She gave a little sigh. 'I sure could use a long, hard fuck.'

Sam grinned. 'I think that can be arranged.' He was mentally peeling off the Texan girl's underwear with his teeth when a sudden thought struck him. 'Er, did Kris tell you what happened when she met me that evening?'

'She said you bought her a couple of drinks and then called a cab to take her home. Why – was there something else?'

'No, not really,' Sam said vaguely, not wanting to reveal anything that might put Taylor off.

The Texan girl fixed him with her large grey eyes. 'Mom made a move on you, didn't she?'

Sam gave a small nod. 'Yeah. How did you know?'

'I didn't. It was just a hunch.'

'Nothing happened between us, I swear.'

'I know,' said Taylor, who seemed amused rather than angry. 'She's not your type.'

'And what would you know about my type, young lady?'

'I know more about you than you think.' Taylor raised a questioning eyebrow. 'Good christening yesterday, was it?'

Sam looked at her in surprise. 'How did you find out about that?'

'Kirkhulme's a small place. Word gets around.' Taylor paused, before adding: 'And from what I hear you're quite the doting father.'

'I know how it looks – but my wife and I . . .' Sam took a deep breath as he prepared to deliver the lie. 'We really are just ships that pass in the night.'

'To be honest, I don't really care. I like you; you like me.' Taylor gave a half-shrug. 'I'm only here for the summer. I just want to have some fun. So all I need to know is: are you up for it?'

Sam broke into a grin. This girl really was something else. 'You bet I am,' he said, knowing that, for two pins, he could have taken her right there and then, up against the trunk of a Norway spruce. 'So when can we get together?'

'How about tomorrow evening?'

Sam hesitated. He and Laura had tickets for a jazz gig in town. 'Great. I did have some vague plans, but I can easily cancel them.'

'Are you sure?'

'Absolutely. What do you fancy doing?'

Taylor's eyes lit up. 'I want to party. Let's go into Delchester and hit a few nightclubs.'

Sam looked doubtful, knowing he couldn't risk word of his night out getting back to Laura. 'I don't know if that's such a good idea. We're bound to get recognized and then the local gossips will have a field day.'

'Oh shit, yeah. I wasn't thinking.'

'We could always have a little party of our own, here at St Benedict's. I've got a lot of friends here ... very discreet friends. I could arrange for us to have dinner in one of the private rooms.'

'Sounds great,' said Taylor. 'I don't suppose ...' She looked around anxiously, although the nearest golfer was more than thirty feet away. 'I don't suppose you know where a girl can get some candy cane around here, do you?'

Sam frowned. 'Candy cane?'

'You know ... cocaine,' Taylor said in a low voice.

'Oh right. Yeah, sure.' Sam smiled inwardly; this girl was full of surprises. He glanced at his watch. 'I can sort you out now, if you like, but we'll have to be quick. I'm teaching a master class in fifteen minutes.'

Taylor linked her arm through his. 'In that case, lead the way.'

In the club shop, Ace was busy with a customer who'd come to check out the new range of canine clothing. An uppercrust Miss Marple lookalike in a tweed skirt and brogues, the woman had insisted on bringing her border terrier into the shop. Strictly speaking, animals weren't permitted anywhere on club premises, but because the shop was quiet Ace had relented.

'I'm afraid the dog won't be able to try anything on,' he said as he escorted them to a rail of miniature outfits.

Miss Marple tutted irritably. 'Whyever not?'

'Health and safety.'

'But Douglas is scrupulous about his personal hygiene,' the woman said indignantly.

'I'm sure he is, but I've already bent the rules by letting him in the shop.' Keen to keep the woman in a high-spending frame of mind, Ace squatted down to stroke her pet's otter-like head. 'Douglas is an unusual name for a dog,' he remarked.

The woman smiled. Her false teeth were small and perfectly white, the sort you might find on the necklace of a cannibal chieftain. 'I named him after my late husband,' she said. 'They have identical temperaments.'

'Really,' said Ace, standing up quickly as a foul retort issued from the beast's nether sphincter. He gestured to the rail of dog wear. 'Were you after anything in particular?

'A coat,' she said. 'Something lightweight and shower-proof.'

Ace snapped his fingers. 'I've got just the thing.' He began thumbing through the rail of tiny coat hangers until he arrived at a navy parka. 'These are gorgeous – and hot off the catwalk.' He put his index finger to his chin. 'Or should that be *dog*walk?'

The woman wasn't amused. 'It's not terribly dignified, is it?' she said, tweaking the jacket's fur-trimmed hood. 'I had something more classic in mind.'

'Righty-ho,' said Ace patiently. He returned the parka to the rail and selected a sober waxed jacket. 'This is practical *and* stylish.' Bending down, he held it up against the bored-looking terrier to check the size. 'Look at this, boy. You'll be the classiest mutt in town in this little number.'

'*Mutt?*' the woman exclaimed in horror. 'I'll have you know that Douglas is a pedigree. He won Best of Breed two years running at the Kirkhulme Dog Show.'

'My humble apologies,' said Ace, tugging his forelock. 'I didn't realize I was in the presence of a champion.'

The woman gave him a sharp look. 'Don't get clever with me, young man, or I'll have you up before the manager.'

'It was a joke,' said Ace wearily. 'In any case, I *am* the manager.'

The woman didn't even have the good grace to look embarrassed. 'Well, in that case, you ought to know better,' she snapped.

Ace counted silently to five. 'So,' he said with a fake smile. 'What do you think of the jacket?'

The woman reached out and rubbed the fabric between forefinger and thumb. 'It feels cheap.'

'But this is a top-notch designer brand. I can assure you that only the highest-quality materials were used in its manufacture.' Ace unfastened the jacket, exposing the tartan lining. 'See this? This was made using wool from a special breed of angora goats found only in the foothills of Patagonia,' he ad-libbed. 'Feel how soft it is.'

Pursing her lips, the woman did as she was told. 'Yes, you're right; it *is* soft,' she conceded. 'Douglas will like that.' She lowered her voice, as if worried the dog would overhear. 'He's dreadfully fussy about what he wears next to his skin.'

Scenting a sale, Ace went in for the kill. 'This is actually the very last one in this range,' he said. 'I only put them out at the weekend, but they've been flying off the shelves.' He smiled encouragingly at the woman, expecting her to be impressed – but her face told a different story.

'Douglas is a fashion leader, not a follower,' she said spikily. 'He'd die a thousand deaths if he bumped into another dog in the village wearing the same coat.'

'Sensitive soul, isn't he?' said Ace through gritted teeth.

The woman nodded emphatically. 'He certainly is; just like his namesake.' She gave a loud sniff. 'It was the fifth anniversary of my husband's death yesterday. I still miss him terribly.'

Ace who, up to now, had thought the woman rude and condescending, felt a sudden pang of sympathy for her. In any case, he couldn't possibly let her leave without making a purchase. Not that Ace ever had any problem meeting his sales targets; it was simply a matter of pride.

'I've just had a thought,' he said. 'Some new stock came in this morning that I haven't even had a chance to unpack. I've a feeling I can find something that might just meet young Douglas's exacting requirements.' He gestured to the leather armchair outside the changing cubicles. 'If you'd like to take the weight off your feet, madam, I'll see what I can do.'

'Very well,' the woman said. 'But don't be long. Douglas is terribly impatient.'

The terrier gave a little shake of his head, as if to say, *just ignore her.*

As Ace made his way to the stockroom, he noticed Dylan, who was on his fifth tea break of the day, sitting in the staff kitchen with his head in his hands. 'Keep an eye on the shop, will you?' he called out to his colleague. 'I've got to nip to the stockroom.'

'Will do,' came the muffled response.

Frowning, Ace went over to him. 'What's up, Dyl? You've been moping around all morning.'

Dylan lifted his head. His eyes were shining with tears and there was a greenish gobbet of snot congealing on the tip of his nose. 'I've split up with Sorrel.'

'Ah, *maaate,*' Ace said, squeezing his friend's shoulder. 'I'm sorry; you should've said something sooner.'

Dylan shrugged. 'It's too painful.'

Ace nodded sympathetically. 'Of course – I understand.'

Dylan let out a long sigh. 'I caught her in bed with one of the tennis coaches. You know, Guillaume – that flash French bastard with the Patek Philippe and the tight shorts.'

'Puh,' Ace said disgustedly. 'No wonder you dumped her.'

'I didn't.' Dylan's voice sounded wobbly. 'Even after what Sorrel's done, I'd still crawl through shit for her.'

Ace shook his head despairingly. Dylan was barely into his twenties, and still had a lot to learn about the ancient art of treating 'em mean to keep 'em keen. 'So what happened?'

'*She* dumped *me*. She said I was too immature and that, in any case, Guillaume had promised to take her for a long weekend at his parents' villa in St Tropez.'

'Shallow little slut,' Ace muttered. 'Honestly mate, you're better off without her.'

'Am I?' said Dylan disconsolately. 'I'm really going to miss her blow jobs; she has this special trick, you see.'

'Oh yeah?' said Ace, a lascivious grin spreading across his face. 'What's that then?'

'She lets a couple of Alka Seltzers dissolve in a glass of water, takes a sip, holds it in her mouth, and then starts doing the business.' Dylan stared wistfully into the middle distance. 'I tell you what, Ace, I don't know if you've ever had dozens of tiny bubbles bursting all over your cock, but it feels fucking amazing.'

'I'll take your word for it,' said Ace, making a mental note to stop off at the pharmacy in the high street on his way home. 'Anyway, look, Dyl, I don't want to be an insensitive git, but can you get your arse on the shop floor? There's a batty old dear out there who could be busy filling her pockets with golf balls for all I know.'

When Ace returned to the shop a few minutes later, he was clutching a canary yellow rain slicker and matching sou'wester in a dog-size medium. His customer was sitting in the leather armchair, her chin nodding on her chest.

'Madam?' said Ace in a loud voice. The woman didn't respond. He touched her forearm gently. 'Madam?'

The woman's head jerked back. 'Unhand me, you filthy –' She made eye contact with Ace. A look of confusion crept across her face. 'Oh. It's you. I'm sorry – I must've dozed off. I forgot where I was for a minute.'

'That's okay,' said Ace. He pretended to be plucking a loose thread from his vintage Farah polo shirt in order to give the woman a few minutes to collect herself.

The woman patted her silver bouffant self-consciously. 'Did you find what you were looking for?'

'I certainly did.' Ace unfurled the rain slicker and spread it across her lap with a theatrical flourish. '*Voila!*'

'Ooh,' the woman cooed. 'Now that *is* nice. I love the colour.' She pulled apart the Velcro fastenings. 'This'll keep Douglas nice and dry. He does so hate the rain.'

'And that's not all.' Ace produced the sou'wester from behind his back, placing it jauntily on his own head.

The woman clapped her hands together. 'Ah, how perfectly adorable.' She reached down to stroke the terrier, who was lying at her feet with his head resting on his front paws. 'What do *you* think, Douglas?'

The dog lifted his head and yawned fulsomely. His owner beamed. 'I think he likes it.'

'And you can rest assured that no other pooch in Kirkhulme will have one of these,' said Ace. 'Not yet, anyway.'

The woman rose to her feet. 'I'll take it, and thank you for your help; it's much appreciated.'

'It's been a joy and a privilege,' Ace chirruped. He glanced towards the door. Sam Bentley had just come in. 'Hi, Sam,' he called out to the golfer. 'I'll be right with you.' He turned to his younger colleague, who was standing beside one of the mirrors, holding up a Fairway & Green diamond-print sweater to his chest. 'Dylan, can you escort this lady to the till, please?'

Ace walked over to the golf section where Sam was standing with a leggy blonde girl. Her face was turned away as she examined a range of novelty headcovers.

'Nice to see you, mate,' Ace said as he shook hands with Sam. 'That was a lovely party yesterday. Astrid and I really enjoyed ourselves.'

'Yeah, it was fun, wasn't it?'

At that moment, Sam's female companion lifted her head. 'Do you do this in pink?' she said, holding up a furry headcover in the shape of a bulldog.

Ace broke into a smile a mile wide. 'Taylor Spurr! This *is* an honour.' He gave a sweeping bow. 'Welcome to our humble emporium. Ace Murphy, shop manager *extraordinaire*, at your service.'

Taylor giggled. 'You English guys are so funny.'

'We aim to please.'

'You'll have to watch yourself with Ace,' Sam told Taylor. 'This geezer could sell ice cubes to the Eskimos. Don't get out your credit card, or he'll have flogged half the shop to you quicker than you can say, "But I only came in to shelter from the rain."'

'Ooh, Sam, lovie, you certainly know how to make a

boy blush,' Ace said camply. 'So what can I do for you lovely folk today?'

'Taylor would like to make a little purchase,' said Sam.

'But, of course, what was it you were after? Shiny new nine iron? A calfskin ladies' golf glove? A sexy little baseball cap in your trademark powder pink?'

Sam nudged the American girl. 'See what I mean?' He gave Ace a meaningful look. 'Taylor's keen to avail herself of your *special* service. I offered to make the introductions.'

'Ah,' said Ace. 'Right you are.' He glanced over his shoulder and saw that the elderly woman and her dog were preparing to leave. 'Give me a sec, guys,' he said to the golf pros. He sprang to the door and held it open. 'Pop back soon,' he sang to his departing customer. 'We're getting new stock every day.'

'We will,' said the woman. She bent down and stroked the terrier's head. 'Come on, Douglas. The sooner we get home, the sooner you can try on your lovely new raincoat.'

Now that the shop was empty, Ace could get down to the business in hand. 'Right then,' he said, rubbing his hands together. 'What would you like, Miss Spurr? I'd like to assure you that we offer a discreet, reliable service. I can get pretty much anything you care to mention – and, if it's not already in stock, I'll have it for you within twenty-four hours.'

'I want some coke,' said Taylor. 'Maybe, two ... no, uh, better make that three grams.'

'Coming right up.' As he turned to go, Ace noticed

Dylan skulking behind a display of gold-plated golf tees they'd been struggling to shift for months. 'Let me introduce you to my associate.' He beckoned Dylan over. 'Come on, Dyl, don't be shy.' Dylan shuffled over, eyes downcast 'I'm afraid my friend here's just had a bit of bad news, so he's not his usual perky self,' Ace explained.

Taylor mustered a sympathetic look. 'Gee, I'm sorry to hear that.'

'I'm fine, really,' Dylan said, his heart thudding in his chest as he made eye contact with her. 'Just a bit of woman trouble, nothing I can't handle.'

'Dylan, I'm sure I don't need to tell you that this is Taylor Spurr,' Ace said. 'One of the hottest lady golfers on the PGA tour.' He winked at her flirtatiously. 'And I do mean *hot* in every sense of the word. Taylor, this is Dylan. If ever I'm not here, he'll be able to help you. We have another sales assistant too – Harry – but it's his day off.'

'Hi, Taylor,' said Dylan shyly, extending a sweaty palm.

The American girl produced a dazzling smile. 'Pleased to meet y'all.'

'I'm a huge fan of yours,' Dylan said, unable to take his eyes off her. 'And can I just say you're even more beautiful in real life.' His gaze wandered down to the tanned expanse of smooth stomach visible beneath her cropped singlet.

'Put your tongue back in your mouth, Dylan,' Sam snapped. 'You look like a cretin.'

Sensing the golfer's irritation, Ace tapped Dylan on the arm. 'Come on, mate, better get back to work. The Astroturf in that window display could do with a vacuum.'

He began backing away from Taylor, as if he were in the presence of royalty. 'This humble serf shall fetch your merchandise, Your Highness,' he said, bowing deeply. 'He won't be two ticks.'

Taylor laughed. 'He's cute,' she told Sam as Ace disappeared through a door at the back of the shop.

Sam felt a hot surge of jealousy. 'He's a drug dealer,' he said in a low voice. 'Not the sort of man a girl like you should get too close to.'

'Oh no?' said Taylor, taking a step towards Sam and tilting her face upwards so she was looking him right in the eyes. 'And what sort of a man would you recommend for a girl like me?' She leaned forward, so that her lips were almost touching his.

Sam closed his eyes and inhaled deeply, picking out the different components of Taylor's scent ... shampoo, chewing gum, a light perfume with lemony overtones. When he opened his eyes, a teasing smile was playing about her lips. 'Just you wait till I get you alone,' he murmured. 'It's going to be a night both of us will remember for a very long time.'

All of a sudden the shop door flew open. Instantly, Sam stepped away from Taylor and pretended to be engrossed in a carousel of designer sunglasses. St Benedict's was a seething hotbed of gossip and it wouldn't do for him to be caught in a compromising position with a woman other than his wife. Taylor, meanwhile, stared unashamedly as the newcomer made her way towards the sports bras.

'Who's *that*?' Taylor mouthed to Sam as she took up position on the opposite side of the carousel.

'Amber Solomon,' Sam whispered back. 'Otherwise

known as Catwoman. She's married to one of the richest men in Kirkhulme.'

'I thought I'd seen some crazy plastic surgery in the States, but *she* is something else,' said Taylor, unable to take her eyes off Amber's face. 'She looks hideous. Why would anybody want to do that to themselves?'

Sam picked up a pair of Oakleys and tried them on for size. 'Beats me. I guess she must have more money than sense.'

At the other end of the shop, Amber scanned the shelves impatiently. Unable to find what she wanted, she turned towards the window display, where Dylan was busy with the vacuum cleaner.

'Is there any chance of getting some service around here,' she called out to him in an aggrieved tone. Dylan didn't even look up, unable to hear anything above the hum of the vacuum.

Amber snapped her fingers. 'Hey, you in the window, I need some help,' she said loudly. Still she failed to engage Dylan's attention.

Never one to ignore a damsel in distress – even one as frightening as Amber – Sam bent down and pulled a plug out of the wall. Instantly, the vacuum cleaner fell silent. Confused, Dylan looked down at the hose in his hand. 'What's wrong with this stupid thing?' he muttered.

'Mate,' Sam said, as he pointed towards Amber. 'I think your assistance is required.'

'Oh, sorry, Mrs Solomon,' said Dylan, as he squeezed between two mannequins and stepped on to the shop floor. 'I didn't see you there. What was it you were after?'

'Nipple daisies,' Amber said peremptorily.

Dylan frowned, clearly at a loss. '*Nipple daisies*? Erm, I'm not sure if we stock those. What are they for exactly?'

Amber kissed her teeth as if she couldn't believe his stupidity. 'For preventing show-through, of course.'

'*Show-through?*' Dylan repeated. 'What's that when it's at home?'

'Do you want me to draw you a diagram?'

Amber's sarcasm was lost on Dylan. 'Yeah, that'd help,' he said. 'Let me get a pen and paper.'

It was too much for Amber. 'Just forget it!' she shrieked as she charged towards the door. 'I'll find them in another shop – preferably one that isn't staffed by dimwits.' As she passed the carousel of sunglasses, she noticed Taylor staring at her.

'What are you gawping at?' she hissed.

Taylor wasn't cowed. 'Your face,' she said evenly. 'I was staring at your face and wondering what on earth possessed you to have all that work done. It's really quite horrific.'

Amber was taken aback. 'How dare you!' she exclaimed. 'Do you know who I am?'

Taylor folded her arms across her chest and gave Amber a challenging look. 'Do you know who *I* am?'

Amber looked her adversary up and down. 'Some jumped-up little tart, by the looks of things.'

Taylor laughed. 'Jealous, are we?' She ran the back of her hand across her smooth cheek. 'Take a good look, bitch; this is what *real* beauty is.'

Dylan, who had been watching the pair's exchange with interest, decided to interject. 'Now, now, ladies,' he said, scurrying up to them. 'Why don't we all try to calm down?'

Amber shoved him aside. 'Get out of my way, you imbecile.'

'Steady on,' said Sam. 'He was only trying to help.'

Amber glared at him. 'When I need his help, I'll ask for it. Now, where we were ... ah yes.' Then, quite unexpectedly, she raised her hand and brought it down across Taylor's face. 'Perhaps that'll teach you to have a bit of respect for your elders,' she snarled.

It wasn't a particularly hard slap, but it caught the young golfer unawares and she staggered backwards into Sam's arms.

'There was no need for that,' said Sam angrily over the top of Taylor's head. 'I don't care who the hell you are; you can't just go around assaulting people.'

A guttural snort issued from the back of Amber's throat. 'So sue me.'

Dylan laughed softly as he watched the hotelier's wife strut towards the door and exit the shop. 'Never a dull moment at St Benedict's,' he said to no one in particular.

Thirteen

'I didn't think Daniel had such a capacity for cruelty,' Amber sobbed. 'Barring me from my own swimming pool was bad enough, but this ... this is the work of a monster. What am I supposed to live on now – thin air?'

Fiona Mortimer removed the box of tissues from her desk drawer and slid it across the desk. 'I hate to say this, Amber, but you really didn't do yourself any favours by outbidding Daniel at the auction. He was bound to retaliate, and what better way to do it than by freezing your joint account?'

'I thought you were supposed to be on my side,' Amber wailed.

'I am – and rest assured that I'm going to do everything in my power to make sure you get what's rightfully yours,' the lawyer said, fiddling absent-mindedly with one of her Chopard diamond earrings. 'Don't worry about the joint account ... he can't leave you without any means of support; we'll get a court order for interim maintenance.'

Amber dabbed at her dainty nose with a tissue, cringing inwardly as she recalled the previous day's ignominy when she'd taken herself into town to buy a new party dress. In two weeks' time one of her closest friends, Pamela Lamont, the wife of a toilet-paper millionaire, would be celebrating her fiftieth birthday in style with a lavish dinner-dance at St Benedict's. It was no exaggeration to say that Amber's social life had nose-dived since her marriage break-up. Naturally, the corporate invitations had dried up almost immediately, Nancy taking Amber's place as Daniel's official consort at the extravagant fund-raisers, days at the races and other assorted no-expense-spared jollies the wife of a top hotelier could expect. What was more surprising was the fact that several of Amber's so-called friends had been studiously ignoring her in recent weeks. A soon-to-be-divorced woman was not, it seemed, a desirable dinner-party commodity. Of course her oldest friends, like Pamela, had stuck by her, but Amber had been reluctant to meet them for lunch or drinks, certain that people would be laughing at her behind her back: *look, there's the woman who spent a fortune on plastic surgery so she could look good for her husband – and she was still usurped by the ugly, fat, hairy housekeeper.* Now, however, Amber had had enough of mooching around the house with only Couscous for company. Determined to reintegrate herself into Kirkhulme high society, she'd made up her mind that Pamela's fiftieth would be the first step on that painful journey. And, in order to make sure no one missed her grand comeback, she was going to need a show-stopping designer outfit.

After spending the best part of two hours with a Harvey Nichols personal shopper, Amber finally chose a floor-length Vera Wang gown in plum organza. Another hour and she had all the accoutrements: shoes, handbag, jewellery. She was in a good mood as she handed over her platinum card. Amber Solomon may be down, she told herself, but she certainly wasn't out. In her beautiful new dress, she would rise, phoenix-like from the ashes of her marriage and really give people something to talk about. But then Amber's little daydream had come crashing down around her.

'I'm sorry, madam. Your card's been declined.'

Amber fired an icy glare in the sales assistant's direction. 'Don't be ridiculous; there must be a problem with your machine. Try again.'

The girl did as instructed. A few moments later, the card was rejected a second time. 'Do you have some other method of payment?'

With a sigh of exasperation, Amber opened her handbag. Her purse contained a couple of hundred pounds in cash, but that wouldn't even pay for the Swarovski hair crystals she'd picked out from the jewellery counter. Behind her, a queue of shoppers was forming and the old crone at her elbow was already starting to huff and puff impatiently. Amber fumbled in her handbag, knowing it was pointless. She had no way of paying for her purchases – she didn't own any credit cards; Daniel didn't hold with them. She used her debit card for everything; that way, Daniel said, she wouldn't be paying interest on top.

'Is everything all right, Amber dear?' a voice called out.

She turned round to see Wendy Harris waving at her from the back of the queue.

Fucking great, Amber thought to herself. This was all she needed. Wendy, a fellow member of the Kirkhulme's Ladies' Guild, was the village foghorn. Famed for being able to pick up a whispered conversation from forty feet away with her bat-like ears, Wendy spent so long rummaging through other people's dirty laundry it was a wonder she hadn't put the local dry-cleaners out of business. What's more, she'd held a grudge ever since Amber's mince pies (bought from Fortnum & Mason then gently distressed with a rolling pin and dusted with icing sugar to make them look homemade) had beaten her own offerings into second place at the Guild's Christmas bake-off.

'Fine thanks, Wendy,' Amber replied through gritted teeth. 'Just a little problem with my card.' She turned back to the sales assistant. 'I'm afraid I'm going to have to pop to a cashpoint. Could you put these items to one side for me?'

'Certainly, madam; we can hold them till the end of the day.'

As Amber walked past Wendy, she forced herself to smile.

'Poor darling,' Wendy murmured in a singularly unsympathetic tone. 'I'd get your husband to call the bank right away. I'm sure they'd be horrified to know they'd caused embarrassment to the wife of such a high-profile customer.' She put her index finger to her mouth hammily. 'Oops, silly me. I was forgetting . . . you haven't got a husband any more, have you, dear?'

Unable to think of a suitably scathing reply, Amber stuck her chin in the air and flounced off in the direction of the lifts.

At the cashpoint, it was the same story. Despite keying in her pin number on two separate attempts, the machine refused to dispense any money. Amber was confused. She rarely bothered looking at her bank statement, but she knew there must be tens of thousands of pounds in their joint account. She thought longingly of the Vera Wang dress. She'd die if she couldn't wear it to Pamela's party. In a fit of fury, she marched back to the car where Stephen was waiting patiently.

'Successful shopping trip, Mrs Solomon?' he enquired pleasantly as he opened the passenger door.

'Does it look like it?' Amber snapped, holding up her arms, which were free of carrier bags.

Stephen didn't reply. He knew that silence was the best policy when Amber was in one of her moods.

As the Mercedes set off for home, Amber called the bank on her mobile, threatening the customer advisor who had the misfortune to take the call with sacking – and a lot worse besides – unless he sorted out the problem with her card immediately. She was dumbfounded when she heard that Daniel had ordered their account to be frozen until further notice, refusing to believe it could possibly be true until she received confirmation from the lackey's line manager. Less than twenty-four hours after making this shock discovery, she was sitting in her lawyer's office in a monsoon of tears. And now, as she thought of the Vera Wang gown, she felt the floodgates start to open again.

'How quickly will you be able to sort out the interim maintenance?' she asked, reaching for another tissue. 'There's a dress I simply must buy for a birthday party the weekend after next.'

Behind the desk, Fiona Mortimer surreptitiously adjusted the slightly too-tight waistband of her trouser suit. 'I'm afraid it's going to take a little longer than that. In the meantime, I shall have to speak to Daniel's lawyer and arrange some sort of cash advance for you, but it will probably only be enough to cover basic living expenses.'

Amber sighed. She hadn't been prepared for any of this. Several of her friends were divorced, but they seemed to regard their newfound singledom only in positive terms. They talked excitedly of hot, no-strings sex with men young enough to be their sons and the bliss of a life free from stentorian snoring and nasal hair clippings in the bathroom sink. None of them had mentioned the agony of negotiating a settlement – or perhaps *their* husbands had simply been more reasonable than hers.

'Actually, I've got some news for you,' Fiona continued. 'Daniel's made you an offer.'

Amber's elongated eyes widened as far as they could – which, admittedly, wasn't very wide at all. 'Oh?' she said.

'It's what we call a clean break settlement, which means he'll pay you a lump sum, on the condition that you won't make a future claim, either for maintenance or further capital. It basically means you'll be financially independent of one another.'

Amber chewed her lip, silently digesting the information. 'How much is he offering?'

'Five million, plus half the value of the house and its contents.'

'Half the *value*?' Amber repeated.

Fiona nodded. 'An independent surveyor will determine the current market value of the house and its contents.'

'But what about the house itself?' Amber said impatiently.

'The terms of Daniel's offer state that he gets to keep it.'

Amber's nostrils flared. 'In that case, tell him he can stick his offer up his arse.'

'Five million is a generous offer – and enough to keep you in the style to which you've become accustomed, as they say. I wouldn't dismiss it out of hand if I were you.'

'I don't care about the money,' Amber whined. 'Well, actually, that's not strictly true. I want Daniel to reimburse me for the eighteen years I wasted on him, of course I do. But as I've told you until I'm blue in the face, the most important thing to me is the Old Manor. I don't care how you do it, but I want that house as part of my settlement. It's *not* negotiable.'

Fiona leaned back in her chair. Having gone through three divorces of her own, and guided hundreds of well-heeled clients through theirs, she'd heard it all before. Wives were always gung-ho in the beginning, especially the ones whose husbands had cheated on them. They came to her, brandishing a list of demands as long as the waiting list at Nicky Clarke's, imagining naively that their guilt-stricken exes wouldn't put up much of a fight. But, in Fiona's experience, every divorce settlement contained a good deal of compromise on both sides. Unfortunately, most of her clients only acknowledged this after months of stressful and energy-sapping to-ing and fro-ing. Really, Amber would be better off accepting Daniel's offer. Then at least she could get on with her life. But, if she wanted to continue paying her lawyer's hourly fee – which was among the highest in Delchester – then who was Fiona to argue? Even so, she felt duty-bound to give her client a reality check.

'You know, if this ends up going to court, there's no guarantee you'd end up with more money than the five million Daniel's offering. And, at the end of it all, the judge might decide that the house issue is simply too contentious, in which case he could order everything to be sold and the proceeds split between you.'

Amber stared out of the window as she considered her lawyer's words. And then, completely without warning, an image of the manatee-like Nancy swimming ungainly laps in the Old Manor's pool popped into her head. Amber's jaw tightened: she wouldn't give up the house; she *couldn't* give it up.

'I doubt very much it'll get to court. Daniel's anal about wasting money unnecessarily.' She gave a haughty sniff. 'Unless it involves sports cars or Ancient Egyptian artefacts. He won't want to bear the heavy costs of a legal hearing, not if he can help it. I think we just need to sit tight for the time being and wait for him to come back with a better offer.'

'Fair enough,' said Fiona, conceding defeat.

'In the meantime, is there really no way of evicting him? Can't I take out some sort of injunction?'

Fiona steepled her fingers under her chin. 'You'd have to prove his presence was damaging in some way – that he was physically abusive towards you, for example, or an unfit father.'

'Of course he's an unfit father!' Amber cried. 'He's shagging his bloody mistress right under our son's nose.'

Fiona frowned. 'You mean they're having sex in view of Calum?'

'Well, no, not exactly. Daniel takes the trollop up to his quarters on the second floor.'

'I'm not sure a judge would regard that as a moral threat to a boy who's only one year shy of adulthood,' Fiona said. 'Still, it wouldn't hurt to keep a diary, logging all the dates and times that Nancy visits the house. It'll stand you in good stead when – sorry, *if* – we end up in court.'

Suddenly, Amber felt a huge tiredness coming over her, a kind of lethargy in the face of the tangled mess of her life. It was like being forced to choose from a restaurant menu when your brain's exhausted and you can't summon the energy even to glance at the Lunch Specials. 'Yes, yes, I'll do that,' she said in a feeble voice.

'And, listen, no more capers like that business at the auction, okay? We don't want to give the enemy any more ammunition.'

Amber stared down at her lap. 'Mmmm,' she said guiltily.

Fiona gave her a long, hard look. 'Amber? You're not planning something, are you?'

'It's nothing *too* awful ... at least nothing he doesn't deserve.'

Fiona sighed. 'Go on.'

'It was a spur of the moment thing,' Amber said quickly. 'I organized it after Daniel changed the lock on the swimming pool. Luckily, the payment went through before Daniel froze our bank account.' She caught Fiona's grimace of disapproval. 'Don't worry, it only cost a couple of grand.'

'Well, whatever it is, Daniel can't be too annoyed about it. If he was, I'd have had his lawyer on the phone by now.'

Amber licked her lips. 'The thing is, Daniel doesn't actually know about it yet. It took a fair amount of planning; I had to book it several weeks in advance.' She glanced at the fashionably retro wall clock above Fiona's head. 'In fact, it should be going up right about now, just in time for Daniel's drive home from work.'

'Jesus, Amber,' Fiona cried. 'What in Christ's name have you done?'

Amber's nostrils flared. 'Let's just say I've gone public.'

Cindy was feeling very pleased with herself as she drove down the bypass in her sexy black Morgan Roadster – a first anniversary gift from her adoring husband. She'd spent the morning in Delchester, meeting the carpenter who was going to create the intricate fretwork window seats for Amber's music room. It was several weeks since she'd received the commission to redesign the Old Manor's library, and since then Cindy had been busy combing the north-west of England and beyond for materials, furniture and fittings that met with her exacting standards.

Some of Cindy's more demanding clients insisted on personally vetting every fabric swatch, curtain tassel and light fitting – but, once Amber had approved the sketches, she seemed happy to give her designer free rein.

This, perversely, was something of a disappointment to Cindy. An inveterate networker, Cindy had been looking forward to swapping girlie confidences over cups of creamy café latte in Amber's luxurious kitchen. Despite her initial openness, however, Amber had been reserved – and even a little glacial – during Cindy's subsequent visits to the Old Manor. It was as if the hotelier's wife was worried she'd given away too much during their first meeting, and now she'd pulled up the drawbridge. Certainly, Cindy had witnessed no more emotional confrontations with Daniel or Nancy; indeed, she hadn't seen hide or hair of the pair since that first dramatic encounter.

While she was in Delchester, Cindy had collected some wallpaper samples from a little shop that specialized in hand-painted murals, based on original Yuan Dynasty artwork. She'd arranged to drop them off at the Old Manor on her way home. Wallpaper being one of Amber's passions, she was naturally keen to have final say over which design would grace the rear wall of her music room.

Cindy was smiling as she approached the Kirkhulme turn-off, mentally running through the welcome-home dinner she was planning to cook for her husband that evening. Kieran had been away for the past week, teaching golf to underprivileged youngsters in his native Scotland. It was the longest time they'd spent apart since they got married fifteen months ago, and Cindy had missed him terribly.

She was approaching the roundabout at the bottom of the slip road when suddenly she saw something that almost caused her to swerve. Next to the roundabout, in a prominent position atop a grassy verge, was a vast billboard. Usually, Cindy drove past it without a second glance, but not today. It was the photograph that caught her eye first – a large, professional-looking shot of Daniel Solomon. He was wearing a dark suit and a purple tie and sitting on the corner of a desk with his hands clasped together; the sort of thing you'd see in a corporate brochure. Beneath it was a paragraph of text in a huge typeface. Cindy only had time to read the first line before she drove past:

> To the people of Kirkhulme: I'd like it to be known that my husband, Daniel Solomon, is the single most despicable, immoral, underhand human being I have ever had the misfortune to meet.

Open-mouthed, Cindy performed a second, slower circumnavigation of the roundabout, eyes glued to the billboard. The poster must've been put up in the last few hours. She would certainly have noticed if it had been there on her outbound journey.

> Don't be fooled by his suave exterior, habit of standing rounds in the Fox & Hounds and generous donations to charity, because it's all an act. The truth is, there's only one person Daniel Solomon cares about – and that's himself.

> Signed, Amber Solomon.

> P.S. Nancy Coughlin is not only a conniving husband-stealer, but a useless housekeeper to boot. I'd

remove my own gallbladder with a red-hot butter knife before I'd recommend her to anybody in the village.

'Sweet baby Jesus,' Cindy muttered as she indicated right to turn into the high street. She was perfectly aware that the Solomons' separation was anything but amicable, but this . . . this was no ordinary divorce battle.

There was no sign of life at the Old Manor. Usually, when Cindy arrived, there'd be a couple of gardeners hard at it or she'd see Stephen, Amber's driver, buffing the Mercedes with a chamois. Today, however, the grounds were mysteriously quiet. Only the trees moved, their branches buffeted by an unseasonable wind.

It was with a certain degree of trepidation that Cindy emerged from the Morgan, not sure what angry scene she might be about to walk into. Daniel Solomon was an influential figure in the village and the billboard was certain to cause him an enormous amount of embarrassment. Who knew what he might do in retaliation? Bending down, she reached for her handbag, which was wedged in the rear footwell. Suddenly, an insouciant gust of wind snatched at her skirt, blowing it up above her waist. Quickly, she pushed it down, clamping the light-weight fabric to the sides of her thighs as she walked around to the boot, where half a dozen wallpaper books were stashed. Catching a movement from the corner of her eye, she turned to see Calum strolling across the lawn towards her. Instantly she coloured, wondering if she'd just inadvertently flashed her underwear at him.

With one hand still holding her skirt down, she

called out to him, 'Hey, Calum, where did you spring from?'

'I was hanging out at the tree house,' he said, pushing a hand through his shaggy hair. 'I saw your car coming up the drive.'

'Your mom asked me to bring by some samples,' Cindy said. Then, remembering the billboard, she added: 'I hope I haven't called at a bad time.'

'Actually, Mum's not here; she's gone into town for an emergency meeting with her lawyer. I'm not sure when she'll be back.'

'Oh, okay.' Cindy popped the boot and pointed to the wallpaper books. 'In that case, maybe I could leave these with you.'

'Sure. They look pretty heavy; why don't I carry them for you?' Calum said with slightly self-conscious gallantry.

Cindy smiled. 'Thanks.' As she began piling the books into the teenager's outstretched arms, she caught the musky scent of fresh sweat on his skin. It was strong, but not altogether unpleasant. 'Have you been into the village today?' she asked, trying to get a steer on whether or not he'd seen the billboard.

'No. Why, what's happening?'

'Nothing,' Cindy said quickly. 'I just wondered, that's all.' Gathering up the final wallpaper book, she elbowed the boot shut. 'Is your dad home?'

'Nah, he's at work. He should be back quite soon, though; he's meeting Nancy for lunch at St Benedict's.'

'Will he be coming back in the car?'

'Yeah, he always drives to work. Why do you ask?'

'No reason.' Cindy glanced up at the swift, scudding

clouds and shivered. 'Let's get these wallpaper samples inside, shall we? It looks like rain.'

Calum unlocked the front door and pushed it open, stepping aside to let Cindy enter first. No sooner had she crossed the threshold than her eardrums were assailed by a barrage of anguished shrieks. For one awful moment, she thought somebody was being murdered.

'Don't worry, it's only Couscous,' said Calum, seeing the look of horror on her face. 'He always gets antsy if he's left alone for too long.'

Cindy exhaled in relief. 'Maybe we should let him out of his cage for a while. It can't be much fun being cooped up all day.'

'You're joking, aren't you? The little bugger will run riot. He only behaves when Mum's around. The last time Dad let him out of his cage, he bit him on the end of his nose.'

'Oh well, he is a wild animal after all,' said Cindy, unable to keep the censure out of her voice.

'Yeah, I know. I've been telling Mum for years that keeping a monkey as a pet is cruel, but she's not interested in anything I've got to say.' Calum cut his eyes to the side. 'No one around here ever listens to me.' Without waiting for a reply, he set off down the narrow corridor that led to the library.

'When do you think you're going to start work in here?' asked Calum, dumping the wallpaper books unceremoniously on a leather Chesterfield.

Cindy deposited her own cargo on top of Calum's. 'The week after next, hopefully. I'm just waiting to hear back from one of my contractors.'

'I gather you're a bit of a design genius,' Calum said, fixing her with a surprisingly intense stare.

As she met his eye, Cindy found herself thinking, and not for the first time, what a good-looking boy he was. He had big, emphatic features: heavy brows, full lips, his father's strong nose. There was nothing of Amber in him at all, but that was scarcely surprising, given that there was nothing much of Amber in herself these days. 'I do okay for myself,' she said lightly.

'I think you're being modest. Mum's a real perfectionist; she'd only hire the best.'

The designer gave a faux-superior toss of her head. 'Well, since you put it like that, I guess I am pretty darned hot.'

Calum grinned. 'You know she's only having the music room done to piss Dad off, don't you?'

'Hmm … I did have my suspicions. From what I've seen, your parents are pretty combative.'

'Did you hear about Mum outbidding Dad for the Nefertiti ring at auction?'

Cindy nodded. 'I read about it in "Jemima's Diary". I can't think how the paper found out about it.'

Calum gave a little snort. 'From the horse's mouth, of course.'

'What, you mean Amber told them?' Cindy said incredulously.

'Got it in one. Mum doesn't want everyone in the village pitying her just cos Dad's got a new girlfriend. Tipping off "Jemima's Diary" is her way of showing people she can take care of herself.'

'Oh well, whatever helps her get through it. Your dad

must've been pretty mad when he missed out on that ring.'

'He had a shit fit. And then he went and changed the lock on the pool house, so Mum can't use it any more.'

Cindy frowned. 'That seems a little petty-minded.'

'They're like a pair of bloody kids, I'm telling you. But it gets worse . . .'

'It does?' said Cindy eagerly, hungry for more details.

'Yesterday, Mum discovered he'd frozen their joint account.'

'Jeez, poor Amber. What's she going to do now?'

'I dunno. That's why she's gone to see her lawyer. I expect they're plotting how they're going to cut Dad's balls off and feed them through a mincing machine right now.'

'Ouch,' said Cindy. 'Never mind "Jemima's Diary", *that* little exclusive would probably make the front page of the nationals.'

Calum looked at her in alarm. 'Hey, you won't repeat this conversation to anyone, will you?'

'Of course not,' said Cindy, her face a picture of empathy. 'I may be a brash American, but I'm certainly not a gossip.'

'No, I didn't think you were. In any case, I probably shouldn't be talking about this stuff to you. I was just . . . you know . . . letting off steam.'

'It must be hard for you, being caught in the middle of all this.'

'They're doing my fucking head in.' Calum glowered. 'I refuse to take sides, so I just keep my head down and stay out of their way as much as possible.' He kicked the leg of the Chesterfield moodily. 'I wish I could leave college and get a job. Then I could afford to get a place of my own.'

'Is there no one you can talk to?' said Cindy. 'It sounds as if you could use some support right now.'

'Like who?'

'A friend, perhaps? Or one of your college tutors?'

'I couldn't trust them to keep their mouths shut,' Calum sighed. 'Anyway, look, just forget I said anything, okay? I'll deal with it in my own way.'

Cindy reached out and took Calum's hand. 'My parents got divorced when I was eight, so, if it's any comfort, I know what you're going through.'

The teenager cleared his throat, suddenly bashful. 'I'll be fine,' he said gruffly, pulling his hand away.

Sensing that the subject of the Solomons' relationship was now closed, Cindy wandered over to one of the library's focal points: the large, leaded-light window at the far end of the room. 'Would you mind if I checked a couple of measurements while I'm here?' she asked. 'The guy who's making the window seat has changed the dimensions slightly, so I'll need to order extra curtain fabric.'

Calum shrugged. 'Be my guest.'

Pulling an industrial-sized tape measure out of her handbag, Cindy began taking measurements, jotting them down in a small notebook. Calum watched her keenly, mesmerized by her graceful movements. Generally speaking, he preferred his women to be much fuller figured than Cindy who, though well endowed in the bust department, had a slim waist and gently flaring hips. But there was no denying she had a beautiful face, framed by long auburn hair that cascaded down her back like a river of molten copper. He smiled, remembering how her skirt had blown up, revealing peachy buttocks, encased in a minuscule pair of lace-trimmed briefs.

'Do you need a hand with that?' he asked, seeing that Cindy was struggling to reach the top of the window frame.

Looking over her shoulder, she gave him a grateful smile. 'If you wouldn't mind, Calum. Even in these heels, I'm not quite tall enough to reach that finial.' She gave him the tape measure and asked him to hold it up against the existing curtain pole.

'Like this?' Calum said, drawing himself up to his full height of six feet and one inch, so Cindy could see just how manly he was.

'A little higher,' said Cindy, taking his forearm and guiding his hand into position. As she did so, the tips of her impressive breasts grazed his chest.

Calum swallowed hard and tried to imagine what it would be like to have a root canal without anaesthetic – anything to fend off the swelling in his boxer shorts.

'Perfect,' said Cindy, unaware of the effect she was having on the teenager. 'Just hold that there, nice and still.' She took the end of the metal tape and began pulling it towards the floor. As she leaned forward, she unwittingly provided Calum with an excellent view down the front of her camisole top. He could see the tan lines left by her bikini and the dusting of cinnamon-coloured freckles across her cleavage. 'Okay, read off the measurement,' she said.

Dragging his eyes away from Cindy's chest, Calum squinted at the tape measure. 'Seventy-six inches. And a little bit.'

With one finger still pinning the tape to the floor, Cindy looked up. 'I need you to be more precise. Can you do it to the nearest quarter of an –' Before she could finish her sentence, an almighty bang reverberated through the house. It made Cindy jump and, as she did, the tape slipped from her finger and pinged back into its case at high velocity.

Calum let out a yelp and dropped the tape measure. 'Shit,' he said, shoving his injured hand under his armpit. 'That hurt.'

'I'm so sorry,' said Cindy, wincing in sympathy. 'That noise made me jump. What was it?'

'The front door,' said Calum. 'Dad always slams it when he's in a bad mood.'

Remembering the billboard, Cindy licked her lips nervously. 'In that case, I really ought to get going.'

'Don't you want to finish the measuring first?'

Cindy bent down to pick up the tape measure. 'I tell you what. Why don't I come back some other time? I have a feeling your father could do with a little privacy right now.'

Calum waved a hand dismissively. 'Don't worry about him; he's always in a bad mood.'

'Honestly, Calum, I think it's best that I go,' said Cindy, scooping up her notebook and the Waterman Edson fountain pen she'd treated herself to when she bagged her first commission after moving to the UK – a bedroom makeover for an ex-Formula One racing driver.

All at once, an angry voice came bouncing down the corridor. 'Calum? Calum, are you there?'

'In the library, Dad,' Calum called back. He turned to Cindy. 'It sounds as if I'm in the shit. I bet Dad's found my stash of weed.'

'I wouldn't bet on it,' Cindy murmured.

Calum began walking towards the door, but before he could get there it flew open. Daniel stood on the threshold, his face purple with fury and his eyes burning like two hot coals. Without any word of explanation, he seized his son roughly by the shoulders.

'Look, Dad, I can explain,' Calum began.

Daniel didn't seem to hear him. 'You won't believe what your bitch of a mother's gone and done now,' he cried.

Realizing that it wasn't *him* his father was gunning for, Calum let out a sigh of relief. 'What?'

'Have a guess,' Daniel urged, his voice trembling with emotion.

'I really haven't got a clue, Dad,' the teenager replied in a bored tone. 'Why don't you just tell me?'

'All right then, I will,' Daniel bellowed. 'She's made me the laughing stock of the entire village.'

'Really,' said Calum flatly. 'And how has she managed to do that?'

'By hiring a fucking great billboard, plastering my face across it and announcing to the world in letters two-foot high that I'm a complete frigging tosspot.'

'Oh well, I guess that just about evens up the score then.'

At this, Daniel formed his hands into two claws and

gripped an imaginary throat. 'I'm going to make her pay for this, if it's the last thing I do,' he screamed. 'I'm going to sue her for libel. I'm going to creep into her bedroom in the dead of night and put a pillow over that hideous face of hers.'

'Er, Dad.' Calum jerked his head towards Cindy, who was cowering beside by the window, desperately trying to make herself as unobtrusive as possible. 'I think you'd better calm down; we've got company.' The amused look on his face told Cindy that he had deliberately allowed his father to rant on unchecked – though whether this was out of a desire to show her just how bad relations were between his parents, or simply for sport, it was hard to say.

Daniel wore a look of horrified embarrassment. 'Ah, Mrs McAllister, I didn't see you,' he said, smoothing back the hair at his temples as he struggled to compose himself. 'Please forgive me.' He laughed self-consciously. 'You mustn't take my words too literally. I'm afraid I lost my temper for a moment there.'

'It's okay,' said Cindy as she hooked her handbag over her shoulder and made her way towards the two men. 'I was just leaving.'

Daniel clasped his hands together in a gesture of entreaty. 'Please don't go on my account,' he said obsequiously. 'Why don't I get you something to drink? A cup of tea, perhaps?'

'No, honestly, I'm fine.'

Daniel clapped his hand to his forehead. 'Ugh, what was I thinking? You Americans only drink coffee, don't you?

'No, thank you,' said Cindy, more firmly this time.

'Espresso? Cappuccino? Macchiato? I've got a fantastic gizmo in the kitchen that can do just about anything.'

'*Dad*,' said Calum, glaring at his father. 'She doesn't want anything, okay? She just wants to get the hell out of this crazy house – and, frankly, I don't blame her.'

'Yes, of course ... I'm so sorry, Mrs McAllister.' Beads of perspiration were beginning to form on Daniel's brow. 'Look, before you go, can I ask a favour of you?'

'Sure,' said Cindy, inching closer to the door.

'I realize this is rather brazen of me, given that you're working for my wife, but can I please ask you not to repeat anything you've just heard me say? As you know, Amber and I are in the middle of a very difficult divorce and I would hate my words to be taken out of context and used in evidence against me, if you get my meaning.'

'I understand, Mr Solomon,' said Cindy crisply. 'And I can assure you I heard nothing.'

Daniel broke into a relieved smile. 'Thank you, Mrs McAllister. I won't forget this, and if you and your husband ever fancy a romantic weekend away, please let me know. I'd be happy to offer you a complimentary suite in any one of my fine establishments.'

Cindy paused with her hand on the door handle. 'I appreciate the offer, Mr Solomon, but that won't be necessary.' A mischievous smile played about her lips. 'But if those *fine establishments* of yours ever need a redesign, I do hope you'll bear me in mind.' She turned to Calum. 'Can you ask your mother to give me a call when she's had a chance to look through those wallpaper books?'

'Will do.' The teenager walked over to her. 'I'll see you to the door.'

Leaving Daniel alone in the library, the pair made their way back along the corridor. As they crossed the entrance hall, Cindy stopped and turned to Calum. 'Before I go, I want to give you something,' she said, reaching into her handbag. She held out a small black card, embossed with gold writing. 'It's got my home and cellphone numbers on it. That way you can call me if you ever need to talk.'

Calum stared the card in surprise. 'Thanks,' he said. He looked up at her. Their eyes locked together and in that brief moment it seemed to Calum that they were the only two people in the universe. He could feel his heart pounding against his ribcage. It was now or never he told himself.

'Was there something you wanted to tell me?' said Cindy, sensing his hesitation.

Calum took a deep breath. 'Not *say*, so much as *do* . . .'

He placed one of his strong hands behind her neck and drew her towards him. The next thing Cindy knew, the teenager's tongue was in her mouth. It all happened so quickly, she barely had time to react – and then, when she did have time to react, she found herself responding. Two seconds later, she came to her senses.

'What are you doing?' she said, pulling away from Calum and stumbling backwards.

The look of disappointment in his eyes was almost too much too bear.

'Weren't you enjoying that?' he said.

237

'No ... I mean yes ... I mean ...' Cindy sighed. 'I'm married, and you're just a boy.'

Calum puffed his chest out. 'I'm nearly eighteen. In any case, I like older women.'

He seemed so serious that Cindy couldn't help smiling. 'Oh, honey, I'm flattered, really I am. But I love my husband and I'd never dream of cheating on him.'

Calum shrugged. 'Oh well, if you ever change your mind ...'

'It's not going to happen,' said Cindy gently. 'But you're a lovely guy and I'm sure there are dozens of girls out there who'd give their right arm for a date with you.' She gave his arm a friendly squeeze. 'Look, I've really got to get going. I'll see you next time, okay?'

'Okay,' said Calum as he accompanied her to the front door. He felt a strange sense of abandonment as he watched Cindy's Morgan disappear down the driveway. Still, he consoled himself, at least he had the image of her peachy arse forever burned into his brain. That delicious vision would fuel his wank fantasies for a good month or more.

Fourteen

Laura leaned back on her heels and surveyed the kitchen floor. Earlier that morning, as she'd breakfasted with the girls, Birdie had managed to knock an almost-full bottle of olive oil off the table, sending it smashing on to the limestone tiles. This was the reason Laura had been on her hands and knees, scrubbing brush in hand, for the past half an hour. She'd managed to clean up the worst of it, but despite several applications of Ajax, followed by bleach and finally white spirit, a greasy stain the size of a dinner plate clung stubbornly to the floor. Forced to admit defeat, Laura tossed the brush carelessly into the washing-up bowl beside her. A small tsunami of bleach solution slopped over the bowl's edge, splattering the sleeve of her favourite red cardigan.

'Shit, shit, shit,' Laura groaned, peeling off her rubber gloves and rushing to the sink. As she held her sleeve under the cold tap, she glared at Tiger, who was reclining beside the Welsh dresser in his baby rocker. 'I suppose you think this is funny, don't you?' she said.

Tiger blew a raspberry, whereupon a bungee rope of spittle appeared at the corner of his mouth and began its unattractive descent down the front of his T-shirt.

'Yes, that's right, you have a good laugh at Mummy's expense,' said Laura, examining her sopping wet sleeve, upon which white spots were already beginning to form.

She waved her arm at the baby. 'Look at this – my favourite cardigan, ruined. And it's all your fault.'

Surprisingly, there was a shred of truth in the accusation. Normally, Laura didn't attend to domestic spillages. She didn't have to; she had a cleaning lady, Mrs Potter, for that sort of thing. Or at least she *used* to have a cleaning lady – for less than twenty-four hours ago Laura had sacked Mrs Potter. It was a rash decision and one which she was already beginning to regret – and the person who was responsible for Mrs Potter's departure, albeit indirectly, was Tiger.

The previous afternoon, Laura had been sitting in her home office drafting a press release about the local am-dram society's production of *A Midsummer Night's Dream*. Once a high-flying executive in a top London sports agency, she had agreed to do some unpaid PR for the Kirkhulme Players, just to stop her brains from curdling. The house, for once, was quiet: Sam was on the golf course, Tiger was asleep in his cot and Marta and Birdie were taking their regular walk through the park to pick Carnie up from school. Downstairs, meanwhile, Mrs Potter was taking advantage of the children's absence to give the playroom a good going over.

Laura had barely composed her first sentence when a shrill cry shattered the blissful silence. Gritting her teeth, she turned her desk fan to top speed, hoping its whirring blades would drown out the racket. She managed to write another few sentences but then, realizing he was being ignored, Tiger decided to pump up the volume.

'Typical, bloody typical!' Laura cried as she flung down her pen. Wrenching open the office door, she stalked into the nursery to confront the source of the nuisance.

'The whole world doesn't revolve round you, you know,' she bellowed at the screaming infant. 'Can't you see I'm trying to work?' When her words failed to have any effect, Laura grabbed the rails of the cot and shook them. 'Shut up!' she cried. 'Shut up, you little shit, before I put you up for adoption.'

'You oughtn't to speak to him like that,' a stern voice declared.

Turning round, Laura saw Mrs Potter standing at the top of the stairs, feather duster in hand. Her first feeling was one of embarrassment that she'd been caught in the act of trying to reason with a two-month-old. In the next instant, she became defensive. 'He's my son,' she snapped at the cleaner. 'And I'll speak to him any way I like.'

Mrs Potter clasped her hands self-righteously beneath her shelf-like bosom. 'Babies need love and cuddles, not shouting at,' she said. 'If you carry on like that, you'll give him a complex.'

'Oh, please, spare me the cod psychology,' Laura said. Feeling the need to explain her actions, she added. 'Look, I know I shouldn't have shouted at him, but I haven't been sleeping at all well lately; my nerves are frazzled.'

'That's as may be, but you shouldn't go taking it out on the kiddie. Threatening to have him adopted . . .' The cleaner shook her head disparagingly. 'It's not nice, not nice at all.'

'Oh, for God's sake, I lost my temper with him *once* – big deal.'

Mrs Potter pursed her thin lips. 'But it's not the first time. Is it, dear?'

'I don't know what you mean,' Laura said, suddenly feeling flustered.

'I've heard you shout at him before – *and* use bad language.'

Laura narrowed her eyes. 'Have you been spying on me?'

'Certainly not,' said Mrs Potter. 'But I'm here five days a week . . . I can't help overhearing things.'

Laura felt a cold, hard knot twisting in the pit of her stomach. 'Perhaps if you put as much effort into cleaning the house as you did eavesdropping, I wouldn't have to spend so much time tidying up after you.'

The cleaner blinked hard. 'I beg your pardon.'

Laura leaned over the cot and picked Tiger up, determined to prove to Mrs Potter that she wasn't a neglectful mother. 'Well,' she began, raising her voice so she could be heard over the baby's breathless yelps, 'yesterday, there was a distinct tide mark round the bath after you'd supposedly cleaned it.'

It was a low blow: Mrs Potter was, generally speaking, an excellent cleaner, but in recent months an arthritic hip had prevented her from performing certain domestic tasks – notably those requiring a degree of bending or stretching – to her previous high standards.

'I'm sorry about that,' Mrs Potter said, a mottled rash breaking out across the folds of her jowly neck. 'I must have been having an off day; it won't happen again.' She frowned at Laura, who was rocking Tiger roughly back and forth in her arms. 'He'll be sick if you jiggle him around like that.'

Suddenly, all the resentment that had been welling up

inside Laura over the past eight weeks came pouring out. 'Oh, leave me alone, you interfering old crone,' she snarled. 'When I want your advice, I'll ask for it.' She took a couple of steps towards the startled cleaner. 'I've put up with so much from you over the years, and this is the thanks I get.'

Mrs Potter opened her mouth to protest, but Laura silenced her with a poisonous glare. 'I know you've been stealing from me,' she said in a hard voice.

'Now look here,' Mrs Potter began indignantly, but Laura began talking over her.

'I daresay you see it as a perk of the job – a toilet roll here, a half-empty tin of furniture polish there – but, technically speaking, it's still stealing. I've always turned a blind eye because I know how much you need this job.'

'Pah!' said Mrs Potter. 'I could get another job tomorrow.'

'In that case, I suggest you start looking for one.' Laura glared at Tiger, whose wails were now threatening to shatter the windowpanes. 'As you can see, I've got my hands full, so I hope you don't mind seeing yourself out. Oh, and I'd be grateful if you could leave your front door key on the dining-room table.'

Mrs Potter opened her mouth but, finding herself temporarily rendered speechless, she closed it again and walked towards the door.

Afterwards, Laura felt thoroughly ashamed of herself. She wasn't an innately spiteful person and she'd certainly never resorted to name calling before. She didn't know what was wrong with her; ever since Tiger's birth she'd been irritable and out of sorts with everyone. Now, as she looked at her son, asleep (just for once) in his rocker, she found herself thinking back to that day on the escarpment. If only she'd had the courage to push the pram over the edge, her life would be a whole lot simpler. In addition to the burden of caring for a child she didn't love, she now had the unenviable task of finding a replacement for Mrs Potter. Good cleaners were highly prized commodities in Kirkhulme and usually had to be lured away from their existing employers with promises of biannual pay rises and private healthcare. Sighing wistfully, Laura gazed out of the kitchen window, looking out towards the lawn where her younger daughter was sitting beside the undulating box hedge, pulling up handfuls of daisies. She couldn't help smiling. Birdie reminded her of herself as a child: wilful and inquisitive. Then, realizing that Marta was nowhere in sight, Laura's smile faded. After delivering Carnie to her Montessori school, the au pair was supposed to engage in an hour of interactive play with Birdie. It was part of a strict regime that Laura had devised to encourage her daughter's cognitive development. After checking that Tiger was still asleep, and safely buckled into the baby rocker, she pulled back the folding glass doors that gave on to the garden and called out to her daughter. 'Where's Marta, darling?'

'On da phone,' Birdie said in her funny little sing-song voice. 'Talking to her boyfwend.'

Laura's top lip curled. 'Is she now?' She walked over to Birdie and hoisted her on to her hip. 'Come on, sweetpea. Let's go and see Marta.'

They found the Spanish girl in the old orchard. She had her back to them and a mobile phone was clamped to her jaw. Stopping momentarily, Laura raised a finger to her lips. 'Let's sneak up on Marta and give her a surprise,' she whispered to Birdie.

Nodding enthusiastically, the toddler clapped her hand over her mouth.

As Laura crept through the orchard, snatches of Marta's conversation drifted towards her. 'I don't mean to be jealous,' the au pair was saying. 'But I can't help it. What was I supposed to think when I walked into that bedroom and found you half-naked with Keeley?'

Laura knew about the incident at the christening party because Keeley had mentioned it to her the following day over lunch. Her friend had laughed off the suggestion that she and Harry were anything more than friends but, by the sound of things, Marta wasn't convinced.

Suddenly, the au pair gave an enormous sigh and began walking away. 'I *do* believe you,' Laura heard her say in an earnest tone. 'Please, Harry, let's not fall out over this.'

Laura tiptoed after her, hoping to catch more of the conversation. As she negotiated the gnarled remnants of a pear tree, she stepped on to a dry twig. It broke beneath her foot with a loud snap, instantly alerting Marta to her presence. The au pair glanced up, making eye contact with her employer. 'Look, I've got to go,' she gabbled into her mobile. 'I'll call you later.'

'Boyfriend trouble?' Laura asked casually, walking over to the au pair.

'You could say that.' Marta hung her head submissively. 'I'm sorry, Laura, I know I shouldn't be making personal calls when I'm supposed to be looking after Birdie.'

Laura shook her head as if Marta's neglect of her young charge was inconsequential. Having already alienated one valuable member of her support network, she wasn't about to risk losing another. Bending down, she set Birdie on her feet. 'Look at the robin redbreast on that branch, darling. Why don't you go and say hello to him?'

As she watched Birdie totter off, Laura draped a friendly arm round Marta's shoulders. 'I couldn't help overhearing what you said about catching Harry in a compromising position with Keeley,' she remarked. 'You don't think they're sleeping together, do you?'

'I don't think so. Harry says she was just helping him dry his shirt,' Marta said glumly, before launching into a detailed account of what had happened in the Bentleys' spare bedroom.

Laura affected surprise, giving no indication that Keeley had already delivered her own, strikingly similar, version of events. 'Goodness, I think I'd be suspicious too if I was in your position,' she said when Marta had finished. 'I don't mean to be unkind, but I wouldn't be at all surprised if Harry wasn't still holding a torch for Keeley.' She mustered a pitying half-smile. 'I've seen the way he looks at her.'

Marta looked aghast. 'What do you mean, *still* holding a torch for her?'

'Well, they did have that fling last summer, after all.' Laura saw the look of surprise in Marta's eyes. 'Didn't Harry tell you?'

'No,' said Marta quietly.

'Oh yes, it didn't last very long, but it was quite a passionate affair by all accounts.' Laura was surprised how easily the lie slipped out. She knew full well that Keeley's relationship with Harry was casual in the extreme and had ended the moment she'd got together with Ryan.

Marta swallowed hard, as if she were fighting back tears. 'Why did they break up?'

'I think Keeley felt Harry wasn't ambitious enough,' Laura said. Twisting the knife further, she added, 'And, you know, she does have a point. He *is* only a shop assistant, after all . . . hardly the catch of the century.'

'I see.' Marta rubbed her eye. 'So you really think they might be seeing each again?'

Laura paused, formulating her words carefully. 'Don't get me wrong – I love Keeley to bits – let's just say she's the sort of girl who always wants what she can't have.'

'But she seems so in love with Ryan; I can't believe she'd cheat on him.'

Laura shrugged. 'It wouldn't be the first time she's been unfaithful.'

Marta frowned as she tried to digest the implications of what Laura was saying. 'Things were going so well between me and Harry,' she said in a quavering voice. 'We've even talked about moving in together when the contract on my house share runs out at the end of the summer.'

'Ooh, goodness, I think that would be jumping the gun a bit, don't you?' Laura said quickly. 'I mean, if the man can't be trusted . . .'

'We don't know that for sure,' said Marta, suddenly defensive. 'I'd like to give him the benefit of the doubt.'

'Then why didn't he tell you that he and Keeley used to

be fuck buddies?' said Laura. 'Unless, that is, he's got something to hide.'

'Perhaps he was just trying to spare my feelings.'

Laura nodded. 'Perhaps.'

'Has Keeley said anything to you – about her and Harry, I mean?'

'Not a word, I promise you.'

'Well, that's a good sign,' said Marta, breaking into a smile.

Laura wrinkled her nose. 'Is it?'

'Yes. You and Keeley are good friends; surely she'd tell you if she was seeing Harry in secret?'

'Not necessarily,' Laura said. 'Keeley plays her cards very close to her chest – and, given the fact that you work for me, she's hardly likely to admit she's shagging him, now is she?'

The au pair wrung her hands together. 'I guess not.'

'Let's face it, the only way you'll know for sure is if you actually catch them red-handed.' Laura let her arm slip from Marta's shoulders. 'I'd better get back indoors; I've left Tiger asleep in the kitchen. Why don't you stay out here and play with Birdie? And try not to worry too much about Harry and Keeley. I dare say this will all turn out to be a storm in a teacup.'

Laura was feeling smug as she made her way back to the house, knowing that the seeds of doubt had been sown in Marta's mind; now all she had to do was feed them with a little fertilizer.

Later that evening, when the children were in bed and Sam was slumped in front of Sky Sports, Laura phoned

Keeley at home. Without any preamble, she went straight to the purpose of her call. 'Listen, Kee, I've got a favour to ask.'

'Fire away,' said Keeley, who was hunched on the sofa in her cramped studio flat, painting her toenails.

'It's Marta and Harry. I want to split them up and I need your help to do it.' At the other end of the phone, there was silence. 'Keeley, are you still there?'

'Yeah, I'm here. Do you mind running that by me again?'

Laura repeated herself.

'I thought that's what you said.' Keeley drew breath sharply as a droplet of vermilion polish landed on her handmade Persian rug – a gift from a Far Eastern shipping magnate she'd had a brief fling with after he'd eyed her up on the croquet lawn at St Benedict's. 'But I don't understand ... why on earth would you want to split them up? I think they make a lovely couple.'

'They're getting far too cosy for my liking,' said Laura mysteriously.

'But aren't you pleased for Marta? Harry's a good, solid bloke; she could do an awful lot worse, you know.'

Laura made a huffing noise. 'No, I am *not* pleased. Their relationship's starting to have a negative impact on family life.'

'I thought Marta's family lived in Seville.'

'Not Marta's family, *my* family.'

'Ah, I see. You mean now that she's all loved up, her mind's not on the au pairing any more?'

'Marta's certainly distracted – there's no doubt about it – and, if things carry on the way they are, they'll be setting up home together before the summer's out. And you know what'll be next, don't you?'

'A trip to Ikea?'

'No, silly! She'll be getting pregnant and handing in her notice, that's what. I know I must sound like a complete bitch, but honestly, Kee, losing Marta would be my worst nightmare. I'd go insane without her, I really would.'

'It wouldn't be so difficult to get another au pair, would it?'

'I could find someone to take care of Birdie and Carnie, sure; they're no trouble at all. It's Tiger who's the problem. He's such a difficult, unlovable child. I honestly don't think many girls could cope with him the way Marta does.'

Keeley giggled. 'Oh, come on, that's a bit harsh. I know Tiger can be grizzly, but he's certainly not unlovable.'

'Isn't he?' said Laura tightly. 'I know my own son and I'm telling you he's utterly revolting.'

Thinking that Laura must be joking, Keeley played along. 'Of course he is,' she said. 'He's a whiny, snotty-nosed little brat and an absolute disgrace to the Bentley name.'

'So you'll help me then?' said Laura eagerly.

'I don't see how I can.'

'It's easy, I want to set a honey trap – with you as bait.'

Another long silence. 'You're having me on. This is all a big joke, right?'

'No, I'm deadly serious.' Laura's tone softened. 'Don't worry, I don't expect you to sleep with Harry or anything.'

'Oh, well, that's all right then,' said Keeley dryly. 'So what *do* I have to do?'

'Call him up and invite him to meet you for a drink in the Fox & Hounds after work. Say there's something urgent you need to discuss with him.'

'*Okaaay*,' said Keeley warily. 'So we go for a drink ... and then what?'

'You wait till Harry's a bit pissed – that way, he'll be thinking with his dick and not his brain, then you tell him you've still got the hots for him.'

'No way!'

'Hang on, hear me out – it's not as bad as it sounds.'

Keeley sighed. 'Go on.'

'Next, you make a move on him.'

'When you say, *make a move* . . .'

'You know, act like you're up for it – put your hand on his thigh, nuzzle up to him a bit.' Pretending not to hear Keeley's groans, Laura continued outlining her scheme. 'And when he's all fired up, so to speak, you invite him into the beer garden for a bit of a snog.'

At this, Keeley broke into a fit of the giggles. 'Oh, Laura, this is absolutely ridiculous.'

Laura ignored her. 'Meanwhile, back at my house, Marta will be finishing up. She's been getting the bus to work recently because her car's in for repairs. So, being the thoughtful employer I am, I'll offer to give her a lift home.'

'What about the kids?' Keeley asked. 'Who'll be looking after them?'

'I don't know. I haven't worked out all the details yet,' said Laura impatiently. She moved on swiftly, before her friend could raise another objection. 'Then, as I'm driving past the pub, I'll ask Marta if she fancies popping in for a quick drink.'

'I can see exactly where this is going,' Keeley sniggered. 'What if Marta says no?'

'She won't, okay?' Laura snapped. 'And, just to make sure of it, I'll see to it she has such a shitty day at work. She'll be gagging for a stiff gin by the end of it.'

Keeley sighed. 'You're actually serious about this, aren't you?'

'Of course I am,' said Laura irritably. 'So ... are you going to help me or not?'

'Sorry, Laura, the answer's no.'

'Oh, don't say that. Won't you at least think about it?'

'No,' said Keeley firmly. 'I'm with Ryan now. How do you think he'd feel if he knew I was leching over another bloke behind his back?'

'It's not like you to take the moral high ground,' Laura said airily.

'What do you mean?'

'Well, let's face it, you have shagged a few married men in your time.'

'Yes, but that was just a bit of fun,' said Keeley. 'I wasn't trying to break up anyone's relationship. In any case, I never slept with a man whose wife I'd actually met.'

'But all I'm asking you to do is *snog* Harry. I promise you that's all it'll take ... as soon as Marta sees you two playing tonsil tennis in that beer garden, she'll dump him like a shot. Job done.'

Keeley could hardly believe her ears. 'How can you

be so cold-hearted? This is Marta we're talking about; I thought you were fond of her.'

'I *am* fond of her,' said Laura. 'But, don't you see, we'd be doing her a favour? Isn't it better that she realizes what Harry's like now – rather than finding out in a year's time when she's up the duff?'

'I'm sorry, Laura, I'm not getting involved and I really think you should forget the whole stupid idea.'

'Without you on board, it looks as if I'm going to have to,' Laura said tightly.

'Don't be cross with me. You need to get this whole thing in perspective. Who says Marta's going to get pregnant? And, even if she does, I bet it won't be for ages yet – by which time Tiger will probably have grown out of his "unlovable" phase and be a perfect little darling, just like his sisters.'

'I'm not holding my breath,' Laura muttered. 'Anyway, just forget I asked, okay?'

'Promise me you won't try to interfere in Marta and Harry's love life?'

Laura sighed. 'I promise. Now can we change the subject?'

'Sure.' Having finished painting her toenails, Keeley set down her bottle of polish on the large wooden blanket box that doubled as a coffee table. 'Actually, I'm glad you phoned because I've got some rather exciting news. But, if I tell you, you've got to promise to keep it a secret.'

'Of course,' said Laura. 'My lips are sealed.'

'Get this . . .' Keeley paused for an imaginary drum roll. 'A top London football club is sniffing around Ryan.'

'Gosh, how exciting.'

'Nothing's signed yet; his agent's still in negotiations, but it's practically a done deal.'

'But what's going to happen to you two if he does move to London?' Laura asked. 'All that commuting's bound to put a strain on your relationship.'

Even though there was no one to see her, Keeley was wearing a grin as big as Cheddar Gorge. 'I won't *be* commuting,' she said smugly.

'What, you mean Ryan's asked you to go with him?'

'Not in so many words,' Keeley conceded. 'But I'm sure it's only a matter of time. God knows, I'm at his apartment so much we're practically living together already. Actually ...' She ran her tongue round her lips. 'Ryan doesn't know that I know he's about to leave Delchester FC.'

Laura frowned. 'So who told you?'

'We were at a bar in town the other night and one of his friends' girlfriends let it slip when we were chatting in the queue for the ladies. She obviously assumed I already knew, so I just nodded and acted like Ryan had told me all about it.'

'But why *hasn't* he told you? Surely he'd want to share an important piece of news like that with you?'

'That's what I thought – and I must admit I was a bit miffed at first. But the more I thought about it, the more it made sense. You see, the thing is, I reckon Ryan's getting ready to propose.'

'Oh, Kee, do you really think so?'

'Yes, I do,' said Keeley, hugging herself in delight. 'You know how cautious Ryan is. I reckon he's just waiting until that contract's signed, so that it's all official, then he's going to hit me with a double whammy: a new life in London and a fuck-off ten-carat yellow diamond on my ring finger.'

Knowing how long Keeley had waited to meet the man of her dreams, Laura was almost as excited as her friend. 'That's wonderful news, darling! I'm so pleased for you both. You will call me the instant he pops the question, won't you?'

Keeley laughed. 'You'll be the first to know, I swear.' Suddenly, she caught sight of the digital display on her DVD player. 'Shit, is that the time? Look, Laura, I've got to dash. Ryan's picking me up in an hour and I haven't even decided what I'm wearing yet.'

'Where's he taking you?'

'Some posh house party in the village.'

'Ooh, lovely. Anyone I know?'

'I don't even know them myself, to be honest; they're friends of Ace and Astrid's.'

'Oh well, it's always nice to meet new people.'

'I suppose so,' said Keeley. 'It's certainly going to be an interesting evening, one way or another.'

Fifteen

Keeley was feeling uncharacteristically nervous as she waited for Ryan to arrive. She'd been to balls before and gala dinners, not to mention countless nightclub openings and charity fundraisers – but when it came to swingers' parties, she was a complete novice. As a former model with a wardrobe crammed full of contemporary and vintage fashions, Keeley usually had the knack of knowing exactly what to wear to any event. But tonight she was flummoxed, rejecting four different outfits before settling on a knee-length charcoal wrap dress and a pair of Pedro Garcia slingbacks. After experimenting with several different hairstyles of varying degrees of sophistication, she finally decided to wear her long hair loose. Her make-up too was subtle, as she eschewed her usual sophisticated evening look in favour of tinted moisturiser, mascara, blush and a slick of nude lip-gloss.

Ryan was ten minutes early. Usually, he rang Keeley's doorbell, but that evening he was impatient, beeping his car horn until she threw open the living-room window.

'Aren't you coming in?' Keeley called down to him. She was hoping they could have a quick drink together for Dutch courage before they set out.

'Nah, we'd better get a move on,' Ryan shouted back. 'Ace says it's best to get there early.'

'Fine,' muttered Keeley. She closed the window and

grabbed her bulging handbag from the sofa. Instead of her usual girlie paraphernalia, the bag contained a list of items that had been emailed to her by Astrid the day before – 'essentials', as the Swedish girl had described them: wet wipes, deodorant, breath mints, condoms, lubricant. Astrid had even suggested she might like to bring a sex toy or two, but Keeley – who, it must be said, possessed a collection of vibrators to rival any branch of Ann Summers – had balked at this. The truth was, she wasn't looking forward to the party as much as she'd thought she would. She'd never been averse to casual sex in the past, but those encounters had always been spontaneous. Swinging, by contrast, seemed so dreadfully premeditated. As if to emphasize the point, Astrid had even gone so far as to offer some etiquette tips in her email:

Don't turn up empty-handed.

Be friendly and polite with everyone, even if you're not interested in them sexually.

Remember that 'no' always means 'no'.

Don't bring any drugs – or you'll be asked to leave!

Set a code word or signal, so that you can indicate to each other if you start to feel uncomfortable.

As Keeley jogged down the three flights of stairs that led to the communal entrance, she couldn't help wishing that she and Ryan were spending a quiet night in together, instead of attending what was, in practical terms, a mass orgy. She hadn't been keen on the idea from the start but, carried along by Ryan's enthusiasm and not wanting to seem like a prude, she'd found herself agreeing and it was too late to back out now.

She didn't get her usual kiss when she slid into the passenger seat of Ryan's BMW. Instead, the footballer looked her up and down and, judging by his raised eyebrows, he was unimpressed by her appearance.

'What's with the dress?' he asked, as he pulled away from the kerb.

Keeley smoothed a hand over the soft jersey fabric covering her thighs. 'What's wrong with it?'

'It's not very sexy.'

'Astrid said this party was going to be a classy affair. I didn't want to look slutty.'

'Yeah, but c'mon, Kee, there's a world of difference between looking slutty and looking as if you're going to a job interview.'

Keeley sighed. 'I can go back and change if you like.'

'There's no time,' said Ryan curtly.

For the next few minutes, they drove in silence. Ryan seemed tense and preoccupied. 'Is something wrong?' Keeley asked at last.

'No,' said Ryan, without taking his eyes off the road.

'Could've fooled me,' Keeley muttered. 'I'm not sure I want to go to this party if you're going to be in a shitty mood all night.'

Instantly, Ryan's demeanour changed. 'Sorry, babe,' he said, taking his hand off the gear stick and placing it on her knee. 'I shouldn't have been rude about your dress. It's just that you're all covered up, and I want the other guys at the party to see how hot you are.'

Keeley wrinkled her nose. 'I'm not sure I like the idea of loads of strange blokes drooling over me.'

Ryan laughed. 'Well, that is the point of tonight, isn't it?'

'I guess so.' Keeley stared out of the window as the countryside flashed by. 'Neither of us has to do anything we don't feel completely comfortable with, right?'

Ryan sighed. 'I thought we'd already been through this.'

'I was just checking.' Keeley opened her handbag and began rummaging for the breath mints.

'You know, if you want to get the most out of tonight, you're going to have to enter into the spirit of things,' Ryan said. 'There's no point being a wallflower all evening.'

'I don't intend to be.' Keeley held out the mints. 'Do you want one of these?'

'Yeah,' said Ryan, opening his mouth so Keeley could drop a sweet on his tongue. 'I reckon we're in for a great night,' he said. 'We just need to let go of our inhibitions and go with the flow.'

'Hmm . . . just so long as we don't get *too* carried away,' Keeley said. 'Speaking of which, we need to set a code word.'

'A code word? What for?'

'It's a sort of secret SOS. If one of us says the code word, it means we're not enjoying ourselves and we want the other one to come to the rescue, so to speak.'

'Don't you think that's a bit unnecessary? I can always tell when you're not having a good time: your bottom lip sticks out and you get this glazed look in your eyes.'

'Yes, but you might not be able to see me; you could be too busy snogging the face off some other woman.'

'Okay, okay,' said Ryan, in the weary tone of a parent acceding to a child's request for ice cream. 'What word shall we use?'

Keeley thought for a moment. 'How about *penalty*? Given your profession, it seems like as good a choice as any.'

'*Penalty* it is,' said Ryan as he indicated to turn right into a private road. A few moments later, the car pulled to a halt in front of a steel security gate. 'So ... here we are then.'

Keeley looked anxiously at the grand property that lay on the other side of the gate. In typical art deco style, it was a vast white rectangle with curved glass windows and geometric blocks around the front door, which mimicked the entrance to some exotic temple. She'd passed the house hundreds of times before and had often wondered what lay beyond its stunning facade. Now she was about to find out. She looked at Ryan. 'Are you feeling nervous?'

'A bit,' he replied.

'I'm absolutely bricking it.'

'Don't worry, babe, a couple of drinks and you'll soon loosen up.' Reaching through the BMW's open window, Ryan pressed the button on the video intercom.

There was a crackle of static and then a disembodied male voice answered. 'Good evening.'

'Er, hi,' the footballer began hesitantly. 'We're here for the party.'

'Your names?'

'Ryan and Keeley.'

'And you are guests of?'

'Oh, er, right. Ace and Astrid invited us?' Ryan's voice went up at the end of the sentence, the way it always did when he was feeling unsure of himself.

There was no reply, but a few seconds later the gate slid smoothly open.

When Keeley and Ryan stepped out of the car, their host was waiting at the front door. A powerfully built man of forty or thereabouts, he was dressed in a white shirt and trousers of loose Byronic elegance. As Keeley walked towards him, she realized that his face didn't match up to his impressive physique. His eyes drooped at the corners and the skin around his cheeks was slack. The overall effect was that of a slab of Camembert left too long in the sun.

'Welcome,' he said pleasantly. 'I'm Jonny.' His eyes flickered over Keeley's body. 'I'm so glad you could come; Astrid's told me all about you.'

'Has she?' said Keeley. 'I didn't realize you two knew each other so well.'

'Ah yes, the lovely Astrid and I are intimately acquainted.'

Ryan handed over the bottle of Krug he'd pulled from the fridge before leaving his apartment. 'Here you go, mate.'

Jonny beamed. 'Thank you, that's most generous.' He pressed himself against the door and waved them into the house. 'Come in, won't you? Most of the others are here already.'

Keeley and Ryan found themselves in a curved

entrance lobby, decorated in minimalist black and white. The floor was plain polished parquet and towards the rear a spectacular wrought-iron staircase swept upwards in a giant spiral. Keeley stared around her in awe. 'This place is so cool,' she said. 'I've always wanted to see inside it.'

'I'll give you a guided tour later, if you like,' said Jonny, smiling wolfishly.

Keeley felt herself blush. 'That would be great,' she said, grabbing Ryan's hand. 'I'm sure you'd like to see the house too, *wouldn't you, darling*?'

They followed Jonny into a large living room, decorated like an ultra-chic ocean liner with maple veneered walls and large pieces of streamlined furniture. There were a dozen or so couples already there, some of whom shot interested glances in the newcomers' direction.

'Let's get you both a drink,' said Jonny, striding towards an elegant 1930s cocktail cabinet. 'We've got pretty much everything.' He smiled at Keeley. 'What'll it be?'

'Just a white wine, thanks.'

'Sancerre do you?'

'Lovely.'

'Ryan?'

'I'll have a whisky and soda, but I'm driving so you'd better make it a small one.'

Jonny gave him a quizzical look. 'Aren't you staying over? Most of the others are.'

'Oh no, we have to get back home tonight,' Keeley said quickly.

'Ah well, if you change your minds, the offer's there.'

As their host poured the drinks, Keeley surreptitiously

checked out the other party guests. All seemed to be in the twenty-five-to-forty-five age bracket and – somewhat to her surprise – many were strikingly attractive. Despite Ryan's concerns, she was relieved to discover that she *had* chosen her outfit appropriately. The other women were also dressed conservatively in summer dresses or stylish designer separates, while the men wore suit trousers with open-necked shirts, or chinos and polo tops. They could have been at any smart cocktail party in Kirkhulme – except, that is, for the palpable air of sexual electricity and the long, lingering looks that passed between relative strangers. Suddenly, Keeley spotted Astrid across the room. She was talking to a tall man with a leonine mane of blond hair. They were standing very close together and Astrid kept tossing her head flirtatiously.

Jonny handed Keeley a drink in an expensive-looking lead crystal wine glass. 'Why don't you go and say hello to Astrid?' he said, nodding towards the Swedish girl. 'I'll keep Ryan entertained.'

Keeley looked at her boyfriend, reluctant to leave him to his own devices so early in the evening.

'Off you go then,' the footballer said, taking a slow, deliberate sip of whisky.

'I'll only be a minute.'

Ryan shrugged. 'Take as long as you like; it doesn't bother me.'

After a moment's hesitation, Keeley turned and began walking across the room.

When Astrid spotted her friend and sometime client, she waved. Then she placed her hand provocatively on the blond man's chest and whispered something in his ear. He smiled and whispered something back before walking away to join another group of partygoers.

'Keeley, I'm so glad you made it,' cooed Astrid as she greeted her friend with a kiss.

'This place is amazing,' said Keeley. 'It's like being on the set of some glamorous thirties film noir.'

'Jonny's a dotcom millionaire,' said Astrid matter-of-factly. 'He likes to collect beautiful things.' She pointed to an impossibly chic brunette in a fuchsia shift, standing beside a large display cabinet, which groaned under the weight of Clarice Cliff. There were two men with her, both staring at her admiringly. 'That's Jonny's wife, Selina. She used to be a Givenchy model.'

'I'm not surprised; she's stunning.'

Astrid made a face. 'Hmm, but not exactly blessed in the brains department. Rumour has it she's got an IQ lower than the setting on my thermostat.'

Keeley giggled. 'You are awful, Astrid.'

'Still, I don't suppose it really matters tonight. It's not as if anyone's going to sit around discussing the meaning of life.' Astrid gave her friend a meaningful look. 'You might be interested to know that Selina swings both ways.'

'Does she now?' Keeley purred. Her gaze drifted back to the former model. She took in the elegant neck, the coltish legs, the high breasts, which were surprisingly full for such a slender woman. 'Nice . . .' she murmured.

Astrid leaned in closer. 'You should go for it. From what I've seen, she's happy to accommodate all-comers.'

Keeley sighed. 'It's a tempting thought, but I couldn't – not with Ryan here.'

'Doesn't he know you like to dabble?'

'You're joking, aren't you?'

'But Ryan's a broad-minded lad; I'm sure he wouldn't raise any objections ... especially if you let him watch.' Astrid arched an eyebrow. 'I daresay Ace wouldn't mind being part of the viewing gallery either.'

Keeley made a horrified face. 'Oh God, I don't like the sound of that. I don't think I'd ever be able to look Ace in the eye again.' Looking over her shoulder, she surveyed the room. 'Where is Ace, anyway?'

'Pressing some flesh, so to speak.' Astrid nodded towards a set of connecting doors that separated the main living room from a smaller room beyond. The doors were half closed and through the gap between them Keeley could see Ace talking to a statuesque female with a boyish crop. He was holding the woman's upper arms in a gentle, affectionate way and then, to Keeley's surprise, the shop manager leaned forward and tenderly kissed the woman's décolleté.

Unable to stop herself, Keeley let out a gasp. Astrid, by contrast, appeared utterly unfazed by her boyfriend's actions.

'The blond guy I was talking to earlier is that woman's husband,' she told Keeley. 'They've been swinging for years. Ace and I had some fun with them at the last party we went to.'

'Oh,' said Keeley. 'That's nice.' Suddenly feeling territorial, she looked around. Ryan was nowhere to be seen.

'What is it?' Astrid asked, sensing her friend's concern.

'It's Ryan; I can't see him.'

'Relax, sweetie, I expect Jonny's taken him upstairs.'

Keeley's anxiety levels went up another notch. 'Why would he do that?'

'To show him the pleasure rooms.'

'Pleasure rooms?'

'Jonny's created three gorgeous themed bedrooms where guests can have a little privacy. My personal favourite – for obvious reasons – is the torture room.'

Keeley gulped. 'Torture?'

'It's all very playful … silk blindfolds, fur-trimmed wrist restraints, ostrich feather ticklers. In other words, nothing that's going to cause any real injury.' Astrid smiled cruelly. 'More's the pity. Next door to the torture room is the rococo boudoir. It's got stunning chinoiserie wallpaper and a massive Chippendale four-poster, which sleeps three comfortably. There's an antique washstand in the corner of the room, and if you slide open the drawer you'll find a great collection of strap-ons.'

'Smashing,' said Keeley, who was beginning to feel faintly overwhelmed. 'And the third room?'

'The Barbarella. There's all this amazing futuristic furniture specially designed for having sex in, and con-cealed projectors that beam psychedelic shapes all over the occupants.

'No Orgasmatron?' Keeley quipped.

Astrid grinned. 'People don't usually need any help in that department.'

'It certainly sounds as if no expense has been spared.'

'Jonny's a sociable guy, and he's got plenty of time – not to mention money – on his hands.'

'How often does he throw these parties?'

'As often as the mood takes him,' Astrid replied. 'Which I have to say is pretty often.'

'How do people get to hear about them – does he advertise?'

Astrid looked at Keeley as if she were mad. 'God, no. Jonny's very particular; he doesn't want any old Tom, Dick or Harry beating down his door. It's all done through word of mouth. New people are only allowed to come if they've been personally recommended, the way I recommended you and Ryan.' She gave a little smile. 'Jonny was very impressed that I knew a Premiership footballer.'

'I do hope he hasn't been shooting his mouth off about it,' said Keeley. 'The papers would have a field day if they found out Ryan was into wife-swapping.'

Astrid winced. 'For God's sake, don't let anyone hear you using that expression; it's dreadfully passé. And you don't need to worry about Jonny, or anyone else for that matter. Everyone here is very discreet. They'd all have a lot to lose if their activities became public knowledge.' She pointed to a tanned man with a Ralph Lauren sweater looped casually round his shoulders. 'That guy's a high-court judge.' She sighed wistfully. 'He gives great anal.'

At this, Keeley almost choked on a mouthful of wine. 'You're so blasé about this wife-swapping – sorry, *swinging* lark.'

Astrid shrugged 'Why shouldn't I be?'

'It just seems weird, that's all.'

'In my opinion, it's the monogamists who are weird,' Astrid said loftily. 'When you consider that we're basically on this earth to procreate, having sex with multiple partners is the most natural thing in the world.'

'I suppose so,' said Keeley. 'I'm just having a little difficulty getting my head round it.'

'Don't worry, these parties are always a little daunting for first-timers.'

Keeley took a sip of wine. 'Can I ask you a question?'

'Sure, ask me anything you like.'

'Do you actually watch Ace having sex with other people?'

Astrid nodded enthusiastically. 'Yep – and *he* watches *me*; it's what's called *open swinging*. That's just our personal preference; it's not for everyone.'

'Don't you ever get jealous?'

'Of course, but swinging has definitely made our relationship stronger. When I see Ace with someone else, it just makes me want him even more.' Astrid wrinkled her nose. 'Does that make sense?'

'Kind of. I'm just not sure I want to see Ryan shagging another girl. Especially if she's got bigger tits than me.' Keeley looked down at her modest breasts. 'Which, let's face it, is just about everyone.'

Astrid laughed. 'You've got a great little body. Believe me, you'll be beating them off with a stick later on. And, listen, there's no law saying you have to watch Ryan on the job. You two can always go in separate rooms. That's what known as –'

'*Closed swinging?*'

'Hey,' Astrid said approvingly, 'you're catching on fast.'

Keeley's gaze turned to the ceiling. 'I wonder what

268

Ryan's doing up there. You don't think he's hooked up with someone already, do you?'

'No way, it's still early; people are just getting warmed up. This part of the evening's all about mingling and seeing who you might want to play with later. You'll see a bit of kissing and fondling, but nothing too hardcore. Speaking of which . . .' Astrid took Keeley's elbow. 'Come on, girlfriend, it's time we started working the room.'

It wasn't long before Keeley began to relax. All the people Astrid introduced her to seemed reassuringly normal, and when a guy called Pascal with a sexy French accent started flirting outrageously with her, she found herself responding. Barely ten minutes into their conversation, Pascal leaned in close, as if he wanted to whisper something. A moment later, Keeley felt the Frenchman's tongue wetly probing the inner recesses of her ear. Feeling pleasantly tipsy after a second glass of wine, she allowed him to continue, placing her hand on the back of his neck and drawing him closer. As she did, she noticed that Ryan and Jonny had re-entered the living room. Although she felt rather naughty, as if she'd been caught with her hand in the cookie jar, Keeley made no attempt to pull away from Pascal. Instead, she watched over his shoulder as the two men refilled their empty glasses at the cocktail cabinet. Afterwards, Jonny patted Ryan on the back before striding off towards another group of guests. For a few moments, the footballer stood there alone, one hand in his pocket, the other clutching his whisky glass. It wasn't long before he spotted his girlfriend, wrapped around a handsome stranger.

When Keeley made eye contact with Ryan she half expected him to storm over in a jealous rage, but instead he just smiled and raised his glass in a silent toast. Then he leaned against the wall, crossed one foot over the other and watched, quite calmly, as Pascal's hands began to explore Keeley's body. Realizing that Ryan was enjoying the show, Keeley smiled. Then she closed her eyes and let her head loll on Pascal's shoulder, as he continued to feel her up. Suddenly the stereo, which had been blasting Vivaldi all evening, fell silent. When Keeley opened her eyes she saw Jonny standing beside the fireplace with a remote control in his hand. Her fellow party-goers had abandoned their conversations and were looking at him expectantly.

'Okay, folks,' Jonny began in a cheery tone. 'I think it's time to play a little game, just to help break the ice.'

His suggestion met with a murmur of approval.

'How about . . .' Jonny looked around at his guests, 'sexy dice?'

'Ooh, yes!' squealed a fox in six-inch spike-heeled stilettos.

Johnny smiled. 'I'll get the dice,' he said, and walked towards a handsome walnut sideboard.

Without waiting for further instructions, the guests began congregating in the centre of the room.

'What's happening?' Keeley asked Pascal.

'You'll see,' he said, taking her hand and leading her towards the others, who had formed themselves into a loose circle.

As she took her place in the circle, Keeley noticed that Ryan was standing directly opposite her. She tried to catch his eye, but he seemed more interested in checking out the willowy brunette standing beside him. Immediately, Keeley turned to Pascal and gave him a pouting, sexy look. He responded by snaking an arm round her back and squeezing her left buttock.

When Jonny returned, the circle automatically parted, allowing him to step into the centre, before closing round him. He held two large wooden dice aloft, one white and one black. Both had words written on them instead of numbers, but Keeley couldn't make them out.

'Who wants to go first?' Jonny asked, as he began walking slowly round the circle.

A few people raised their hands in the air, but Jonny kept on walking until he came to Keeley. 'I think it's about time we initiated our newcomer,' he said in a mellifluous voice.

'Good idea!' someone else called out. Keeley looked around to see who had spoken. It was the blond man who had been talking to Astrid earlier.

Keeley shook her head. 'But I don't know how to play,' she said, suddenly feeling self-conscious.

'The rules are simple,' Jonny said. 'You'll pick it up in no time.'

'Honestly, I'd rather just watch.'

'Don't be nervous. Trust me, you're going to love it.'

Still Keeley hesitated. She looked towards Ryan, silently willing him to lend her some support.

The footballer looked at her blankly. 'Go on, Kee,' he said. 'Don't be a spoilsport.'

Keeley sighed. 'Oh, all right then.'

'Enjoy, *ma cherie*,' Pascal murmured as Keeley stepped into the centre of the circle.

'Before we begin, could someone pass me a couple of those cushions,' Jonny said, pointing to the sofa. 'We want our player to be comfortable, after all.'

The brunette who had caught Ryan's eye handed two of the oversized velvet cushions to Jonny.

'These should do the trick,' said Jonny, as he squatted down and arranged the cushions end-to-end on top of an expensive-looking rug. 'Okay, sweetheart,' he said, looking up at Keeley. 'Do you want to strip down to your undies?'

Keeley's mouth felt as dry as the Sahara. Generally speaking, she enjoyed the spotlight, but there was a big difference between being the centre of attention and stripping off in a room full of strangers before undergoing some sort of ritual that, she strongly suspected, included a hefty dollop of sexual deviancy.

'There's no need to be shy – we're all friends here,' said Johnny as he set the two dice on the floor. 'I'll even take some clothes off too if it makes you feel more comfortable.' Without waiting for a reply, he crossed his hands over his chest and pulled off his shirt. His chest was impressive, with well-developed pectorals and a six-pack that put even Ryan's to shame. After slipping off his loafers, he unzipped his flies and removed his trousers. 'There you go,' he said, standing with his hands on his hips, legs aggressively akimbo.

'I think I'll join you,' a woman said. Recognizing the voice, Keeley turned towards Astrid. The Swedish girl was hastily unbuttoning her blouse, while next to her a grinning Ace had bent down to unlace his shoes.

Within seconds, a number of other guests began to follow suit, shedding their clothes without a hint of bashfulness. Soon, everyone was in their underwear and the floor was covered in piles of designer clothing. Touched by their solidarity, Keeley began undoing her wrap dress, feeling a surge of confidence as she remembered that she was wearing her sexiest Agent Provocateur lingerie – a cream satin bra with French lace edging and matching knickers that tied at the sides with a silk bow. As she dropped her dress on the floor with a flourish, there was a ripple of applause.

'Bravo,' Jonny declared, grinning from ear to ear as she kicked off her slingbacks. 'That's the difficult bit over. Now all you have to do is lie down and enjoy yourself.'

Keeley did as she was told, half-sitting, half-reclining on the soft cushions. Jonny loomed over her, a dice in each hand. He turned them over and over in front of Keeley's eyes, so she could see that the words written on the white dice were all body parts, and the words written on the black dice were all actions.

'Okay,' said Jonny, stepping back into the circle. 'Who would you like to take the first turn at rolling the dice? If you don't know people's names, just point.'

Keeley looked around. Several of the men were smiling, willing her to choose them. She smiled back at them; it was nice to be lusted after. She studiously avoided looking at Ryan; instead, her gaze turned to Pascal. She looked him up and down, taking in his muscular legs and the snug-fitting Calvin Kleins that showed off a generous crotch bulge. 'I'd like *monsieur* over there,' she said.

The Frenchman smiled. '*Merci, madmoiselle*,' he said, taking the dice from Jonny's outstretched hand. He squatted down beside Keeley and tossed the dice on to the rug, crying, '*Fantastique!*' when he saw what he'd rolled.

'What have you got, Pascal?' someone called out.

'The white die says *massage* and the black die says *buttocks*.'

'Lucky boy,' said Jonny as he tapped his wristwatch. 'You've got five minutes, starting from . . . now.'

Pascal grinned at Keeley. 'Turn over, *ma cherie*, and I will show you exactly what a Frenchman can do with his hands.'

Keeley's heart was pounding in her chest as she rolled on to her stomach. She couldn't quite believe what was about to happen. Still, she comforted herself, at least she was lying face down so she wouldn't have to see the twenty pairs of eyes that were fixed on her body.

Pascal placed a hand in the small of her back. 'Are you ready?'

'Mmm,' Keeley mumbled into the cushion.

A moment later, she felt Pascal's strong hands cupping her butt cheeks. '*Verrry* nice,' he said as he began moving his palms in a circular motion, gently nudging her knickers northwards, so that more of her skin was exposed. After a few moments, he began using his fingers to knead her flesh. Keeley gave a little groan. Her bottom had always been her favourite erogenous zone and Pascal's confident manipulations brought back memories of her *tukta* sessions with Astrid. She lifted a head from the cushion. 'Harder, *monsieur*,' she commanded.

Pascal laughed softly. 'I like a woman who knows what she wants.'

As he worked on Keeley, some of the other guests moved in closer to get a better view, while others shouted encouragement from the sidelines.

'Her arse is all red,' Keeley heard one of them say in a hoarse voice. 'It looks beautiful.'

Sighing, she ground her pelvis into the cushion, not caring if anyone saw. Pascal had just started to administer a series of deliciously firm chopping strokes when she heard Jonny's voice. 'Sorry, guys, I can see how much you're enjoying yourselves, but I'm afraid time's up.'

'*Que c'est dommage*,' Pascal muttered as he rose to his feet. 'I was enjoying that.'

'Me too,' said Keeley.

'Don't worry, there's plenty more where that came from,' Jonny said. 'Which lucky guy's going to be next?'

Keeley rolled on to her side and rested her head on her hand. 'Do the rules say it has to be a guy?' she said, throwing a defiant look in Ryan's direction.

Jonny raised an eyebrow. 'Absolutely not.'

'In that case,' Keeley said, arching her back provocatively. 'I'd like Selina.'

'Good choice,' Jonny purred. He looked at his wife. 'Darling?'

Selina stepped into the circle, looking like a burlesque starlet in a black basque and matching ruffled panties. 'How perfectly delicious you look,' she remarked, sinking gracefully on to the rug.

'Thanks,' Keeley said. A long look passed between the two women. All at once, Selina reached out and began tracing the outline of Keeley's lips with a forefinger. 'You're very beautiful,' she said softly.

Impulsively, Keeley opened her lips and drew Selina's finger into her mouth.

Selina pretended to look shocked as Keeley sucked on her finger. 'You nasty girl; I haven't even thrown the dice yet.'

'Yeah, come on, Selina, throw the dice,' said Jonny, who was in a visible state of sexual arousal. 'Let Keeley see what you're really made of.'

Smiling, Selina removed her digit from Keeley's mouth and scooped up the dice. She shook them in her fist, blew on them for luck and tossed them on to the rug. 'Well, well, well,' she said when she saw the result. 'The white die says *lick*, and the black die says *nipple*.'

A susurrus of excitement spread round the circle like a Mexican wave. Keeley, too, was pleased with the result.

'I'm all yours,' she said, stretching out languidly on the cushions, her earlier inhibitions forgotten.

Selina needed no further encouragement. Assuming a kneeling position she raised one of her legs, so that she was straddling Keeley's body. Sensing that they were about to witness something very special, the partygoers crowded around them, so that instead of the elaborate ceiling rose, all Keeley could see when she looked up was a mass of faces. She gasped as Selina took the lace-trimmed demi-cups of her bra between forefinger and thumb and pulled them down so that both her breasts popped out. As she felt Selina's warm mouth engulf her left nipple, Keeley let out a little mew of pleasure. For the first time that evening, it occurred to her that actually, despite her reservations, she could get used to this swinging lark.

While Keeley was playing with her newfound friends, elsewhere in Kirkhulme, Marianne was about to embark on a sexual adventure of her own. For the past half an hour she'd been sitting outside All Hallows in her Audi, waiting for the church to empty. Friday evenings meant choir practice and, with a big society wedding scheduled for the following day, tonight's rehearsal seemed to be going on forever.

'Get a move on, can't you?' Marianne groaned, drumming her fingers on the steering wheel impatiently. It had been three days since her last assignation with Simon and she was – not to put too fine a point on it – gagging for it.

It was just after 10 p.m. when the church door finally opened and members of the choir began spilling out, chattering excitedly as they made their way to their cars and bicycles. Marianne watched from across the road as the car park emptied. As soon as the coast was clear, she exited the Audi and made her way towards the church, her head covered by a black lace mantilla to conceal her identity, just in case any stragglers remained.

Inside, the church lay quiet and still. Most of the lights had been turned off but beneath the vestry door a light still burned. Quickly, Marianne went to the door and knocked on it gently.

'Simon. Are you there? It's me – Marianne.'

A moment later the door flew open. Simon stood there, handsome as ever in his clerical shirt and dog collar. He smiled when he saw what Marianne was wearing. 'You look ravishing in that,' he said, running a hand over the mantilla. 'Whatever brings you here at this hour?'

'I wanted to see you,' Marianne replied, pulling of the mantilla and letting it float to the ground. 'I've missed you terribly.'

'And I've missed you too,' Simon murmured into her hair. 'More than you can imagine.'

Marianne caught a whiff of alcohol on his breath. 'Have you been drinking?' she asked him.

'Just a little snifter of Communion wine,' Simon said diffidently. 'I know I shouldn't, but it's been a long day.'

'Well, it's lucky I'm here to help you unwind,' said Marianne as she cupped the vicar's balls through his church-issue black polyester trousers.

'Isn't it just?' said Simon. 'Shall we go back to mine?'

'Honestly, darling, I don't think I can wait,' said Marianne, yanking down his flies before working a hand into his Y-fronts.

The vicar groaned in appreciation as she massaged him with her cool, quick fingers. 'You're very good at that,' he said. 'How did you learn that stuff?'

'Years of practice, darling,' Marianne replied, sinking to her knees.

Simon watched as she took his cock in her mouth, sighing as an ambrosial tingling spread through his groin. After less than a minute, he set a hand on her bobbing head. 'Just a minute.'

Marianne looked up at him. 'What is it?'

'Might I be permitted to make a little adjustment?'

Marianne shrugged. 'If you like.'

Bending down, Simon picked up Marianne's discarded lace mantilla and draped it over her hair and face. 'There we are,' he said. 'Now, my love, I'm all yours.'

Sixteen

Daniel Solomon was alone in his office. Lying on the desk in front of him was a large padded envelope that had just been delivered to the house by courier. For a few moments, he eyed the package nervously, wondering if the contents would live up to his expectations. Tomorrow was his nineteenth wedding anniversary and Daniel was determined to make it a day to remember, divorce or not. For the first time in five years, he'd gone to the trouble of choosing a gift for his wife himself. In the past, he'd had his secretary select some overpriced bauble – a hand-painted Limoges to sit uselessly on Amber's dressing table, or a crystal caviar bowl which, having been briefly admired, would quickly be relegated to the back of a kitchen cabinet. But this year was different. This year, Daniel wanted to show his wife just how much she meant to him. To this end, he'd gone to a lot of time and trouble to acquire a unique love token – and now he was about to discover if all his efforts had been worth it.

Picking up his paperknife, Daniel sliced the envelope open and drew out the well-wrapped item inside. He rubbed his hands together in anticipatory pleasure before parting the folds of tissue paper. 'Wow,' he said out loud as he stared at the gift. It was much more beautiful than he'd imagined, and the workmanship was absolutely top notch. He picked it up in both hands, smiling as he savoured its weight and texture. 'Happy anniversary, my sweet,' he said, safe in the knowledge that tomorrow would be a day his wife would never forget; not for as long as she lived.

For the past week, Amber had been staying at her widowed mother's house in the Peak District. She'd been hoping for a relaxing break, but instead she found herself facing a daily inquisition as Elsie, her mother, struggled to comprehend how her daughter had managed to 'destroy' her life by letting a 'prize catch' like Daniel get away. Amber had pointed out that it was Daniel, not *she*, who had sabotaged their marriage by having an affair – and that, in the circumstances, divorce was the only sensible option. But still her mother had railed against her, insisting that she could – indeed, *should* – have been more accommodating.

'Daniel has a very stressful job. It's only natural that he needs to let off steam every now and then,' Elsie had argued. 'You should've turned a blind eye and let him have his bit on the side. Your father was constantly unfaithful and I never let it bother *me*.'

This was news to Amber. 'Daddy had affairs?' she said incredulously.

'Your father was like a dog,' Elsie replied. 'He humped anything with a pulse.'

'And you just let him get on with it?'

'Of course I did. Otherwise I would've ended up like you – *single*.' She virtually spat the word, as if it tasted sour in her mouth.

'I can think of worse fates,' Amber retorted.

'Such as?'

'Goodness, all sorts of things ... cancer, penury, the death of a child.'

'How on earth would you know?' Elsie said, shooting her daughter a disdainful look. 'You've never *been* single.'

Although she was annoyed at her mother's lack of support, Amber couldn't help thinking she might have a point. She'd always known that life as a single woman was going to be tough, but only now was she beginning to realize just how tough. There were the practical concerns for one thing: with no husband to hand, who would bring in the wood for the fire on cold winter evenings, unscrew a stiff lid from a pot of jam, take responsibility for booking the Mercedes in for its annual service? And what of her social life? Girlie lunches were all well and good, but how on earth could she be expected to attend a glamorous evening function without an escort? She did have a fallback, it was true, in the form of Sebastian, an attractive gay man of her acquaintance. But everyone would know he was nothing more than a walker. Furthermore, his services didn't come cheap – the going rate being a designer suit and various other sundry expenses. Then there was the small matter of sex; this, unfortunately, fell well beyond Sebastian's capabilities.

After a difficult week with her mother, Amber was relieved when Stephen came to take her back to Kirkhulme on what was, she noted bitterly, her wedding anniversary. She was silent in the car as she reflected on the events of the past month, imagining how things might have been different. It was beginning to dawn on her that she might have been a little hasty in filing for divorce.

Perhaps if she'd done what her mother had suggested, and allowed Daniel a little room to manoeuvre, he would eventually have tired of Nancy and all this heartache could have been avoided. Still, she told herself firmly, it was too late for regrets. She'd made her bed and now she was going to have to lie in it.

As Stephen pulled up outside the Old Manor, Amber was pleased to see no sign of Nancy's VW Polo. With any luck, Daniel had taken the little slut away for the weekend. At least then Amber wouldn't have to listen to them copulating like a pair of alley cats. In recent weeks, Nancy had become increasingly vocal, forcing Amber to dig out the pair of pink furry earmuffs she'd last worn skiing in Val d'Isère. She was convinced the housekeeper was hamming it up with her shrieks and moans of delight, just to rub Amber's nose in it. For Daniel, she knew from personal experience, wasn't *that* good in bed.

'Can you bring the luggage up to my bedroom?' she asked Stephen as he held the passenger door open for her.

The driver grimaced apologetically. 'Sorry, Mrs Solomon, I'm not allowed.'

'What are you talking about?' Amber said impatiently. 'You always carry my bags in.'

'Not any more,' Stephen replied. 'It's what was agreed in your interim settlement. Mr Solomon's lawyer sent a copy to me a couple of days ago. From now on, I'm only permitted to drive you from A to B. Anything more than that and I'll be in breach of my contract.'

'Oh, for heaven's sake,' Amber cried, 'that's the most ridiculous thing I've ever heard.'

Stephen scratched the end of his nose. 'Your signature

was on the paperwork, so I assumed you'd agreed to the terms.'

Amber cast her mind back to the eight pages of densely typed legalese that Fiona Mortimer had faxed through to her at her mother's house. The document had contained dozens of tediously nit-picking clauses and conditions, so that by page four Amber had lost the will to live. Assuming her lawyer wouldn't have agreed to anything too outrageous, she'd simply signed her name on each page, as requested, and faxed it back.

'Surely those terms were just guidelines,' Amber told Stephen in a buttery tone. 'There's no need to take them literally.'

'I'm afraid I must, Mrs Solomon.'

Amber gave a disapproving sniff. 'In that case, why did you put my suitcase in the boot of the car when you picked me up from my mother's house?'

'I shouldn't really have done that,' Stephen admitted, rubbing an imaginary smear on the windscreen. 'But I didn't think it would matter, seeing as we were miles from home and Mr Solomon wasn't likely to see us. But now that we're back ...' He licked his lips nervously. 'I don't mean to be difficult, but it is your husband who pays my wages, after all.'

'Fine,' Amber snapped. 'Have it your way. I'll just give myself a hernia then, shall I?' She jabbed an impatient finger at the car. 'At least open the bloody boot, can't you?'

A few moments later, Amber was dragging her Gucci suitcase towards the front door, wincing as the soft leather underside scraped against the gravel. She never travelled light and the suitcase contained enough clothes to dress a concert party. After unlocking the front door, Amber began hauling the bag into the house, sighing as it caught on the raised stone sill that separated the porch from the entrance hall. '*Waaarghhh!*' she cried like a weightlifter, tugging it as hard as she could with both hands. The next moment she found herself stumbling backwards, propelled by the weight of the suitcase. She landed in a heap on the floor, with the bag resting on her shins.

'Damn you, Daniel Solomon!' Amber screeched as she kicked the suitcase away and staggered to her feet. Rubbing her sore coccyx, she hobbled over to the Louis XV chair and threw down her handbag. It was then that she noticed the candy-striped gift box sitting on top of the radiator cover. It was ostentatiously tied with a huge gold bow and next to it was an envelope addressed to her in Daniel's handwriting. Frowning, she tore open the envelope. To her amazement, it contained an anniversary card. The picture on the front showed two polar bears, nose to nose on an ice floe. Amber was nonplussed. Daniel never forgot their anniversary, but she hadn't for one moment expected him to acknowledge it this year. Inside the card was a message.

To my darling wife. Thank you for 19 unforgettable years of marriage. Please accept this gift as a small token of my appreciation. Yours, Daniel x

Amber's heart gave a little leap. Despite everything, Daniel still had feelings for her. Perhaps it wasn't too late after all; perhaps he was also having second thoughts about the divorce and this was his way of reaching out to her – the first tentative step towards their reunion. She laid the card down and turned her attention to the gift box. With trembling fingers she untied the gold bow and eased off the lid, gasping in delight when she saw what lay inside: a dainty, chocolate fur stole, nestling in a swirl of purple silk. Greedily, Amber picked it up and lay it along the length of her forearm. It was exquisite and beautifully made, just the sort of thing she might have chosen herself. She couldn't imagine where Daniel had found it, for in today's politically correct world such things were hard to come by. As she held it up to the sunlight that was streaming in through the window, Amber wondered if it might be vintage. Probably not, she told herself; the condition was mint and it didn't have the slightly musty smell of a second-hand piece.

Draping the fur round her neck, Amber went to the mirror. The stole looked wonderful, a true one-off; no one else in Kirkhulme would have anything like it. Amber smiled triumphantly at her reflection. There was no doubt in her mind that this was Daniel's way of apologizing for his cruel behaviour. Why else would he have gone to so much trouble and expense? She wondered if he had any other anniversary surprises in store. A bottle of Dom Perignon chilling in the fridge? A reservation at their favourite Italian restaurant?

With a sigh of pleasure, she pressed the stole to her face and closed her eyes. The fur felt soft against her cheek . . . and also strangely familiar. Suddenly, Amber's body froze in a rictus of horror. Her eyes snapped open. 'No,' she gasped in a terrified whisper. 'He wouldn't . . .' She yanked the stole from her neck and studied it again. A sick realization was beginning to dawn. With a ragged sob, she went tearing across the hall, bursting through the door of the drawing room and running full pelt to the orangery. It was then that her worst fears were confirmed: Couscous had disappeared. In the place where his cage once stood was a pair of cane armchairs and a matching sofa that she'd never seen before. It was, quite simply, as if the little capuchin had never existed. Distraught, Amber fell to her knees and began dry retching. She never ate breakfast – it was one of the ways she managed to stay so thin – but, if she had, she would certainly have regurgitated it on the orangery's marble floor.

Upstairs, Calum was enjoying a post-masturbatory roll-up in his bedroom when all at once he became aware of a distant, high-pitched wailing. At first, he didn't think anything of it. Since his parents announced they were getting divorced, the Old Manor had regularly reverberated with the sound of raw emotion. It seemed to Calum that whenever Amber and Daniel's paths crossed, a slanging match ensued as each accused the other of perpetrating some fresh outrage. Inevitably, the arguments would be punctuated with assorted screams, bellows, slammed doors and even, on occasion, deliberately smashed ceramics. Usually, the skirmishes were short-lived and afterwards his parents would scuttle off to their respective lairs – Daniel to his study, Amber to the drawing room – to lick their wounds. But this time, the wailing went on and on until finally Calum decided to investigate.

He found Amber in the orangery. She was lying on the floor in a foetal position, clutching a damp scrap of fur to her breast and keening like a vixen who'd lost her cub. Feeling awkward, he squatted down beside her and laid his hand on her shoulder. 'Mum, are you all right?' he asked her tenderly.

Amber turned her mascara-streaked face to her son. 'Do you think I'd be lying on the floor in a nine-hundred-pound Pucci dress if I was all right?' she growled, as she raised herself into a sitting position.

'Um, er, I guess not,' said Calum, who knew that only one person could be responsible for his mother's anguished state. 'What's Dad done now then?'

'What's he done? What's he *done*?' Amber shrieked. 'He's only gone and ripped my heart out, that's all.'

Calum frowned. 'Meaning?'

'Meaning that he's a fucking murderer.'

Knowing his mother's propensity for exaggeration, Calum sniggered. 'Yeah, right.'

Amber grabbed Calum's T-shirt and pulled him towards her. 'This isn't a laughing matter, sunshine. Why don't you look around the room and tell me what's different?'

The teenager did as he was told. 'The monkey cage . . . it's gone,' he said.

'And do you know why?'

Calum shook his head.

'Because your sick bastard of a father has killed Couscous, that's why.' Amber gave a loud sniff. 'It was his anniversary present to me.'

Calum looked at his mother disbelievingly. 'Dad

wouldn't do that. This is probably just his idea of a joke.'

Amber's huge lips quivered. 'Is *this* a joke?' she said, holding up the tear-sodden stole.

Calum took it from her. 'What is it?'

'It's Couscous,' Amber said in a tremulous voice. 'Or rather what's left of him.'

'Jesus,' said Calum, dropping the stole on the floor as if it had burned his hands. 'Are you sure about that?'

'Of course I'm sure. I raised that monkey from a baby; I'd recognize his coat anywhere.' Amber let out a giant sob. 'What was I thinking of . . . going to my mother's and leaving Couscous alone with that evil man.'

A sudden thought occurred to Calum. 'Hang on, didn't you arrange for those pet-sitting people to come in and feed Couscous, like you normally do?'

'Yes, and I left them strict instructions to call me if there were any problems whatsoever. I even gave them a set of keys, so they could let themselves in when no one was home. I suppose your father must've called them and told them we wouldn't be requiring their services after all.' Amber pushed some stray strands of hair out of her face. 'He was always jealous of my relationship with Couscous; I bet he enjoyed watching him die.'

Calum gave a little shudder. 'Do you think Dad killed him with his bare hands?'

'I wouldn't put it past him. I just hope poor Couscous didn't suffer too much.' Amber gave her a son a hard look. 'Obviously, I'm not holding *you* responsible for any of this . . .' she began

'Cheers, Mum,' Calum muttered.

'But didn't you notice Couscous had gone? Dismantling that cage must've involved a fair amount of disruption. It seems strange that you didn't see or hear anything.'

'I've hardly been here for the past week,' Calum said. 'I've been staying at Tony's; he's got a music studio in his shed.'

'Tony? You've never mentioned *him* before.'

'He's our new lead singer; the band are trying to get a demo together.' Calum touched the back of Amber's hand. 'I'm really sorry about Couscous, Mum. If I'd known what Dad was up to, I would've stopped him.'

'I know you would, darling,' Amber said, attempting a smile. 'Where is your father anyway?'

'Playing squash at St Benedict's. He's meeting a business contact for lunch afterwards, so he won't be back for ages.'

'Good,' said Amber as she wiped her fist across her snotty nose.

She stood up, hungry for revenge. For Daniel to vent his frustration on her was one thing, but to take it out on a defenceless animal was nothing short of barbaric. Her husband had to be punished – and Amber knew just where to hit him where it hurt. With Calum in her wake, she stalked out of the drawing room and down the corridor that led to Daniel's study but, to her surprise, when she turned the door handle it refused to budge. 'Since when has your father taken to locking this door?' she asked.

Calum shrugged. 'Dunno.'

'Where does he keep the key?'

Another shrug.

Amber thought for a moment. Then she turned round and marched back to the entrance hall.

'What are you doing?' asked Calum, watching his mother drag the Louis XV chair towards the stone fireplace.

'Using my initiative,' she replied as she clambered on to the chair and reached towards the pair of medieval poleaxes that formed a cross on the wall. Daniel had bought them at a specialist weaponry auction soon after they bought the Old Manor. Amber was horrified when she saw the scary-looking things, but by the time Daniel had cleaned them up and mounted them above the fireplace, she had to admit they looked pretty impressive.

'Hey, be careful,' said Calum, holding the back of the chair as Amber yanked the axe free. He knew he should try to talk his mother out of whatever it was she intended to do but, like a lot of teenagers, he enjoyed mindless violence. What's more, he was keen to see just how far Amber was prepared to go in her bid to avenge Couscous's death.

Together, they walked back to the study. After telling her son to stand well back, Amber raised the axe above her head and brought it down on the door. Its steel head made light work of the soft, 400-year-old oak, cleaving the door right down the middle.

'Go, Mum!' Calum cried, leaping up and down excitedly.

Amber propped the axe against the wall and dusted off her hands. 'Well,' she said proudly. 'That was easy.' She pointed to the shattered wood. 'Finish that off, will you?'

Pleased to be of use, just for once, Calum leapt into action, aiming a series of vicious kung-fu kicks at the door until finally it caved in. 'After you,' he said, with a small bow.

Inside Daniel's study, everything was in meticulous order. On the desk, the spines of his auction catalogues were precisely lined up. Beside them, a row of freshly sharpened pencils lay in the shadow of the anglepoise, which was twisted to its usual ninety degrees. Out of habit, Amber ran her fingertips along the top of the nearest exhibit case. They came away clean, indicating that either Nancy had been pressed into service, or Daniel had broken the habit of a lifetime by picking up a duster. Realizing that a new exhibit case had been added to the collection, Amber went over for a closer look. Inside lay a necklace composed of azure beads, interwoven with tiny clay figurines. The identification card beneath it bore the words: *faience necklace, 18th Dynasty, 1470 BC.*

'That must've cost your father a pretty penny,' Amber remarked, depressing a small catch at the back of the exhibit case and carelessly flipping open the lid. 'How upset he's going to be when I trash it.'

Calum, standing in the doorway, gave a sharp intake of breath, but he said nothing.

Reaching into the exhibit case, Amber lifted the necklace from its custom-made red satin cushion. 'I'm going to enjoy this,' she said in a cold, hard voice. She held the jewellery aloft and, without a moment's hesitation, yanked her hands in opposite directions. The 3,000-year-old necklace fell apart easily, sending dozens of bright blue beads bouncing across the room. Some of the clay figures shattered the moment they hit the floor-boards. Others, miraculously, survived the fall – but their respite was short-lived. With a manic grin, Amber raised her foot and began systematically grinding each one to dust beneath the heel of her Miu Miu Mary Janes.

Calum let out a nervous high-pitched laugh. 'Dad's going to go ballistic,' he said.

'He is, isn't he,' Amber agreed, moving to the next exhibit case, which contained a reddish pottery vase, made from Nile silt and dating from the reign of Rameses II, according to the accompanying card. Seconds later, the floor was covered in shards of ancient earthenware. 'Oops, clumsy me,' Amber trilled, putting her hands to her cheeks in the manner of a pantomime dame.

With her son looking on in appalled fascination, Amber's rampage continued. She moved from case to case like an automaton, systematically annihilating Daniel's precious collection without an ounce of equivocation or remorse. As Calum watched her dash a rare pre-dynastic drinking vessel in the hearth like a guest at a Greek wedding, he couldn't help wondering where his parents' bitter and bloody battle was going to end.

She saved the statue of Nefertiti for last. It was Daniel's favourite piece and had been in his collection for more than ten years. Amber could still remember the precise day the statue had entered their lives. It was a cold January afternoon and she was sitting in front of the fire with a copy of *Tatler* when Daniel came waltzing, quite literally, into the morning room with his latest auction prize.

'I can hardly believe she's mine,' he said to Amber as

he twirled around the room with Nefertiti in his out-stretched arms. 'Isn't she the most beautiful thing you've ever seen?'

'I'll take your word for it, darling,' Amber replied, smiling at her husband indulgently. 'You're the connoisseur, not me.'

All at once, Daniel grew serious. 'Actually, I lied,' he said, stopping his dervish dancing and setting the sculpture down on the mantelpiece.

'Oh?'

Daniel went over to his wife and knelt at her feet. '*You're* the most beautiful thing I've ever seen,' he said, taking both her hands in his. 'And I mean that with all my heart.'

Of course, this was long before Amber embarked on her obsessive round of cosmetic surgery. Back then, her eyes were a normal shape, her lips formed a gentle cupid's bow, her nose was strong and proud. She'd never even entertained the notion of submitting to the surgeon's knife. Why would she when Daniel was hopelessly in love with her?

Leaning forward, she kissed her husband on the mouth. 'You do say the nicest things.'

They'd hugged each other and then Daniel had taken her upstairs to bed. The ancient queen had been for-gotten, albeit temporarily. Afterwards, as they lay in bed, limbs entwined around each other, Daniel had stroked her hair.

'I don't know what I'd do without you, Amber,' he said. 'I'd die if you ever left me.'

Remembering those words now, Amber felt a fresh

rush of grief – not just for the death of Couscous, but for the loss of the husband who'd once adored her. Blinking hard, she opened the final exhibit case and lifted out the fifteen-inch limestone figure. As she stared at the features that had shaped her own, she hesitated. It did seem an awful shame to destroy something so beautiful. Still, if a job was worth doing, it was worth doing well, as her father had often told her.

'This one's for you, Couscous,' said Amber, as she raised her hands above her head and flung the statue to the floor with as much force as she could muster.

Calum giggled as Nefertiti's freshly amputated head came rolling towards him.

'Kick it,' Amber commanded her son. 'Kick the bitch's head as hard as you can.'

'You're the boss,' said Calum. He swung his leg back and directed a hefty kick at the head.

'Bravo,' cried Amber when it smashed against the skirting board and shattered into half a dozen pieces.

Calum walked into the centre of the room, his trainers crunching over hundreds of thousands of pounds worth of ruined artefacts.

'D'you feel better now, Mum?' he said.

Amber nodded. 'Much better, thanks.' She lifted a hand and cupped the side of her son's face. 'You didn't see or hear anything, okay? I don't want you getting into trouble with your father over this.'

'Sure,' Calum said. 'But I want you to know that I don't blame you for this. Killing Couscous was a shitty thing to do.' He added quickly, 'Not that I'm taking sides, mind.'

'Thank you, Calum. I appreciate your support.' Amber

began walking towards the place where the door used to be. 'There's something I've got to do. Will you be a love and stick that poleaxe back on the wall? Then you'd better make yourself scarce. It's probably best if you're not here when your father gets back.'

'Hey, Mum.'

Amber looked over her shoulder. 'What is it?'

'You do know Dad's going to get you back for this, don't you?'

Amber sighed. 'Your father's murdered my best friend. How much worse can it get?'

The violence of Amber's emotions had left her feeling drained. She longed for a cup of soothing camomile tea and a lie down, but first she had some unfinished business in the orangery. On the floor, the fur stole still lay in a bedraggled mound. Amber picked it up and went to a Provençal-style armoire, where she kept a small selection of hand tools for tending houseplants. Having selected a potting trowel, she unlocked the glazed door and went out into the garden. Usually, she avoided being outdoors when the sun was high in the sky, obsessed as she was with premature ageing. But, she told herself, there were times when one had to set one's own selfish needs aside, and this was one of them.

After some little deliberation, Amber made her way towards a flowerbed, where her favourite honeysuckle was in full bloom, filling the air with its sweet scent. She'd had it imported from Holland the year they moved into the Old Manor, and each year its flowers had grown larger and more abundant. Kneeling down beside it, she set the fur stole aside and began digging a hole in the loose earth. As she worked, she reflected on the havoc she'd wrought in Daniel's study. She didn't feel a shred of guilt; her husband had got exactly what he deserved. In fact, he should count his lucky blessings that only a fraction of his treasures had been on display, or she would quite happily have destroyed the entire collection.

Satisfied that the hole was deep enough, Amber picked up the stole. 'Goodbye, Couscous,' she whispered as she lowered it gently into the ground, before covering it with earth and levelling the ground flat. Afterwards, she closed her eyes and said a silent prayer, remembering all the good times she and Couscous had had together. She knew he was only a monkey, and there were certainly those among her friends who thought she was crazy for lavishing so much time and attention on a mere pet. But the little capuchin had brought a great deal of pleasure into her life, and he'd always been there for her when she'd needed him – which was more than she could say for most humans.

Aware that her left cheek was starting to burn in the sun's searing heat, Amber rose to her feet and brushed the earth from her knees. 'I'll never forgive you for this, Daniel,' she said, brushing a tear from the corner of her eye. 'Never.'

Seventeen

Sam Bentley stared in the bathroom mirror and was pleased with what he saw. 'Looking good, old son,' he said, running a hand through his thick hair. 'Looking good.' Sam was thirty-seven, but on a good day he could easily pass for thirty, thanks to a strict regime of facials, gym workouts and spray tanning. The only thing that gave the game away was the sprinkling of grey around his temples. He'd thought about dyeing his hair and then decided against it. The grey showed his maturity and, for lots of women, maturity signalled skill in bed. That was certainly true in Sam's case. He was a perfectionist, who strove to excel at everything he did, be it golf, public speaking or down 'n' dirty fucking. It wasn't that he was unselfish; far from it. To Sam, it was simply a matter of pride that the woman had a good time in bed; it didn't matter if she was his wife or someone he'd just picked up in a bar.

The golfer turned his face to the right, checking his profile. Although he'd shaved less than eight hours ago, his jaw was already peppered with incipient stubble, giving him a rugged, macho look. He picked up a bottle of Ralph Lauren cologne and sprayed it into the air above his head, turning his face upwards as the mist descended; that way, its effect would be more subtle. Sam might be a ladykiller *par excellence*, but he didn't want to reek of aftershave like some oily Casanova.

As he returned the cologne to the bathroom cabinet, he heard the sound of footsteps, followed by a loud thump on the door. 'Sam?' came his wife's voice. 'How much longer are you going to be in there?'

'A few minutes,' Sam replied. 'Why?'

'I need to bath the kids.'

Sam squirted a generous measure of hand cream into his palm. 'There are three baths in this house,' he said, working the cream into his cuticles. 'Can't you use one of the others?'

'But Carnie likes *that* bath,' Laura said impatiently.

Sam glanced at his watch: seven fifteen; time he was leaving anyway.

'You're a bit late with the girls tonight, aren't you?' he said as he opened the door. 'Birdie's usually in bed by now.'

'Yeah, well, I've had a ton of cleaning up to do,' said Laura, pushing past him. 'I'm starting to feel like flaming Cinderella these days.'

'And whose fault's that?'

Laura reached over Sam's shoulder and snatched a jumbo-sized bottle of bubble bath from the cabinet. 'I know I made a mistake letting Mrs Potter go; there's no need to rub it in.'

'The food hamper didn't work then?'

Laura sighed. 'Evidently not. It was delivered two days ago, together with my grovelling letter of apology, but I haven't heard a word from Mrs P.'

'That was a waste of a hundred quid.'

Laura cleared her throat. '*Two* hundred, actually. I went for the luxury champagne hamper in the end.'

'Great,' said Sam. 'I guess we'd better start looking for another cleaner.'

'That's easier said than done. Practically every family in the village has got one; there simply aren't enough to go round.'

'Can't we ask Marta to muck in, just in the short-term?'

Laura frowned. 'Oh no, we don't want to do that; it's not in her job description.'

'What are you talking about? Plenty of au pairs do cleaning.'

'No, Sam, we'll end up driving her away,' Laura said firmly. 'Oh, and that reminds me. What time will you be back tomorrow? Only it's Marta's day off and I need you to look after the girls while I take Tiger to the doctor's.'

A look of concern flitted across Sam's handsome face. 'What's wrong with him?'

'I want to get him referred to a sleep clinic.'

'Why?'

Laura sighed in irritation. 'Why do you think?'

'So what if the kid doesn't sleep through the night? It isn't such a big deal, is it?'

Laura slammed the bubble bath down on the side of the bath. 'It may not be a big deal to *you*, but you're not the one who's up half the night seeing to him.'

'Look, sweetheart,' said Sam. 'I'd love to help more with the night-time feeds, you know I would. But I'm a professional sportsman; I need my beauty sleep or I can't function properly.'

'You and me both,' Laura said under her breath. She knew she was fighting a losing battle. Sam had very traditional views: he was the breadwinner; she was the homemaker. That was the way it had been their entire marriage. She knelt down beside the bath and turned on the taps. 'So, anyway, the doctor's appointment's at five. Can you make sure you're back by then?'

'Yeah, course I will.'

Laura spoke over her shoulder: 'What's the name of the hotel you're staying in, just in case I need to contact you?'

'Erm, I can't remember off-hand; Phil did all the bookings. You'll be able to get me on my mobile, though.' To switch the conversation away from the subject of where he was going to be spending the night, Sam went over to Laura and ran an affectionate hand over her voluptuous rump. 'It's a pity Phil wanted it to be a boys-only thing, otherwise we could've dumped the kids at your mother's and made a weekend of it.'

'Another time, perhaps,' said Laura, smiling wistfully at the thought of a child-free weekend. 'Don't forget to wish Phil a happy birthday from me, will you?'

'I won't,' said Sam, planting a kiss on his wife's cheek. 'I guess I'd better get going; I'm supposed to be meeting the guys at the station in half an hour.'

'Have fun,' Laura called out as Sam disappeared through the door. She wouldn't have been quite so generous-spirited if she'd known he wasn't really going to be spending the night in a swanky hotel on the moors in advance of a day's clay-pigeon shooting, to celebrate his golfing buddy's fortieth birthday. Instead, her husband had planned a night of hot sex with one of America's finest lady golfers.

Sam had been having a full-blown affair with Taylor Spurr for the past three weeks. He was used to women with healthy sexual appetites, but Taylor was something else. The nineteen-year-old was up for it any time, any place, anywhere. A couple of days earlier, they'd both been putting in some practice on the fairway at St Benedict's – the golf course being one of the few places they could spend time together in public without arousing suspicion. Dusk was approaching and the course was practically deserted but, even so, Sam was shocked when Taylor suggested they sneak into the copse that guarded the four-teenth green for a quick knee-trembler. He demurred at first, but the American girl could be very persuasive, and when she bent down on the pretext of picking up a golf ball to reveal she wasn't wearing any underwear, Sam was powerless to resist.

Their first date had been a good indication of things to come. As promised, Sam had hired a private room at St Benedict's for an intimate dinner à deux. The cost of staging such an event was considerable, for nothing at St Benedict's came cheap. Sam had done it partly to show off, though there was an ulterior motive for his largesse. Neither golfer wanted their rendezvous to become public knowledge, and the waiting staff who serviced the private rooms were renowned for their discretion. Admittedly, there had been a slight slip in standards the previous summer when one of the waitresses – a part-timer, work-ing to fund her university education – claimed she'd been impregnated by Sam during a debauched stag night. Her revelation, which had been made at the club's annual gala dinner in front of dozens of appalled guests, had caused a good deal of concern. All kinds of liaisons were conducted in the private rooms – not just sexual shenanigans, but drug-taking, dodgy business deals and illegal gambling too. Members had always assumed their clandestine activities would remain precisely that, which was why they were more than happy to pay the club's exorbitant fees. In the wake of the pregnancy scandal, however, bookings for the private rooms nosedived, and several well-connected and exceedingly wealthy individuals threatened to withdraw their memberships. Desperate to restore St Benedict's reputation, the management tightened up employment procedure, so that all waiting staff were now required to sign confidentiality contracts. It did the trick, and soon the private rooms were bustling with life once again.

Taylor had arrived for their soiree dressed to kill in a black halter dress and a sophisticated up-do that made her look at least five years older than she actually was – which, in Sam's opinion, was a bit of a shame. As they talked and flirted across the table, an exceedingly deferent waiter served them honey-roast duck and a £300 bottle of Château Lafite Rothschild. Before Taylor's arrival, Sam had issued the waiter with strict instructions to keep his companion's wine glass topped up at all times, but in the event the American girl required minimal lubrication.

After dessert, without a hint of self-consciousness, Taylor produced the bag of cocaine she'd bought in the club shop and begun expertly chopping it on one of the glass place mats.

'Dinner was lovely,' she said, after they'd both snorted a fat line through a rolled-up fifty. 'But we both know what we're here for, so let's cut to the chase, shall we?'

And with that, the little minx was all over Sam, straddling him where he sat and grinding her pelvis hard against him like she wanted it bad. Sam had her dress off in an instant, and was thrilled to discover she looked even better naked, with her all-over tan and her gently rounded butt. Her breasts were a bit on the small side, but very firm and deliciously tip-tilted.

They'd gone at it like a pair of wild animals first time round, right there on the reproduction Regency chair, and it was all over pretty quickly.

'Jeez, I needed that,' Taylor said as she eased herself off Sam's lap and into a standing position.

'Me too,' said Sam, who hadn't had sex for several months, not since before Tiger was born. As the golfer registered this fact, his thoughts turned fleetingly to Laura. He loved his wife and it had never crossed his mind to leave her, but one woman would never be enough for him. According to Sam's twisted logic, he wasn't being unfaithful; he was simply satisfying a perfectly natural physiological urge. In any case, he told himself, Laura was tired of him pestering her for sex and would prob-ably be relieved to know he was getting it elsewhere. He pulled Taylor's slender hips towards him and kissed her belly button. Her skin was soft and smelled like rainfall.

'How about a digestif and another line of coke before

we go again?' he said, as he buried his face in the V between her legs.

And now here he was, dozens of shags later, driving towards Taylor's house, which lay on the other side of the village. Taylor was keen to keep their relationship a secret from her mother, so the rented cottage they shared had previously been out of bounds. But, with Kristina out of town for a couple of days, visiting a relative in London, the ban had been temporarily lifted. Tonight, Sam would spend an entire night with Taylor for the very first time, and it was an opportunity he intended to take full advantage of.

Riverside Cottage was a pretty, chocolate-box affair, covered in rambling roses and wisteria. Towering hollyhocks filled the well-maintained flowerbeds and the front lawn was a licentious moist green, in defiance of the unforgiving summer sun. Sam parked his 4×4 with its distinctive personalized number plates behind a box hedge, so it couldn't be seen from the road. Afterwards, he went round to the boot and removed a huge bouquet of flowers that he'd been keeping in a bucket of water in the garage all day, away from Laura's prying eyes. He carried them to the house and rapped on the front door with the brass knocker that was shaped like a pineapple. Then, on impulse, he hid his face behind the flowers, so that only his torso and lower body were visible. Sam waited until he heard the door open, then he took a step forward.

'For *modom*,' he said, putting on the fake posh accent that always made Taylor laugh. 'With the compliments of Lord Bentley-Boothe-Crumpett of Kirkhulme.'

Immediately, the flowers were snatched from his grasp: 'Gee, thanks, Sam, I didn't know you cared,' said a deeply sarcastic voice.

Sam stared at the speaker in horror. 'Kristina,' he said, forcing a smile. 'This is an unexpected pleasure.'

The caddie stuck her nose in a sprig of freesia and inhaled deeply. 'Do you mean to say these beautiful flowers ain't for me?'

Sam swallowed hard. 'Actually they're for your daughter,' he said, wondering where Taylor was and why she hadn't phoned to warn him her mother had returned home a day earlier than expected.

'And why on earth would you be bringing my daughter flowers?' Kristina said, eyebrows raised.

'I ran into her on the golf course earlier and she gave me some great tips for improving my putting technique,' Sam lied. 'I just popped by to say thank you.'

Kristina threw back her head and laughed. 'Oh, Sam, is that the best you can do, sugar?'

Sam scowled. He didn't like being laughed at. 'I don't know what you mean,' he said.

'Oh, I think you do.' Smiling, Kristina stepped back from the door. 'Won't you come in? Taylor's waitin' on you. The little darlin's spent the whole day slavin' over a hot stove — but I have to warn you her cookin' ain't half as good as her golf.'

Feeling very confused, Sam stepped into the cottage.

'Taylor, come and look at these lovely flowers Sam brought you,' Kristina called out as she led the golfer into a cosy living room with a beamed ceiling and lots of overstuffed furniture.

Seconds later, Taylor appeared. She was wearing a blue-and-white striped apron and her cheeks were red from the heat of the kitchen.

'Hey, Sam,' she said.

Sam smiled nervously. 'Hi,' he said, not knowing whether or not it would be appropriate to kiss her on the cheek.

Taylor nodded towards the bouquet in her mother's arms. 'Thanks for the flowers – they're gorgeous. Mom, would you mind putting them in some water for me?'

'Sure,' said Kristina. She looked at Sam. 'Can I fix you a drink? How about a glass of my homemade fruit punch? It's an old Texan recipe – been handed down through four generations of my family.'

Sam would've preferred a cold beer, but he didn't want to seem impolite. 'Lovely,' he said, trying to sound as if he meant it.

The minute Kristina was gone, Sam grabbed Taylor's hand and pulled her towards him. 'What the fuck's going on?' he hissed in her ear. 'Why didn't you tell me she was back early?'

'Relax,' said Taylor, smiling lazily. 'I've told Mom everything.'

Sam stared at her open-mouthed. 'She knows we're sleeping together?'

'Yep.'

'Are you out of your mind?'

'I had no choice. Mom turned up out of the blue a couple of hours ago. Apparently, she had some sort of falling out with her cousin, so she decided to come home early. She walked into the kitchen to find me up to my elbows in guacamole and every dish in the kitchen dirty. It was obvious I was expecting company.'

'Yeah, but you didn't have to tell her you were expecting *me*. Couldn't you have lied?'

'I tried to. I said I'd invited my coach to dinner, but Mom didn't buy it; she knows I wouldn't go to all that trouble just for him. And then I thought to myself: fuck it, I'm a grown woman; I'm going to tell her the truth and, if she doesn't like it, tough.'

'I bet she was thrilled,' Sam said sarcastically. 'Her precious daughter going out with a much older, married bloke – especially one she'd earmarked for herself.'

'Actually, once she'd gotten over the initial shock she was totally cool about it.'

'But, Taylor, I'm *married*. Surely she can't be cool with that.'

Taylor rolled her eyes. Sam got the impression she was keen to change the subject. 'I guess she understands this is just a bit of fun for both of us. I mean, you've got your family and I'm going back to the States next month. It's not as if we're about to go falling in love and running off into the sunset together.'

Sam covered his face with his hands. 'You know, if this gets out, we'll both be in the shit. My marriage will be history and you'll be labelled a home-wrecker.'

Taylor reached out and gently pulled his hands away. 'It won't get out. Mom's not going to breathe a word, trust me. You can ask her yourself if you like; she's going to have dinner with us.'

Sam groaned. 'Look, Taylor, I really think I should leave. This whole thing feels seriously weird.'

'But your wife isn't expecting you back till morning.'

'I'll drive into Delchester and stay in a hotel. In fact ...' Sam's face lit up. 'Why don't you come with me?'

Taylor pouted sexily. 'But I've spent the whole day cooking.' She pressed her nubile body against his. 'Mom will be disappointed too. She really wants to get to know you.'

Sam hesitated. He'd always found it difficult to resist a beautiful woman.

'Pretty please?'

Sam laughed. 'All right then. I'll stay for dinner, but I'm not spending the night.'

Taylor's face fell. 'Awww ... why not?'

'It wouldn't be appropriate. In any case, I don't think I'd be able to ... you know, *perform*, with your mum in the next room.' Hearing a sound, he glanced towards the door. Kristina was hovering on the threshold with a tray of drinks. Sam wondered how long she'd been there. Feeling uncomfortable with Taylor's arms wrapped round his waist, he stepped away from her.

'It's okay, Sam, you don't have to stand on ceremony,' said Kristina as she walked into the room and set the tray down on a low table. 'I know exactly what you've been doin' with my daughter – and, if it's okay with her, then it's okay with me.'

'Thanks,' said Sam. 'I appreciate that. And I want to assure you of my absolute discretion.' He smiled at Taylor. 'Your daughter's a very special person, and I'd hate to see her name dragged through the mud because of me.'

Kristina threw him a sharp look. 'I think *you've* got more to lose than Taylor if this gets out.'

Sam gave a small nod. Kristina was right: Laura had overlooked his previous indiscretions, but she wouldn't be so forgiving this time.

The atmosphere at dinner wasn't as bad as Sam had feared. They ate in the kitchen, sitting round a well-worn farmhouse table. Despite Kristina's warning, Taylor proved to be a reasonable cook and Sam was touched that she'd gone to so much trouble for him. The food was traditional Texan – shrimp cocktail, quesadillas with all the trimmings and banana pudding, washed down with more homemade punch. As they ate, they talked. The two women were keen to hear about Kirkhulme's dark underbelly and Sam made them laugh with his tales of vegetable sabotage in the run up to the village's annual Produce Fair. To his surprise, there was no further discussion about his relationship with Taylor. He'd been expecting Kristina to give him the third degree but, curiously, she seemed satisfied that his intentions towards her daughter were entirely dishonourable.

Afterwards, they repaired to the living room, where Kristina pressed more punch on to Sam, though he couldn't help noticing that she and Taylor had switched to Perrier with lemon. It was only when the golfer stood up to empty his bladder that he realized he was pissed. 'Blimey,' he said, putting a hand to his head. 'What was in that punch?'

'Grenadine, rum, vodka, pineapple juice and lime,' Kristina drawled. 'It's pretty potent stuff.'

'You can say that again,' said Sam as he held on to the mantelpiece for support. He looked through the window at the darkening sky. 'I'd better get going soon. I need to get into town and find myself a hotel for the night.' He patted his jacket pockets, feeling for his mobile, then realized he'd left it in the car. 'I'm in no fit state to drive. Would one of you mind calling me a cab? I can pick my car up tomorrow, if that's all right.'

'Don't be silly,' Kristina said. 'You can stay the night here.'

Taylor rolled her eyes. 'I've already told him that, Mom.'

Sam smiled. 'Thanks for the offer, but I think I'll stick to the hotel.'

Kristina shrugged. 'Suit yourself.'

When he returned from the bathroom, Sam found that his punch glass had been refilled yet again. 'One for the road,' said Kristina, 'and then I'll call you a cab.' Somehow, one drink became three and before he knew it Sam's chin was nodding on his chest.

The grandfather clock in the hall had just struck three when Sam woke with a start. The room lay in darkness and for a second he didn't know where he was. His shoes had been removed and there was some sort of counterpane covering him. Then he realized he must've fallen asleep on Taylor's sofa, Kristina's punch having clearly got the better of him. Groaning, he lifted his head to see if there was a half-drunk glass of Perrier within arm's length. It was then that he saw he wasn't alone. A shadowy figure was kneeling at the foot of the sofa, head bowed. Sam closed his eyes, thinking that in his still-drunken state, he might be seeing things. When he opened them again, the figure was still there.

'Hello?' he said experimentally.

The figure shifted slightly and all at once Sam felt a hand fumbling with the zip of his chinos under the counterpane. Smiling, he lowered his head back on to the arm of the sofa.

'You're a very bad girl, Taylor,' he slurred.

Suddenly, his nesting cock was yanked from his boxer shorts.

Sam laughed. 'Easy!'

The next moment, a cool hand was gripping his penis and administering a series of businesslike pulls. Sam moaned softly as he felt himself rise to the occasion. After his lover had been servicing him for several minutes, he lifted his head and groped in the darkness, hoping to make contact with Taylor's naked body. His fingertips brushed against a bare shoulder.

'Your skin's so soft,' he murmured. 'Come here, I want to taste you.'

His request was ignored. Instead, the shadow leaned forward and took his penis in her mouth. Usually, Taylor was very gentle when it came to oral sex – too gentle, if truth be told – but tonight there was an unmistakable urgency about her technique. She had a new trick up her sleeve too, using the tip of her tongue to stimulate the ridge of his glans as if she were licking the cream from a chocolate eclair.

'Mmmm, that's nice,' said Sam, gasping in pleasure. 'How come you've never done that before?'

His praise seemed to spur her on to further naughtiness. Releasing Sam's cock from captivity, she wrapped her lips around his testicles and began to hum. Sam laughed softly as her actions transmitted wave after wave of delicious vibrations. 'You filthy minx,' he said. 'You really *have* been hiding your light under a bushel, haven't you?'

After a little while, she switched her attentions back to his cock, her lips gripping him like a vice as she worked them up and down his shaft. Sighing in pleasure, Sam closed his eyes and surrendered to his lover's ministrations. A few moments later, he caught a whiff of Taylor's perfume. When he opened his eyes, the young golfer was leaning over him; he could feel the ends of her long hair tickling his chin.

'Come here, you,' he said, cupping the back of her neck with his hand and drawing her face towards him.

As their lips mashed against each other, Sam pushed his tongue deep into Taylor's mouth. She responded eagerly, and as she kissed him she reached for his hand and used it to push down the front of her silky nightdress so that his hand was touching her naked breast. It took Sam's alcohol-fugged brain several seconds to work out that, if Taylor's lips were on his, they couldn't be simultaneously wrapped round his cock.

'What the fuck . . .?' said Sam as he twisted his face away from her.

'Relax,' Taylor whispered, nuzzling against his neck, showering it with little nips and kisses. 'Just enjoy it.'

Meanwhile, the mouth that was expertly sucking his cock didn't slow its pace, not for a second.

'Aaargh,' cried Sam as he felt himself hurtling towards orgasm. 'Stop!'

But it was too late.

When it was over, Sam lay there breathing heavily, too stunned to say a word.

And then Taylor, who was still lying across his chest, spoke. 'Nice work, Mom.'

Her voice jolted Sam into action. Shoving her aside, he leapt off the sofa. The moment he stood up, his chinos fell to his ankles, causing him to stumble and crash to the floor. In the darkness, he heard Kristina's distinctive throaty cackle.

'This isn't funny,' he said, as he stood up, now trouser-less, and groped for the light switch. 'You've just sexually assaulted me.'

Kristina gave a cluck of dissent. 'Assaulted you? Don't make me laugh. Go on, admit it, that was the best goddamn blow job you ever had.'

Sam's fingers found the switch and as the overhead light came on he threw his arm across his eyes, momentarily blinded. When he dropped his arm, he saw Kristina and Taylor sitting next to each other on the sofa. They were wearing matching black satin nightdresses and self-satisfied expressions.

Sam stared at the women in appalled disbelief. 'Is this your idea of a joke?' he roared, stuffing his flaccid penis back into his boxer shorts.

'Absolutely not,' Kristina said coolly. 'We like you, Sam; we thought you'd find our little conceit erotic.'

'Erotic?' Sam stammered. 'It's repulsive.' Still unable to believe what had just occurred, he turned to Taylor.

'I thought you and I had something special. How could you do this to me?'

Taylor shrugged; her expression was strangely serene. 'I did it so we could go on seeing each other.'

Now Sam was really confused. 'What?'

'Mom said she wouldn't make a fuss about our relationship.' Taylor smiled languidly. 'Just so long as I agreed to share.'

'What?' said Sam, clutching his chest. 'You mean to say if you agreed to share *me*?'

Taylor nodded. 'Uh-huh.'

'But how could you even countenance something so utterly depraved?'

Taylor giggled. 'Oh, Sam, you're making a big ole fuss over nothing. We all enjoyed ourselves, didn't we?'

Sam gaped at her, open-mouthed, too stunned to remonstrate further.

Suddenly, Kristina stood up. 'You're not going to run out on us, are you?' she said. 'That was just the appetizer; the main course will blow your mind, darlin'.'

Sam began backing towards the door. Kristina was an intimidating woman. Even in her bare feet, she was almost as tall as him and beneath the spaghetti straps of her nightgown, her biceps bulged menacingly. 'I'm not interested,' he said. 'You two are twisted, do you know that?'

Kristina took a step towards him. 'Now, now, there's no need to be nasty.'

As Sam's hand closed around the door handle, Kristina made a sudden lunge for him. Yelping like a puppy that's just been kicked, Sam turned and bolted for the front door. 'Get away from me!' he shrieked as he yanked the door open and went running outside in his stockinged feet. It was only when he reached his car that he realized he didn't have his keys. Or his trousers.

He turned back to the house, half-expecting to see Kristina tearing towards him with a large club in her hand. To his relief, there was no sign of her. Taylor stood alone in the doorway with a pile of his clothes in her arms.

'Spoilsport,' she spat, hurling his trousers, jacket and shoes on to the drive. 'Don't you dare come sniffing round me again. You've burned your bridges big time, mister.' Then she stepped back inside the house and slammed the door.

Eighteen

It was a Sunday morning in mid-August and the north-west of England was basking in a heatwave. In Marianne's garden, Keeley, Laura and Cindy were gathered round a rustic picnic table, poring over the latest edition of the *Kirkhulme Gazette*. It was several weeks since they'd all been together and there was plenty to catch up on.

Marianne, who was sitting slightly apart from the others, picked up a tall pitcher of iced tea and began filling glasses. 'It's on page fifteen,' she said, nodding towards the newspaper. 'The lead item in "Jemima's Diary", would you believe? The wretched woman even had the gall to phone me for a quote. I don't know how she got my number; I'm ex-directory.'

'What did you tell her?' asked Keeley.

'"No comment," of course. You know what these journalists are like – you give them the slightest bit of encouragement and the next thing you know they're on your front doorstep, demanding an exclusive interview and a saucy photo shoot.'

Keeley giggled. 'This is the *Kirkhulme Gazette* we're talking about, not the *News of the World*.'

Marianne flicked her hand like a Roman emperor. 'They're all the same – and I don't pose in my lingerie for anyone.' She pouted suggestively. 'Well, not unless they're six foot two with blue eyes and abs of titanium.'

Laura shook her head. 'You're incorrigible, Marianne.'

'I don't know what you mean,' said Marianne, all wide-eyed innocence.

Keeley flipped the pages of the newspaper impatiently. 'Page fifteen, you say? Ah, here it is.' She gave a little whoop. 'Hey, there's even a picture!'

She scrutinized the colour photograph, which showed Marianne standing beside a gravestone, looking elegant in a Chanel suit and revoltingly expensive jewellery. 'Hang on, wasn't that taken outside the church at Tiger's christening?'

Marianne nodded. 'Don't you remember, the *Gazette* sent a photographer? Jemima must have wet her control pants in excitement when she realized the paper already had a picture of me on file.'

'You look fabulous in that outfit,' said Cindy. 'No one would ever guess you were fifty-six.'

Marianne sighed. 'How many times do I have to tell you, I'm fifty-*two*.'

Cindy clapped her hand to her mouth. She knew how sensitive Marianne was about her age. 'Oh, honey, I'm so sorry,' she said. 'I've never been very good with figures.'

'No need to apologize,' said Marianne icily. She picked up the pitcher and gave Cindy an unnecessary refill, deliberately slopping iced tea over the top of the glass, so that it ran between the slats in the picnic bench and splashed on to Cindy's lap.

Recognizing a reprimand when she saw one, Cindy knew better than to make a fuss.

'Why don't you read the story aloud, Keeley?' she said,

pulling a tissue from her handbag and discreetly dabbing at the damp patch on her skirt.

'Ooh yes,' said Laura. 'And take it nice and slow. I want to savour all the juicy details.'

Keeley smiled. 'Righty-ho.' She pushed her sunglasses into her hair and started to read.

Missionary position for randy Rev

I do so hate to be the bearer of bad news, but word reaches me that Reverend Simon Proctor has quit All Hallows in disgrace after being caught romping with a member of his flock on church property. Rumours have been circulating about the Rev's closeness to attractive divorcée Marianne Kennedy for weeks – and, late on Friday night, the precise nature of their, ahem, 'friendship' was exposed when police were called to the church by a concerned local resident.

Master butcher Henry Glossop was walking his miniature dachshund Millie in Church Lane when he spotted a light through the vestry window. Fearing that a burglary was taking place, the community-minded chap dialled 999. Police were on the scene in minutes, and soon discovered that nocturnal naughtiness was indeed occurring on All Hallows' consecrated ground – though not the sort they were expecting.

When the boys in blue burst into the vestry, they discovered they weren't the only ones with their truncheons at the ready. According to my very reliable source, the partially clothed Rev Proctor, 42, was locked in an intimate embrace with fifty-something Mrs Kennedy, who owns a £1.5m property in Kirkhulme's ultra-exclusive Woodlands Way.

'The police told me they were going at it hammer and tongs,' a shocked Mr Glossop whispered in my shell-like. 'I think it's disgusting. This is a respectable community. They should both be thoroughly ashamed of themselves.'

The Bishop of Delchester has ordered an inquiry into the incident – and, if found guilty of a charge of 'unbecoming conduct', Rev Proctor could be banned from working as a minister. Still, it's not all gloom and doom for the vulgar vicar. My spy tells me he now plans to become a missionary and hopes to fly to South Africa at the end of the month to work with the Quakers in Cape Town. Ah well, that's one position he should feel right at home in . . .

'Blimey,' said Keeley, tossing the newspaper down on the table. 'That's quite an exclusive.'

'Personally, I don't know what all the fuss is about,' said Marianne. 'We're two consenting adults, after all, and it's not as if either of us is married. Besides which, Simon's only human, and he has needs just like the rest of us.'

'Yeah, but doing it in the vestry,' said Keeley. 'Isn't that sacrilegious?'

'We couldn't help ourselves.' Marianne sniffed. 'The Reverend's a very passionate man.'

Laura flashed her friend a sympathetic look. 'How embarrassing, getting caught in the act like that.'

'I know,' said Marianne. 'It's all that interfering bloody butcher's fault. Suffice to say, that's the last time I get my Christmas turkey from Glossop's.'

'Oh well,' said Cindy. 'Try and look on the bright side. What was it Oscar Wilde said? There's only one thing in the world worse than being talked about, and that's not being talked about.'

Marianne glared at the newspaper. 'I don't know about that; it's never nice having one's private affairs offered up for public consumption.' She ran a hand over her platinum chignon, smoothing imaginary stray hairs. 'Still, I look pretty damn hot in that photograph, though I do say so myself.'

'Will you miss him?' asked Keeley.

'Simon?' said Marianne. 'I'll miss the sex, that's for sure. He may have taken Holy Orders, but that man was positively wicked in bed.' She affected a shudder. 'He gave oral like no man I've ever met – and I bet he didn't learn *that* at the seminary.'

Cindy couldn't help wincing. She'd always found Marianne's frankness about sexual matters somewhat distasteful and, when she'd heard about her friend's dalliance with the vicar, she'd had a feeling it was all going to end in tears. 'So has he really been sacked from All Hallows?'

Marianne shrugged. 'I wouldn't know. I haven't seen or heard from him since that night in the vestry. I called him at the vicarage the next day, but there was no reply. So later I stopped by the church and Marjorie, who does the flowers, told me he hadn't turned up for Morning Prayer. Apparently, no one in the village has seen him since. He must be absolutely mortified; no wonder he's keeping a low profile.'

'Do you think you'll ever see him again?'

'I shouldn't think so, not if he's heading out to Africa, but to tell you the truth I don't really care.' Marianne crossed one leg languidly over the other. 'I've got a new man now.'

The admission caused Keeley to choke on her iced tea. 'Fuck, Marianne, you don't hang about, do you? Where did you meet him – at St Benedict's?'

Marianne shook her head. 'I found him on the internet.'

'You've started internet dating?' said Laura. 'That's very adventurous of you.'

Marianne smiled enigmatically. 'You know me – I like to cast my net as wide as possible.'

'Is it going well?' asked Cindy eagerly.

'Oh yes,' purred Marianne. 'This one's definitely for keeps.'

Keeley's eyes widened. 'I've never heard you say that before. Have you shagged him yet?'

'Within ten minutes of meeting, we were naked in bed together.' Marianne cocked her head kittenishly to one side. 'We've barely come up for air since.'

'How exciting,' said Laura. 'I know it's only early days, but I'd love to meet him.'

'Then meet him you shall,' said Marianne. 'He's here now.'

Laura frowned. 'What – in the house?'

'Mmm-hmm. He's upstairs in bed, having a lie-in.'

Keeley grinned. 'I expect he's knackered. I know what *you're* like, madam.'

'Actually, Brad's got amazing stamina,' Marianne said loftily. 'He can even outlast me, which is saying something. And he has a torso to die for. I couldn't have designed it better myself.'

'Sounds like my kind of guy,' said Keeley. 'Has he got any brothers?'

'Yes, quite a few actually. I can fix you up, if you like.' She looked at Laura and Cindy. 'In fact, I can fix all of you up. Believe me, you won't regret it.'

'I'm a happily married woman, thank you very much,' said Cindy primly.

'Ah, but you see with a man like Brad you can have your cake and eat it.'

Laura frowned. 'How?'

Marianne stood up. 'Come on, girls, I'll show you.'

The three women swapped bemused looks.

'You're going to introduce us *now*?' said Keeley.

'Absolutely.'

Cindy looked around anxiously, as if she were expecting hordes of lascivious Brad-a-likes to come rampaging across the lawn. 'Won't he be embarrassed when we all barge into the bedroom?' she said. 'Shouldn't you give him a chance to put some clothes on first?'

'Don't be silly,' said Marianne. 'Brad's an exhibitionist; he won't be in the least bit self-conscious.'

'Well *I'm* up for it,' said Keeley, draining her glass of iced tea.

'Me too,' said Laura, rising to her feet. 'I never turn down the opportunity to ogle a semi-naked man.'

'Cindy?' said Marianne, looking at the American woman expectantly.

Cindy sighed. 'Oh, all right.'

As the four women trooped into the house, there was much girlish giggling.

'How old is Brad?' asked Keeley.

'You know, I'm not entirely sure,' Marianne replied. 'Thirty or thereabouts, I should think.'

Laura gave her friend an admiring look. 'Honestly, Marianne – you and your toy boys; I don't know how you do it.'

'Oh, finding Brad was easy,' said Marianne immodestly. 'A couple of emails was all it took.'

'Wow, I'm impressed,' said Keeley. 'Friends of mine who've tried internet dating haven't had much luck.'

'They obviously don't subscribe to the right website,' said Marianne mysteriously. When she reached the foot of the staircase she paused. 'I'm warning you, Brad's not my usual type.'

'If you like him, then I'm quite sure we will too,' said Keeley.

'I hope so,' said Marianne. 'Because he's made me a very happy woman.'

A few moments later, they were standing outside the door of the master bedroom.

'Shouldn't you check he's awake before we go in?' asked Cindy.

Marianne sighed. 'Stop fretting, darling. I've already told you it'll be fine.'

'Please,' said Cindy. 'Just to make me feel more comfortable.'

Marianne sucked in her cheeks. 'Oh, all right, if you insist.' She pushed open the door and stuck her head round the side. 'Morning,' she chirruped. 'Are you decent? Good, because we've got company.'

She stepped back and pushed the door open. 'Ladies, I'd like you to meet Brad.'

Keeley didn't need a second invitation. 'Hey, Brad, it's nice to meet you,' she said, stepping across the threshold. 'I'm Marianne's friend, Keeley.' All at once, her smile faded. 'What the . . .?'

Frowning at the confusion in her friend's voice, Laura stepped into the room, followed by Cindy. They, too, were shocked by what they saw.

The man sitting in Marianne's king-size bed, propped up by a stack of duck-feather pillows, was undeniably handsome. He was clean-shaven with startling blue eyes and full lips that seemed made for kissing. With the bedclothes only just covering his pubic hair, it was plain to see that his physique was, as Marianne had indicated, most impressive. He had a six-pack and well-sculpted biceps, not to mention pectoral muscles that would put most body-builders to shame.

For a moment or two, the three women stood there in stunned silence.

'So,' said Marianne, coming up behind them. 'What do you think? He's pretty tasty, eh?'

Keeley turned to face her friend. 'Is this some kind of joke?'

'Oh no,' said Marianne with a straight face. 'Brad's no joke in bed, I can assure you of that.'

'But . . . but . . .' Laura stuttered. 'He's a dummy.'

'Shush, Brad's very sensitive. You'll hurt his feelings.'

Cindy broke into an appalled grimace. 'Marianne, please. You're freaking me out.'

At this, Marianne threw back her head and burst out laughing. 'Oh, girls, you should see your faces.'

Laura placed a relieved hand on her chest. 'Thank God

for that. For one awful moment, I thought you'd gone stark raving mad.'

'Very droll,' said Keeley. 'But you didn't really expect us to believe you'd have sex with a mannequin, did you?' She turned back to Brad. 'Although I have to say, he *is* incredibly lifelike.'

'That's because he's made from high-grade silicone,' said Marianne. 'It's the same stuff they use for Hollywood special effects. And for your information, I *do* have sex with him.'

Cindy groaned. 'Please tell me I'm hearing things.'

'Don't be so squeamish. You've all got vibrators, haven't you?'

'Yes, but that's different,' said Keeley.

'I don't see how. Honestly, darling, you don't know what you're missing. Just feel him.' Marianne took Keeley's hand and led her over to the bed. 'See,' she said, placing Keeley's fingertips on Brad's chest.

'Oh my God, that's amazing,' Keeley squealed. 'It feels just like real skin, only cooler.'

Marianne stroked Brad's shock of dark hair. 'Before we have sex, I wrap him up in an electric blanket,' she said. 'That way, he feels just like the real thing.'

'Jesus,' Cindy muttered as she walked over to the bed for a closer look.

'Do you mind me asking how much he cost?' Laura asked.

'Not at all, darling. He wasn't cheap; I didn't get much change out of four grand.'

The others stared at her as if she were mad.

'Honestly, girls, he's worth every single penny and

I took full advantage of the customized options the website people were offering. I got to choose his hair and eye colour, as well as his facial expression. Oh, and look at this.' Marianne grabbed Brad's left arm and twisted it round to reveal a heart-shaped tattoo. There was a banner running through the middle of the heart with the word *Marianne* emblazoned across it.

Keeley let out a long, low whistle. 'That's so cool.'

'Ah, but you haven't seen the pièce de résistance,' said Marianne. She grabbed the bedclothes and yanked them back. 'Ta-daaah!'

All three women gasped in amazement.

'Wow,' said Laura as she took in the erect penis, projecting from a pair of generous gonads. 'It looks just like the real thing.'

'I ordered a selection of attachments,' Marianne said, as if she were discussing a new vacuum cleaner. She pulled out a drawer in the bedside cabinet to reveal six prosthetic appendages of varying girth and length. 'That way I can switch them around depending on my mood. There's even a flaccid one, in case I just feel like cuddling.'

Keeley eyed the specimens hungrily. 'Can I touch one?'

'Of course you can,' Marianne said, picking out a sturdy, nine-inch model and slapping it into Keeley's palm. 'They're all dishwasher safe,' she continued gaily. 'The manufacturer really has thought of everything. In fact, my only criticism of Brad is his eyes.'

'What's wrong with them?' said Laura, who was growing more envious of Marianne by the minute.

'They're dreadfully empty, don't you think? Sometimes

I find it so disconcerting I have to put sunglasses on him.'

Keeley pressed the penis into Cindy's hands. 'If I had a boyfriend with a dick *that* big, I don't think I'd be spending much time gazing into his eyes.'

Cindy fluttered her eyelashes like a Victorian lady in need of the smelling salts as she traced the line of one of the bulging veins that decorated Brad's silicone member. 'But surely you'd rather have a real man,' she said to Marianne. 'Brad may be well endowed, but he can't take you out for dinner or tell you how beautiful you are.'

Marianne shook her head. 'Real men are too high-maintenance. As far as I'm concerned, Brad's the perfect partner: he doesn't pick his nose or fart in bed, he's never irritable or short-tempered, he doesn't cross-examine me about where I'm going and who I'm with and, best of all, he's always ready for action.'

'You've certainly convinced *me*,' said Keeley with an impish grin. 'Hell, I might even have to get the address of that website off you.'

Cindy looked at her peevishly. 'I expect Ryan would have something to say about that, wouldn't he?'

'I shouldn't think he'd give a toss,' Keeley replied.

'Hang on a minute,' said Marianne. 'I thought you two were love's young dream.'

Keeley sighed. 'So did I. But Ryan's been acting pretty strangely lately.'

'What do you mean?'

'He doesn't return my texts and calls straight away like he used to, and when we *are* together he seems distracted.'

Laura frowned. 'That's not like Ryan; he's usually so

attentive. I expect he's just got a lot on his mind, especially with a move to London in the pipeline. Have you two had a chance to discuss that properly yet?'

Keeley stuck out her bottom lip. 'That's another weird thing. I kept waiting and waiting for him to mention it, but he never did. So a couple of nights ago, I decided to bring it up myself. I pretended I'd heard a rumour at St Benedict's that he might be about to leave Delchester United and I asked him if it was true.'

'What did he say?' said Cindy, pressing the penis into Laura's eager hands.

'Not much. He admitted that a London club had approached his agent, but he insisted they were a long way from signing any kind of deal. So then I asked him what would happen to us if he *did* move down south.'

'And?' said Laura, giving Brad's glans an experimental squeeze.

'He just gave me a blank look and said, "We'll cross that bridge when we come to it, shall we?" Then he changed the subject. He definitely knows more than he's letting on – I'm sure of it.'

'That's not very satisfactory, is it?' said Marianne. 'You need to know where you stand.'

'I really think he's going off me,' said Keeley glumly. 'At the moment, it feels as if we're growing further apart by the day.'

'I'm sure it's not too late to get things back on track,' said Cindy. 'Why don't you take up some sort of joint hobby? That way you'll be able to spend more time together. Kieran and I have just joined a book group. New members are always welcome; we meet on the second Thursday of every month, if you're interested.'

'Sounds riveting,' Marianne muttered.

Cindy glowered at her. 'Do you have any better ideas?'

'What about tennis?' Marianne suggested. 'I know you're not very sporty, Keeley darling, but you could have great fun dressing up in all those cute little outfits.'

Keeley smiled shyly. 'As a matter of fact, Ryan and I *have* just taken up a new hobby.' She paused. 'If you can call it that.'

Somewhere in the distance, Marianne's mobile phone started ringing.

'Do you want to get that?' Keeley said.

'No, don't worry; it'll go to voicemail in a minute.' Marianne gave Keeley a nudge. 'Come on, darling, what's this new hobby of yours?'

Keeley took a deep breath. 'Swinging,' she said, then, unable to look her friends in the eye, she stared hard at the cream wool carpet.

Cindy's jaw dropped open. 'What, you mean like wife-swapping?' she said in a horrified voice.

Keeley nodded. 'Except that nobody calls it that any more.'

Cindy's hands flew to her cheeks. 'I can't believe I'm hearing this.'

'Oh, for goodness' sake,' said Marianne. 'There's nothing wrong with indulging one's sexual fantasies from time to time. You ought to try it, Cindy. Perhaps then you wouldn't be quite so uptight.'

'I'm not uptight,' Cindy said huffily. 'I just have certain standards.'

'Then maybe you should think about lowering them,' Marianne retorted. 'Believe me, you'd have a lot more fun.'

'Ladies, please,' said Laura, extending an arm towards each woman like a referee in a boxing ring. 'We're supposed to be supporting Keeley, not launching into a moral debate.'

'Yes, of course we are,' Cindy agreed. She put her hand on Keeley's shoulder. 'I'm sorry, honey, please don't think I'm judging you. I'm just a bit shocked; I didn't think you were into that kind of thing.'

'Neither did I,' admitted Keeley. 'Ryan was the one who talked me into it. But after I got over my initial nerves, I started to really enjoy myself. In fact, I find the whole thing quite liberating.'

Laura looked thoughtful. 'I always thought swinging died out in the seventies.'

'Don't you believe it,' said Keeley. 'Of course, the whole scene's moved on a lot since then. The swinging parties I've been to have been incredibly sophisticated.'

'Swinging parties?' Laura repeated. 'Here in Kirk-hulme?'

Keeley nodded. 'You'd be amazed how many people are into it; there are parties most weekends.'

'Well I never,' said Marianne. 'How come I've never seen any of these events advertised?'

'Swingers are very discreet; it's all done through word of mouth,' Keeley explained. 'And not just anyone can come along. For starters, you have to be recommended by somebody who's already active on the scene. Even then you won't get through the front door unless you're rich or beautiful, or preferably both.' She gave a smug little smile. 'I've met some of the wealthiest and most influential people in the village through swinging.'

'Like who?' Marianne said eagerly.

'I'm sorry, I can't name names. It's part of the swingers' etiquette.'

Cindy's eyebrows shot up. 'You're telling me these people have a code of conduct?'

Keeley glared at her. 'I thought you said you weren't going to judge.'

Cindy held her hands up. 'Sorry.'

'So what's the problem?' said Marianne. 'It sounds like fun.'

Keeley gave a great sigh. 'It is, and in the beginning I really thought it would help bring us closer together, the way it seems to have done for other couples we know. But now it just seems to be tearing us apart.'

'Because of jealousy?' said Laura.

'Not exactly; I can handle seeing Ryan with other women because at the end of the day I know it's me he'll be taking home.'

Cindy frowned. 'So what is it then?'

'I know this might be hard for you to understand, Cindy, but having sex with a complete stranger can be very exciting.'

Cindy gulped. 'I'll take your word for it.'

'So now normal sex seems dull by comparison. Ryan and I hardly ever do it in private any more. Don't get me wrong, *I'm* still up for it. It's Ryan; he never seems to be in the mood these days. It's as if he can't get turned on unless other people are involved.' She folded her arms across her chest. 'Either that, or he just doesn't fancy me any more.'

Laura opened her mouth to offer some words of reassurance, but before she could speak Marianne's distinctive ring tone struck up again.

Keeley jerked her thumb towards the door. 'Are you *sure* you don't want to get that? It might be important.'

'Honestly, don't worry about it,' said Marianne. 'If it's that important, they can call back.'

'So what do you think I should do?' asked Keeley.

'The answer's obvious, isn't it?' said Cindy. 'Give up the swinging parties.'

Keeley scowled. 'It's not that simple. I've already suggested to Ryan that we at least give it a break, but he wouldn't hear of it. He said if I didn't want to do it any more, he'd find someone who did.'

'But that's emotional blackmail,' cried Laura.

'Of course it is,' agreed Marianne. 'Honestly, darling, if that's his attitude, I really think you're better off without him.'

'But I love him,' Keeley wailed, her eyes filling with tears. 'He's rich, kind, funny ... okay so he may not be the best-looking guy in the world but I can live with that.' She pulled a paper tissue from the gold-plated dispenser on Marianne's bedside table. 'I can't bear the thought of being single again.'

'You'd find someone in an instant,' said Marianne, wrapping a comforting arm round her friend's shoulders. 'You always do.'

'Yes, but I'm not getting any younger, am I? And there's so much competition for eligible men. Have you seen how many gorgeous girls there are at St Benedict's? You can hardly move for pert buttocks and silky blonde hair.'

Cindy tutted. 'What are you talking about, Keeley? You're twenty-eight years old.'

'I think what you need to do is sit down with Ryan and have a serious talk,' said Laura. 'It's no good bottling these things up. You need to tell him exactly how you're feeling – and if he can't give you the reassurance you need, Marianne's right: you should dump him.'

Keeley managed a smile. 'Thanks for the advice, girls. I know you're right. I just have to find the courage to confront Ryan.' She gave a long sigh. 'I really hope we can work things out.'

'If it's any comfort, there are couples going through a tougher time than you two,' said Cindy. 'The Solomons, for example.'

'Ooh, what's the latest?' asked Laura eagerly. 'From what I hear, the Old Manor is staked out like a battle-ground.'

Cindy shook her head. 'I really can't comment ... client confidentiality and all that.'

'Spoilsport,' Keeley muttered. 'You've been working at the Old Manor for weeks; I bet there's all kinds of juicy gossip you could tell us.'

Marianne cocked her head to one side. 'Can't you feed us one tiny morsel?' she said hopefully.

'Honestly, girls, there's nothing to tell,' Cindy replied. 'In any case, I've finished Amber's music room now, so I guess I won't be going back to the Old Manor again.'

Keeley folded her arms in front of her chest. 'I heard

a rumour that Daniel killed Amber's pet monkey in retaliation for that business with the billboard.'

Cindy burst out laughing. 'I knew there were some crazy stories doing the rounds, but that's got to be the craziest.'

'I do feel sorry for the Solomons,' said Laura. 'It must be bad enough going through a divorce, but then to have people making up cruel stories about you …' Realizing she was still clutching one of Brad's appendages, she set it down on Marianne's bedside table. As she did, she caught sight of the digital display on Marianne's alarm clock.

'Shit, is that the time?' she groaned. 'I'm really sorry, girls, but I'm going to have to make a move. I promised Sam I'd be back in time to make the kids' lunch.'

'Oh, but, darling, you've only just got here,' said Marianne. 'Surely Sam can manage on his own.'

Laura shook her head. 'You'd think so, wouldn't you? Sadly, Sam's utterly useless in the kitchen. He can't even heat a bottle of formula without supervision.'

'I thought you were breast-feeding,' said Cindy.

'I gave up in the end,' said Laura. 'Neither of us seemed to be enjoying it very much.'

'Are you still finding it tough going with Tiger?' Marianne said gently.

''Fraid so, but I'm just going to have to get on with it, aren't I?' Laura heaved a sigh. 'Still I try to look on the bright side … only another seventeen years and ten months to go.'

'To go before what?' said Cindy.

'Before I can legally disown him.'

Keeley's face crumpled with concern. 'Oh, Laura, is it really that bad?'

Laura nodded grimly. 'Yep.' She leaned over to kiss her friend. 'Anyway, don't worry about me. You've got enough on your plate at the moment. Give me a call in a couple of days and let me know how things are going with Ryan, okay?'

'I will,' said Keeley, pressing her lips to Laura's cheek. 'That offer of babysitting still stands, by the way, so if things get on top of you and you need to get out of the house for a while . . .'

'That goes for me too,' said Marianne.

Cindy smiled. 'And me.'

'Thanks,' said Laura. Feeling suddenly emotional, she kissed the other two quickly and began walking towards the door. 'I'll see you all very soon.'

The others watched her go, not knowing that the next time they saw her she would be changed forever.

Nineteen

As Laura collected her handbag from Marianne's garden and set off on the short drive home, she could feel her good mood evaporating, knowing that all she had to look forward to was a not-very-stimulating afternoon of childcare and assorted domestic chores. She had been hoping she and Sam could take the children to the Delchester Country Park, where there was a petting zoo and lots of other activities to keep small minds occupied. But as they lay in bed that morning, discussing their plans for the day, Sam had revealed that he intended to head to the golf course the minute Laura returned from Marianne's.

'But it's Sunday,' Laura pointed out. 'Surely you can take one day off from practice to spend time with your family.'

'There's nothing I'd like more,' Sam replied, not very convincingly. 'But it's the Portugal Masters next month and I've really got to work on my bunker shots if I'm going to improve my European ranking.'

Laura gave a snort of displeasure. 'Just so long as that's *all* you're working on.'

This, Sam knew, was a veiled reference to the affair he'd had with his caddie the previous summer – an affair that had ended in tragedy, though not, Sam reassured himself for the umpteenth time, through any direct fault of his own.

'Oh, sweetheart,' he said, summoning up a wounded expression from his well-rehearsed repertoire. 'How can you say that?'

'Because you've done it before,' Laura said in a monotone.

Resisting the temptation to raise the small matter of his wife's own past infidelity, Sam stared deep into her eyes. 'Read my lips, Laura: I am *not* having an affair.' Technically speaking, it was the truth, for – to his enormous relief – Sam hadn't seen or heard from Taylor or Kristina since that embarrassing night at the cottage.

'I'm sorry, darling,' Laura said, stroking his hair. 'I didn't mean to bring all that up again. I know we agreed to put it behind us. I just can't help feeling a little insecure sometimes.'

'What have you got to feel insecure about? You're a gorgeous, intelligent woman and you've given me three wonderful children.'

'I don't know about the "intelligent" bit,' said Laura. 'I spend so much time at home I sometimes feel as if my brain's turned to mush. And as for the "gorgeous" ... let's face it, after three kids, my figure's not what it was.'

'You're still beautiful to me,' said Sam. He drew Laura towards him and gave her a slow, lingering kiss. After a few moments, his hand moved from the back of her neck to her swollen breasts.

Wincing, Laura pushed his hand away. 'Sorry, darling, they're awfully tender. I think I need to express some milk.'

Sam sighed. 'No problem,' he said, rolling away from her. 'I'll go downstairs and make some tea, shall I?'

Laura watched as Sam yanked his robe off the hook on the back of the bedroom door and wrapped it tightly round his muscular frame.

'I know how frustrating this must be for you,' she said, sensing his disappointment. I just don't feel up to sex yet.'

'Look, don't worry about it, okay?' Sam held up his right hand. 'I've still got this, haven't I?'

Laura smiled, but despite Sam's reassurances she knew it was only a matter of time before he looked elsewhere for sexual gratification. That is, if he hadn't already.

Laura had left Marianne's quiet, tree-lined road and was waiting at the traffic lights halfway down the high street when she heard her mobile cheep. With one eye on the lights, she reached into her handbag and pulled out the phone: eight missed calls, all from Sam. Because he hadn't bothered leaving a message, Laura assumed he was simply eager to get to the golf course and was phoning to chivvy her along. Feeling slightly piqued at her husband's harassment tactics, Laura decided to delay her return by stopping at the newsagent's for a Sunday paper and a king-size Snickers, followed by a leisurely browse of some estate agents' windows.

When she finally arrived back at the house, Laura immediately noticed the garage door was open and Sam's 4×4 was missing. Her first thought was that Tiger must have embarked on one of his marathon crying jags and Sam had taken all three children for a drive in a desperate attempt to lull him to sleep. She couldn't help smiling to herself, pleased – in a slightly sadistic way – that Sam hadn't had an easy morning of it. Now at least he'd had a taste of what *she* had to put up with, day after day. As she let herself into the house, Laura registered that Sam hadn't bothered to double lock the door, *or* set the alarm. 'Lazy sod,' she muttered, hooking her handbag over the coat stand in the hallway. 'It would've served you right if we'd been burgled.'

She went to the kitchen, intending to have a quiet read of the newspaper before Sam arrived home with the children. For several minutes she busied herself making a pot of tea to go with her Snickers and washing up her favourite oversized cup and saucer. It wasn't until she went to get the milk that she noticed a note pinned to the fridge door with one of the kids' alphabet magnets. She sighed when she saw it had been written on a page torn from Carnie's much-loved Winnie-the-Pooh colouring book. Sam should've known better; Carnie would be outraged when she discovered what he'd done. Laura plucked the page from the fridge, frowning as she tried to decipher Sam's barely legible scrawl. The note was brief and had obviously been written in a hurry.

I'm taking Tiger to A&E at Delchester General. Get there as soon as you can.

The piece of paper fell from Laura's hand and fluttered to the floor. A wave of panic rose in her stomach as she ran through the possibilities: a cut, a fall, a scalding. Whatever injury Tiger had sustained, she knew it must be serious to necessitate a trip to casualty. She picked up the phone that was lying on the kitchen table and dialled Sam's mobile number. All she got was his voicemail. 'Shit,' she said as she tossed the phone down and grabbed her car keys.

Laura drove to the hospital as fast as she could, beeping at any driver who dared slow her progress and almost running down an elderly man on a pedestrian crossing. She reached Delchester General in less than twenty minutes, where she miraculously managed to find a space in the hospital car park. With trembling fingers, she stuffed pound coins into the ticket machine, unsure how long she was going to be there. She ran into A&E and queued at the reception desk, eyes casting wildly around for any sign of Sam.

'I'm Tiger Bentley's mother; his father brought him in about an hour ago,' she said when finally it was her turn to be seen. As the receptionist tapped on her keyboard, Laura added, 'He's only a baby,' hiccupping as her breath caught in her throat.

The receptionist stared at her computer screen. 'Your son's been transferred to the special care baby unit,' she said gently. 'You need to go back outside, turn left and follow the yellow signs.'

At the mention of 'special care', Laura's blood ran cold. 'What's wrong with him?' she demanded, gripping the reception desk until her knuckles turned white. 'Has he had some sort of accident?'

'I'm sorry, I'm afraid I don't have that information. The staff in the unit will be able to tell you more.'

Fighting the urge to scream, Laura turned and fled from the building. A few minutes later she was standing at a second reception desk, her heart thudding painfully against her ribs. As she waited impatiently for the receptionist to finish speaking on the phone, she heard a familiar voice call out her name. Turning, she saw Sam standing at the end of a long, brightly lit corridor. Even from twenty feet away, she could see the concern etched across his face.

'Thank God you're here,' he said.

Laura began walking towards him. 'What's happened?' she said. 'Where's Tiger?'

'Let's go somewhere more private.'

Putting his arm round his wife's shoulders, Sam led her into a nearby room that was painted a soothing shade of taupe and furnished with comfy sofas and a large television.

'Please, Sam, just tell me what's wrong with him,' Laura begged him.

Sam ran a hand through his hair. Laura could see tears forming in his eyes. Sam hardly ever cried; rarely showed any sign of vulnerability at all. She knew then the situation must be grave.

'They're doing tests,' Sam said. 'The doctors don't know what's wrong with him.'

Laura screwed up her face. 'Tests? What sort of tests?'

'All kinds of stuff: blood samples, chest x-rays, a lumbar puncture.' Sam took a deep breath. 'The doctors say his condition's critical. They think it might be meningitis.'

Laura suddenly felt sick, saliva flowing into her mouth

as if she were about to gag or vomit. When Sam opened his arms, she collapsed into them.

'I don't understand,' she said as she struggled to take in the shocking news. 'He was fine earlier on.'

The minute the words were out, Laura realized they weren't strictly true. As she'd dressed Tiger that morning, she'd noticed that he seemed even crankier than usual, grunting and flaring his nostrils as she tried to pull an organic cotton T-shirt over his head. His skin seemed a little warm to the touch too, but because it had been a balmy night and she was keen to get to Marianne's she hadn't been concerned, hadn't even thought to mention his symptoms to Sam before she left. As she pressed her face into her husband's broad chest, she felt a sharp stab of guilt, knowing that she would probably have cancelled her plans and stayed home if Carnie or Birdie had been even vaguely out of sorts.

'Don't blame yourself,' said Sam, apparently reading her thoughts. 'The doctor says the early symptoms of meningitis can be very subtle.'

Laura looked up at her husband. 'But *you* knew he was sick,' she said, her voice quivering with emotion.

'Yeah, I thought at first he was just a bit tired, but when I picked him up he felt floppy and he kept rolling his head from side to side. I wasn't sure what to do, so I called you on your mobile but it just rang and rang.'

'I didn't hear it,' Laura said. 'I'd left my handbag in Marianne's garden while we went indoors.'

Sam's chest heaved up and down. 'So then I decided to phone the out-of-hours GP service. When I described Tiger's symptoms, they said it sounded like colic and not to worry. I waited another half an hour and then I noticed he seemed to be breathing a bit quicker than usual, and his skin had gone a funny colour. I knew then I had to get him to hospital as soon as possible. I kept calling and calling you, but I couldn't get through. I tried Marianne's mobile too but she didn't pick up either. I did think about driving round to her house, but she lives in the opposite direction to the hospital and I didn't want to waste any time.'

'You did the right thing,' Laura said quietly. 'What happened when you got to A&E?'

'The duty doctor took one look at him and whisked him out of my arms.'

At this, Laura began sobbing uncontrollably.

'Shush,' Sam whispered into her hair. 'It'll be all right. Tiger's a tough little fellow; he'll come through this, you'll see.'

'But he's so tiny,' Laura wailed. 'And now he's in a room somewhere with loads of strangers sticking needles into him. He'll be terrified; he'll think we've abandoned him.' She let go of Sam and rummaged in her handbag for a tissue. 'How long is it before they get the test results?'

Sam shrugged. 'I don't know ... a few hours at least. The doctor says he'll come and see us the minute there's any news.'

'I can't believe this is happening,' said Laura, slumping on to the nearest sofa. 'What if he doesn't make it, Sam?'

'You mustn't think like that. We've got to stay strong for the girls.'

Laura looked at her husband in horror. 'The girls!' she cried. 'Who's looking after them?'

'Relax,' said Sam. 'I brought them with me to the hospital and then, as soon as I realized Tiger's condition was critical, I called Marta. She was having lunch with some friends, but when I explained the situation she very kindly agreed to drop everything and pick the girls up. She's taken them back to ours; she says she'll stay the night if we need her to.'

Laura blew out a puff of air through pursed lips. 'Marta's a good girl. I don't know what I'd do without her.' She rested her elbows on her knees and buried her head in her hands. 'And I don't know what I'd do without Tiger.' And, with that, her tears started up afresh.

The rest of the day passed in a blur. Sam and Laura spent most of their time in the relatives' room or pacing up and down in the corridor outside, fortified by endless cups of bitter vending-machine coffee. At various points, members of hospital staff came to update them on Tiger's condition, which remained critical – but, frustratingly, there was still no diagnosis. Despite this, the doctors had already embarked on an aggressive treatment programme, consisting of intravenous administration of broad-spectrum antibiotics. Without this, the Bentleys were told, Tiger could die within hours if he were indeed suffering from meningitis.

When all the tests were completed, Sam and Laura were allowed to visit their son in intensive care. They clung to each other as they walked towards the incubator, afraid of what they might find. Inside, Tiger lay asleep, wearing nothing but a nappy and a knitted bonnet, every inch of his pale body covered in tubes and monitors.

'Oh, Laura,' Sam said as he stared down at his infant son. 'I feel so helpless. What has Tiger done – what have any of us done – to deserve this?'

Laura wiped her puffy eyes with the back of her hand. 'It's my punishment,' she replied.

'Your punishment for what?'

'For being a bad mother.'

'Don't say that,' Sam said angrily. 'You're a brilliant mum.'

'You don't know the half of it,' Laura whispered, her words muffled by the sterile mask she was wearing.

Throughout the night, the Bentleys kept a vigil beside their son's incubator. For once, Tiger slept right through, his body severely weakened by the infection that was coursing through his veins. As Laura watched him, she felt dazed – not just by the cruel blow fate had dealt them, but also by the strength of her emotions. Countless times she'd wished that Tiger were dead; on one occasion she'd even considered killing him herself. But now that his life hung in the balance she realized that, more than anything else in the world, she wanted him to survive.

Around 7 a.m., Sam went in search of breakfast. Neither of them had eaten a thing since lunchtime the previous day, their appetites dulled by fear. Soon after he left, Tiger woke up. Immediately, he began squawking – a sound that would previously have made Laura's jaw clench in irritation. Now, however, she felt only a deep pain and a suffocating desire to comfort him.

'It's all right, sweetpea, Mummy's here,' she said, reaching into the incubator and stroking his feverish cheek.

Tiger's blue eyes swivelled in her direction. They were huge and pleading. *Get me out of here*, he seemed to be saying. Laura chewed the inside of her cheek, desperately trying not to cry.

'I know you're hurting, but Mummy's going to make it better, I promise,' she said.

As she touched the back of Tiger's tiny hand, being careful to avoid the IV that was taped to the back of it, he reached out and curled his fist around her index finger. Instantly, Laura's eyes brimmed with tears.

'Don't leave me,' she whispered. 'Don't you dare leave me.'

Twenty

While the Bentleys were anxiously waiting for Tiger's test results, back in Kirkhulme, Amber Solomon was concerned with the altogether more trifling matter of a tea party. For some weeks now she'd been struggling to rebuild her social life and restore her hitherto-very-high standing in the local community. She had hoped that her stunt with the billboard would stir up a bit of sympathy and that the village's movers and shakers – the very same people who'd taken advantage of her own lavish hospitality so many times in the past – would open their ranks and welcome her back into the fold. Perversely, however, Amber's very public declaration appeared to have had the opposite effect. Her phone remained resolutely silent, and her eighteenth-century French escritoire, once littered with stiff cards requesting the pleasure of her company at this glamorous party or that fund-raising auction, now contained only bills and densely typed letters from her lawyer. Even on her occasional forays into the high street, casual acquaintances seemed reluctant to meet her eye, preferring instead to feign a sudden interest in the contents of their shopping bag. Only the village children continued to stare, mesmerized by her supernatural face.

But Amber was a fighter and, after giving the matter some considerable thought, she decided that the key to her rehabilitation lay in the Kirkhulme Ladies' Guild – or, more specifically, in regaining her place on the board of directors. Despite its genteel title, the Guild was one of the most influential organizations in the village and those within its highest echelons were afforded a generous measure of respect. As well as the more mundane coffee mornings and cake sales, the Guild was also responsible for organizing a wealth of evening events. Most of these masqueraded as charity fundraisers, but those in attendance were less concerned with swelling the coffers of the local donkey sanctuary than with flaunting their designer outfits and necking as much all-inclusive champagne as possible. It was this giddy social whirl that Amber longed to reacquaint herself with. Not only would it provide a welcome relief from long, lonely nights at home, but she might also find herself a new love interest. Or, if not love, at least some satisfying, no-strings sex.

Amber had once been a leading light in the Guild; indeed, its annual garden party, staged in the grounds of the Old Manor and heavily subsidized by the Solomons, was the highlight of its summer calendar. Six weeks earlier, however, she had resigned her position as director. With so much else on her plate, she no longer felt able to commit to the weekly board meetings – or bear the pitying looks of her fellow directors. Since then she'd had no involvement with the group and she knew that some serious brown-nosing would have to be done if she were to get back in favour. To this end, she had invited the Guild's chairwoman, Lady Emmerson – a member of one of Kirkhulme's oldest families – and her two deputies, Hattie and Marilyn, to afternoon tea. Amber had been bracing herself for excuses but to her surprise all three had instantly accepted, motivated, she suspected, more by plain old-fashioned nosiness than any desire to be supportive.

It was the first time Amber had invited guests to the Old Manor since the breakdown of her marriage and she was feeling understandably nervous at the prospect of entertaining three such important figures. Normally, she would have relied on a small army of staff to help her stage such an event: caterers, florists, waiters and so on. But, with her interim maintenance settlement yet to be finalized, she was operating within a very limited budget. Earlier that day, she'd visited the village bakery to purchase a selection of scones and cream cakes, as well as thinly-sliced bread for the sandwiches, which she made herself using free-range eggs from the farm shop and a tin of salmon she'd found at the back of the larder.

With the weather forecast promising a fine, dry day, Amber had decided to host the tea party outdoors, as far away from the house – and, more to the point, as far away from Daniel – as possible. Following the dramatic events of their wedding anniversary, the two were no longer on speaking terms, though sternly worded lawyers' letters had been simultaneously exchanged, each advising the other party against further 'wilful destruction of personal property'. Both the Solomons appeared to have heeded the warning and, for the past week, a fragile truce had been in place. That wasn't to say Amber had reached any sort of understanding with Daniel. Far from it. His callous dispatch of Couscous had simply made her even more determined to hang on to the Old Manor at all costs.

The location Amber had chosen lay in a secluded corner of the garden, overlooking the Italianate fountain she'd had commissioned for Daniel's fortieth birthday. Inspired by the Fountain of Love at Cliveden, where the couple had once spent a romantic weekend, the ornate piece was situated in the middle of a pond and featured voluptuous female nudes and cherubs cavorting beside a giant shell. Usually, silvery streams of crystal-clear water cascaded gently from the dozen or so jets concealed in the shell, having been pumped through a sophisticated filtration system. But that morning, as Amber dragged the heavy, wrought-iron table and chairs across the lawn – breaking a fingernail in the process – she noticed that the fountain wasn't working. Flaring her nostrils in annoyance, she stood on the pond's grassy bank and stared into the murky water, which was rich with plant life. She supposed that the pump had given out – and, with her guests arriving within the hour, there was no time to call the maintenance company. It was disappointing, but Amber wasn't about to let a minor detail like a faulty fountain spoil her big day.

Once the garden furniture was in position, Amber set about dressing the table. Keen to make a good impression, she dug out her cream Irish linen tablecloth and the monogrammed napkins that were a wedding present from her parents, folding them so that the intertwined *D* and *A*, hand-stitched in gold thread, were facing inwards. Afterwards, she laid out her best bone china plates and teacups, as well as the sterling silver cutlery that she kept for special occasions. Finally, she filled a Persian vase with a colourful – if slightly clumsy –

arrangement of tea roses, helianthus and spiky eryngium that she'd filched from the Old Manor's well-stocked flowerbeds. After placing it in the centre of the table, she stepped back to survey the finished result. Then, satisfied that her efforts would pass muster with the exceedingly pernickety Lady Emmerson, she went indoors to relay last-minute instructions to Calum who, after some cajoling and a small financial incentive, had agreed to act as waiter for the afternoon.

Amber found her son in the kitchen, heaping a scone with jam and cream. As usual, a tinny percussive hiss was emanating from his person.

She waved at him to get his attention. 'You'll go deaf if you insist on having the volume that loud.'

Calum pulled out one of his earphones. 'What?'

'I *said* … oh, never mind.' Amber caught sight of the clock on the kitchen wall. 'Gosh, is that the time? My guests will be here in fifteen minutes. Hadn't you better get changed?'

Calum looked down at his hoodie and combats. 'What's wrong with what I'm wearing?'

'Oh darling, you look like a drug dealer. Lady Emmerson's going to have an attack of the vapours if you come within ten feet of her.'

Calum sighed. 'What do you want me to wear?'

'A suit.' Amber said firmly. 'What about that nice black one we bought you for your grandfather's funeral?'

'Oh, *Muuum*,' said Calum through a mouthful of scone.

'Please, darling, you'd be doing me a huge favour.'

'*Okaaay*,' said Calum, sending a shower of scone crumbs on to the floor.

'And don't eat any more of those or there won't be enough to go round,' said Amber, pulling the Coalport dish of scones towards her and re-securing the clingfilm cover.

'When should I bring the stuff out?'

'Three thirty promptly,' said Amber, pulling a large glass tea press from one of the kitchen cupboards. 'You do know how to use this, don't you?'

'Uh, I think so,' Calum mumbled.

'It's very simple. You put two spoonfuls of Earl Grey and one of lapsang formosa in the infuser basket, add the boiling water and push down the plunger.'

'Cool.'

'All the food's there on the counter. All you have to do is put everything on to a tray and bring it out to us in the garden and arrange it nicely on the table. Do you think you can manage that?'

Calum rolled his eyes. 'I'm not a fucking idiot, you know.'

'Of course you're not, darling. I don't mean to be patronizing, but this is a big day for me and I don't want anything to go wrong. Speaking of which ...' Amber cocked her head, ears straining for any sound of movement. 'Do you know if your father's home? I haven't seen him this morning.'

'He's in the garage. He said he needed to check the tyre pressure on the Harley.'

Amber frowned. 'I didn't know he still had that old bike. Is he planning to go out for a ride?' she said, knowing that she'd be able to enjoy the afternoon a lot more if Daniel made himself scarce.

Calum shrugged. 'Dunno. But don't worry – he's promised to keep out of your way today.'

Amber looked at her son. 'What do you mean?'

'I told him about the tea party.'

Amber's jaw tightened. 'You did *what*?'

'I told him about the tea party.'

'*What* did you tell him?' Amber hissed.

'That you were having some old crones over from the Ladies' Guild. I couldn't remember their names.'

Amber drove the heel of her hand into her forehead. 'I wish you hadn't done that, Calum,' she said, struggling to remain calm. 'I didn't want your father to know about this.'

Calum sighed. 'Honestly, it's no big deal. Dad was fine about it. He said he was pleased you were getting back in touch with some of your old friends and that he hoped you had a nice time.'

'He did?'

'Yeah.' Calum patted Amber's shoulder. 'Stop stressing, Ma, it'll be fine.'

Amber sighed. 'It had better be.'

While Calum went upstairs to change, Amber headed into the hall to check her appearance in the mirror above the console table. Not wanting to look as if she were trying too hard, she'd settled on a low-key outfit – loose-fitting navy trousers and a silk blouse, teamed with diamond earrings and a matching solitaire pendant. She stared hard at her reflection, noting that her eyes looked tired and the skin around her neck seemed a little saggy. Financial constraints meant she'd had to put her plans for further cosmetic surgery on hold, but as soon as her interim maintenance settlement was agreed, she would speak to Dr Lawrence about getting some more work done. She might even have the vaginal tightening procedure she'd been thinking about for months.

As she checked her forehead for new furrows, Amber heard the crunch of tyres on gravel. Turning towards the window, she saw Lady Emmerson's chauffeur-driven Bentley winding its way sedately up the drive. Her guest was more than twenty minutes early. Amber knew it was a deliberate tactic: Lady Emmerson, who regarded herself as the best party-giver in Kirkhulme, famously liked to push other hostesses to the limit and had doubtless been hoping to throw Amber's preparations into disarray by arriving before she was expected. Amber, however, was one step ahead. *You've got to get up pretty early in the morning to catch me out, you old witch*, she thought to herself as she walked to the front door.

By 3.05, all Amber's guests had arrived at the house. She was pleased to see they'd made an effort with their outfits – a clear sign that, despite Amber's new single status, they still thought she was Somebody Worth Bothering With. Lady Emmerson, who believed dressing down showed bad breeding, looked like a grand dowager duchess at a wedding in a flamingo-pink two-piece and a matching hat, trimmed with marabou. Hattie, her right-hand woman, had opted for a floaty bias-cut affair that strained unappetizingly across her spare tyre, while side-kick number two, Marilyn, was stylish in an elegant

Matthew Williamson shift that Amber had been salivating over for weeks after seeing it in the window of one of Kirkhulme's designer boutiques.

'Thank you all so much for coming,' Amber said in a honeyed tone as she led them towards the fountain and her carefully laid tea table. 'I'm sorry I've been keeping such a low profile recently, only I've had rather a lot on my mind.'

'Yes, you poor thing,' Hattie twittered, easing her ample rump into a garden chair. 'Your marital troubles are the talk of the village.'

Amber smiled tightly. 'Really? Haven't people got anything better to gossip about?'

'Oh, but you've brought it on yourself,' Lady Emmerson snorted.

'It's not as if I *asked* my husband to have an affair with the housekeeper,' Amber said, sensing – even at this early stage of the proceedings – that the afternoon was going to be something of an ordeal.

Lady Emmerson patted the back of Amber's hand. 'Of course not, my dear; after all, what woman wants to suffer the abject indignity of being upstaged by the hired help?' Her eyes bored into Amber, hard and cold as chips of ice. 'Still, you didn't have to air your dirty laundry in public.'

'She's talking about the billboard,' Marilyn added helpfully.

'Ah,' said Amber.

'We were all terribly shocked when we saw it, weren't we?' Hattie said, gazing at her mentor worshipfully.

Lady Emmerson nodded. 'It was a dreadfully vulgar

tactic, if you don't mind me saying. I daresay you were upset, but you really didn't do yourself any favours. A lot of folk felt sorry for Daniel when they saw his face plastered across that hoarding.'

'Really?' said Amber.

'People in the village are very fond of him,' said Lady Emmerson. 'Especially since he made that sizeable donation towards the refurbishment of the cricket pavilion.'

'But Daniel doesn't give a shit about the cricket club,' Amber said indignantly. 'That donation was *my* idea. I read about the fund-raising effort in the *Kirkhulme Gazette* and insisted Daniel put his hand in his pocket.'

Lady Emmerson glowered at Amber. 'Don't be petty, dear; it's most unbecoming. All I'm saying is you need to conduct your private affairs more discreetly if you're hoping to rejoin the Guild's board of directors.' She studied Amber the way a spider sizes up a fly, caught in its web. 'That *is* why you've invited us here today, isn't it?'

Amber bowed her head deferentially, though it almost killed her. 'Yes, Lady Emmerson. The truth is, I think I may have been a bit hasty in stepping down.'

'Quite – *and* on the eve of the jam-tasting gala too,' said Marilyn, folding her arms across her chest. 'You really left us in the lurch, Amber. It was very hard finding another judge at such short notice.'

'I'm truly sorry. My head was a mess. I was so devastated by Daniel's infidelity, I just wasn't thinking straight.' Amber paused, waiting for some sign of sisterly sympathy, but none was forthcoming. She licked her lips tentatively. 'You haven't found a replacement director yet, have you?'

'No,' Lady Emmerson conceded. 'But we'd have to think very carefully about letting you return. A place on the board isn't a right – even for an ex-director; it has to be earned.'

'I understand,' said Amber, though actually she thought it was Lady Emmerson, not she, who was being petty. Unable to look the chairwoman in the eye, she gazed out across the lawn. This tea party was turning out to be a lot more difficult than she'd expected. Suddenly, she caught sight of a gangly figure loping towards them. It was Calum, his face almost concealed by the heavily laden cake stand he was carrying on a tray. Amber smiled, glad of the distraction. 'Ah, good,' she said. 'Here's my son with the tea.'

For the next few minutes, she fussed with the tea-pot and handed round sandwiches, pretending not to notice as Lady Emmerson inspected her butter knife before polishing it vigorously on the corner of the table-cloth. With everyone fed and watered, the conversation turned once again to the subject of Amber's failed marriage.

'It must be very difficult living in the same house as one's estranged husband,' Marilyn mused out loud.

'It's perfectly horrible,' Amber admitted. 'Although we do our best to stay out of each other's way.'

Hattie gave her hostess a sly look. 'Does he bring *her* back?'

'Her?'

'You know ... the charwoman.'

Amber sighed. The last thing she wanted to do was confide in this catty trio, but she had a feeling that serving up a few tasty titbits was the only way to get herself back in their good books.

'All the time,' she said, lifting the teacup to her lips. 'And judging by the racket coming from Daniel's room I can say with reasonable confidence that copious bodily fluids are being exchanged on a regular basis.'

Marilyn batted her hand in front of her face as if she were having a menopausal flush. 'Ooh, I say. Talk about rubbing your nose in it.'

For a few moments, the Guild harpies were silent as they gleefully imagined how they would set about disseminating this piece of information.

'How's your little monkey?' Hattie asked, helping herself to a third mini éclair.

Amber decided to really give them something to gossip about. 'Couscous? He's very dead, thank you.'

Lady Emmerson peered over the top of her glasses. 'Did you say *dead*?'

Amber nodded. 'I did indeed. I'm afraid the cricket club's esteemed benefactor killed an endangered species and served him up to me as an anniversary present.'

At this, Hattie started choking on her cake.

'How utterly appalling,' said Marilyn, patting her fellow deputy chairwoman on the back in an attempt to loosen the wedge of choux pastry lodged at the back of her throat. 'I've never had monkey stew before. What does it taste like?'

Amber crossed one leg over the other. 'Oh no, Daniel didn't cook him; my husband's much more original than that. He had poor, innocent Couscous made into a fur stole.'

Lady Emmerson's eyes lit up. 'A monkey stole! Now that's something I'd like to see.'

Amber took a swallow of tea to wash down her distaste. 'I'm afraid you can't. I've buried it. Naturally, I'd find it far too upsetting to wear what remained of my faithful companion.'

Hattie, who had now recovered from her near-asphyxiation, smiled sympathetically. 'I'd be exactly the same if anything happened to George, my darling Springer spaniel.'

'Don't worry,' said Amber archly. 'I got my own back.'

'May we enquire how?' asked Marilyn, leaning forward eagerly.

'I smashed his precious Egyptian artefacts on the floor of his study and ground them to dust under the heel of my shoe.'

Hattie clapped her hands together delightedly. 'Good for you, Amber!'

Even Lady Emmerson's lip curled in amusement. She picked up one of the tiny crustless sandwiches, which Amber had painstakingly trimmed into circles using a cookie cutter, and popped it in her mouth. Instantly, her smile evaporated. 'Is this *tinned* salmon?' she asked imperiously.

'I'm afraid so,' said Amber unapologetically. 'Daniel's frozen our joint bank account, so I've had to cut back on certain luxuries for the time being.'

Lady Emmerson raised her napkin to her lips and spat

out a well-chewed mouthful of sandwich. 'How long have you been married – twenty years, isn't it?'

'Nineteen.'

'I hope you're planning to take him to the cleaners.'

Amber blinked slowly. 'Of course.'

'Have you got a decent lawyer?'

'Fiona Mortimer. She's the best in the north-west, with fees to match.'

'Good, then there's no reason you won't emerge from this messy business with a sizable settlement.' Lady Emmerson gave Amber a sharp look. 'I presume you're making a demand for the house.'

'Abso-bloody-lutely.'

'I'm pleased to hear it.' Lady Emmerson shook her napkin on to the grass and then spread it across her knees. 'Because it would be hard to find a finer backdrop for the Guild's annual garden party.'

Amber's heart gave a little flutter. This sounded more promising. It looked as if she were still in the running for the director's position after all. 'Let me pour you some more tea,' she said, reaching for Lady Emmerson's cup. 'And then you must tell me all about that talented grandson of yours. He's going up to Oxford next month, isn't he?'

'That's right,' said Lady Emmerson smugly. 'The boy comes from a long line of geniuses, though I do say so myself.' She nodded towards the Minton jug. 'Plenty of milk, please.'

Amber did as she was told, then she reached across the table to hand the teacup back to Lady Emmerson. At that very moment, a loud revving shattered the calm of the garden, startling Amber and causing her hand to jerk. She watched aghast as the teacup went flying into Lady Emmerson's lap.

With an ear-splitting shriek, the chairwoman jumped up from the table.

'Oh my goodness, I'm so sorry,' said Amber, rushing round to tend to her guest.

Luckily the tea was only lukewarm, thanks to the generous helping of milk; in any case, the thick linen napkin on Lady Emmerson's lap had taken the brunt of the spillage.

'Look at my skirt. It's ruined, ruined!' Lady Emmerson cried.

'It'll soon dry in the sun,' said Amber as she dabbed at the flamingo-pink fabric with her own napkin. 'And if the stain doesn't come out, I'll pay for it to be dry-cleaned.'

'With what?' the chairwoman sneered. 'You can't even afford fresh salmon.'

Amber chewed her lip to stop herself saying something she might regret.

'What was that noise anyway?' said Marilyn, putting a hand over her eyes and scanning the landscape. 'It seemed to come from over there.' She pointed towards the row of garages that housed Daniel's car collection.

Amber looked up. In the distance, she could see a figure standing beside a highly distinctive motorcycle: a 1945 Harley Davidson Knucklehead, to be precise.

'It's Daniel,' she said. 'It looks as if he's working on his bike.'

She'd barely finished speaking before another series of deafening revs rent the air. Sighing, Amber turned back to her guests. 'I'm sorry about this, ladies. Hopefully, Daniel will be finished soon.'

'I didn't realize he was a motorbike enthusiast,' said Marilyn.

Amber raised an eyebrow. 'Neither did I. He hasn't touched that old Harley in years.'

'Look, he's putting on a helmet now,' said Hattie excitedly. 'He must be taking it out for a spin.'

The four women watched as Daniel kicked the bike off its stand and began motoring along the driveway towards the Old Manor's gated entrance.

'Thank goodness for that,' said Lady Emmerson as she settled back into her chair. She glared at Amber who was still crouching at her feet, napkin in hand. 'My skirt still feels very damp,' she added sniffily. 'But I suppose it'll have to do.'

Thus dismissed, Amber retreated back to her own chair. 'Now, what were we talking about?' she said, keen to get the afternoon back on track. 'Ah yes, Lady Emmerson's grandson. Just remind us of those amazing A-level results again.'

'Three As and a B,' Lady Emmerson crowed. 'But Oxford were so keen to have Jonty they made him an unconditional offer . . .' Her voice tailed off.

'Whatever is he doing now?' she said, scowling into the distance.

Amber followed her gaze and saw that Daniel had veered off the driveway and was following the snaking Cotswold stone path that led to the fountain. She gave a hard sigh. 'Who knows? That man's a law unto himself these days.'

She waited until Daniel was a few feet away, then called out to him, mindful that her guests would be scrutinizing every second of their interaction with interest. 'What do you think you're playing at?' she said in a cool, calm voice. 'Can't you see I have guests?'

Daniel didn't reply. Instead, he put one foot on the ground and revved the engine. A pungent cloud of fumes belched from the exhaust and drifted towards the tea table, causing the ladies of the Guild to cough and bat their napkins in front of their faces.

Amber stood up and took a step towards her husband. 'I thought you told Calum you were going to leave me in peace this afternoon.'

Daniel twisted the accelerator again. He looked menacing in his black leather jacket and the crash helmet with its tinted visor.

'Sorry, what was that?' he said, putting his hand to the side of his head. 'I can't quite hear you.'

'Then turn the fucking engine off!' Amber snapped. She cleared her throat, trying to regain her composure. 'Please.'

Daniel turned the key in the ignition and the engine puttered out. He pulled off his helmet and gave the tea party a dazzling smile. 'Good afternoon, ladies, and how are we this afternoon?'

'Very well, thank you,' Hattie simpered, looking at Daniel adoringly.

Amber rolled her eyes in disgust – but she knew that, for his age, her husband cut a dashing figure.

Lady Emmerson pressed the back of her hand to her forehead. 'Unfortunately, I can't say the same. I can feel one of my heads coming on, thanks to those ghastly fumes and that infernal engine noise.'

Instantly, Daniel's face was a picture of concern. 'Oh, Lady Emmerson, how dreadfully inconsiderate of me. I was just blowing the cobwebs out of the old girl.' He looked the chairwoman up and down. 'You're looking particularly lovely today, if I may say so. Pink really suits you.'

Lady Emmerson broke into a smile. 'Why, thank you,' she said, batting her eyelashes like a prize heifer.

Amber felt her guts clench. She found Daniel's toadying positively vomitous but, not wanting to make a scene, she held her emotions in check.

'Was there something in particular you wanted?' she snapped.

'Not really, I just thought I'd come and say hello.' Daniel fired up the engine again. 'I'll stick the bike back in the garage and leave you girls to enjoy the rest of your afternoon in peace.'

'Thank you,' said Amber, forcing herself to smile. 'That would be much appreciated.'

Daniel wheeled the bike round, then, almost as an afterthought, he paused and gestured to the pond. 'It's such a pity the fountain's not working,' he said to no one in particular. 'It really is quite spectacular when it's in full flow.' The next moment he was gone.

For the next half hour or so, Amber's tea party continued without interruption. Once the subject of Lady Emmerson's grandson's educational achievements had been exhausted, the conversation turned to the Guild's Harvest Supper. Held in the village hall at the end of

September, the annual event was a chance for members to show off their culinary skills and usually attracted a good-looking, well-heeled crowd. For the past five years, Amber had played a pivotal role at the supper, sitting at the top table with the other directors during the sumptuous, cordon bleu-standard meal, before taking to the podium to officiate at the requisite charity auction.

'This year's Supper's going to be the best ever,' Lady Emmerson declared. 'The tickets have been sold out for weeks; there's even a waiting list for returns.' She looked at Amber reproachfully. 'It's such a pity you didn't feel able to contribute this year.'

Hattie nodded her agreement. 'Trying to rustle up those auction prizes was a complete nightmare. We really missed not having your business contacts, Amber.'

Amber forced herself to look contrite, though she was tired of apologizing. 'You should've called me,' she said in a neutral tone. 'I could've given you some names and numbers.'

'We thought you didn't want anything more to do with us,' said Marilyn. She flashed a sly look at Lady Emmerson. 'Didn't we?'

'That's right,' the chairwoman confirmed. 'But now it seems Amber's changed her mind.'

To hide her discomfiture, Amber picked up the teapot; then realized it was empty. 'It was never my intention to abandon the Guild altogether,' she said. 'I simply needed a break, so I could deal with a personal crisis.'

Lady Emmerson smiled, a mirthless, leering grin. 'Ah, if only I could have a break whenever I was experiencing an emotional hiccup. Unfortunately, my sense of loyalty to the Guild simply wouldn't allow me to.'

'I promise I'll make it up to you,' Amber said, hating the note of desperation in her voice. 'If you'll just give me the chance.'

Lady Emmerson eyed Amber with the vicious aspect of a terrier on the lookout for something to sink its teeth into and shake until its backbone cracked.

'We're looking for another volunteer for the Harvest Supper,' she said coolly. 'Verity Brown broke her ankle last weekend during a tango lesson and she's going to be out of action for weeks.' She shook her head. 'Tango dancing? A woman as inelegant as Verity? It was always going to end in tears.'

'I'd be glad to step into the breach,' said Amber eagerly. 'You know how much I've always enjoyed presiding over the auction. I'm sure I can coax our guests into raising a record amount this year.'

'The auction's already taken care of; Marilyn's kindly offered to do the honours.' Lady Emmerson scratched the end of her long nose. 'It would be nice if you could be a little more hands-on this year, Amber dear.'

Amber nodded. 'Just tell me what you want me to do.'

'Washing-up,' said Lady Emmerson. The note of glee in her voice was unmistakeable.

'You want me to wash up?' Amber repeated.

'That's right. We'll need you in the kitchen all night, so there'll be no time to mingle with the guests I'm afraid.'

Amber looked down at her lap. This wasn't the glorious Guild homecoming she'd imagined.

'Of course, if you feel it's beneath you …'

Amber's head snapped back up. 'No, no, of course not.' She smiled weakly. 'I'd be glad to help in any way I can.'

'Good, that's settled then.' Lady Emmerson nodded towards the teapot. 'Are you going to put the kettle on?'

'Yes,' Amber said, mentally adding, *you hatchet-faced old sow*.

'A few more of those delicious scones wouldn't go amiss either,' said Hattie. 'Are they homemade?'

'Absolutely,' Amber lied. 'It's my grandmother's special recipe.'

'In that case, you can make some for the Harvest Supper,' said Lady Emmerson. Shall we say four dozen?'

Amber cursed inwardly. 'Fine,' she said, rising to her feet and picking up the teapot. 'I won't be long.'

She'd taken no more than half a dozen steps when suddenly she stopped and stared in surprise at the pond that surrounded the fountain. The surface of the water was bubbling fiercely, as if it were boiling.

A few moments later, Hattie's voice drifted over to her. 'Is everything all right, Amber?'

'Something strange is happening to the water,' Amber replied, as she peered into the pond's murky depths. 'I think the pump may have started up again.' She turned to her guests and smiled. 'Perhaps you *will* be able to see the fountain in action, after all.' And with that, she set off across the lawn towards the house. Forty-five seconds later, the first blood-curdling scream rang out.

Amber spun round, her heart in her mouth. At first her eyes couldn't make sense of what they were seeing.

The fountain was working again – but the usual gentle sprays of water, which caressed the stone figures before tumbling back into the pond, were nowhere to be seen. Instead, high-pressure jets arced from the stone shell across the lawn like a water cannon – and they all seemed to converge in one place: the tea table. What's more, the water wasn't clear and fresh, but thick, dark and smelly. As more anguished shrieks filled the air, Amber flung the teapot to the ground and went charging towards the fountain. As she ran, she realized to her horror that her three guests were writhing on the grass, having apparently been knocked to the ground by the force of the water. Every time they tried to get back up, one of the jets blasted them back down. All three were drenched, their expensive outfits découpaged with mud, slime and pondweed. Lady Emmerson's immaculate coiffure now hung in rat's tails and her skirt had ridden up to reveal a flesh-coloured pantie girdle.

'Don't just stand there,' she yelled at Amber above the roar of the water. 'Do something!'

Amber thought about running into the maelstrom and forcibly dragging Lady Emmerson clear, but quickly rejected the idea, realizing that she, too, would be knocked to the ground in an instant. 'Stay on the ground,' she shouted to the women. 'You need to roll *under* the jets.'

'We can't hear you!' said Hattie, yelping as a particularly powerful jet pummelled her posterior.

In desperation, Amber turned and ran towards the fountain, bending low so she could dodge the jets. She knew that the pump had a cut-off switch, if only she could remember where it was located. As she scuttled round the pond, she saw Daniel standing a short distance away. He was leaning against an oak tree and laughing fit to burst. Suddenly, the penny dropped.

'You!' Amber cried, the cut-off switch momentarily forgotten. 'You're responsible for this, aren't you?'

Daniel shrugged. 'I plead the fifth amendment.'

Amber felt her rage flare up like a lit match tossed into a pool of petrol. 'You bastard!' she shrieked as she went charging towards him. 'Have you got any idea what you've done! They'll never take me back on the board now. Never!'

Daniel caught Amber in a bear hug, pinning her arms to her sides. It was the closest they'd been to each other in months.

'I'm going to kill you for this!' Amber screeched as she struggled to free herself. 'And, believe me, I'm going to make it a slow, agonizing process.'

'Do it,' Daniel taunted her. 'Anything's got to be better than living with you – even death.'

'I hate you!' Amber cried, as she kicked his shins. '*IhateyouIhateyouIhateyou!*'

Suddenly, she heard a voice behind her. 'For God's sake, can't you two give it a rest for five minutes?'

It was Calum and, judging by the wobble in his voice, he was on the verge of tears. 'Let her go, Dad. Just let her go, all right?'

Daniel released his wife. Immediately, Amber brought her knee up sharply between his legs. 'After killing Couscous, I didn't think you could sink much lower,' she said as her husband doubled over in agony, hands crossed over his crotch. 'But yet again you've proved me wrong.'

She turned to her son just in time to see him angrily swipe a tear from his cheek. 'It's all right, darling, don't go upsetting yourself.' She fired a look of disgust in Daniel's direction. 'See what you've done with your stupid antics? I hope you're proud of yourself. Now turn off that wretched fountain before one of those old bags has a heart attack.'

Calum gave a loud sniff. 'It's okay, Mum, I've already done it.'

Amber turned towards the tea table, where three bedraggled figures were standing in a state of shock. Two were openly sobbing. 'Oh my God,' she said. 'I'm never going to live this down.' She turned to Daniel. 'I want you to go over there and apologize to those ladies,' she said firmly. 'Then I want you to admit complete responsibility and offer to cover their dry-cleaning bills. Really, it's the very least you can do.'

Daniel looked up. 'Calum,' he said in a strangulated voice. 'Tell your mother to go fuck herself.'

Twenty-One

It was Dylan's day off and, as usual, he'd spent most of it on the golf course at St Benedict's, exercising his employee privilege of half-price green fees. A scratch golfer, Dylan had been working as a sales assistant in the club shop for the past three years but he hoped that one day, in the not too distant future, he'd qualify as a PGA professional. Coaching jobs at St Benedict's were always hotly contested – not least because they afforded pros the opportunity for one-on-one time with the many beautiful and/or wealthy females who wanted to improve their game. Dylan met plenty of women in the shop, but he was always overshadowed by his colleagues, Ace and Harry, who were better looking than him and more extrovert. If he were working as a coach, on the other hand, there'd be no competition and Dylan was convinced that, once news of his easy manner and brilliant technique spread around the club, girls would be queuing up to grip his shaft, so to speak. But first he had to get his handicap up to the minimum requirement of plus two, which meant cramming in as much practice as possible.

As the sun started to descend over the fairway, Dylan shouldered his golf bag and set off towards the clubhouse. He'd planned to go straight home to the flat he rented in a neighbouring village, but after securing his gear in the staff locker room, he decided on impulse to pop into the Chukka Bar for a cheeky half. It was a Monday evening and the bar was quiet. As he carried his drink to an empty table, Dylan noticed Taylor Spurr sitting in one of the corner booths with a much older woman. They were drinking cocktails and seemed relaxed in each other's company. Taylor caught his eye and waved. Dylan waved back, amazed that the American girl even recognized him following their one brief encounter in the club shop more than a month earlier.

Before he sat down, Dylan reached into the back pocket of his Farahs and pulled out a dog-eared lads' mag he'd found lying on one of the benches in the locker room. Then he settled into a leather armchair and began perusing its well-thumbed pages. He was engrossed in the centre spread, across which a well-known glamour model posed topless on all fours, when he realized he had company. He glanced up to see Taylor standing beside him. She was resting one hand on the chair's high back and wearing a friendly expression.

'Hi,' she said. 'It's Dylan, isn't it?'

Dylan grinned. 'Hey, you remember my name.'

'Of course I do,' said Taylor, pushing her long hair back behind her ears. 'You made quite an impression on me when we met in the shop.'

Dylan frowned. 'I did?'

'Sure.' Taylor nodded towards his lap. 'Interesting reading, huh?'

Dylan looked down at the magazine. 'Oh, this?' he said, as casually as he could manage. 'It's just something I found lying around the locker room.'

Taylor leaned over his shoulder so she could study the

centre spread more closely. As she did so, a skein of her silky hair grazed Dylan's cheek, sending a powerful surge of sexual electricity through his groin.

'She's got great tits, hasn't she?' said Taylor, stroking the model's breast with her fingertips.

Dylan's throat felt dry. He longed to reach for his drink, but that would mean moving away from Taylor. 'They're not bad,' he concurred.

Taylor turned her head towards him. Their faces were now mere centimetres apart. Even this close up, Dylan could see that the golfer's skin was flawless, except for a tiny indentation above her left eyebrow that might have been a chickenpox scar.

'Do you reckon they're real or fake?'

'What?' said Dylan, who was lost in the dark pool of Taylor's chocolatey irises.

'Her tits – real or fake?'

Dylan dragged his eyes away from Taylor's and looked down at the magazine. 'They look fake to me.'

'Me too,' said Taylor. 'Which do you prefer?'

Dylan forced himself to swallow. 'Erm, I don't really mind, to be honest.'

Suddenly, Taylor straightened up and thrust out her chest, which was encased in a tight pink T-shirt. 'Do you think *I* should get a boob job?'

Dylan stared at Taylor's modest, but undeniably perky offerings. 'They look just fine to me,' he said. 'You're so slim, I think you'd look out of proportion if they were any bigger.'

'Aw, thanks,' said Taylor, smiling as if he'd just paid her the most enormous compliment. 'Listen, Dylan, the reason I came over was, my mom and I were wondering if you'd like to join us.'

Dylan turned to look at the woman in the booth. She was staring right at them. 'Oh, is that your mum? She doesn't look old enough,' he said – not because it was true, but because it seemed like the right thing to say. He closed the magazine and tossed it on the table. 'Yeah, okay then. It's not as if I've got anything to rush home for.'

Taylor's lips formed a surprised 'O'. 'What – no girlfriend?'

'Nope, I'm footloose and fancy free.'

Taylor shook her head. 'What a waste.' She picked Dylan's drink up from the table as if she were worried he might be about to change his mind. 'Come on, Mom's dying to meet you.'

To begin with, the conversation was pretty mundane. Keen to make a good impression and still unsure of Taylor's motives for inviting him over, Dylan stuck to safe territory: golf. Both women reacted enthusiastically when he told them about his ambition to make it as a club pro and Taylor even offered to take him out on to the course for a practice session. 'It'll have to be in the next couple of weeks, though,' she warned. 'Mom and I are heading back to Texas at the beginning of September.'

'That's a shame,' Dylan said boldly. 'It would've been nice to get to know you a little better.' Then, for polite-ness' sake he added: 'Both of you, I mean.'

Kristina leaned over and squeezed his hand. 'The

night's still young, darlin'.' Noticing his empty glass, she turned to her daughter. 'Why don't you get us some more drinks, Taylor?'

'Oh no, let me,' said Dylan, reaching for his wallet.

Taylor smiled. 'How 'bout you get the next one?'

'Cool,' said Dylan, smiling back at her.

He watched her as she walked to the bar, admiring the way her arse moved under her short denim skirt.

'Taylor's pretty cute, huh?' Kristina remarked.

'She's absolutely gorgeous,' Dylan said dreamily.

'I was a bit of a peach in my day – Miss Wichita Falls 1978, no less.'

'Really?' said Dylan, trying not to sound too surprised. Kristina wasn't wholly unattractive, but he'd never have had her down as a former beauty queen: her skin was leathery and lined with crows' feet and she had forearms like a champion shot-putter.

'Oh yeah, I had guys queuing up to ask me out,' Kristina continued. 'And then I made the biggest dumb-ass mistake of my life by agreein' to marry Taylor's dad.'

Dylan glanced at the caddie's left hand and noticed that she wasn't wearing a wedding ring. 'It didn't work out then?'

'Uh-uh,' said Kristina. 'He left me for another man.'

'Blimey,' said Dylan, desperately fighting the urge to smirk. 'I bet that was tough.'

'I haven't been able to trust another guy since.' Kristina's eyes flickered over him. She had the carnivore look of a wild pack animal. 'How old are you, Dylan, if you don't mind me asking?'

'Twenty-one.'

Her eyes went to his crotch and then back to his face. 'Do you like older women?'

Dylan coughed nervously, not sure what she was getting at. 'I like all kinds of women, Mrs Spurr.'

At that moment, Taylor returned with their drinks. Dylan was surprised to see that instead of cocktails the two women were now drinking sparkling water.

'I got you a double,' Taylor said, handing Dylan his requested vodka tonic.

'This had better be my last one,' said Dylan as Taylor slid in beside him, so that he was now sandwiched between the two women. 'I'm driving home.'

'We'll make sure you get back safely, won't we, Mom?' A knowing look passed between mother and daughter, as if they were sharing a private joke.

'Oh yes,' said Kristina. 'Don't you worry about a thing, young fella. Taylor and I plan to take very good care of you.'

A couple of hours later, Sam Bentley happened to be crossing St Benedict's front lawn, en route to the car park following a late session on the floodlit driving range. As he passed the clubhouse, he spotted Dylan standing under one of the art deco street lamps.

'Hey, Dyl,' he said, walking over to the young man. 'What are you up to?'

'Just waiting for someone.' The shop assistant was wearing a silly smile and appeared to be rather the worse for wear. 'You'll never guess who's invited me back to her place for a nightcap.'

Sam's face lit up. 'You mean to say you've pulled?'

'I've done more than pull,' said Dylan. 'I've hit the fucking jackpot.' He pulled the lever on an imaginary one-armed bandit. 'Ker-ching!'

'Oh yeah, and who's the lucky girl?'

Dylan rubbed his hands together, barely able to contain his excitement. 'Taylor Spurr, that's who.'

Sam's mouth fell open. 'You're kidding me!'

'I know, I can hardly believe it myself. You should've seen her in the Chukka Bar – all over me she was … touching me up under the table and everything. Trust me, mate, that girl wants it bad.' Suddenly Dylan clapped a hand to his forehead. 'Oh shit, sorry, mate, she's a friend of yours, isn't she? I didn't mean to disrespect her.'

Sam shrugged, affecting a don't-care attitude. No one at the club knew about his little dalliance with Taylor and that was the way he wanted it to stay. 'Don't worry about it; she's more of an acquaintance really. I showed her the ropes when she first arrived at the club, that's all.' He looked around. Taylor was nowhere in sight. 'So where is she then?'

'She's nipped to the ladies with her mum. Our cab's due any minute, so I said I'd come out here and wait for it.'

Sam frowned. 'Hang on a minute, did you say you're going back with Taylor *and* her mum?'

'Yeah, Kristina seems pretty cool about Taylor having guys back.' Dylan performed a series of cartoon-like pelvic thrusts. 'Let's just hope she's got a good pair of earplugs, eh?'

Sam stroked his jaw thoughtfully. He liked Dylan and he knew that, sexually speaking, the sales assistant was pretty inexperienced. He'd hate to see his friend used and abused the way *he'd* been. 'Why don't you take Taylor back to yours?' he suggested. 'That way you two will have a bit more privacy.'

'No way,' said Dylan. 'My place is a complete shithole. The sink's full of washing up and I haven't changed my sheets for months.'

Sam glanced towards the clubhouse again. There was still no sign of Taylor and Kristina. 'Look, mate,' he said, taking Dylan's arm and speaking in a low voice, 'I don't want to piss on your parade but, take it from me, those Spurr women are dangerous.'

Dylan started sniggering. 'Dangerous? Are you having me on?'

'No, Dyl, I'm deadly serious.' Sam leaned in closer. 'Taylor and Kris have got this kinky double act. Believe me, you don't want to go back with them. They'll eat you alive.'

Dylan screwed up his face. 'What are you on about?'

Sam sighed. 'They're into threesomes.'

Dylan's eyes threatened to pop out of his head. '*Noooo*!'

'I know, it's freaky shit.'

'Hang on,' said Dylan. 'I thought you said you didn't know Taylor all that well.'

'I don't, but they pulled a friend of mine,' said Sam hastily.

'So what happened?'

'They lured him over to their house, got him drunk, turned the lights off so he didn't know what was going on and then both of them took advantage of him.'

'Wow,' said Dylan. 'That sounds awesome.'

Sam looked at Dylan in shock. 'Come on, Dyl ... mother and daughter? You've got to agree, that's seriously sick.' Suddenly, he caught sight of two figures emerging from the clubhouse. 'Look, they're coming over now. You're drunk, mate; you're not capable of making a rational decision. Why don't you let me give you a lift home?'

Dylan looked at him as if he were mad. 'What – and miss out on the opportunity of a lifetime?' He looked towards the approaching women and grinned. 'I don't think so.'

Sam sighed. 'Suit yourself. Just don't say I didn't warn you.'

He began walking away briskly, keen to avoid a confrontation with the Spurrs. A minute later, he turned to look over his shoulder. Taylor and Kristina each had an arm linked through Dylan's and the older woman's head was resting against him. It gave Sam a sickening sense of déjà vu. Suddenly, Taylor glanced in his direction. As their eyes locked together, she raised her hand behind Dylan's back and, very slowly and deliberately, gave him the finger. Sam turned away and hurried to the car park, head bowed.

Twenty-Two

Sam pumped the consultant paediatrician's hand. 'I'm so grateful for everything you've done, Dr Sheridan.'

'That goes for me too,' said Laura. 'You've been fantastic; all the staff have.'

Dr Sheridan smiled. 'That's what we're here for – to make people better.'

'You did more than make Tiger better,' Laura said, as she kissed the doctor on the cheek. 'You saved his life and for that I thank you from the bottom of my heart.'

'You're absolutely welcome,' the doctor replied. 'It was just fortunate Sam brought Tiger in when he did. Another couple of hours and the outcome might have been very different.'

Laura shuddered. 'Just thinking about it makes me go cold.' She looked at Tiger, lying peacefully in her arms. 'And you're quite sure he won't suffer any long-term ill effects?'

Dr Sheridan shook his head. 'There's no way we'd let him leave the hospital if we didn't think he was com-pletely recovered. We've given him a thorough check-up and everything – his reflexes, eyesight, hearing and so on – are all perfectly normal. In fact, they're better than normal. They're excellent.'

Sam stroked Tiger's downy head. 'Did you hear that,

son? You're a perfect physical specimen; we'll have you scoring your first hole in one in no time.'

Laura grimaced apologetically. 'You'll have to forgive my husband, Doctor. I'm afraid he's one of those pushy sports dads.'

Dr Sheridan laughed. 'You take care of that boy of yours, okay?'

Laura looked down at Tiger and felt a sudden and overwhelming rush of love for him. 'Oh, I intend to.'

It was six days since Tiger had been admitted to Delchester General. Six days during which the Bentleys' lives had been put on hold, their thoughts consumed entirely by their infant son's battle to survive. The diagnosis, when it finally came after an exhaustive round of tests, had surprised everyone. Not meningitis after all, but group B streptococcal septicaemia, an acute bacterial infection, unwittingly carried by the mother and passed to her baby during labour. Dr Sheridan had explained that eighty per cent of the time the illness manifested itself during the first two days of an infant's life. Tiger, however, was one of the rarer, late-onset cases. The consultant also delivered the chilling news that, if left untreated, group B strep could give rise to all sorts of complications, including meningitis, pneumonia and even, in extreme examples, respiratory arrest. Thankfully, Tiger had been one of the lucky ones, for the antibiotics, administered as a precautionary measure from day one, had stopped the infection spreading further into his bloodstream.

While Sam went to the nurses' station to hand out bottles of champagne to the staff who had cared for his son, Laura carried Tiger outside to the car. As she strapped him into his baby seat, she kissed him on the forehead.

'We're going home, sweetheart; we're starting again,' she whispered. 'I'm so sorry for all those horrid things I said to you before. But I'm going to make it up to you, I promise. From now on, I'm going to be a proper mother and I'm not going to let anything or anyone hurt you.'

Tiger gurgled and grabbed hold of one of Laura's dark curls. Despite the trauma of the last six days, for the first time in his short life he seemed utterly contented.

Back at the house, Marta was eagerly awaiting their arrival. She'd been an absolute rock while Tiger was ill, caring for Carnie and Birdie virtually round the clock, so that the Bentleys could spend as much time as possible at the hospital. The au pair was delighted to be reunited with her young charge, smothering him with hugs and kisses, to his obvious delight.

Later that day, Sam took the girls to Delchester Country Park for their long-overdue visit to the petting zoo, leaving Marta and Laura to catch up over coffee in the kitchen.

'It sounds as if the girls have had a great time over the past few days,' Laura said as she arranged shortbread fingers on a plate, adding wryly: 'Carnie tells me Uncle Harry has a very impressive selection of magic tricks.'

Marta blushed. 'He came to the house a few times while you were away. I didn't let him stay the night or anything. I hope you don't mind.'

'Don't be silly,' said Laura carrying the biscuits over to

the table. 'I just hope he didn't find the girls too exhausting.'

'No way,' said Marta. 'He was fantastic with them. I think he'll make a great dad one day.' She smiled shyly. 'Actually, I've got something to tell you.'

Laura took a sip of coffee. 'Go on.'

'Harry and I are moving in together.'

'Oh, Marta, that's wonderful news!' Laura exclaimed.

The Spanish girl blinked in surprise. 'You mean you approve?'

'Of course I approve. I know how you feel about Harry.'

'Oh,' said Marta. 'It's just that I got the impression you weren't too happy about our relationship.'

'Oh dear, I didn't realize I'd made my feelings so obvious,' said Laura, wincing. 'It isn't that I don't like Harry; it's just that you seemed to be getting very serious and I was worried that . . .' She paused and stared into her coffee cup.

'That I'd quit my job and you'd be left to cope with Tiger on your own?'

Laura broke into an embarrassed grin. 'Am I really that transparent?'

Marta picked up a shortbread finger and chewed it meditatively. 'Let's just say I could see you were struggling with Tiger. I've tried to help you as much as I can.'

'I know you have,' said Laura, giving the au pair's arm a grateful squeeze. 'And I honestly don't know what I would've done without you. But it was selfish of me to expect you to stay single forever; you're young and you've got your own life to lead.' She sighed. 'I daresay you and Harry will be thinking about babies of your own soon.'

Marta snorted. 'No way; not for a good five years at least.' She looked Laura in the eye. 'Don't worry, I'm not going anywhere. I love my job and I love the kids.'

'And *we* love you,' said Laura. 'Sam and I are so grateful for everything you've done for our family, especially over the last few days. In fact, we'd like to give you something to show our appreciation – a new car to replace that dodgy old Citroen of yours.'

Marta's hands flew to her mouth. '*¡Icanastos!* Are you sure?'

Laura nodded. Sam's already made a few enquiries and a dealer in Delchester has offered him a great deal on a brand-new Beetle.' She smiled at the au pair. 'God knows, you've earned it ten times over.'

At that moment Tiger – who'd been lying on the floor in his baby rocker, good as gold – began cooing loudly.

Laura laughed. 'See, Tiger agrees with me.' She leaned forward and scooped up her son, nestling him in the crook of her arm and staring at him adoringly. 'Don't you, pumpkin?'

'You two seem to be getting on very well,' said Marta, taking Tiger's foot in her hand.

Laura nodded. 'We are, aren't we? When I saw him lying in that hospital incubator for the first time, so tiny and helpless ... well, it just brought home to me how much I cared about him.'

'Tiger seems a lot more relaxed too,' said Marta. 'Which is amazing, considering what he's just been through.'

'I've noticed that too,' said Laura. 'But, then again, it's

no wonder he was always so crabby when he had that nasty bug in his system since birth, just waiting to attack his immune system.' She beamed at Marta. 'Call me a hopeless optimist, but I think motherhood is just about to get a whole lot easier.'

While Laura was revelling in her newfound domesticity, her friend Keeley was trying to put her own house in order, metaphorically speaking. In recent weeks, Keeley's relationship with Ryan had become increasingly strained, and things had come to a head as they returned home from a swinging party. Keeley was annoyed because Ryan had spent most of the evening holed up in a bedroom with a TV producer, who was tall and slender and wore heavy-framed black glasses – the kind that beautiful women wear to signal they're smart, and yet so beautiful they can get away with wearing ugly accessories. Keeley, meanwhile, had received enthusiastic cunnilingus from the producer's husband in a separate bedroom, before politely declining his offer of full sex. Afterwards, she got dressed and walked down the hall, intending to go downstairs for a glass of wine. En route she passed an open door. Beyond it, an indeterminate number of people lay in a writhing heap on the vast four-poster. On another occasion, Keeley would have stopped to watch. If she'd been feeling particularly energetic, she might even have joined in. But that evening, she was revolted by what she saw and heard. 'Animals,' she muttered under her breath as she hurried past the door.

Finding herself overwhelmed by a sudden desire to be at home, curled up on the sofa with a mug of hot chocolate, she went in search of Ryan, banging on each of the half dozen or so bedroom doors and calling his name until she found him.

He came to the door in his underwear. 'What is it?' he asked irritably.

Over his shoulder, Keeley could see the TV producer sprawled naked on the bed. A torn condom wrapper lay on the floor beside her.

'I want to go home,' Keeley said.

Ryan glanced at the showy, diamond-encrusted Audemars Piguet on his wrist. 'But it's not even ten o'clock yet,' he said.

'I don't care; I've had enough.'

The goalkeeper glanced over his shoulder, whereupon his playmate blew him a kiss. It was a harmless enough gesture, but it made Keeley sick to her stomach. When Ryan turned back to her, he was grinning like a lovesick schoolboy. 'Just give me another half an hour, okay?'

'No,' Keeley replied. 'I want to go now.'

'Oh, *baaabe.*'

'Remember the rules,' Keeley said in a tight voice. 'The minute one of us has had enough, we go.' Then, just to show she meant business, she held out her hand. 'Give me the keys. I'll wait for you in the car.'

Ryan was in a bad mood when he finally joined Keeley in the BMW, a good fifteen minutes later.

'What you did back there was very rude, you know,' he said sulkily as they waited for the ubiquitous security gates to swing open. 'I didn't like leaving Felicity in the lurch like that.'

'Well, you're not Felicity's boyfriend, are you?' Keeley snapped. 'You're mine.'

They drove in silence for a minute or two, and then Keeley announced. 'You know, I really don't want to do this any more.'

'Do what?'

'Swinging – I've had enough.'

Ryan glanced across at her. 'I thought you enjoyed it.'

'I used to, but tonight I just felt cheap.'

The footballer gave a mocking laugh.

'What's so funny?'

'Let's not go there, okay?'

Keeley glared at Ryan. 'Come on, if you've got something to say, say it.'

'What you said about feeling cheap . . . it just sounds a bit ironic, that's all.'

'Meaning?'

'Meaning you used to have a bit of a reputation.'

Keeley's cheeks began to burn. 'What are you talking about?'

'Come on, Kee, you were the biggest gold-digger at St Benedict's; everyone knows that. You'd sleep with any fella, just so long as he could keep you in Cristal and diamonds.'

'You bastard,' Keeley spat. 'You fucking bastard.'

Ryan seemed unmoved. 'Don't have a go at me,' he said lightly. 'All I'm doing is telling the truth.'

'So why did you go out with me then, if I'm such a slapper?'

Ryan sighed. He hated confrontation. 'I thought you

were a nice person,' he said, fully aware of how lame he sounded.

'*Nice?*' said Keeley. 'Is that it?'

'What more do you want?'

'Oh, I don't know ... how about *fascinating* or *gorgeous* or *sexy?*'

'Well, yeah, you're all of those things too.'

'You might try sounding like you mean it.'

'Jesus, woman, can't you stop nagging me for one minute?' said Ryan, banging his palm against the steering wheel.

Keeley bit her lip, fighting back the tears. 'What's got into you?' she said. 'You used to be so romantic and caring, but now all you try and do is put me down at every opportunity. I feel as if I hardly know you any more.'

Ryan looked straight ahead, stony-faced. He *had* been bad-tempered with Keeley lately. Her clinginess irritated him and just recently she was liable to go into a sulk at the slightest thing. He'd hoped the swinging would loosen her up a bit and help put their relationship on a more casual footing, but it had only succeeded in making her even more possessive.

'Don't exaggerate.'

'You're secretive too.'

'What are you on about?' said Ryan, his voice full of weary exasperation.

'The transfer deal ... I don't understand why you're being so cagey about it.'

Ryan sighed. 'How many times do I have to tell you? My agent's in talks with a club in London, but nothing's been agreed.' He felt a twinge of shame as he spoke the words, but quickly brushed it aside. Keeley would discover the truth, soon enough. He knew he was being cowardly, but he couldn't bear emotional scenes with women. This way, he told himself, things would be a lot easier for both of them.

'Fine,' Keeley said curtly. 'I'll just have to take your word for it then, won't I?'

They lapsed into silence again. Keeley's mind was churning. There was so much she wanted to say, but she didn't know where to begin.

'So there's nothing wrong then?' she said after a while. 'With us, I mean.'

'Course not.'

'And you still love me.'

The tiniest pause. 'Sure.'

Keeley put her hand on Ryan's thigh. 'I hate it when we argue.'

'Me too.'

Another silence. 'So, about the swinging ...' Keeley ventured.

Ryan flicked on his indicator. 'Can we talk about this later? I'm really not in the mood.'

'Okay,' said Keeley meekly, not wanting to make him cross again.

A moment later, the BMW pulled up outside Keeley's building. She'd assumed Ryan would be staying the night, but in the event, he didn't even bother putting on the handbrake.

'I won't stay over,' he said. 'I've got an early start tomorrow. I'm helping a friend move house.' He leaned over and kissed her clumsily on the side of her face.

'Suit yourself,' said Keeley as she climbed out of the car and slammed the door shut behind her.

The BMW roared away before she even had her key in the lock.

For three days, Keeley heard nothing from Ryan. She, in turn, resisted the temptation to contact him. She was still sulking over the footballer's refusal to stay the night and was determined that he should be the one to make the first move. And, if he really wanted to make amends, she told herself, then a small gift – some jewellery perhaps, or a new handbag – would grease the wheels of forgiveness. Then, on the evening of the second day, as Keeley stood in her cramped kitchen preparing an avocado salad while the local TV news burbled in the background, she heard her boyfriend's name. As a Premiership footballer, Ryan was regularly mentioned on TV and Keeley was always keen to hear about his latest achievement – even if he *was* in her bad books. Picking up her plate, she walked through to her tiny living space and stared at the TV screen, which was filled with a huge, grinning photograph of Ryan.

'Delchester United player Ryan Stoker will be unveiled as the new goalkeeper of Hampton Rangers at a press conference on Friday,' the sports anchor said. 'Stoker, who passed his medical last week, has agreed a two-year deal with the London club for an undisclosed fee. Rangers beat the transfer deadline to complete the signing earlier today, following weeks of negotiations. The club's chairman, Freddy Davies, told *North West Tonight*:

"Ryan has a lot of natural talent and he will be a huge asset to the team."'

Keeley's salad plate landed on the coffee table with a clatter as she collapsed on to the sofa. She felt like a house shaken by some nearby gas explosion: tiles had fallen, windows had blown in, the chimney stack was leaning at a precarious angle. The house was still standing – but only just. Her mind was buzzing as she tried to absorb the implications of the brief news report. If Ryan had completed a medical for Rangers last week, there must have been a deal on the table at that point. And, even if he'd been sworn to secrecy by the club, why hadn't he at least phoned to tell her the good news earlier that day, as soon as contracts were signed? Amidst all the confusion, only one thing was certain: Ryan had lied to her. She picked up the cordless phone and punched in Ryan's home number. It rang unanswered. She tried his mobile. It cut straight to voicemail. She hurled the phone on the floor. Then, after only a few moments, she picked it up and called the number of the local taxi firm.

Half an hour later, a mini cab pulled up outside the Piano Factory, a luxury apartment block in one of Delchester's most fashionable postcodes. After paying the driver, Keeley marched up to the building's imposing entrance. A resident was on his way out and smiled at her as he held the communal door open – even with her hair scraped back in a ponytail and minimal make-up, she was still stunning. But Keeley was oblivious to his admiring look and walked straight past him towards the lift. She was almost there when a voice called out.

'Miss Finnegan, may I have a word, please?'

Not bothering to hide her irritation, Keeley whirled round and glowered in the direction of the concierge's desk. 'What is it, William? I'm in a hurry.'

The concierge folded his arms across his chest. 'Have you come to see Mr Stoker?'

'Why else would I be here?' Keeley snapped.

'He's not at home.'

Keeley shrugged. 'Never mind, I've got a set of keys. I'll let myself in and wait for him to come back.'

The concierge came round from behind the desk. 'Unfortunately, that won't be possible. You see, Mr Stoker moved out two days ago.'

Keeley's mouth dropped open. 'Is this some sort of joke?'

'Absolutely not, Miss. I believe he's gone to London.'

'But he can't have.'

'I'm afraid he has.'

There was a moment of silence while Keeley digested the information, and then she put back her head and let out a loud wail.

Immediately, the concierge came round from behind the desk. 'There, there, no need to go upsetting yourself.'

'I've been dumped,' Keeley sobbed. 'Haven't I?'

'I really couldn't say.' The concierge glanced anxiously towards the lift. An illuminated display told him somebody on the fourth floor was waiting to board it.

'That bastard!' Keeley shrieked. 'He didn't even have the guts to tell me. He just went sneaking off, like the sly, underhand, devious little scumbag he is.'

'Come now, Miss Finnegan, let's get you into a cab

now, shall we?' The concierge took Keeley's arm and began leading her towards the door.

Keeley leaned in the opposite direction and dug her heels into the marble floor. 'I'm not going anywhere. Not until you give me Ryan's forwarding address.'

'I'm not at liberty to divulge that information.'

'Give ... me ... the ... fucking ... address!' Keeley bellowed.

Behind her, the lift doors slid smoothly open to reveal an elegant, middle-aged man and his pet dachshund.

'Is everything all right, William?' the man said.

'Yes, Mr Stern,' the concierge said with a forced smile. 'This lady's had some bad news; I'm just helping her to a cab.' He jerked Keeley's arm hard. 'Are you going to leave quietly or do I have to call the police?' he hissed.

'All right, all right, I'm going,' Keeley said. 'Now get your hands off me.'

The concierge let go of her arm and opened the communal door. 'Good day, miss.'

It was one in the morning before Keeley finally returned home. She was rather the worse for wear having spent several hours in a city centre wine bar, downing glass after glass of chilled Sauvignon Blanc, only one of which she'd had to pay for herself. At precisely the same time Keeley was falling out of a cab with her shoes in her hand, Amber was exiting the Old Manor – but she wasn't going far.

The full moon cast an eerie glow as Amber crept across the damp grass. Shivering, she tightened her grip on the plastic bag she was carrying and quickened her pace. When she arrived at her destination a few minutes later, she reached into the pocket of the angora cardigan she was wearing over her nightdress and removed the remote control she'd stolen from Daniel's briefcase earlier that day. Pointing it at the row of garage doors, she clicked a series of buttons. One by one, the heavy doors began to lift on their well-oiled hinges. As she waited for them to open fully, Amber set her precious cargo down on the ground. The carrier bag was heavy and the plastic handles had cut into her hand, but she felt no pain, only a mounting sense of excitement.

The first garage housed two of Daniel's favourite cars: a six-month-old Maserati and a vintage Lamborghini. Amber flicked a switch by the door and immediately the garage was flooded with light. Without any deliberation, she opened the door of the Maserati and reached across the driver's seat. The smell of Italian leather greeted her nostrils like an old friend. She released the handbrake and put the gear stick into neutral. Then she took hold of the doorframe and started pushing the car out on to the driveway. To her relief, it was light and moved easily across the smooth tarmac. Afterwards, she went back for the Lamborghini. Then it was on to the next garage, which was home to the Jag and the Lotus. And finally to garage number three, home to the stately Aston Martin and its English cousin, the Bentley Continental. When all the cars were lined up outside in a colourful display that would make most grown men weep with longing, Amber returned to her shopping bag. Inside was a fifty-five-pound sack of millet, and nestling beside it a plastic detergent scoop. Without further ado, Amber tore open the sack and plunged the scoop into its gritty contents. As she sprinkled the seeds over the Maserati's bonnet with gay abandon, she looked up at the sky. Dawn would be breaking in less than an hour, and then the carnage would begin.

Twenty-Three

Daniel sat at the breakfast bar in striped pyjamas and a black silk dressing gown. At his elbow was a half-eaten *pain au chocolat* and a double espresso. He was next to useless until he'd had his morning shots of sugar and caffeine. Nancy was always on at him to kick the habit, fearing for his blood pressure and cholesterol levels. Her concern touched him. It was yet another sign – as if he needed it – of just how much she cared. Daniel knew his friends wondered what he saw in the former house-keeper. She wasn't young or beautiful or rich – but she was bright and funny and, best of all, she was real – not like the silicone-fed bimbos his friends lusted after.

A few moments later, Calum wandered in. He was wearing a camouflage jacket and there was a guitar case slung across his shoulders.

'Morning, son,' said Daniel. 'Are you off to college? I'll give you a lift to the bus stop if you like.'

'I'm not going in; it's a study day,' Calum replied as he helped himself to a banana from the fruit bowl. 'I'm heading over to Tony's to rehearse. He's picking me up in five minutes.'

'Doesn't that rather defy the object of a study day?'

Calum looked at his father blankly.

'Shouldn't you be *studying*?'

'Nah, band practice is far more important; we've got a gig tonight.'

Daniel sighed. He knew he should be stricter with Calum, but he had a lot on his mind. It was Nancy's birthday the following week and he had organized a special surprise: a champagne breakfast at St Benedict's followed by a balloon ride, during which he planned to propose. They'd only been together for a few months but he knew, beyond a shadow of a doubt, that Nancy was the woman he wanted to spend the rest of his life with. She'd been away for a few days, staying with an old school friend. They wouldn't be able to marry until he got his decree absolute, of course – and who knew when that might be. Several months had passed since the divorce papers had been filed and he was still no nearer to reaching a settlement with Amber. With both parties refusing to concede the house, it seemed increasingly likely that the matter would have to be decided by the courts. Just thinking about it was enough to bring Daniel out in a cold sweat. Mustering a smile, he asked his son what time he would be home.

'I'm staying the night at Tony's,' Calum said, squeezing a conference pear to test it for ripeness.

'You seem to be spending more time at Tony's than you do at home.'

The teenager shrugged. 'Do you blame me?

Daniel brushed some stray crumbs from his lap. 'Not really, I'm sure it must be a nightmare living with your mother and me.' He cleared his throat self-consciously. 'Listen, Cal, I'm sorry about the other day.'

'Sorry you ruined Mum's tea party?'

'No, said Daniel. 'I mean I'm sorry you had to get involved.'

Calum gave his father a reproachful look. 'If I hadn't, Mum would've ripped your throat out.'

'You're probably right,' said Daniel, grinning gleefully. 'I don't think I've ever seen your mother quite so pissed off.'

'It's not funny, Dad.'

'Oh, come on,' said Daniel. 'It was bloody hilarious.'

The corners of Calum's mouth began to twitch as he recalled the sight of a bedraggled Lady Emmerson, rolling on the ground, skirt bunched up around her hips. 'How did you do it, Dad?' he asked. 'Those jets of water were freaking awesome.'

'It was easy. That's a state-of-the-art pump in that pond; all it took was a few subtle adjustments to the settings.'

'Okay, so yesterday *was* pretty funny,' Calum admitted. 'But killing Couscous . . . that was bad, Dad.'

Daniel nodded. 'I know, and that's something I regret. Still, it's not as if I wrung his neck myself. I took him to the vet's and had him put down humanely.'

'That doesn't make it any better.'

'No, I don't suppose it does. But I was just so mad at your mother after her cruel trick with the billboard, I wanted to hurt her . . . badly.' Daniel shrugged half-heartedly. 'And that was the best way I knew how.'

'I wish you and Mum would hurry up and sort out this stupid divorce settlement. Then you could go your separate ways and life could get back to normal.'

'Believe me, so do I,' said Daniel. 'And I've tried to be

as reasonable as I can. I've made your mother a very generous financial offer, but her bitch of a solicitor is determined to play hardball.'

'All she really wants is the house, Dad. Can't you just let her have it?'

Daniel's bushy brows knitted together. 'Never,' he growled. 'I was the one who found this place and I'm the one who's been paying the mortgage all these years. It's mine by rights.'

'Whatever,' Calum muttered. 'But if you two don't stop your stupid game of tit for tat, someone's going to end up getting hurt.'

Daniel's expression softened. 'Look, Cal, I don't like this situation any more than you do. After yesterday, I reckon your mother and I are just about even so, if she's agreeable, I'm prepared to call a ceasefire.'

Calum gave a hard laugh. 'I think it might be a bit late for that.'

'What makes you so sure?'

Calum jerked his head towards the window. 'Mum's arranged a little surprise for you. Outside.'

Daniel slammed down his coffee cup. 'Why didn't you say something before?'

'Because I didn't want to be here when the shit hit the fan.' Calum stuffed the fruit in his pockets and began walking towards the utility room. 'See ya, Dad. Wouldn't wanna be ya.' A moment later, the back door slammed shut behind him.

Daniel stood up and walked to the window. The back garden was bathed in early morning sunshine; nothing seemed odd or out of place. He went to the back door and stepped outside, still in his Prada slippers. Pushing his hands deep into his dressing-gown pockets, he sniffed the air experimentally, like a bloodhound trying to pick up the scent of death. He detected only the rich fragrance of honeysuckle, followed by a subtler undertone of fresh-cut grass. He walked a few paces across the reclaimed flagstones that formed a small patio area, then turned and looked back up at the Old Manor. Amber's bedroom window was open a fraction, but the blackout curtains she couldn't sleep without were tightly drawn. Wondering if Calum might be having a joke at his expense, Daniel began to walk slowly round the house, scanning the landscape for anything unusual. The garden was more his wife's domain than his and he couldn't imagine that any act of sabotage she might have enacted would affect him in any significant way. It was only as he rounded the east wing that Daniel realized he might have seriously underestimated his wife. For there, in the distance, was his prized fleet of vehicles, lined up like a row of racing cars on the starting grid. This, in itself, was an anomaly. No one but Daniel had a remote control for the garage block, not even Stephen, Amber's chauffeur, who kept her Mercedes housed in a separate outbuilding. A ball of phlegm rose in Daniel's throat. He swallowed it back down and set off towards the cars at a brisk jog. As he drew nearer, he noticed something else odd. Half a dozen or so wood pigeons were perched on the bonnet of his flame-red Maserati. At the sound of his approach, they took fright and fluttered skywards.

It wasn't until Daniel was practically within touching distance of the cars that the full horror of what Amber had done struck him. Every vehicle was plastered from front bumper to rear in bird shit. This by itself was bad enough, for Daniel knew how easily the highly acidic droppings could fade the three-coat pearlescent paint finishes favoured by top-end car manufacturers. But bird mess could be hosed off. Less easy to remove were the hundreds of chips and scratches that dimpled the cars' roofs and bonnets, seemingly caused by the sharp beaks and claws of many, many birds. Light-headed with shock and outrage, Daniel ran from car to car. Not one inch of paintwork had escaped unscathed; the damage ran into thousands. The assault seemed almost biblical in proportion, and at first Daniel didn't understand how it could have happened. Then he saw that the area in front of the garages was peppered with white grains. Bending down, he picked up a few grains on his fingertips: millet. Suddenly, it all made perfect, agonizing sense. He stared up at the sky. Above him, the cluster of wood-pigeons wheeled hungrily. He picked up the nearest stone and hurled it into the air. 'Fuck off, you bastards!' he cried, his voice hoarse with emotion.

'Temper, temper,' came an amused voice behind him.

Daniel whirled around. Amber was standing a few feet away. She was wearing a multicoloured kaftan and a vengeful smile.

'You cow,' he snarled, fists clenching and unclenching at his sides. 'You absolute fucking cow.'

Unperturbed, Amber walked slowly towards the Jaguar and ran her fingertips across its damaged bonnet. 'Goodness, those birds *were* hungry,' she said. 'Your pretty penis extensions have all been ruined.'

'You've gone too far this time,' said Daniel, his voice trembling as he struggled to keep his rage under control. 'My lawyer warned you about causing any further damage to my property. I'm going to speak to him about taking out a restraining order; you're a bloody lunatic.'

'And you, dearest, are a bloody *murderer*!' Amber screeched.

Daniel took a step towards his wife. 'You're never going to get your hands on this house, Amber; the sooner you get that into your thick skull the better.'

'I've *earned* that house,' Amber screamed in his face. 'You were just a two-bob businessman when I met you. You'd be nothing without me, *nothing*!'

'No, Amber, you're the one with nothing: no real friends, no high-flying career, no lover to hold you at night.'

'And what have you got?' Amber sneered. 'A load of pompous business cronies and a girlfriend who's so ugly she gives Freddy Krueger nightmares.'

'You're a fine one to talk,' Daniel bellowed. 'I'm amazed you've got the nerve to go out in public without a bag over your head.'

As the pair continued to trade insults, their voices drifted towards the entrance to the estate, where Calum was still waiting for his lift. Reaching into his pocket, he pulled out his iPod. He'd intervened between his parents yesterday but that, he'd already decided, would be the very last time.

Back at the garages, the Solomons' argument was reaching a crescendo. They stood nose to nose, attacking and parrying like a pair of Olympic-standard fencers.

'I'm going to fight you every last step of the way,' Daniel spat. 'You'll have the Old Manor over my dead body.'

'I despise you,' Amber hit back. 'I despise you with every last breath in my body.' She turned away. 'See you in court,' she called out as she stormed back towards the house, her kaftan billowing about her ankles.

Daniel massaged his eyeballs with his thumbs. He was sick of this constant battling; it was physically and emotionally draining. What's more, he hated the effect it was having on Calum. Suddenly, he felt a sharp pain in his chest. He slumped against the Jaguar, gasping as the air was crushed out of his lungs. Thinking he must be having a heart attack, he tried to call out to Amber's retreating back, but his voice emerged as a whisper. A wave of panic gripped him as he slid down the Jag's shit-splattered passenger door and landed with a bump on the tarmac. For several minutes, he sat there, watching the wood pigeons circling overheard like vultures. And then, after what seemed like an eternity, the pain began to subside to a dull ache. Still clutching his breastbone, Daniel staggered to his feet, realizing with relief that what he had suffered was heartburn, probably brought on by the coffee and the gobbled *pain-au-chocolat*.

He stared at the Old Manor, standing there in all its glory, and thought that the rich Cheshire brick, whose sandblasting he had personally supervised, had never looked more beautiful. He knew that Amber would never give in, no matter how much alimony he agreed to give her; the hard-faced bitch wouldn't be satisfied until the house was hers. But the way things were going the divorce battle would be rumbling on for months, years even – especially if it went to court. What was the point of proposing to Nancy when he didn't have the remotest idea when he'd be a free man? In that moment, Daniel knew there was only one option open to him; one way to get them all out of this horrible mess. If *he* couldn't have the house, then no one would.

The next day was a Saturday, Amber's favourite day of the week. As usual, she rose early and made a refreshing cup of mint tea. Once showered and dressed, she packed a small backpack and headed off to St Benedict's for a round of treatments in the club's luxurious spa. Following her latest confrontation with Daniel, Amber was looking forward to her weekly pampering session even more than usual. It would be a chance to escape the highly charged atmosphere at the Old Manor and forget about her problems for a few short hours.

Daniel was watching from his bedroom window as Amber crossed the garden, heading towards the gate that gave on to the golf course at St Benedict's. The millionaire hotel mogul had never been a procrastinator and, with his wife safely off the premises and Calum presumably sleeping off a hangover at Tony's, he wasted no time putting his plan in motion.

Within minutes of Amber's departure, Daniel was making his way towards one of the brick outhouses that were dotted about the estate. The building was used as a store and contained miscellaneous items: garden tools, tins of paint, some battered traffic cones, and several propane gas cylinders, which were used to supply the patio heaters on the terrace. Daniel worked quickly and with a steely determination. Only by keeping his mind utterly focused on the job in hand would he be able to prevent himself from having second thoughts. When all the cylinders had been rolled across the lawn and were sitting outside the house, he dragged them into the entrance hall, one by one, and ranged them round the foot of the staircase. With a sad smile, Daniel stroked the cherrywood balustrade for the last time. He couldn't help thinking what a shame it was to use such a wonderful example of craftsmanship as kindling – but, he told himself, needs must.

Five miles away, Calum was slowly returning to consciousness on Tony's bedroom floor. His head ached, his neck was stiff and when he tried to moisten his parched lips, he found that his tongue was inconveniently stuck to the roof of his mouth. Gingerly, he raised himself up on to his elbows and stared, blurry-eyed, around the room. Beside him, on the bed, Tony was exhaling king-size snores, dead to the world. Spotting a can of Coke on the carpet, Calum picked it up and tipped the last remaining inch of liquid into his mouth. Instantly, he began coughing, remembering belatedly that Tony had been using the drink can as an ashtray the night before. As he wiped his mouth and lay down again, fragments of the previous night began filtering back to Calum: a half-empty pub back room … the audience booing them off … going back to the drummer's house … getting wasted on cider and spliff … a pretty girl sitting on his knee as she thrust her tongue down his throat. Despite his raging hangover,

Calum broke into a smile: the gig might have been a complete disaster, but who cared when he'd actually snogged a girl! Closing his eyes, he tried to recall more details of the tantalizing encounter ... Lucy, her name was. Or was it Lisa? She'd been well built, pretty too, and before she left she'd punched her phone number into his mobile. Seeking confirmation that he hadn't dreamt the entire episode, Calum rolled over and reached for his camouflage jacket, which was lying in a crumpled heap on the floor, together with his jeans and trainers. Thankfully his phone was still in the pocket, and the display told him he had a voicemail message. Realizing it was from one of his parents, he played it back:

'Hey there, it's Dad. Hope the gig went well last night; I'm looking forward to hearing all about it. Listen, Cal, I don't know what your plans are for today, but I want you to stay at Tony's until I call you. Something's happening down at home, something to do with the divorce, and I need a bit of privacy. I repeat: do *not* come home until I give you the all clear. Any probs, give me a call.'

Calum frowned. The message seemed odd in the extreme; what's more, his father had sounded jittery and slightly breathless. Pushing Lucy/Lisa to the back of his mind, he dialled his home number. After a few rings, Daniel picked up.

'It's me,' Calum said.

'Hi, son, did you get my message?'

'Yeah, what's going on, Dad?'

'It's nothing for you to worry about. Are you at Tony's?'

'Yeah, I just woke up.'

'Good, then do as I say and stay there for the time being.'

'Where's Mum?'

'At St Benedict's; it's her spa day.'

Calum rubbed the side of his jaw. 'You're up to something, aren't you, Dad?'

Daniel didn't answer.

'Look, I know you must be pissed off about the cars, but don't do anything stupid; remember what you said about that ceasefire?'

Another silence.

'Dad?'

'I've got to go now, Cal. You stay at Tony's until I tell you it's safe, okay?'

The hairs on the back of Calum's neck stood to attention. '*Safe?* What are you talking about?'

'Nothing, it's just a figure of speech. I'll see you later.'

'But, Dad . . .'

It was too late. Daniel had hung up.

A minute later, Calum was pulling on his jeans with one hand and shaking Tony awake with the other.

'Come on, Tone,' he said as his friend's eyes flickered open. 'Some bad shit's going down at my house; I've got to get back. Can you give me a lift?'

'You're joking, aren't you?' Tony croaked. His breath smelled strongly of alcohol and cigarettes. 'I'm still half-cut.'

Calum sighed as he let Tony go and started pushing his feet into his trainers. He felt sick with foreboding as he jogged down the stairs. Only the day before, he'd promised himself he wasn't going to get involved in his parents' machinations, but this was different; this time he knew in his guts that his father was going to do something really terrible. He just hoped he could get back in time to stop him.

After grabbing a two-litre bottle of water from Tony's fridge, Calum set off on the long walk home. He'd been hoping to hitch a ride, but it was still early and the country lanes were deserted. As he walked, he weighed up the pros and cons of calling his mother, eventually deciding not to. If she suspected his father were up to something, she'd go flying back to the house in a fit of hysteria and probably make the whole situation ten times worse. If only there were someone in Kirkhulme he could call: someone he could trust, someone who could go to the Old Manor at short notice and provide a distraction, just until he got back. And then Calum had a brainwave. Reaching into his jeans pocket, he pulled out his wallet and rifled through the contents, not even sure if he still had it. But there it was, the small black business card bearing the words: *Cindy McAllister, Interior Designer.*

Cindy was in her home gym when she received the call, performing a complicated stretching routine in preparation for her morning jog. She was stunned when she heard Calum's request.

'Don't you think you might be overreacting, honey?' she asked him as she sat down on a weights bench.

'Absolutely not,' said Calum. 'Something bad's going to happen if I don't get back home and stop it. Don't ask me how I know, I just do.'

'But your dad seems like a well-adjusted man, surely he wouldn't do anything too awful.'

'The divorce has completely messed with his mind,' said Calum, his tone more urgent now. 'I honestly think he's capable of anything; he killed Couscous, for fuck's sake.'

Cindy gulped. 'I thought that was just a rumour.'

'No, it's true, and I dread to think what he's going to do next.'

'But I can't just turn up announced.'

'Yes, you can – say my mum invited you round to take some measurements or something.'

'But I finished work on the music room two weeks ago.'

'Then pretend you left something behind … I don't know, your tape measure or something. And then all you have to do is keep him talking until I get back.'

Cindy sighed. 'Wouldn't it be easier if I just picked you up in the car and brought you home?'

'I'm miles away; there isn't time. Please, Cindy, you're the only one who can help.'

Cindy thought for a moment. There was no mistaking the desperation in Calum's voice and, though she didn't like to admit it, she found the prospect of getting involved in a drama at the Old Manor too tempting to resist. She dreaded to think what her husband would say if he knew what she was about to do – but Kieran was asleep in bed and what he didn't know, wouldn't hurt him.

'*Okaaay*,' she said, managing to sound rather more

reluctant than she felt. 'I can be there in less than five minutes.'

She heard the explosion just as she was turning into the isolated lane that twisted and turned for a third of a mile before coming to a dead end at the Old Manor. There was a deafening roar and then the road beneath the Morgan's wheels seemed to shake. Being a native Californian, Cindy thought at first it was an earthquake. Then she noticed a vast plume of what looked like smoke emerging above the treetops. Stunned, she pulled over to the side of the road and got out of the car. She scrambled up the grass verge and peered through a gap in the line of towering horse chestnuts. Beyond them lay the Old Manor. Or, rather, what was left of it. For a moment Cindy stood there, rooted to the spot and barely able to make sense of what her eyes were telling her. But then commonsense kicked in and she went back to the car. 'Fire brigade,' she said breathlessly into her mobile. 'And please hurry.'

Unusually, given the wealth and status of its occupants, the Old Manor had no security gates. Instead, the entrance was marked by two massive stone pillars, which were covered in lichen and had probably been there for centuries. When Cindy arrived she found the gap between the pillars filled by a row of mismatching traffic cones. A handwritten sign, taped to the tallest cone, bore the warning: DANGER! KEEP OUT. More confused than ever, she parked the Morgan on the opposite side of the road and cleared the cones away, so that the fire engine would be able to pass unhindered. Then, without any thought for her own safety, she ran towards the dense grey cloud that seemed to fill the sky.

The scene that greeted her was apocalyptic. The Solomons' beautiful home had been razed to the ground and in its place lay a gigantic mound of rubble. What Cindy thought was smoke wasn't smoke at all, but a choking pall of dust. A strong smell of gas hung in the air and in one area of the mound, a small fire blazed among some ancient roof timbers. Pressing the sleeve of her sweatshirt to her mouth and nose, Cindy surveyed the devastation in a state of shock. She couldn't believe Daniel had destroyed the home he so obviously loved – but, then again, divorce did strange things to people. She wondered how he had done it: some sort of remote detonation, she supposed. The hotelier was probably miles away by now, waiting – quite literally – for the dust to settle. Calum's premonition had been right, but even he couldn't have foreseen devastation on this scale. Suddenly, a strange and surreal sight caught her eye: one of the Old Manor's mighty chimney stacks was lying perfectly upright and virtually intact on the lawn, a short distance away from the main site. When she looked harder, she saw to her horror that, behind it, a body lay unmoving. With a loud gasp, she ran towards it.

He was barely recognizable – his face was badly burned and his clothes hung about him in charred shreds, but Cindy knew it was Daniel. Bile rose in her throat and for a moment she thought she might be sick. As she dropped to her knees beside him, she realized that part of the chimney stack was resting, gruesomely, on his torso. Without further ado, she put two fingers to the side of his neck; there was no sign of life. 'Oh, Daniel,' she murmured. 'What have you done?'

Her thoughts turned to Calum. He would be home soon; she couldn't let him walk into this holocaust. She must drive to the bottom of the lane and intercept him. Shaking her head in disbelief, she stood up and started walking back towards the car. She hadn't gone far when she saw a figure stumbling towards her through the dust cloud. It was Amber. Bizarrely, she was wearing a swimming costume and a rubber cap, studded with garish plastic flowers. She stopped when she saw Cindy and stood shivering on the lawn.

'I heard the explosion,' she said. She looked as if she were in shock and her hand was shaking as she pointed at the mountain of rubble. 'My house ... my precious house.' Her voice had a strange strangled quality, as if she'd swallowed a sharp object and couldn't get it all the way down. Suddenly, her eyes hardened. 'What the fuck happened?'

Cindy shoved her hands in the front pocket of her sweatshirt. 'I'm not entirely sure,' she said tentatively. 'Calum called me from his friend's house and asked me to get over here as soon as possible. He had a bad feeling Daniel was going to do something silly – and it looks as if he was right.' The American woman looked back towards the spot where the Old Manor had once stood. 'But I must admit, I wasn't expecting this.'

'So you're absolutely sure Calum's safe?' Amber said.

'Yes, he's fine; he's on his way back now.'

The news seemed to breathe new life into Amber. 'Just wait till I get my hands on that idiot husband of mine,' she shrieked as her hands performed a wringing action. 'He's going to wish he'd never been born.'

'Ah,' said Cindy. 'I'm afraid I've got some very bad news on that front.'

Amber snorted. 'Don't tell me, he's on the next plane to Acapulco,' she said sarcastically.

'No.' Cindy took a deep breath. 'There's no easy way of saying this, Amber, so I'll just come straight out with it . . . Daniel's dead.'

'What?' said Amber, her huge lips wobbling like a crème caramel.

Cindy pointed towards the chimney stack. 'He's lying over there; I've already checked and there's no sign of a pulse. I'm so sorry, Amber.'

At this, Amber let out a long, inhuman howl. 'No!' she cried as she ran towards her husband's lifeless form. 'He isn't dead! He can't be!' She flung herself on the ground and grabbed his shoulders with both hands. 'Wake up, Daniel! Wake up, you fucking bastard.' Then, realizing that nothing would rouse him, she slumped over his body and began crying, great gulping ragged sobs that seemed to come from the very core of her being.

Cindy touched her shoulder. 'You'd better come away,' she said gently. 'It's not safe; that chimney stack could come crashing down at any minute.'

Amber looked up at the chimney and saw that Cindy was right. Then, turning back to Daniel, she bent down and kissed his bluish lips. 'Goodbye, my love,' she whispered.

Despite the heat of the afternoon, Cindy felt a shiver travel up the entire length of her spine. Somewhere in the distance she could hear the plaintive wail of a siren.

Epilogue

It was the first week in November. A brisk north-easterly had blown through Kirkhulme overnight and the grounds of St Benedict's were covered in brightly coloured autumn leaves. In the Ladies' Lounge, Marianne, Keeley, Cindy and Laura were enjoying a champagne brunch at their favourite table, overlooking the eighteenth green. Their main topic of conversation was the long-awaited result of the coroner's inquest into Daniel Solomon's death, which had been fulsomely reported in the previous day's newspapers. A post-mortem had revealed that the unfortunate hotelier suffered second-degree burns in the explosion; however, the cause of death was given as internal injuries, inflicted when a half-ton chimney stack struck him as he attempted to flee the scene.

The coroner recorded a verdict of death by mis-adventure, for there was no evidence to suggest Daniel had been suicidal. His grieving mistress Nancy testified that he'd been in good spirits when he'd telephoned her on the eve of the accident, and the two had talked excitedly about a Caribbean holiday they were planning. An upmarket jeweller in Delchester also came forward to say that Daniel had recently commissioned a sapphire-and-diamond-engagement ring. These were not, the coroner reasoned, the actions of a man intent on taking his own life. Then there was Calum's heart-rending recollection of the strange phone call with his father, just minutes before the explosion, and Daniel's promise to call him when it was 'safe' to return. The most likely scenario, the coroner declared, was that Daniel's plan had simply been to destroy the house and its contents as a way of bringing to an end the bitter dispute with his estranged wife over the future ownership of the Old Manor.

After bringing three propane cylinders, each containing about thirty pounds of pressurized gas, into the house the hotelier had apparently opened the cylinders' safety valves. Forensic experts calculated that he would've been outside the building when he ignited the highly flammable cloud of vapour – probably by tossing a lighted rag through an open window – and had failed to accurately predict the strength of the resulting blast, which created a shockwave of some 400 yards. It was, the coroner said in his summing up, the act of a desperate man, worn down by months of legal wrangling, and should serve as a warning to other divorcing couples who found themselves at loggerheads as they attempted to divide the spoils of their union.

'Poor Daniel,' said Marianne as she chased a forkful of Gruyère and asparagus omelette round her plate. 'I always thought he seemed like such a sensible man. I suppose he must just have had a moment of madness.'

'It's Calum I feel sorry for,' said Cindy. 'To lose your dad at that age is dreadful, and in such appalling circumstances too.' She gave a great sigh. 'If only I'd gotten to the Old Manor a few minutes earlier, I might have been able to stop him.'

Marianne patted her hand. 'You mustn't blame

yourself, darling. Once a man like Daniel Solomon has made up his mind to do something, there's nothing and no one that can stand in his way. In any case, if you'd arrived any earlier it might've been *you* lying under that chimney.'

'I guess,' said Cindy, stroking the rim of her champagne glass thoughtfully.

'It seems to me that the only winner here is Amber,' Keeley remarked. 'Okay, so she lost her home and all her possessions but, hey, she *is* thirty million pounds richer.'

Laura frowned. 'Didn't the housekeeper get anything?'

'No,' said Cindy. 'According to "Jemima's Diary" Daniel never got round to changing his will, which means Amber and Calum were the sole beneficiaries.'

'And Calum, lucky lad, is going to have a tasty ten million pound trust fund waiting for him when he hits eighteen in a few months' time,' Keeley added. 'Something tells me he's going to find himself very popular with the girls all of a sudden . . .' She looked around the table with a mischievous grin. 'I might even make a move on him myself.'

'You stay away from that boy, Kee, or you'll have me to answer to,' Cindy said firmly. 'Calum's been through a tough time and he doesn't need any more complications in his life right now.'

'I wonder what he's going to do with all that money,' Marianne mused out loud.

Cindy shrugged. 'Who knows, but I'm sure he'd rather have his dad back – and so, I suspect, would Amber.'

'I thought she hated him,' said Laura.

'Oh no, that was all an act,' Cindy replied. 'I reckon she loved Daniel every bit as much as the day they got married.'

'How very tragic,' said Marianne. She took a sip of Cristal. 'The funeral was well attended; Daniel certainly had plenty of friends.'

'I think a lot of people at that graveside hardly knew him,' said Cindy. 'They just went along for the spectacle.'

Marianne smiled thinly. 'People like me, you mean?'

'Oh no, I'm sure you genuinely wanted to pay your respects,' Cindy said hastily.

'Actually, you were right the first time,' Marianne remarked. 'I love a good funeral. They make me feel so –' She gave a little shudder – '*alive*.'

Keeley pushed her half-eaten French toast to one side. 'Did you see that bunch of freaks in the long white dresses, lurking under the trees while they were lowering the coffin into the grave?'

'Yeah,' said Laura. 'Who *were* they?'

'Amber told me they were business associates of Daniel's,' said Cindy. 'Apparently they shared his passion for Egyptology. They even set up some weird secret society, dedicated to Queen Nefertiti.'

Her voice tailed off as Jeremy, the maître d', approached their table. He was carrying a baby bottle on a silver tea tray. 'Your milk, Mrs Bentley,' he said, offloading the bottle on to to the table. 'Heated to thirty-seven degrees precisely.' He offered a glutinous smile. 'And how is the little fellow today?'

'He's absolutely adorable,' said Laura as she lifted Tiger out of the carrycot placed on the velvet-covered banquette beside her. 'It's very good of you to let me bring him in here. I know children aren't usually allowed in the Ladies' Lounge.'

'No problem,' said Jeremy smoothly. 'You and Mr Bentley are highly valued customers at St Benedict's; we're happy to make an exception to the rule.' He gave a little bow and retreated.

The other women watched approvingly as Laura settled Tiger into the crook of her arm and began feeding him.

'He looks incredibly healthy,' Keeley said. 'You'd never know he'd been so poorly.'

Laura smiled. 'He's incredibly good-natured too. I can't believe the difference; it's almost like having a brand-new baby.'

'I'm so pleased it's all worked out for you, darling,' said Marianne. 'At one point, I was quite worried.' She made a little moue. 'I really thought you might do something, you know ... silly.'

'You were right to be concerned,' said Laura. 'There were a few times when I came close to the edge.' She bit her lip, remembering that day on the escarpment. 'Quite literally.'

Cindy groaned. 'Oh, honey, you should have said something to one of us. We're your friends – we'd do anything to help.'

'I know you would. I was just so tired and so very resentful I couldn't think straight.' Laura looked down at Tiger, who was sucking greedily on the bottle's plastic teat. 'But I know now I'd never do anything to harm him ... never.' As a flood of emotion threatened to overwhelm her, she turned quickly to Marianne. 'So how are things going with Brad? Is he still keeping you up all night.'

Marianne's bosom heaved. 'Just thinking about that nine-inch detachable cock makes me go weak at the knees.'

'Please Marianne, not when there are children present,' said Cindy.

'Oh, he doesn't mind, do you, Tiger?' Marianne reached out and stroked the baby's cheek. 'What about you, Keeley – any sign of romance on the horizon?'

The younger woman screwed up her face. 'No, worst luck. And it's only fifty-two days till Christmas, so I'd better get a move on.'

'Surely spending Christmas as a single girl wouldn't be so bad,' said Cindy.

Keeley speared a hash brown crossly with her fork. 'I'd rather drink my own bathwater, quite frankly. Just think of all those lovely presents I'd be missing out on.'

'What about all those well-connected people you meet at those swinging parties?' said Marianne. 'Can't you bag yourself a rich lawyer?'

'I've knocked swinging on the head,' Keeley said. 'It was fun at first, but the novelty soon wore off. I know you lot think I'm a terrible flirt, but when all's said and done I'm a one-man woman.'

Laura lay a sated Tiger back down in his cot and tucked the blankets in around him. 'Did you ever hear from Ryan? Sam tells me he's making quite an impression at Hampton Rangers.'

Keeley's face clouded over. 'No, and God help that

man if I ever set eyes on him again.' She gave a great sigh. 'Anyway, there's no point dwelling on the past; I'm looking forward to the future now.'

Cindy dabbed the corners of her mouth with her napkin. 'I wonder where we'll all be a year from now.'

'Sitting at our favourite table in the Ladies Lounge, drinking champagne and putting the world to rights?' Marianne suggested.

Laura smiled. 'Do you know what, I can't think of anywhere I'd rather be.'

'Me neither,' said Cindy. She raised her glass. 'Here's to another year at St Benedict's.

'St Benedict's,' the others chorused.

LEONIE FOX

PRIVATE MEMBERS

Four gorgeous girls.
One naughty playground for the rich and famous.

Cindy
A new member at St Benedict's, an exclusive country club with more millionaires
per square foot than the Hamptons in midsummer.

Laura
Unhappily married to playboy golfer Sam Bentley and the former lover of Jackson
West, an enigmatic Formula One driver whose career went up in flames. Literally.

Keeley
The ultimate party girl about town, with a Premiership footballer for a boyfriend
– and Premiership debts mounting up faster than a Jaguar S-Type.

Marianne
The decadent widow with a taste for the finer things in life – and depraved tastes
in the bedroom.

Cindy is amazed at the intrigue bubbling beneath the steamy waters of the St
Benedict's jacuzzi … barely is she on top of everyone's extramarital exploits
when the reappearance of Jackson sends temperatures soaring in the sauna – and
the scene is set for an unforgettable climax at the club's legendary Gala Dinner.

Calling all girls!

It's the invitation of the season.

Penguin books would like to invite you to
become a member of Bijoux – the exclusive club for
anyone who loves to curl up with the hottest reads in
fiction for women.

You'll get all the inside gossip on your favourite authors
– what they're doing, where and when; we'll send you
early copies of the latest reads months before they're
on the High Street and you'll get the chance to attend
fabulous launch parties!

And, of course, we realise that even while she's
reading every girl wants to look her best, so we have
heaps of beauty goodies to pamper you with too.

If you'd like to become a part of
the exclusive world of Bijoux, email
bijoux@penguin.co.uk

Bijoux books for Bijoux girls

He just wanted a decent book to read ...

Not too much to ask, is it? It was in 1935 when Allen Lane, Managing Director of Bodley Head Publishers, stood on a platform at Exeter railway station looking for something good to read on his journey back to London. His choice was limited to popular magazines and poor-quality paperbacks – the same choice faced every day by the vast majority of readers, few of whom could afford hardbacks. Lane's disappointment and subsequent anger at the range of books generally available led him to found a company – and change the world.

'We believed in the existence in this country of a vast reading public for intelligent books at a low price, and staked everything on it'
Sir Allen Lane, 1902–1970, founder of Penguin Books

The quality paperback had arrived – and not just in bookshops. Lane was adamant that his Penguins should appear in chain stores and tobacconists, and should cost no more than a packet of cigarettes.

Reading habits (and cigarette prices) have changed since 1935, but Penguin still believes in publishing the best books for everybody to enjoy. We still believe that good design costs no more than bad design, and we still believe that quality books published passionately and responsibly make the world a better place.

So wherever you see the little bird – whether it's on a piece of prize-winning literary fiction or a celebrity autobiography, political tour de force or historical masterpiece, a serial-killer thriller, reference book, world classic or a piece of pure escapism – you can bet that it represents the very best that the genre has to offer.

Whatever you like to read – trust Penguin.

read more
www.penguin.co.uk